Through YOU

Also by Ariana Godoy

Through My Window

Through the Rain
FALL 2023

Ariana Godoy

Through YOU

An imprint of Wattpad WEBTOON Book Group

English translation by Susy Alvarez

Published in Canada by Wattpad WEBTOON Book Group,

a division of Wattpad Corp.

36 Wellington Street E., Suite 200, Toronto, ON M5E 1C7 Canada

www.wattpad.com

First W by Wattpad Books edition: January 2023

ISBN 978-1-99077-844-5 (Trade Paper original)

ISBN 978-1-99077-845-2 (eBook edition)

Library and Archives Canada Cataloguing in Publication information is available upon request.

Printed and bound in Canada

1 3 5 7 9 10 8 6 4 2

To all my Wattpad readers—
Thanks to you, the Hidalgo's trilogy made it this far
and is able to reach more hearts.
Thank you, now and always, for loving all of them:
Ares and Raquel, Artemis and Claudia,
And now Apolo.
I love you all.

Prologue

ARTEMIS

July 4th

The sound of fireworks booms throughout the main square. The night sky explodes with colorful circles that expand and then quickly vanish. The people around cheer, shout, and clap. I wipe my sweaty palms on my pants.

Why am I so damn nervous? Because it's her.

I turn to watch her at my side. I am rethinking everything, calculating. I rehearse in my head what I need to say, how I should say it, if I can actually say it. We're sitting on the grass, and she's smiling, her gaze fixed on the spectacle. The fireworks shine on her face and give it a multicolor glow.

She's been by my side since childhood. As the years have passed, part of me has always known that what I feel for her goes beyond friendship. I want more. It's taken me weeks to build the courage, to confess my true feelings and let her know where I stand.

I'm ready.

I stare up again at the sky streaked with vibrant colors. I slowly run my hand through the grass until I reach hers, and place mine on top. My heart is racing, and I feel like a fool because I'm losing control. I don't like feeling this vulnerable. I never thought I could feel this way about anyone, and didn't expect to find something like this. She remains silent, but doesn't move her hand away.

I feel her eyes on me, but I'm unable to look at her or speak. Words have never been my forte.

Then I finally make my move, and the swiftness of my advance takes even me by surprise. My free hand moves to her neck, and I pull her toward me and press my lips to hers. However, the brush of our lips, like the fireworks in the night sky, is short-lived. She pushes me off and quickly moves away. Her reaction leaves me breathless.

Bitter rejection settles in the pit of my stomach. My heart tightens. She seems about to say something, but then quickly closes her mouth. She doesn't want to hurt me and is unsure what to say—I can tell by looking in her eyes. But it's too late. I clench my jaw, stand up, and turn my back to her. I don't want her pity.

"Artemis . . ." she whispers. But I am already walking away, leaving her behind.

That night I decide to put her in the past, and close myself off. I will never be vulnerable like this again or let anyone hurt me this way. It's not worth it.

One

Why don't you ever want to talk about him?

CLAUDIA

July 4th, five years later

"What's it like to live with three very attractive guys?"

"You are so lucky."

"I'm dying of envy!"

"Living with those absolute gods, what a privilege!"

"How can you stand living under the same roof?"

"Have you ever slept with one of them?"

"Can you get me their numbers?"

I've heard these kinds of comments from the moment the Hidalgo brothers became the leading men in the fantasies of every girl and boy around town. Although we're not family, I grew up with Artemis, Ares, and Apolo Hidalgo. And out there, on the streets, they cause never-ending swooning and sighing.

How did we end up living under the same roof? Well, my mother was hired to work as a housekeeper for the Hidalgo family when I was a little girl. Mr. Juan Hidalgo, their father, opened his doors and allowed us to live in his home. A year ago, when my mother fell ill and could no longer work, Mr. Hidalgo let me take her place as housekeeper. I am forever grateful to him for his kindness.

Many envy my position and think I have the perfect life because I live in close proximity to three very attractive guys. This is far from my reality. To me, there is more to life than relationships, sex, boys, etc. Relationships only lead to problems, disagreements. Sure, sometimes they may bring happiness, however, it's fleeting, and not worth the risk. Or at least I don't believe it is. I prefer stability and tranquility a thousand times over what a relationship may offer. So I keep a safe distance from all these complications. I have too much on my plate already.

I'm not only talking about love. It's also difficult for me to make friends. I have no time for friendships. I work for the Hidalgos during the day. During my breaks, I look after my mother. And in the evenings I attend university. My day starts at four in the morning and ends close to midnight. I hardly have time to sleep. At the age of twenty, I should have many friends, yet I only have one, and that's simply because we're in the same classes. Of course, I also consider the boys my friends. Well, Ares and Apolo. With Artemis, it's a different story.

The truth is, growing up, Artemis and I were very close. Then everything changed five years ago, that Fourth of July night, when I rejected him after he kissed me. From that moment on, our relationship ceased to be easy and comfortable, and turned tense and distant. Now he'll only speak to me when necessary.

Although they never asked questions, Ares and Apolo noticed the change. I appreciate their discretion. It helped me avoid the discomfort of having to explain what happened between their brother and me.

It was easy for Artemis to avoid me. At the end of that summer he started university and left home to live on campus, where he remained for the five years of his program. A month ago he graduated. And now he's coming home. Today.

Life can be full of irony when it wants to be. Out of all the days, he had to come back today, on the exact date of that night, five years ago. I must admit that I'm nervous. The last time I saw him was six months ago. It was a brief encounter—he came by the house to pick up a few things, and didn't even say hello.

To be completely honest, I hope we can manage to be civilized. Five years have gone by. I doubt he evens remembers what happened that night. I don't expect us to be as close as we once were, but I hope we can at least be friendly.

"Is the food ready?" Martha, my mother, asks while zipping up the black dress I need to wear for the surprise party the Hidalgos planned for Artemis.

"Claudia, are you listening to me?"

I turn and smile at her.

"Everything is in order, Mother. Don't worry, and go to sleep. Okay?" I help her lie down then pull up her blanket and kiss her forehead. "I'll come back soon."

"Don't get in trouble. You know it's always best to keep one's mouth shut and avoid . . ."

"Being honest?" I finish her sentence. "I understand."

She caresses my cheek. "You never know, some of the people coming to this party may be rude."

"I'll stay out of trouble, Mom. I'm a grown-up."

I kiss her forehead one more time and walk away. I stand

in front of the mirror to make sure I look okay. The Hidalgo matriarch, Sofia, has ordered me to wear this sleek black dress to match the attire of the rest of the staff. She wants the servers looking after her guests to be elegantly dressed, and I can't be the exception. I check that the bun I've made with my red hair is perfectly in place. I'll be in charge of the distribution of the food so can't have my hair down. I turn off the light and walk out of our room, moving quickly, and my black heels make clicking sounds, announcing my every step. And though I rarely wear high heels, I'm very good at walking in them.

When I reach the kitchen, I find four people waiting: two men wearing waiter uniforms and two women in the same dress I have on. I know them very well. They all work for the catering company that Mrs. Hidalgo frequently hires for these occasions. She prefers to hire the same staff each time because they're familiar with how parties are hosted at the house. One of the women is the one friend I have from university, Gin. I helped her get this job.

"And how is everything?"

"Everything's going well," she replies. She points to the other young woman. "Anellie has prepared a few cocktails and stocked the minibar with champagne and wine."

"Great. And who will be in charge of preparing drinks?" I ask while fixing a tray with hors d'oeuvres. "Is it Jon?"

Jon nods. "Yes, of course. I am, after all, the best bartender in the world." He winks at me.

Gin rolls her eyes. "Um, excuse me? I make the best margaritas in the world, okay?"

Miguel, who has been quiet all this time, finally comments. "I concur."

Jon flips them off.

I check my watch. The guests are about to arrive. "It's showtime."

They all exit, except Gin, who stays behind, hoping to walk out with me.

"How are you feeling?" she asks.

I give her a shrug.

"Fine. How else should I feel?"

She snorts. "You don't have to pretend around me. You haven't seen him in months. You must be nervous."

"I'm fine," I repeat.

"Did I tell you that I caught a glimpse of him a few days ago in this business magazine? Did you know that he's one of the youngest CEOs in the country?"

I do know, but Gin carries on with her update. "He was appointed CEO of Hidalgo Enterprises before he even finished his degree. They added a blurb in the article noting that he graduated with honors. He's a fucking genius!"

"Gin." I turn and grab her by the shoulders. "I adore you, but can you please shut up?"

Gin snorts again. "Why don't you ever want to talk about him?"

"Because there is nothing to talk about."

"You'll never convince me that nothing happened between you two. He's the only Hidalgo brother you never want to discuss."

"Nothing happened," I respond as we approach the living room. The furniture has been removed and replaced with small high tables adorned with centerpieces. Tall glasses filled with champagne and appetizers have been carefully laid out on each table.

Sofia and Juan are by the entrance, ready to receive their guests. I notice Apolo, their youngest son, wearing a beautiful suit and standing by their side. Sofia looks behind her then around, as if looking for someone, and I furrow my eyebrows before realizing who we're missing. Where is Ares?

I know these boys, so I quickly head up the stairs. Ares was partying last night, and came home early this morning. And though it's already six o'clock in the evening, it's very likely that he's still fast asleep. I let myself into his room without knocking, and am not surprised that it's dark inside. I wrinkle my nose; the room stinks of alcohol and cigarettes. I open the curtains and the fading sunlight shines on the figure of the eighteen-year-old boy I know so well. He's lying on his bed, shirtless, with his face buried in his pillow, the sheets pulled up to his torso. I'm not shocked to find a blond girl fast asleep next to him. I've never met her; it's likely she's a one-night stand.

"Ares!" I punch him lightly on the shoulder, and he groans in annoyance. "Ares!" This time I squeeze his shoulder and make sure he opens his eyes—blue, and very much like his mother's.

"Aaaagh, the light!" he complains, throwing his hand over his eyes.

"The light is the least of your problems." I stand up straight and place my hands on my waist.

"What's going on?" He sits up and rubs his face.

And I utter the only name he needs to hear in order to understand why I'm here.

"Artemis."

I watch as the information finally registers. He springs from the bed, only wearing boxers. I would be in awe if I had never seen him wearing just that.

"*Shit!* It's today!"

"Hurry, go shower," I order. "Your suit is hanging by the bathroom door."

Ares is about to run to the bathroom when he notices the girl in his bed, who is still asleep. "Oh shit."

I arch an eyebrow. "I thought you were taking a break from one-night conquests."

"I was. Argh, damn alcohol." He scratches the back of his head. "I don't have time for the effort and drama it will take to get her out of here." He comes closer to me. "Clau, you love me, right?"

"I'm not going to get rid of her for you. You have to take responsibility for your actions."

"But I don't have the time. Please," he begs. "If I have to take care of her, I won't make it on time to welcome my brother."

"All right. But this is the very last time. For real." I shove him toward the bathroom. "Hurry."

I sigh, and proceed to wake the girl up. I try to respect her privacy as much as possible while she puts on her clothes, although it's uncomfortable. Even though I hate to admit it, I'm used to situations like this. It's hard not to be when you live with an eighteen-year-old boy in the midst of his sexual awakening. Apolo, on the other hand, is still very innocent and I'm grateful for that. The blond is very pretty, and I feel terrible for her.

"Come on, I'll call you a taxi and take you to the exit out back."

She looks offended. "The back door? Who do you think I am? And you still haven't told me who you are."

I get what she's asking. My dress is too elegant to indicate that I'm just the house staff.

"That's not important. We're hosting a party downstairs. I suggest using the back exit for your own good. Unless you'd rather make your way out past dozens of strangers while looking like that." I gesture to her tangled hair and rumpled dress.

She shoots me a murderous glare. "Whatever."

How ungrateful.

I know I'm doing Ares's dirty work. Though I don't endorse his actions, I know him well—he's brutally honest with these girls and lets them know exactly what he wants. If they agree to sleep with him under his terms but then change their minds afterward and expect more, well, that's on them.

After I make sure the girl leaves, I descend the stairs, taking the room in: the shining marble floors, the exquisite black-and-white paintings on the walls. The Hidalgos are not the type of family who have a lot of things to show off; they're more into quiet luxurious details. Many guests have already arrived, and the room swarms with elegant dresses, expensive jewelry, and designer suits. I put on my best smile and begin to courteously serve those in attendance. I laugh at their jokes, even when I don't find them funny. And I offer compliments, even though they're fake.

I become more nervous as the time passes and the room begins to get crowded with guests. After all, this is a surprise party. Artemis has no idea that all these people are waiting to welcome him home after all these years away. The time of his arrival is getting closer. I don't know why I'm so anxious.

Sofia gets everyone's attention, and asks them to be quiet. Jon dims the lights, and everyone waits in complete silence while the doors start to open.

Artemis has finally arrived.

Two

Girls aren't only interested in sex.

CLAUDIA

There are moments in life, especially when emotionally charged, that unfold in real time yet feel as if they are playing in slow motion. The door begins to open. The lights are turned on. And the sound of everyone clapping in unison echoes throughout the room.

It bothers me that my heart beats faster when I see him. Artemis. I can't help but notice how much he has changed. He's no longer the bright-eyed seventeen-year-old boy who held my hand on that long-ago Fourth of July. He is a fully grown man dressed in a suit that makes him look older. His parents greet him, and a crowd of guests follows him around. He's changed a lot—he doesn't smile as much, and his gaze is cool and subdued.

I can't deny that he's more handsome than before. His features have matured, and he has a light, scruffy beard. I manage to take my eyes off him, and notice the redhead who stands next to him.

She's beautiful—curvy, with very generous cleavage. I assume they're very close by the way she clings to his side. She places a lock of her red hair behind her ear and smiles at Artemis's mother.

And why should that matter to me?

I shake my head. I'm about to turn around when his gaze finds mine. His brown eyes, which I have always found beautiful, meet mine. I can't breathe. The air around me feels different. And I can sense a tension between us. It feels as if, in this crowded room, we're connected by a cord threaded with so many emotions. I turn away. I'm not brave enough to hold his gaze.

Gin is behind me. "He's even more handsome in person," she says.

I walk on by without replying. Jon greets me with a big grin at the bar. "Why are you always so serious? Smiling isn't a crime, you know."

I give him a tray with empty champagne glasses that need to be filled. "I don't have a reason to smile."

Jon presents me with a fresh tray of full glasses. "You don't always need a reason." He leans on the bar. "You're really pretty when you smile."

I raise an eyebrow. "I told you before, your flirty lines won't work on me."

Gin comes to stand by my side. "But of course they don't work. Claudia prefers guys with beards."

Jon pouts. "I'll grow a beard just for you."

I'm about to speak when a pair of strong arms circle me from behind. I recognize the cologne, and can tell that it's Ares who is hugging me tightly.

"Thank you, you rescued me," he says quietly.

I free myself from his embrace and turn around. "That is the last time."

He flashes all his teeth. "I promise."

"You said the same thing the other last time."

"I double promise, okay?" He gives me the same sheepish look he has undoubtedly used to make girls fall for him. I abstain from answering. Instead, I flick one finger against his forehead. Ares laughs. I look over his shoulder and notice that Artemis and the redhead are approaching, most likely to greet Ares.

And that is my cue to leave.

"I have to go and get more appetizers," I whisper, and leave Gin, who is about to challenge my excuse, since we both well know there's plenty of food circulating.

The kitchen is my safe place. It's where I grew up, where I scribbled and doodled at the table while my mother cooked and cleaned. It's the room in the house that the Hidalgos most rarely frequent. It's my territory. I didn't intend to turn this small space into my refuge, it just happened that way. I rearrange what is ready to serve, and try to make myself look busy in case someone comes in. I'm simply wasting time. If Mrs. Hidalgo finds me here she'll likely scold me. I'm not sure why I'm avoiding Artemis.

In my head, this evening was going to unfold very differently. I never imagined I would act like a coward, retreating to the kitchen. What is wrong with me?

I'm just surprised by how much he's changed, that's all.

I've never let anyone intimidate me. I can't let him be the first.

"Is everything okay?" Apolo's voice startles me.

I turn around to face the youngest of the Hidalgo brothers.

"Yes, everything is going well."

Out of the three brothers, Apolo is the innocent one. He's very cute, with big brown eyes and a childlike smile. I'm willing to bet that of the three, he'll turn out to be the most handsome. And of course, he'll be the one with the nicest personality.

"Okay." He leans on the counter and crosses his arms. "So how come you're hiding here?"

"I'm not hiding."

Apolo arches an eyebrow. "Then what are you doing?"

I open my mouth but close it immediately. I stall while I try to come up with an excuse. And then one pops into my head.

"I am—"

"Wasting your time," Sofia Hidalgo interjects as she makes her entrance. "Can you please explain where have you been for the past twenty minutes?"

"I simply wanted to make sure that—"

"Shush!" She shuts me up. "I don't want to hear your excuses. I want you out there tending to my guests."

I promised my mom that I would be on my best behavior, so I bite my tongue. I walk past Apolo and begrudgingly make my way back to the event. I resume my duties. I serve drinks and smile like an idiot. I keep my eyes and mind off the evening's center of attention.

I become preoccupied with avoiding Artemis at all costs. This unfortunately leads me straight into the chest of the last person I expected would be here: Daniel. His eyes sparkle when they meet mine.

"My beautiful genius."

Shit.

"Hi." I raise my hand to greet him. I'm about to walk past him when he grabs me by the arm and stops me in my tracks.

"Hey, there, wait." He turns me around so I can face him. "You're mistaken if you think I'm going to let you get away this time."

I free myself from his grip.

"I'm really busy right now."

"Why aren't you taking my calls?" This was the conversation that I wanted to avoid. "I get that you're playing hard to get, but ignoring me for two months is taking it too far, don't you think?"

Ugh, Daniel.

In short, what happened with Daniel was too much alcohol mixed with pent-up sexual frustration, resulting in a one-night stand. He plays on the same soccer team as Ares. And he is fucking hot. And though he's a bit younger that I am, he is incredible in bed. And the sex was amazing. But that's all it was. Sex.

And yes, I am quite forward and honest about both my sexuality and my needs.

Women should be free to sleep with whomever we want, whenever and however we want. Society can go screw itself. As long as I'm careful and play it safe, what I do is no one else's business but mine. Some people may judge me, but frankly, I don't give a damn.

I'm not interested in relationships. However, on occasion, I happen to enjoy sexual intimacy with a man who is attractive and knows what to do. Is there something wrong that? My life is mine to decide what to do with. This doesn't mean I disagree with people who prefer to commit to more serious relationships or that I disapprove of those who think sex is sacred. I respect the beliefs of others, and hope to receive the same respect in return.

"Daniel, you're very handsome."

He smiles.

"Thank you."

"But it was a one-night thing. Please, leave it in the past."

The smile vanishes from his face and a look of confusion takes its place. "What . . . ?"

I rub my face with frustration as I stand surrounded by all these people. I worry that Mrs. Hidalgo will find me again not doing my job.

"Daniel, it was just a night of sex, okay?" I say curtly. "I'm not playing hard to get, I just wanted to sleep with you. I did it, and it's over."

"I don't believe you."

"Why not?"

"Girls aren't interested in only sex."

"What a terrible generalization. I regret to debunk your theory, but I am one hundred percent certain that I only wanted that and nothing more."

"I'm not sure what kind of game you're playing with me, Claudia, but stop. You don't need to make it harder—I'm interested in you."

Why is it difficult to believe that a woman could only want sexual gratification and nothing else?

"I'm not playing any games and I just—"

"Something wrong here?" Ares joins us.

I smile at him. "No. I was about to leave." I rush away before Daniel can say anything more.

The party proceeds without complications. When the reception is over, Gin and the rest of the hired staff help me clean up. After I check that my mother is sleeping, I return to the kitchen and make sure everything is in order. I rub my face with my hands and let out a deep sigh.

"Tired?"

My breath stops when I hear him speak. His voice has changed—it's deeper, more masculine and commanding than I remember it. I turn to face him for the first time in a long while.

Artemis.

Three

Surprise!

ARTEMIS

"Oh, come on, how about a tiny smile?" Cristina begs while giving me a look of reproach.

I don't answer. My focus is fixed on the road, this route I know so well. I'm not feeling the least bit enthusiastic about returning to the house of my childhood, a place filled with bitter memories.

Cristina, on the other hand, looks radiant and happy. She loves these kinds of occasions.

"Why so serious?"

I leave her question hanging, unanswered. I'm not in the mood to explain, and she takes the hint. "I hate it when you switch to extreme silent mode—it's irritating."

But she leaves me in peace, and moves to fix her makeup even though she looks great. She is stunning in a red dress that hugs her curves perfectly. Her red hair is loose and lightly curled on the bottom. I'm pretty sure that my mother will adore her. Cristina is elegant and comes from a very good family; to my mother, that's all that matters. When my cell vibrates in the pocket of my pants, I place the Bluetooth piece in my ear and answer the call.

"Sir." I hear the voice of David, my right-hand man, on the other end. "Sorry to bother you today, I know that—"

"David, get to the point."

"Of course, sir." There's a pause. "We have a problem: the machinery department has reported an accident involving one of the bulldozers."

Hidalgo Enterprises is one of the biggest construction firms in the country. We have offices in various states, and I'm in charge of headquarters. The bulldozers are the most expensive type of machinery, used for large-scale excavation. I let out a sigh before muttering my reply. "This must be good. What happened?"

"It was at the work site where they're building the new canal. From what I heard, the bulldozer slid off a side and landed in the water. They used a crane to retrieve it, but the machine is out of commission."

"Shit," I say, and Cristina looks at me with worry. "And its operator, is he okay?"

"Yes, sir." I'm relieved. "Where would you like us to send the machine? Back to the manufacturer? Or should we repair it in-house?

"Send it to our repair shop. I trust our mechanics. And keep me posted."

I hang up right after I hear his confirmation. I can feel Cristina's eyes on me.

"Is everything all right?"

"Yeah. Just machinery issues."

I park the car and unbuckle my seat belt.

"I have to say, I'm feeling pretty anxious," she confesses, and laughs nervously.

I get out of the car and walk over to other side to open the door for her.

She grabs my hand and together we head to the main entrance.

My home . . .

In the past five years, I haven't lived here, though I have made short visits. Yet I'm overcome by a feeling of familiarity, and my mind flashes to a set of black eyes that unsettle me every time I think of them.

"It's very quiet. Aren't we supposed to be attending a party?" Cristina asks in a whisper as she puts her ear to the door.

"Oh yes, we are. My mother expects it to be a surprise." I place my hand on the handle. "So please act accordingly."

"Surprise!" a crowd shouts in unison the moment I open the door.

I make an effort, and force a polite smile. I've only seen these people on a few occasions, often at events hosted by my mother. At last, I spot my parents. The wrinkles on my father's face have deepened, and the dark circles under his eyes are quite visible. The stress of life lived has left a stamp. My mother gives me a wide smile, and my father shakes my hand. My younger brother Apolo welcomes me with a quick hug. I put my hands in my pockets and proceed to introduce them to Cristina.

"And this is my girlfriend, Cristina."

"A pleasure to meet you." Cristina greets them with her best smile and shakes hands with my parents and Apolo. "You have a beautiful home."

"Well, thank you very much." My mother looks her over and seems pleased with what she sees.

While my mom proceeds to ask Cristina a lot of questions, I scan the room and find that pair of black eyes. *Claudia*. I clench my hands, still tucked inside my pockets. I'm in awe at how pretty she looks, and for a brief moment I feel short of breath. It's obvious that these past years have done wonders for her. I feel satisfied when she avoids my gaze. *Can't even bring yourself to look at me?*

The rest of the evening goes by in a blur. I make small talk with friends, listen to their boring stories and offer a few comments here and there. From time to time, my eyes, of their own volition, examine the room in search of a redhead different from the one standing next to me. Claudia tends to the guests. She slips away anytime I approach a group she's looking after, reacting as if I was the plague. *Can't even stand to be near me?*

Later in the evening, after we say good-bye to the last of our guests, Cristina, my parents, and I sit in the living room.

"Cristina, I'm very impressed. You are a fascinating young woman."

I take sip of my whisky while my mom showers Cristina with compliments. There is a twinkle in her eyes as she talks, and it's very clear that Cristina meets all the expectations my mother has for my ideal match. My father informs us he is exhausted and leaves.

"It's bedtime." She turns to address Cristina. "I'll tell Claudia to get the guest room ready for you." My mother gets up, but I grab her wrist gently.

"Please don't bother. Cristina will sleep with me." I look at Cristina and she blushes, her gaze turning downward. My lips curl into a grin. She needs to drop the innocent act, especially after all the naughty things she's done with me.

My mother gives me a disapproving look.

"Artemis . . ."

"Mother, we're adults. And you're not protecting anyone's chastity here." I let go of her wrist and get up. "I'll ask Claudia to bring extra towels and a few snacks up to my room."

I can tell my mother wants to protest my decision but won't do it in front of Cristina. I place my whisky glass on the side table and brush my hands on the side of my pants as I make my way to the kitchen. I come to a sudden stop when I reach the doorframe and notice her. Claudia is finishing with the cleanup. While her back is to me, I make use of the opportunity to examine her carefully for the first time this evening. Her body has changed, and her curves are more pronounced. The dress she is wearing fits her like a glove. Her fiery-red tresses are now pulled back into a high ponytail. She is no longer the fifteen-year-old girl I innocently declared my love to years ago. She's a woman now, and would certainly look incredible lying naked in my bed. She's a woman I would fuck, hard. I shake my head in an attempt to rid myself of these stupid, lustful thoughts.

"Tired?"

She turns to face me and is visibly unsettled. She looks at me briefly, and her eyes are full of fire and something else. Fear? Desire? I'm not sure. The air changes. And a tension that I've never felt before begins to grow.

Her voice is soft but curt. "No."

A part of me wants to ask about her mother and school. But I shouldn't be interested. She is not my childhood friend. She is simply the house staff, and I want to make that explicitly clear.

"*No?* I believe the correct answer is *No, sir*. Or maybe you've forgotten how to address your boss?"

Her eyes harden. I can tell she wants to challenge me.

"No, sir." She stretches the last word, infusing it with a hint of anger. Claudia has always been as fiery and intense as the red of her hair. She was never one to submit to others, and this fuels my desire to break her into submission.

"Bring fresh towels and some appetizers to my room," I order her in a chilly tone.

She nods, and I exit the room.

Four

You are the exception.

CLAUDIA

He wants me to call him sir?

Artemis is definitely not fond of me. I can't believe he's still holding a grudge for what happened so long ago.

He needs to get over it, and turn the page. Or maybe he doesn't even remember, or it doesn't matter to him, and he'd rather just treat me like a member of the staff. I knock on his door reluctantly. I carry the towels in one hand and the appetizers on a tray in the other. Knowing that he's waiting inside is doing a number on my nerves, and I swallow hard with anticipation.

Artemis opens the door. I tighten my grip on the towels. He's wearing his shirt unbuttoned to the waist, revealing a nicely sculpted chest. I look away and offer the items he requested.

"Your towels and appetizers . . . sir."

I hate using this title when I speak to him. I turn to face him when I don't get an answer, and realize that he's moved farther inside the bedroom.

"Put the towels on the bed and the food on the night table."

I don't want to walk inside his room, but I follow his instructions. As I step inside, I hear the sound of running water coming from the shower, and a female voice shouts from the bathroom. "Artemis, I'm waiting for you!"

I narrow my eyes. Oh, his girl is here, with him, in his room. This brings back an old memory: he and I playing Monopoly, sitting on the floor at the foot of his bed.

"You'll scare off the girls if you don't tidy up your room," I told him while checking out the mess.

"No girls are allowed in my room," Artemis replied with absolute determination.

I raised my eyebrow. "And what am I?"

"You are the exception."

I guess this no longer applies.

I pretend that I'm fine, but a strange feeling settles in the pit of my stomach. I don't want to admit that this is having an effect on me, because it shouldn't. Artemis stands on the other side of the bed with his arms crossed over his chest. He studies me, and his eyes search for mine. I need to leave immediately, so I do my best to quickly place everything where he instructed. I become fixated with folding the towels neatly on his bed. I freeze when I turn around and realize that Artemis is now standing in the way, blocking the door.

Undaunted, I start to walk toward the door. But he doesn't get out of the way.

"Excuse me, sir."

He remains silent.

The sound of the shower fills the room. I freeze when I notice he's undoing the last button of his shirt. His shoulder muscles flex as he removes the garment. I fix my eyes on the wall. It bothers me that I'm blushing. What in the hell is he doing? I hear his footsteps coming closer, and once again, I can't bring myself to look directly at him.

"Sir . . ."

My defenses are triggered when he leans over me. I'm about to push him away just as he whispers in my ear.

"Wash this. It's one of my favorites." He puts the shirt in my hands and heads to the bathroom. "And close the door."

I'm out of there in a flash. I walk down the hallway in such haste that I don't even see Apolo until I run straight into him.

"Hey, why are you in such a hurry?"

His hair is messy and he's wearing pajamas. He looks sweet, and I smile.

"It's nothing. I'm just tired."

His eyes dart over to the door of Artemis's bedroom. And then they land back on me. "Is everything okay?"

"Yeah, everything's fine."

He grabs my hand. "Want to come to my room?"

Apolo and I have grown closer in the past months. Sometimes, after I'm done with work, we watch movies until midnight, although I often end up falling asleep midway through. The blush that appears on his face gives him away. At first, I thought we were simply bonding like siblings do, as if he was my younger brother. But recently I've noticed a change in his manner, and he may be misreading our relationship, hoping for more. Or maybe it's just my imagination playing tricks on me. Either way, he's sixteen now; I can't keep treating him like a kid.

"I'll have to take you up on that another night," I reply.

He gives my hand a squeeze. "Are you sure?"

I nod as I pull my hand away. "Good night, Apolo."

"Good night, Claudia."

As I try to fall asleep, the vision of Artemis's bare chest torments my thoughts.

A few days pass and I don't run into Artemis at all. Maybe he's busy with work—who knows. One thing is certain, I feel calm and grateful. Artemis doesn't intimidate me, but I feel unsettled in his presence. He's been away for so many years that it's going to take some time to get used to him being around again.

On Saturday morning, I wake up as usual, assist my mother to the bathroom, and help her get dressed. I opt to wear my hair in two braids; it makes work easy and keeps my hair in place. I leave my mom in our room and make my way to prepare breakfast. I let out a yawn and stretch my arms as I enter the kitchen.

I jump when I notice someone sitting at the table. "Oh my god!"

Artemis is dressed in an impeccable black suit paired with a dark-blue tie, arms folded across his chest. The rays of sunshine streaming through the window shine on his hair, bringing out the few strands of blond that are usually invisible to the casual eye.

It's the first time he's come to the kitchen since the night of the party, and his impassive face and stone-cold eyes make me uneasy.

"Good morning, sir."

Without even a greeting, he says, "I've been waiting for twenty minutes to eat breakfast."

"It's seven o'clock in the morning. I serve breakfast at seven thirty when Ares and Apolo are about to leave for school, and on weekends when they wake up."

"Well, I'm ordering that you change your schedule to suit my needs."

I flush with irritation. "You don't have to talk to me that way."

"I'll address you whichever way it damn well pleases me." He glares at me.

The voice of my mother plays in my head. *Behave*. I fight to control my urge to talk back and tell him where to go. I bite my tongue—literally.

"And in the spirit of getting things straight . . ." He points to a uniform on the table, which I hadn't noticed. "From now on, you wear this."

"I beg your pardon?" I snap. That's the last straw.

"You heard me." He pushes the uniform toward me. "I think you need to wear this to remind yourself of the place you occupy in this house. My brothers have failed to set boundaries where you are concerned."

I let out a sarcastic laugh. "You are a fucking idiot."

Though he arches a brow in reaction to my insult, he at least seems a bit shocked. "What did you call me?"

I make sure to emphasize each word. "You. Are. A. Fucking. Idiot. Artemis."

I notice his jaw is clenched when he gets up from his chair. He leans in and places both hands on the table. "Apologize immediately."

I shake my head. "No." I sound more determined than I truly feel, and in an act of cowardice, I retreat toward the door. But he is way too fast for me, and grabs one of my arms. His strong hand tightens its grip, and pulls me between him and the wall.

"You're not going anywhere."

We've never been this close. I can smell the subtle yet masculine scent of his cologne and his shampoo.

"Let me go." I keep my gaze fixed on his tie.

He takes my chin and forces me to look up at him.

"You have forgotten your place in this house." He looks directly into my eyes as he speaks. "You are an employee here. The help. I could fire you if you crossed the line and disrespected me. I am not my brothers. And I most certainly am not my father. You behave this way again and I will, without hesitation, kick you out of this house."

"You are not my boss." I struggle to free myself from his grip. "I report to Mr. Juan."

"Trust me when I tell you this, Claudia— if I want you out of this house, I can make it happen." This is the first time that he has addressed me by my name, and given the circumstances, I don't like how it sounds.

"I'm your boss now." His gaze briefly moves to my lips. "The roof over your head, your future, your stability, all of it is in my hands. For your own good, I suggest you bite that insolent tongue of yours and follow my orders."

He lets me go and returns to his seat. He grabs the newspaper and proceeds to open it. I close my hands into fists and press them to my sides. Then I grab the uniform, grudgingly.

I hate him.

I never expected he could be this cold. The Artemis I grew up with was a quiet boy. He did not express much of what he felt, but he was warm and would have never treated me this way.

Shortly after, I catch a glimpse of myself in the bathroom mirror, and the way I look bothers me immensely. The uniform looks like a fucking Halloween costume. I wonder how the idiot managed to get the right size.

When I get back to the kitchen, I notice that Artemis has company. Apolo is with him. I can't contain my embarrassment.

"Sir." I pause. "I put on the uniform. May I get back to work?"

Artemis keeps reading the newspaper and avoids looking my way. "As long as you know your place in this house, you may return to your duties."

I purse my lips and make a Herculean effort to reply civilly. "It is evident that, in this house, I am just a maid, sir."

"Good." He puts the newspaper aside, grabs a cup of tea, and spills its contents across the table. "Then you should clean this."

"Artemis!" Apolo's sweet voice helps me remain calm. Artemis gives him a cold stare. He's testing me and wants me to fail so he can run me out of this house. I never thought he would hate me this much. I really underestimated his disapproval.

My eyes fill with tears, but I keep them from falling. I will not give him the satisfaction. I keep quiet and look for a rag. "As you wish, sir."

"Artemis." I'm startled by the anger in Apolo's tone.

No one has ever treated me like this. Not even the lady of the house, and she isn't too fond of me.

Apolo's attempt to remedy the situation clearly irritates Artemis. He says, "Go ahead, try to do something about this, and I'll go straight to our father and let him know about your drunken binges. She's just the house help. She's not worth the trouble, Apolo."

His words are fiery hot and burn me. Regardless of how I feel, I go back to doing my work. A hand grabs my arm to stop me from cleaning. I look up to find Apolo's warm gaze.

"Enough."

I don't want to cause any problems between him and his brother, so I loosen my arm from his grip.

"Sir asked me to clean, and I must do as he's asked."

Apolo shakes his head and grabs my arm again. "'Sir' has gotten enough of this."

Out of nowhere, Artemis shows up right next to us and abruptly grabs Apolo's wrist. "Don't touch her." Apolo and I furrow our brows in confusion. "Go to your room, Apolo."

"Only if you leave her alone."

Artemis lets out a sigh. "Whatever. You two, get out of my sight."

I don't think twice and make my exit as quickly as possible. There will be enough time later to get breakfast ready. It is clear that this Artemis Hidalgo is not the caring boy I grew up with. This man is a shell of his former self. He is cold, and I despise him.

Five

I have asked you to forget that name.

ARTEMIS

"Wow . . . that was . . . enthusiastic." Cristina is out of breath as she rolls the hem of her skirt back down. After I rearrange my boxers, I pull up my pants. She wipes her face with one hand.

I don't say anything and walk to the private en suite bathroom in my office. I clean myself, fix my tie, and return to my desk. "What are you doing here?" I ask. She knows I don't like visits at work.

She arches a brow and smiles. "Oh, now you ask?"

I jumped her bones the second she entered my office. I didn't even greet her or give her a chance to speak, for that matter. I needed the quick release of sex.

She sits on the other side of my desk. "We haven't spent any time together in days, and I wanted to see you."

"I've been swamped with work." She is aware of this. One of the reasons we work well as a couple is that Cristina doesn't make any demands and never complains. She knows me well and has adapted to my needs.

"I know. But I still miss you." She sighs deeply.

I glance over and notice she is looking down, hoping to hide her sadness.

"Would you like to go out for dinner tonight?"

She looks at me with the biggest smile. "Of course."

I smile back. "Then I'll make reservations somewhere nice."

She comes around the desk, leans over, and gives me a quick peck on the mouth.

"All right. I'll see you tonight."

She walks to the door, passing the general manager of purchasing, Hannah, on her way out. Hannah greets me with a smile as she enters my office and then proceeds to drop a file on my desk. "Good afternoon, sir."

"I hope you have good news."

"Yes, indeed. The bulldozer that was damaged has been fixed and is in perfect working condition. This file contains all relevant information about the machinery, the parts sourced, the cost of labor, etcetera. If you need anything else, please let me know."

I let out a sigh of relief. The bulldozers are the most expensive machines we have in our inventory.

"Great. Thank you very much."

She smiles politely and leaves. My doctor has strongly recommended that in order to avoid stress, I need to stop involving myself in every single detail that pertains to the operation of this company. Per his instructions, I need to trust my staff and delegate more, which I am unable to do, even though I've tried. I feel an overwhelming sense of obligation. My father placed his trust in me, and I would hate to disappoint him. I rub my face and sink back in my chair. I close my eyes and massage my temples. I'm exhausted. My sleep-deprived nights are catching up with me.

"Well, this is a discouraging sight." Alex's voice catches me by surprise. When I open my eyes, he's sitting next to my desk with his arms crossed. "I don't mean to offend you, but you look awful."

I met Alex, my best friend, in university. We were in the same faculty, although he studied finance. I hired him when I took over the reins of the company. He is one of the few people I trust. I try to ease the tension in my shoulders.

"What are you doing here?" I ask.

His broad smile lights up his face. Alex is a cheerful type. "Always the charmer. What, I can't drop by for a visit with my best friend?"

"I'm working."

"Really? Because you look like you're about to pass out from exhaustion."

"It's fine."

"If you die, I'm not attending your funeral."

I try to seem stern, but my eyelids are heavy. "I'm fine."

"Are you sure?" Alex makes himself comfortable, puts his hands behind his head, and leans backward. "I ran into Cristina in the hallway. I was under the impression you didn't mix work with pleasure."

I roll my eyes. "What are you insinuating?"

"Well, she looked like she'd just been screwed."

"Please don't talk about her like that."

He removes his hands from behind his head and slowly stands. "My apologies, m'lord. You're in a crappy mood today." He pauses and pretends to ponder. "But then again, you always are."

When I don't reply, he studies me attentively. Alex knows me so well. "You're more frustrated than usual. What's going on?"

"I told you, I'm doing just fine."

"Look, you can keep deflecting, and I can keep asking if you're okay until I wear you down and finally manage to extract a confession, but why don't we save ourselves the time and you just tell me what's going on?"

I sigh. "I think I might have come down too hard on someone."

He pretends to be shocked. "No."

"You don't believe me?"

"If you're actually feeling guilty, then you must have been pretty harsh. Who was it?"

I look away and sink deeper in my chair. Alex arches an eyebrow.

"Don't tell me . . ."

"Alex."

"Oh—I know that look. It was Claudia, wasn't it?"

I don't even know how he remembers her. "I told you to forget that name."

He rolls his eyes.

"It's hard to forget the name that my best friend called out every time he'd get drunk all through first year."

"That belongs in the past."

He sits down.

"Sure thing. What did you do to her?"

My mind flashes back to that moment, me watching her clean the tea I'd spilled. It's been tormenting me—I don't understand why I'm overcome with anger whenever I'm near her.

"You'll slap me when I tell you what I did."

Alex's jaw drops. "Wow. That bad, huh?"

The memory of Claudia's expression tortures me. But I keep that to myself.

Alex is looking at me intently. "Artemis, after all these years, you need to let her go. Stop harboring this grudge over something that's in the past."

"I'm not holding a grudge. I feel nothing for her."

"You can lie to yourself, and to others. But we both know that's not the truth. The anger and lack of self-control that take hold of you come from those pent-up feelings."

"Enough. I shouldn't have said anything."

"Apologize to her, turn the page, and then be civil to her!"

I don't respond. Instead, I get up and leave my office. Once I'm down the hall, I continue on my routine walk around to check on daily operations. Alex will get the hint.

After Cristina and I have our dinner, I drop her home and head back to mine. I loosen my tie the moment I enter and massage my neck to ease the tension. I can hear noise coming from the kitchen as I head there to get a glass of water. I haven't been in the kitchen since the morning I put Claudia in her place. I won't deny that remorse has been eating at me ever since.

The sound of Claudia's voice spreads throughout the kitchen. She's singing. I stand quietly and watch her from the doorway. I never expected the uniform I forced her to wear would look this good on her. She sings while cooking, and holds the spoon as if it was a microphone.

I can't help but smile. She has a lovely voice, and it brings back old memories, like that Sunday afternoon when we were younger, enjoying the pool.

We were sitting together on the edge, with our feet dipped in the water.

"Do you have a dream?" I asked her, out of curiosity.

She shook her head. "No. People like me can't afford to entertain dreams."

I frowned at her response. "Why not?"

"Because it's a waste of time to give in to illusions that will never come true."

I took a sip of my soda.

"You're quite the pessimist. You know that, right?"

"And you are too quiet. You know that, too, right?"

That made me laugh. "But never with you," I said.

"Yes, I know. But it's an entirely different story with others. You need more friends."

"Does it bother you that you're my only friend?"

She placed a loose strand of hair behind her ear and smiled. "No, it doesn't bother me."

We sat in comfortable silence for a bit, then Claudia started to hum a song.

"I know your dream," I told her.

She moved her feet through the water.

"Hmm, tell me more . . ."

"Well, you love singing. Wouldn't you want to be a famous singer one day?"

She looked down, her gaze lost in the crystal clear water.

"That would be—"

"What are you scared of? Admitting the truth won't hurt anyone."

She bit her lip and looked at me. The glint in her eyes gave her away.

"Yeah, that could be my dream. But I'll deny it if you ever tell a soul." She sighed before she smiled. "I would love to be a singer."

Watching Claudia now, as she works and sings in the kitchen, I wonder if she kept that dream. *Ah, what business is it of mine?*

I clear my throat. She freezes on the spot, then gives me a quick glance and places the spoon inside the dishwasher. I'm surprised by the annoyed expression I see on her face when she turns around. I thought she would be embarrassed. Quite the contrary; she looks irritated. I suppose she has every right to be.

"Is there anything I can do for you, sir?" I'm surprised by how cold her voice sounds.

She isn't irritated. She's furious.

Her body language tells me that she's one word away from exploding into a barrage of curses directed at me.

This is textbook Claudia; I have not intimidated her in the least. She will obey and bite her tongue because she has to in order to keep her job, not because she's afraid of me—which doesn't surprise me in the least. Even my brothers are a little terrified of me, but not her, never her.

"I'd like a cup of tea," I reply, and take a seat at the kitchen table. She gives me a cold-eyed stare that almost makes me put my head down. "Please," I finish my request, clearing my throat.

She sighs and prepares the tea in silence while I watch. Her red hair is pulled into a long braid that starts at the crown of her head and falls down her back. Although I can only see her side profile, the hairstyle perfectly emphasizes her features. She rubs her shoulder and grimaces slightly, looking tired. It appears she's had a long day. That makes two of us.

I flash back to what happened the other day, and the feeling of remorse resurfaces. I'm not usually one to experience regret, so the unpleasant feeling is uncomfortable.

Distractedly, I glide my finger along the edge of the table. A cup of tea appears. I look up to see her standing in front of me. Her icy stare is unsettling.

"Your tea, sir." There isn't a shred of respect in her tone, only disgust.

"Thank you."

She turns around and carries on with her work.

I take a sip. I try to enjoy my tea but the awareness that I did something terrible is stuck in the back of my mind. She must feel my stare on her, because she turns to face me. She puts a hand on her cocked hip.

"If you're going to apologize, you can do it now."

It's the first time she's spoken to me in a familiar way, and surprisingly, it doesn't bother me. She must read the confusion in my face because her expression immediately changes. She seems to have realized that she blurted out what she was thinking.

"Forget it." She heads toward the kitchen door.

Before she can exit, I blurt, "I'm sorry." She stops in her tracks but doesn't turn around. I'm grateful she allows me to continue. "I deeply regret what happened the other morning. It was too much. I was an idiot. And it will never happen again."

I don't expect an answer. I know her well. An apology is not enough to make amends. *Oh, you know her? More like you used to know her. You hardly know her now. And are not in the least interested in knowing anything about her.*

"Are you sorry?" She turns around. The fury is noticeable in her eyes. "You treated me like shit and humiliated me in front of your brother. And now you're sorry?"

I get to my feet. "Claudia."

She takes three steps toward the table. She takes my tea and empties the cup on the table. She turns and grabs a rag, which she throws at me. I barely catch it.

"Clean it—sir." Her black eyes are bright with ire; I admit that I'm a bit scared of her. "And if you ever treat me that way again, I will punch you where the sun don't shine. Apology accepted."

Now that she's facing me up close, I'm able to get a good look at her features. The faint bags under her eyes don't diminish how beautiful she is. I remain silent while I wipe the table clean and she stares at me with her arms crossed over her chest.

"I've apologized and I'm done cleaning," I inform her once I finish. "I believe we're even now."

She curls her lips. "I suppose. Now let's try to behave professionally. I'm the staff at this house and you are the son of my boss—period."

"So that's all I've ever been to you, the son of your boss? In that case, you're the hired help and nothing more."

"Agreed." She casts one last cautious glance my way before she disappears through the kitchen door.

She leaves me alone with a reminder of the distance that she always placed between us. It's a distance so immense that it makes it difficult for me to feel her presence even when she's right in front of me.

Six

Apolo, what are you doing?

CLAUDIA

Even though his apology is not enough, Artemis sounded sincere.

It makes me think that maybe he doesn't despise me as much as I thought he did. It makes me hopeful that we can manage to be amicable. I walk without consciously thinking where to go, climbing the stairs and finding myself standing outside Apolo's bedroom. I underestimated how much I need to unload with someone, to interact with another human being.

I also enjoy talking with Ares, but he's hardly ever home. He has a very active social life. Apolo on the other hand likes to spend his time in his room, reading or busy with other things.

I knock on the door and wait for the "Come in" as my cue to enter. Even though it's late, Apolo is sitting on the small sofa next to the window, holding a book open in his hands. His lips turn into a smile and he looks at me with tenderness. He closes the book and places it on his lap. "And to what do I owe the pleasure of this visit?"

I let out a sigh and sit on his bed facing him. "I've had a long day."

His eyes study my face with worry. "Did Artemis bother you again?"

"No."

"Is Martha okay?"

"Yes." My mother's health has remained stable lately, which has been a relief. Living with chronic liver disease has its ups and downs. "I'm just tired, I guess."

He gets up and moves closer until he's right in front of me, forcing me to bend my neck up.

"Would you like a massage?"

Apolo gives the best massages. I smile and nod. He climbs on his bed and kneels behind me. His hands go to my shoulders and move to the dip where they meet my neck. He puts pressure on this point. I close my eyes and give in to pure bliss.

"You're tense," he informs me as he keeps working.

It feels so good. I start to relax and swallow a soft groan. "The past days have been stressful," I admit with an exhale.

Apolo's hands are now on my back and his thumbs are applying pressure. They move alongside my spinal cord, hitting all the main points and making me whimper. Apolo stops and I open my eyes.

"Sorry. It is just too relaxing."

He leans forward. I can feel his breath close to my ear. "Then relax. When a massage is this good, it's normal to make those noises."

His breath tickles, and I have a hard time swallowing. There's a shift of energy in the room. I feel a weird vibe grow between us, and I can't explain why. It's not the first time he's given me a massage. His hands go up my back and stop midway. My breathing comes to a halt when his hands move under my arms and come to rest on my abdomen. His chest is lightly brushing against my back.

"Inhale deeply. This is an antistress technique."

Despite the strange proximity, I do as he tells me.

"Close your eyes. And concentrate on your breathing."

I inhale and exhale. The heat of his chest envelops my back. My heart races. To be completely honest, at this moment I feel the opposite of relaxed. His lips lightly graze my ear and I hope it was by accident. It must be an accident.

"Apolo, what are you doing?" I say quietly.

His nose brushes against my ear and his breathing gently caresses my skin. My heart keeps beating fast. What if he can tell? This is embarrassing. *Relax, this is just a massage.*

"Claudia . . ." Apolo whispers in my ear. And I feel a shiver run down my spine. The sweet scent of his cologne wraps around me.

The strange mood is broken when the door is flung open, and I quickly jump to my feet and away from Apolo. A confused Artemis looks at me first, then turns his gaze to Apolo, who is putting his arms down but still kneeling on the bed.

Artemis folds his arm across his chest. "What are you two up to?"

Apolo looks at me before giving him an answer. "We were just . . ." But he doesn't finish his sentence. Artemis arches his brow. "What do you need?" Apolo says.

"You haven't answered my question."

Apolo looks annoyed. "I don't have to."

Artemis wasn't expecting that reaction from his little brother, and furrows his brow. I don't want to spoil the peace accord we brokered earlier in the kitchen—we agreed to remain civil, and I don't want any trouble.

"I was about to leave." I smile at Apolo, turn to the door, and make my exit without looking back. I should not have come up to see Apolo. I need to be more careful now that Artemis is living here. Not because I care what he thinks of me, but because I don't want to cause any problems for Apolo.

I'm on my way down the stairs when a shirtless and barefoot Ares runs past me.

"Ares?"

He holds a phone in his hand, and looks completely frantic.

"I'll explain later!" he shouts as he dashes out the front door.

Back in my room, I text him. I'm worried and know I won't fall asleep until I receive a message from him, so he lets me know that he won't be sleeping at home tonight. Shirtless and barefoot? I have a hunch that this has something to do with our next-door neighbor's daughter. I believe her name is Raquel. I've never seen Ares show this much interest in a girl. Maybe she's the one who will finally melt that frozen heart of his.

I take a seat next to my mother, who is sitting up and resting her back against the headboard. Her short red hair is peppered with gray. The wrinkles in her face are noticeable when she smiles. She takes my hand. "You're back."

I return the smile, and lean over to kiss her forehead. I pull away and caress her cheek.

"You should be sleeping."

"Hmm."

"How are you feeling?" I ask and carefully examine her features. My priority is her well-being.

"Fine." Her fingers glide gently under my eyes. "Look at these bags. You look exhausted. Let's go to sleep."

"Agreed. Let me change."

She examines the uniform and her brow furrows.

"It's a new dress code, Mom. Nothing that concerns you, okay? I have everything under control."

She waits for me while I change out of the stupid uniform. I put on my pajamas and lie next to her.

"Good night, Mom."

"Good night, sweetie."

Sleep, however, doesn't come easy. My mind keeps replaying this evening's events, from Artemis's apology to that moment with Apolo in his room. What was that all about? I want to believe it's just my imagination playing tricks, but then again Apolo is no longer small. He's a teenage boy with raging hormones. Maybe I've been careless and given him mixed signals. Regardless, I need to proceed with caution, or this could get out of control.

Claudia . . . I hear the tender tone of his voice in my ear. I shake my head and stop thinking about that moment. And pray I find peace of mind and get some sleep very soon.

It's cold . . .

I'm freezing and can't stop trembling. The temperature is so low that my lips are cracked and my skin is dry from the cold. I hug Fred, my stuffed bear. He's filthy and smells terrible, yet I can't let him go. The small trailer where we live is dark. It's been a while since the electricity was cut. I find my mother unconscious, lying on the sofa. Her hand is dangling to the side, and there are used syringes on the floor. She has on a very short skirt and a cropped top that exposes her midriff. Her red hair is long, parted in the middle, unkempt and dirty. I place my small hand on her chest.

"Mommy."

She doesn't move or respond.

"Mommy, I'm cold."

I look for a blanket; I think she must be cold too because she is so underdressed. I try to be careful and cover her as much as possible. I'm startled by someone knocking hard on the door.

"Martha! Martha! Open the damn door!"

My heart is beating fast. I'm afraid and shake my mother.

"Mommy! Mommy, wake up!"

But she remains still. I scream when someone kicks the door open.

"You stupid bitch, where are you?!"A tattooed man with earrings and dressed in black storms into our small place. His eyes land on my mother.

"Oh, there you are."

I stand in his way.

"No! Leave her alone!"

He grabs me by my hair and throws me to the side. My stomach makes contact with a side table next to the sofa. The air gets knocked out of me. I hold on to my tummy. The man picks up the syringes and throws them. He proceeds to slap my mother, who barely blinks her eyes.

"Well, well, look at this! You've been tripping on my merchandise."

I struggle to get up, tears in my eyes.

"Leave her alone! Please!"

The strange man climbs on top of my mom, pulling at her skirt. I hit him repeatedly. He turns around, grabs me by the hair, and drags me to the door. He throws me out and I land hard on the snow that's piled in front of our trailer.

"Listen, brat, if you dare come back inside, I'll kill you."

I run away, hoping to find someone who can help. I can't fight that man by myself. My mother told me I should never fight anyone who comes looking for her. She says I should go look for help instead. I stumble and fall. A few inches of snow have fallen on the ground, and I can't feel my feet.

A kind voice speaks in my ear and a pair of strong arms hold me tight out here in the cold.

"Hey, hey. Claudia."

I open my eyes; tears cloud my vision and I'm trembling uncontrollably.

"You're okay. It was just a nightmare." I am as startled by Artemis's voice as I am by the realization that we're standing in the middle of the backyard. Was I sleepwalking? Again?

The fear, the cold, the anguish of the dream still torment my thoughts. I lift my head to look up at the eyes that used to soothe me when I had these nightmares before. I purse my lips to stop myself from crying. But I fail. Artemis holds my face. In this moment, he ceases to be the cold and bitter man others see. He's the boy I grew up with; the one who protected me and held me every time I was tortured by these horrible dreams. The boy who would only act this way when he was with me.

"You're okay," he whispers while his thumbs wipe away my tears.

I can't speak.

"You don't have to say anything. Everything is okay." He hugs me. And I quietly sob, pressed against his chest. His scent calms me down. His hand caresses the back of my head. I find myself unable to summon the will to put up my defenses and push him away. "I'm here, Claudia, you're okay."

I encircle his waist with my arms, and hug him tightly.

I feel too unstable to think clearly. Right now, I need to feel safe in his arms, if only for a brief moment. Just until the fear of imminent peril that is triggered by these nightmares goes away. Simply because these are not just dreams; they are vivid memories.

And he knows this. He is very well aware.

Seven

You're enjoying this. Aren't you?

ARTEMIS

A punch.

And another.

And one more.

My wrapped fists make contact with the leather bag hanging in front of me. I punch it again and again, every time with more force. The sweat rolls from my neck down to my chest and abdomen. My biceps flex with every hit. Yet my mind is stuck in last night.

"I . . ." Claudia stopped hugging me and moved away, her eyes puffy from crying so much. She looked uncomfortable. "I'm sorry. I—"

"You don't have to apologize," I assured her with a warm smile.

She avoided my gaze and cleared her throat. "I have to go."

As I punch the bag repeatedly, I recall her tense shoulders and stiff posture once she recovered from the shock. Most importantly, I remember how good it felt to hold her in my arms. Her scent, so familiar, drives me crazy. I can't let myself be interested in her. She's part of my past. And I have a girlfriend.

"Claudia," I called; she gave me a friendly smile as she started to leave.

"Thank you for . . ." She paused. "Thanks."

And she went back inside the house, bringing our interaction to a close.

Why is she so uncomfortable around me? She acts as if we're strangers. Sure, maybe that's what we are now. But there's history between us. I clench my fists tighter to deliver harder and more punishing blows. The bag swings as I pounce. I remember finding her with Apolo when I went to his room. She looked relaxed and comfortable in his company. Since when are they that close? Why is she at ease with him and so tense with me?

I have to stop thinking about her.

I quit my workout abruptly, grab the bag, and rest my forehead against it. My breathing is heavy and my entire body is drenched in sweat. I reach for a towel then make my way out of the gym with it wrapped around my neck, dressed in nothing other than athletic shorts.

I'm about to climb the stairs to my room but change my mind. I'm in the mood to tease Claudia, just a little. It's the least I can do after spending this whole morning with thoughts of her stuck in my head. In the kitchen, I walk straight to the fridge for a bottle of water, which I proceed to drink.

Claudia has just finished washing a pan. She notices me as she turns around to dry it.

"Oh." The pan slips from her hands and falls to the floor with a clang. "You caught me by surprise, sir."

She has reverted to using the title when addressing me. I wonder why?

She bends down to pick up the pan. As she rises, she takes in my bare chest and my midriff. A flush spreads across her cheeks. I keep quiet, though my lips turn up in a cocky smirk. She walks past me, glancing quickly and discreetly to check out my muscles—I'm certain of it.

I'm not being arrogant, but I've worked really hard to keep in shape. I love working out and I eat as healthily as I possibly can; and when I can, of course. In this regard, my brothers and I are very much alike. Ares has always been athletically inclined. And from time to time Apolo also makes use of our house gym.

After putting the pan away in the cabinet, Claudia walks by a second time. "Are you hungry, sir?"

She has her back to me, and I use the opportunity to watch her.

"Yes."

Her hair is styled in two braids that expose her neck. A few strands have come loose, making a nice contrast with her skin.

Claudia turns, and I look out the window instead.

"What would you like to eat?"

"A fruit salad would be nice."

She nods. "Very well."

I sit across the kitchen table and watch her prepare the salad. I pay attention to how delicately she holds each piece of fruit before she skillfully cuts and chops it, how she bites her lip each time the knife slices through. And how the sunlight brings out the tiny freckles on her cheeks that are often difficult to spot. How can she be this beautiful? What is it about her that I haven't been able to find in other women I've been with? I honestly want to find the answer to this question. Our eyes meet, and the depth of those black eyes makes me forget all about the strictly professional relationship we agreed to have.

"Are you doing okay?" The words come out before I have time to consider them.

"Yes." She puts a plate in front of me. I notice the fruit salad doesn't include strawberries. She remembers I'm allergic, and the gesture almost makes me smile.

"You did a really nice job with this." I don't know why I feel like I need to say this. Why am I trying to start a conversation with her?

She doesn't respond. I put a piece of cantaloupe in my mouth, chewing slowly, my eyes following her every move around the kitchen. Why doesn't she respond when I give her an opening? It's frustrating. I never have to put in this much effort. Often, other people go to great lengths to break my many barriers to engage or interact with me. But with this woman, it's definitely the opposite, and it unsettles me. I wonder if she behaves differently with Apolo. She was in his room, after all, and didn't seem one bit uncomfortable. I need to stop thinking about that moment.

I'm about to get up and leave when I notice something on the floor has caught Claudia's attention. Her frosty expression fades, replaced with an adoring look accompanied by a smile. I'm speechless. My stupid heart beats fast. I want her to look at me that way.

I follow her gaze to a furry white puppy that runs to greet her. It looks like it came in through the back door. Claudia kneels in front of it. The dog places its paws on her lap, starts to lick her hands, and she proceeds to pet it.

"Hi, cutie." She smiles and love radiates from her eyes. Where did this puppy come from?

Claudia suddenly remembers that I'm in the room and shoots up. Her expression turns serious. She moves toward the sink to wash the dishes by hand. The puppy sticks close to her feet.

"I didn't know we owned a dog." And there I go again—another attempt to start a conversation. What has gotten into me this morning?

Claudia barely looks my way. "It belongs to Apolo. He loves to rescue abandoned dogs. He's been volunteering at the dog shelter."

Apolo.

Her voice softens when she mentions my brother's name. It bothers me. I keep eating my fruit.

"How about that, quite the humanitarian."

"He is."

"I thought you stopped liking dogs."

I remember clearly, when we were much younger my dad got us a puppy. We named him Fluffy. Unfortunately, a few months later, he developed an infection that the vet couldn't cure, and Fluffy died. Claudia and I were devastated. We even held a funeral. From then on, dogs became a touchy subject for both of us.

Claudia looks at me with empathy. "I will never forget Fluffy." Her mouth curves down into a sad smile. "I don't know. It's hard to not get attached to the dogs Apolo rescues. They're so cute and want our love so much."

The dog comes around the table next to me. His fur tickles my feet.

I'm lost for words and don't know what to do. I haven't had

contact with dogs since Fluffy. But then I catch the dog raising his left leg, getting ready to pee on my foot.

"Agh!" I stand up in a flash and move away from him. I manage to get away just as he pees. "What the fuck!"

Claudia's laughter echoes throughout the kitchen. She's laughing so hard that she's gasping and holding her belly. I give the dog a murderous look when I notice him coming toward me.

"No! Stay back! Bad dog!"

I can't believe I'm retreating to avoid an animal so little it doesn't even reach my knees. Claudia has turned red. And for a brief moment, I forget about the dog and watch her laugh. God, I missed that sound. She stops when she senses my gaze on her, and tries hard to control her laughter by taking a deep breath and pursing her lips.

"Doggy!" She calls the dog to get him away from me. "Come here, Doggy!"

She leads the puppy out of the kitchen, closing the back door behind it. When she turns to look at me, she's squeezing her lips tight, trying hard to suppress her laughter. The amusement I see in her eyes is refreshing.

"You're enjoying this, aren't you?"

"No, sir." A giggle escapes her lips. It's the first time she's called me sir jokingly and without a hint of disdain.

Acting on an impulse, I walk around the table to get close to her.

"You are definitely enjoying it. Did you train him to do that?"

She laughs some more and tries to regain her composure while backing away.

"Of course not."

I keep advancing and she keeps moving away until she has

her back against the kitchen wall. Her smile has started to fade and she looks nervous. I corner her and place my hands on the wall on either side of her face. She lifts her hands in an attempt to push me away but stops herself when she realizes her hands will make contact with my exposed skin since I am shirtless.

"What are you doing?" she asks.

I raise one eyebrow. "What happened to *sir*?"

She licks her lips. "I don't like calling you that."

"Why not?"

She fixes her eyes on mine, and there is not a sign of doubt or intimidation in them. "You're too young to be called sir."

"Using the title has nothing to do with my age."

"Right. According to you, it's a way to show respect to the bosses in this house." She rolls her eyes. "And as I've told you before, you're not my boss."

"Is that so?"

She raises her chin defiantly. "Yes."

I tilt my head forward and closer to hers, leaving very little space between us. It allows me the perfect view of every single detail of her face.

"If I'm not your boss, then, what am I?" I can tell she's hesitating. Her lips are so close. I just need to move an inch and I'll find out how they taste, how they feel against mine. For too brief a second her vulnerability is exposed. She doesn't seem as sure of herself or as in control as per her usual. She looks indecisive, and I have to admit that I enjoy seeing her like this. I want her to come undone the way I do whenever she's near me. I simply don't know why I say and do the things that I say and do to her. We're breathing hard, and the heat from our bodies mingles. Claudia is looking directly at me.

"I've told you. You're just my boss's son."

But the conviction in her tone has evaporated. She doesn't sound as determined as the first time she made the same proclamation. She pushes one of my arms with her hand in an attempt to escape from my trap. Before she can run too far, I catch up and quickly take her arm. I trap her between my body and the kitchen table.

"That's all I am, huh?" I grab her chin. "Just the son of the boss. I don't believe you, Claudia."

"I don't care if you don't believe me." She frees her chin from my hold.

"If that's the case, why are you always evading me? What are you so afraid of?" I'm not quite sure why I'm asking these questions, or where they're coming from. I place my hands against the tabletop on either side of her waist. Our gazes are locked, and the urge to investigate, explore, and uncover creeps in. I used to know all her vulnerabilities but now she keeps me on the outside looking in. All I get from her is defensiveness and coldness. I don't want that.

"I'm not afraid of anything. And I'm not evading you."

"Liar."

She purses her lips, and her gaze leaves mine, moving to my chest.

"Artemis, you don't matter that much to me," she says.

"I want you to look at me in the eyes and say it one more time." She looks at me and appears to hesitate. We are so damn close that her breasts brush against my bare chest every time she takes in and lets out a breath.

"You . . ." She can't finish the sentence. I inadvertently brush my thumb against her lips, which she immediately opens to release short, rapid breaths.

Damn it, I am dying to kiss her.

The one thing stopping me is Cristina. She's very special to me, and I don't want to be unfaithful. It is inexcusable that I've let this interaction get this far. I don't want to be like my mother. Claudia is watching me in silence, unsure of what is about to happen. Or perhaps, in anticipation of what she hopes may happen. And I know what I want; it infuriates and baffles me at the same time. I hate not feeling in control.

I don't know how but I manage to separate myself from Claudia and make a quick exit from the kitchen before I do something I'll regret. I foolishly believed I was no longer attracted to her, and now it's clear I must proceed with caution.

Maybe I should be with her once so that I can finally leave her behind, in the past. Perhaps having always thought of her as unattainable presents a challenge, or something to that effect. What is plain and clear now is that I won't be able to move on until I have her. I need to possess every one of the groans, whimpers, and moans that must come out of her mouth in the throes of passion.

I always get what I want. That Fourth of July years ago, Claudia became the exception. But this time, she won't be the exception. Not again.

Eight

You are too easy to please.

CLAUDIA

I need to stay away from Artemis.

The distance I was able to establish between us wasn't enough; this is evident in light of our most recent encounters. What was that moment in the kitchen all about? Why was my heart beating like that? I suppose it's because I'm still adjusting to how much he's grown and changed—maybe that's all there is to it.

Nevertheless, I can't get out of my head the image of his face so close to mine. I got lost in his eyes, and was able to appreciate every detail of his scruffy beard and strong jaw.

I'd rather not think about what happened. It was difficult to hide the effect he had on me when he walked into the kitchen shirtless. He's so fit, and he knows it. I can't give him the satisfaction of seeing me stunned by his good looks.

If that's the case, why are you always evading me? What are you so afraid of?

I'm still rattled by the sound of his deep voice and the sensation of his breath grazing my lips. I shake my head. Maybe it's only a physical attraction; after all, he's very handsome—it's normal to notice. That's exactly why my heart was beating that fast. I don't like to admit that I'm attracted to him; however, it helps explain what's happening with me and why my body reacts the way it does when he's near me. Still, I have to forget about that morning. Days have passed, so I don't know why I'm still dwelling on it. Artemis has maintained a safe distance ever since, and I have a feeling he's avoiding me. I'm grateful; it's what's best for the two of us.

I'm dusting the curtains in the living room when I hear noises coming from the rec room. I pause and listen for a second.

Oh. I guess Raquel, the neighbor, finally fell into Ares's trap.

I recall how timid she appeared earlier when she came around asking for Ares. I confess, I'm surprised she was able to resist his charms for so long.

I can't say the same for other girls who've passed through Ares's bed. One look, a few words, and he traps them in a flash. I walk down the hallway to put on some music to camouflage the sounds they're making. Even though Mr. and Mrs. Hidalgo aren't home and Artemis hasn't come from work, I can't help but feel a little embarrassed on their behalf. Sadly, my attempts are in vain when I find Apolo paralyzed, standing right outside the door of the games room.

"I didn't know Samy was over."

I smile. "It isn't Samy."

"Then who?" Apolo raises a brow.

I let out a long breath. "I think it's the neighbor girl."

Apolo can't hide his shock. "Raquel?"

"Yes, that's the one."

"Oh shit . . . I wasn't expecting that. I thought they hated each other."

I shrug. "Sometimes attraction can masquerade as hate."

I head to the kitchen and Apolo follows me. I'm relieved. In here, we can no longer hear Ares and his guest.

"Would you like a turkey sandwich?" I ask.

He bumps his fist with mine. "You know I do."

I can't help but laugh. "You're too easy to please."

"I bet he is," Artemis says from the kitchen door. He's wearing a suit, which means he just got home from work. The good vibe between me and Apolo is put on pause by his brother's sudden appearance.

"Claudia, do we pay you to chat or to work?"

I see. He's in the frustrated and sarcastic idiot mood again.

Apolo moves to stand between us. "Artemis, don't start. Leave her alone."

He remains still, watching us. I prepare the sandwich, place it on the kitchen table, and immediately proceed to make my exit.

I'm barely halfway across the living room when I hear Artemis and Apolo raising their voices at each other. Are they arguing?

Artemis leaves the kitchen. Apolo is right behind him and about to say something when Raquel rushes out of the rec room and slams right into me. Her hair is disheveled and her eyes are teary. She looks completely lost. She is oblivious to our presence and slams the main door on her way out. Artemis, Apolo, and I stare at each other in confusion.

"Wasn't that Raquel?" Artemis asks, which takes us by surprise because he's in the habit of remembering only the things he considers significant.

Apolo clenches his fists and heads to the rec room, probably to lecture Ares, which feels right and necessary. And then I realize he's left me and Artemis alone. This is the first time I've been around him since that morning. Even though he appears tired from work, his suit and hair are impeccable. It's as if elegance comes effortlessly to him.

I walk back to the kitchen. To my surprise, Artemis follows me in silence. What does he want now? Isn't it obvious to him that tension still lingers between us? He leans against the kitchen door while I sort through some documents on the table; I'd brought them in earlier, hoping to make progress with a university assignment that's due very soon.

"Claudia." His voice has gone back to the icy tone he used that morning when he chose to humiliate me with the spilled tea.

I sigh and stop sorting through the papers. And turn around.

"Yes, sir?"

Two can play at the cold-shoulder game.

His impassive expression is void of any amusement or warmth.

"I want to apologize for the behavior I displayed the other morning. It was out of order on my part and it will never happen again." There is no hesitation in his voice; he sounds certain, and his tone is very chilly. "I'd rather keep our relationship strictly professional."

I cross my arms. "I agree, that has always been my intention, sir. I believe the one who was confused is you."

Artemis, I can most certainly kick your ass at this game.

Fine cracks appear on his cold demeanor to reveal . . . something. Is he hurt? Too late—within seconds, he makes a quick recovery.

"All right. That's all."

He throws me one last glance before walking out. And I finally let the air that I had unintentionally been holding out of my lungs. I'm glad that he apologized. And that he made it clear that the relationship between us is simply about work. That's all I've ever wanted.

So why am I not feeling great about it?

It feels like a breakup even though we're not involved. I sit at the table and get back to reviewing my school assignment. Time to remind myself of my priorities: my mother, my career, and keeping this job, which I would put in jeopardy if I was to get mixed up with Artemis. My mind flashes back to seeing him standing there—his cold-eyed stare, wearing that suit and looking stoic, like a damn iceberg!

"It's Friday, bitches!" Gin exclaims, throwing her arms up in the air.

It's almost ten at night and we've just left the university campus. We aced our presentation, and I have to admit I'm relieved. My lips curve up into a grin.

Gin notices and covers her mouth in shock. "Is that a smile? Oh my god! She's capable of smiling."

I slap her on one arm. "Don't start with me."

"You look so pretty when you smile. I don't get why you don't do it more often." She links my arm with hers, and we make our way to the bus stop. The small campus is far from where we live. Fortunately, the buses run late.

"I didn't expect we would do so well," I say.

"Hell, yeah, we did amazing. The professor was totally

impressed with our work." Gin rests her head on my shoulder while we wait at the stop. "We have to celebrate."

"You and your crazy ideas."

She pulls away. "You deserve a break. You said that your mother was already asleep when you left for school so why don't we go out for a drink? My treat!"

"You know alcohol and I don't mix."

"Because it loosens you up and makes you act like the young woman you actually are."

"No. In fact—" She covers my mouth with her hand.

"I don't want to hear any excuses. I have two free passes for a nightclub with an open bar. You're coming with me, Claudia."

I give up, and remove her hand.

"Fine. But just for one drink."

The wide smile plastered on her small features is contagious. "Let's go!"

We board the bus headed downtown, and during our ride, sitting side by side, Gin tells me that she scored these passes when she ran into a very handsome man at a coffee shop, who spilled his drink on her by accident. He gifted her the passes as an apology.

"He's really hot." She lets out a deep sigh. "He seems educated, very confident. And his smile . . ."

I can't help but laugh a little. "Last week it was the pizza delivery guy. And today this man. How do you manage to fall in love so quickly?"

"It's my specialty." She winks at me. "But seriously, this coffee shop guy is on another level. Very much an Artemis-type."

I stop smiling. Gin, who never misses a beat, notices right away. "Anything I should know?"

I shake my head.

She gives me an eye roll. "What is the enigma with this man? At this point, I may very well end up writing a novel à la Harry Potter titled *Claudia and the Mystery of the Hidalgos.*"

"You're crazy. Also, the Hidalgos? I thought you were only interested in knowing more about Artemis."

She holds up one finger and starts to explain. "No. And it's simply because lately I've noticed that each time I mention Apolo you react like there's something going on that you'd rather not talk about. Possibly because you think that it'll go away if you don't talk about it."

"Apolo is only sixteen. You know that, right?"

"Yeah, so? He's cute."

I slap her in the back of her head. "Gin!"

She bursts out laughing. "Anyway, in this state, the age of consent is sixteen."

She winks again, and I slap her one more time.

"I'm just kidding. You know how much I love teasing you. Okay, now let me do your makeup. Right now you look too much like a university student who just finished class."

"Oh really?"

I let her put on makeup, and don't put up a fight when she decides to apply a bright, fiery-red lipstick, which she claims matches the color of my hair.

At last, we get off the bus.

"I don't think we're dressed to go clubbing." I'm in jeans, boots, and a long-sleeved sweater, which is totally appropriate attire for school in the fall, when the breeze is cold. Gin is dressed similarly.

She fixes my hair. "We look gorgeous." She grabs me by the hand and pulls me along as we make our way down the street.

The Rose District, the nickname given to this street, where all the clubs and bars are lined up, is crowded with people. Some are smoking outside venues while others are strolling along the street. The majority are very well dressed—the women clad in short dresses or jeans paired with beautiful tops and shoes. The men are also wearing fancy outfits.

"I really don't think we're dressed up enough," I say.

"Ah, stop it," Gin proclaims as she guides me to the end of the strip to one of the biggest clubs; it looks exclusive. There are no lines to get in, only a sign that reads GUESTS WITH PASSES ONLY.

I open my mouth in complete shock when I look up and read the name of the club.

"You have got to be kidding me."

INSOMNIA.

Apolo's voice echoes in my head: *I went to Insomnia, Artemis's bar, by pure fluke, and I got drunk there.*

But of course Gin has passes for the bar that Artemis Hidalgo owns. What could possibly go wrong?

Nine

Creating a space.

CLAUDIA

Insomnia is a classy club with modern furniture, sleek decorative accents, and a bar that takes up most of the ground floor. Much like the idiot who owns it, this is a very sophisticated establishment.

Despite the club being full, we manage to move around without bumping into others, which is fantastic, and the opposite to every other club we've frequented, where I often find myself crushed by the crowd.

Gin screams in my ear.

"This is too cool! It's the most exclusive club in the city, I am shook!"

Her happiness is contagious, and I smile as we make our way to the bar. Gin orders two drinks.

"You're okay, Claudia. He's not here."

Artemis has had this place for a while. It was gifted to him when he turned twenty-one. Apolo told me that Artemis put someone he trusts in charge of its operation while he was finishing school, and now that he's busy running the family business, he just oversees it. I doubt Artemis frequents the place.

Gin makes a toast, and then we take a sip from our drinks. The flavor is fruity, and the alcohol is strong but bearable.

"What's this called?"

"It's an orgasm."

"You're fucking with me!"

"Nope," Gin says, her eyes fixed on something behind me. Oh my god. Please don't let it be Artemis.

"It's him!"

I turn around to get a look at the person she's screaming about, and I notice a tall blond guy with boyish looks and green eyes. He's quite attractive but not really my type. He's coming our way, and I spot another guy walking behind him. This one is taller, with dark hair and piercing black eyes, the kind of guy who intimidates everyone. His face is manly, with strong features. His hair is styled messy and looks sexy. He is definitely my type.

"Gin." I need to clarify something. "Which one do you like?"

Please say the blond, please make it the blond.

Gin bites her lip. "The blond guy. He gave me the passes."

He recognizes Gin and comes over.

"Claudia, this is Victor. And Victor, this is Claudia."

I put my hand out. "It's a pleasure."

Gin and Victor start a conversation. I look at the dark-haired guy, but he walks past us and moves farther inside the club. He doesn't even acknowledge me. I don't know what I was expecting. He looks like a runway model, so why should he notice me, looking the way I do?

As we chat with Victor, we find out that he's in charge of

the operation of the club, which means he's the person Artemis hired. He takes us upstairs to the VIP area, where can you get table service and enjoy the music, and you don't have to scream to carry a conversation. Victor seems to be trying to impress Gin, and going by how much she's blushing, I have a feeling it's working.

To give them more privacy, I tell them I need to go to the restroom. I walk by other VIP tables until I come to a curtained entryway. Curious, I go through. It's another section of the club, and as I walk by one of the booths, I realize this is where guests come to do god knows what away from prying eyes. I swear I can hear groans and whimpers, so I turn around and head back to where I came from.

Suddenly he's right in front of me: Mr. Black Eyes.

"Are you lost?"

He's even more attractive up close.

"No."

He gives me a quick once-over, checking me from top to toe, until his eyes land on my face.

"You have a gift."

I furrow my brows. "I beg your pardon?"

"How do you manage to look this good while dressed so ordinarily?"

What the fuck? Is this supposed to be some kind of compliment?

"Uh, thank you?"

"My apologies. I didn't mean to insult your choice of clothes. I just . . . I wanted to say that you're very pretty."

"And you're even prettier. As fine as they come."

This is why I prefer not to drink. It gets my hormones going and makes me uninhibited. And I've only had one drink.

Mr. Black Eyes throws me a sexy crooked grin, the kind I bet has made many girls fall for him.

"Can I buy you a drink?"

I curse my mind at this very moment when it flashes back to Artemis's face. I'm not interested in him, and I'm certain that he doesn't care much for me either. Anyway, he has a girlfriend. It's very likely he's enjoying her company right now. If our relationship is purely professional, why should I let him ruin my personal life?

"Sure," I reply and follow him out of the private area.

Gin is too occupied to take notice of us when we get back to our table, mainly because she has Victor's tongue jammed in her throat. Mr. Black Eyes looks at me, amused, and I simply shrug.

He gives me his hand. "Come on, let's move to another table."

The drinks keep coming, one after the other. Though Mr. Black Eyes tells me to slow down and take my time with each glass, I stop listening once the alcohol takes over my body and senses. The more I drink, the more I think about the idiot who owns this club.

What game is he playing?

One day he's about to kiss me and the next he tells me he only wants to keep things strictly professional?

Who does he think he is? Whoever said I wanted anything more than that? What a conceited ass.

Stop it, Claudia. Look at the fine specimen sitting across from you—he looks just like a model. You need to stop thinking about that iceberg. But he's just so . . . arrrrrgh!

I'm about to take another shot of tequila when Mr. Black Eyes grabs my hand midair. "Hey. Wait, wait, take it easy."

I put down the drink. "I'm fine."

"I don't think you are. You look a bit restless. I have nothing against angry drinking, but I think you need to pace yourself."

"Angry drinking?"

"Yeah. You know, drinking in a rage. A friend of mine does it all the time."

"I'd like to meet this friend of yours, sounds like we have a lot in common."

"You don't want to meet him. He's got a very bad temper."

He gently takes my hand and inches closer on the L-shaped couch we occupy. "If you need a distraction, there are other alternatives you could try."

He's got my attention. I bite my lower lip and grin. "Which ones, exactly?"

His free hand caresses my cheek. His face is so close to mine I can feel his breath lightly grazing my lips. "I think you know which ones."

I'm about to kiss him when I hear Gin's voice.

"Claudia!"

Mr. Black Eyes and I turn to find her standing next to us, her hands on her hips.

"Can I talk to you for a second?"

Mr. Black Eyes makes me turn to face him. "Your name is Claudia?"

Gin lets out a snort. "You haven't even learned each other's names! Agh, Claudia, this is Alex. Alex, this is Claudia."

Alex looks horrified. He quickly lets go of me.

"Shit."

"What's wrong?" I ask.

Alex holds his head. "Please don't tell me that you're the Claudia who works at the Hidalgos' house?"

"Have we met?"

"Shit!" He gets up. "I have to go to the restroom. I'll be back."

He leaves without further explanation. Gin takes advantage of the opportunity and sits down next to me.

"I didn't want to interrupt, but Victor asked me to go to his apartment and I don't want to abandon you here. We can take you home or give you money for a cab."

"You can go, don't worry, I'll be fine," I assure her. I knew this was very likely going to happen when we decided to go clubbing.

Gin puts some bills in my hand and gives it a tight squeeze.

"Don't drink any more and call me when you get home." She kisses one side of my head and leaves.

And then I'm sitting by myself on the couch, facing a table littered with glasses and a half-full bottle of tequila. I am alone, like always.

Isn't that what I've always wanted?

I've fought hard to maintain this solitude, this isolation from everyone. It's much safer than opening up and being vulnerable, something I'm not good at. Perhaps it's tied to what I went through as a child. Or maybe I simply want to be alone. I'd rather not be one of those people who blames their parents for the way they turned out. Yes, your childhood shapes some of your personality; however, at the end of the day, we are all human beings capable of facing our issues and doing something about them. Maybe there's no explanation for it: I am the way I am, and that's that.

I admire people who can freely express their emotions and are willing to put everything on the line, who expose their vulnerability without much thought or hesitation. I think back to Raquel, our neighbor, the girl involved with Ares, and how easy it is to read her emotions in her expressions and actions. I'm tormented by a memory from a few days ago when Ares asked me to get her out of his bedroom the morning after they spent the night together. When I reached the top of the stairs, I found her there, standing and waiting, with tears rolling down her cheeks. I didn't have to say anything—she simply nodded, looking resigned. The pain I saw in her eyes was gut-wrenching. It was as if she had heard everything Ares said to me.

How can she let herself be hurt like that? And then pick herself up again?

In my eyes, she's much braver that I am. She doesn't put up walls and hide behind them. She wears her heart on her sleeve.

And ends up getting hurt.

But isn't getting hurt part of life? Sometimes I feel like this safe life of mine is missing something. Do I want to be hurt? Or could it be that I yearn for something different? It's possible that I'm fed up with the monotony of my day-to-day, and the feeling of emptiness that lingers after flings that are purely for physical satisfaction.

I pour myself another shot of tequila, down it in one gulp, and place the small glass in front of me. Where is Alex? I think I need a good dose of noncommitted connection. No strings attached, no promises or corny proclamations. Just raw chemistry between two people who are physically attracted to each other. Wow, I sound so shallow. Sometimes I surprise myself with my opinions about these sort of things. I'm about to pour a third shot when I begin to wonder if Alex is ever coming back.

I thought we were getting along? What happened? How did he figure out I worked at the Hidalgos' house?

I throw my head back as I take the next shot. The alcohol burns my throat and stomach. When I bring my head down, I make out the shape of a person now sitting on the couch right across from mine. I put the glass down on the table, and with my head hanging low, decide to confront Alex. But when I raise my eyes, I find Artemis in front of me instead of Alex. I nearly choke on my own saliva.

Artemis is sitting comfortably with arms stretched across the back of the couch. The position opens his suit jacket, giving me a peek of the dark-blue shirt and black tie underneath.

His chestnut-brown hair appears black under this lighting; the same goes for his eyes. As usual, his face, which I'm sure was chiseled by heavenly gods, remains stoic. It's not fair how damn sexy the scruffy beard looks on him.

I want to ask what he's doing here but I refrain because I don't want to sound stupid. After all, he owns this club and can be here whenever he pleases. A waiter approaches the table. "We've cleared the place, sir. What would you like to drink?"

Artemis's voice is husky and makes my heart race. "The usual, and one more of these." He points to the empty bottle of tequila in front of me.

"Right away, sir."

Cleared the place? I take a moment to look around and the place does looks empty. The music keeps playing and the DJ remains in his booth, but the rest of the club is deserted. When did it . . . ? Maybe I was too absorbed with my angry drinking, as Alex called it. Artemis stares directly and unabashedly at me. His eyes are too beautiful. I've always found a tenderness in them, which contradicts his present cold appearance.

The waiter returns with a whisky for Artemis and one more bottle of tequila.

"I don't want anyone to come up here unless I call," he orders, and I swallow with difficulty.

"Yes, sir." The waiter makes a quick exit.

Artemis leans over and places the bottle in front of me. "Here you go. Keep drinking."

"What are you doing?"

Artemis first takes a sip of his drink then places his arms back across the couch.

"Creating a space."

My breathing hitches, and my mind travels back to distant memories.

"Leave me alone!" I raised my voice and shook Artemis's hand off. He was trailing me closely as I made my way down the academy halls. He pulled me inside an empty room and shut the door. I was furious when I turned around to look him. "I told you that I . . ."

Artemis hugged me tight against his chest and silenced my protests. "It's all good," he whispered as he caressed the back of my head. "Don't pay attention to those idiots. They aren't worth your anger."

He pulled away to grab a couple of chairs and placed them one facing the other. Then he took a seat.

"Come on. Sit."

He could only smile. He looked so sweet that I gave in and took a seat.

"I'm creating a space." That wasn't the first time he'd done this. When I'd had a bad moment, he kept me company and listened to me rant, complain, and curse about anything and everything I damn pleased.

Now, in the dark, empty club, he's doing it again. "I'm all ears, this is your space."

"We're not children anymore, Artemis." I'm still shaking off the anger. "This . . ."

I stare at the man sitting in front of me, and though that sweet smile of his is missing, his ability to listen remains.

"I recall you saying that you wanted to keep our relationship strictly professional," I remind him, while pouring a drink.

"I want a lot of things. But we can't always get what we want." His eyes fix intently on mine, never leaving, not even for a second.

I toss back my drink.

"I don't need space. We're not teenagers anymore."

My reply triggers a slight grin. "We both know that it's healthy to create space to unload."

"And why would you want to hold space for me?" I ask. "You change your mind from one day to the next."

"That complaint is justified," he admits. "However, it's evident to me that you could make use of it. The club is empty, you have all the alcohol in the world at your disposition. What else do you need? Think of me as a stranger, someone you just met who will forget tomorrow whatever you share tonight."

As if I could do that.

Artemis can read between the lines of my silence and arches a brow inquisitively.

"Unless you need to vent about me. In that case, I completely understand if you don't want to share."

Bingo.

"Let it go," I say.

Artemis brings down his arms from where they were resting. He puts his elbows on his knees and intertwines his hands.

"Let what go?"

"This." I gesture with my hand, pointing back and forth between us. "Stop being nice to me."

"Why?" The intensity of his gaze is unbearable. "Are you

afraid that I may bring down those walls you've put up to protect yourself? I made them crumble once, Claudia. And I can do it again; if I put my mind to it, I can make it happen."

"We both know how it ended the last time you tried," I remind him, thinking back to that night on that Fourth of July.

Artemis doesn't appear upset.

"I'm not an insecure teenager who gives up after his first rejection anymore. I'm a man who knows what he wants, a man who won't rest until he gets it."

And what is that supposed to mean?

I clasp my hands in my lap.

"You are also a man with a girlfriend," I remind him, my heart thumping so hard I can feel it in my throat.

The air between us feels heavy, and the mood is hard to read. Is it sexual tension? I mean, the way he's wearing that suit, he looks extremely fuckable. I shake my head. I can't think of him that way. It's definitely the alcohol. I stand up, determined to get out of there. I'm not myself, and I can't be alone with him, especially not after he reminded me of those moments when he would hold space for me. I've only taken one step when he speaks.

"Me having a girlfriend is what's keeping you from being mine?"

My heart is close to jumping out of my chest and I'm pretty sure I'm blushing. I don't dare look at him. What kind of question is that? I turn to face him. He remains seated and looks unbothered, like he's enjoying all the tranquility in the world.

"I am not an object to be possessed by you. Or anyone else for that matter."

He gets up from his seat, walks around the small table, and comes to stand in front of me.

"I didn't mean to offend you. Let me ask you in a different way." He pauses and I take a step back. "The reason you won't let me get close to you, why you won't allow me to"—he extends his hand in an attempt to caress my face, but I lean away—"touch you or show you how well I can fuck you is because I have a girlfriend?"

The crudeness of his statement is infuriating.

"Maybe I'm just not interested in you in that way."

"You're lying."

I say nothing, and he grabs me by the waist and pulls my body against his, his eyes fixed on mine.

"I don't have a girlfriend anymore, Claudia."

Ten

What do you want, Artemis?

CLAUDIA

"This is dangerous."

I feel the heat radiating off Artemis's body and onto mine. He has one arm snaked around my waist, stirring up feelings that I shouldn't be having for him. His proximity allows me to have a clear view of his masculine features and his perfectly kept scruff. Part of me can't help but wonder how his stubble would feel rubbing against my bare skin.

One thing is certain, it's not my wanton thoughts that are pushing this moment into dangerous territory but the determination in his eyes.

For the first time he is totally in control of the situation and his single-minded expression is making it clear that he's made a decision. There are many possible outcomes, to be determined by how I handle this moment. I try to push him away. This makes him tighten the grip he has on my waist and press himself harder against me.

"Why are you always running away from me?"

The intensity of his gaze makes it difficult to swallow.

"I'm not running away from you."

His lips curve into a naughty grin I've never seen on him. It makes him look incredibly confident and sensuous.

Get away from him, Claudia.

My brain is warning me, yet I can't deny how good it feels to be in his arms. His strong, hard body makes me feel safe. I need to get a handle on this situation. I don't want to give up control, and I feel vulnerable when I'm with him. I don't like feeling this way. Artemis is used to having control over those around him. Except for me. Never me. And so I let myself relax and give in to his embrace. And he takes notice. I can read his look of surprise. I bring my hands up and wrap them around his neck.

"Do you think you can handle this?" I ask.

Artemis is visibly taken aback. "What do you mean?"

I give him a trusting smile. "If you had me, could you handle it?"

Artemis raises a brow. "Oh yes, I certainly could."

"Are you sure?" I bite my lower lip and inch my face closer to his.

I watch him swallow. He doesn't pull away. His nose grazes mine.

"Let me prove it to you."

There is hardly any space between our lips. A small move on his part or mine could close the distance. He's slightly taller so I stand on tiptoe and move in. Our breathing mingles. We're looking into each other's eyes, which project the unspoken emotions taking up room in the space between us.

I want to kiss him.

I'm startled by this admission. I didn't mean to start something; my intention was purely to take control of the situation. But his body, his scent, his breathing, his heat, and the desire radiating from his eyes, all these are limiting my ability to think rationally.

"Are you going to tease me all night?" he whispers against my lips.

"Maybe."

He licks his lips. "Claudia."

I get lost in his eyes for a brief second.

"Artemis . . ."

Before it's too late and I end up giving into my desires, I use his confidence to my advantage and catch him by surprise when I free myself and push away.

"I should go."

He strokes his beard, and doesn't seem surprised by my actions.

"Running away won't help. Some things are inevitable, Claudia."

I fold my arms over my chest. "Which things?"

"You and me."

I ignore his answer.

"To be honest, it's late and I do have to go," I tell him.

"I'll take you."

I don't know why his reply makes me laugh. His persistence is formidable.

"No thanks."

"I won't take a no for an answer," he says. "After all, we're both going to the same house."

He doesn't give me a chance to decline, only grabs my hand and drags me along. We come down from the VIP area and walk by the side of the bar where all the bartenders and the staff have gathered to chat. They quickly disperse when they see us coming. It's obvious from their faces that we were the subject of their conversation. Artemis looks directly at the one employee I suspect is in charge of the rest of the staff. "I'm leaving. You can reopen, or leave it closed. Check with Victor and let him decide."

"Yes, sir. I hope you have a very nice evening."

I smile and hold Artemis's hand while tagging along. Once we're outside, we walk to a dark-blue classic car. He's not one to drive sports cars or anything extravagant; his taste is classy and elegant. He lets go of my hand to open the passenger's door. The trip home is quiet and charged with tension. I discreetly take a few glances at the man next to me while he's focused on the road. He has one hand on the wheel and the other on the shifter to switch gears. I can't put into words how, but he looks so sexy when he's driving.

"How's university going?" I wasn't expecting this question but I'm glad he's the one breaking the silence.

"Good. I have one more year to go."

"Are you still terrible at reading?"

I purse my lips, mortified. "I do my best."

He's grinning. And I realize that I'm short of breath.

"Still prone to falling asleep after a reading a few pages?"

Yes.

"Of course not."

He keeps quiet. I stop staring at him like a fool and look

out the window at the houses, buildings, and trees whizzing by. The motion makes the alcohol still in my system act up, making me feel dizzy. So I turn to look at Artemis instead. The watch he has on the arm resting on the wheel reflects the light of every streetlamp we pass. Every aspect of his appearance is immaculate. Anyone meeting him for the first time could easily feel intimidated by his presence, which surely comes across as detached and unapproachable.

They, of course, have not seen his softer side. The side he showed while standing up for his brothers when they were mocked for what happened with his mother. Or that time when he stood up to his dad, who was about to give Ares a beating. And many other instances that no one knows about.

Why is it so easy for me to see through him? Is that the reason he still wants me? I'm not stupid. True, he's no longer the teenager who declared his love underneath a sky illuminated with fireworks, yet the tenderness is still there in his eyes. I can see it when he looks at me.

What do you want, Artemis? Sex? Or something more? Has the fact that you couldn't have me prevented you from moving forward?

A part of me is terrified at the possibility that once he has me he'll move on, simply because he'll no longer be chasing something he can't have. And that's not even the main reason I keep myself at a safe distance from him—it's one of many.

Artemis shoots me a quick glance. "What are you thinking about?"

I keep my eyes on the road ahead of us and refrain from speaking.

"I thought I was a man of few words but you've always bested me at that."

When we arrive at the house, I quickly get out of the car and run to my room to check on my mother, who is sleeping peacefully. I let out a deep sigh of relief. I gently massage my shoulder as I make my way to the kitchen. To my surprise, I find Artemis there, standing at the opposite end, hands resting on the edge of the table behind him. He has removed his jacket and loosened his tie.

"How's your mother?"

I walk past him to get a bottle of water from the fridge.

"She's fine." I don't know why I feel edgy or why my heart is once again beating madly.

You're just horny, Claudia. That's all. He's very desirable. It's normal to be attracted to him.

The tension between us is heavy and thick. It's as if it's been slowly mounting as the night progresses.

Just seeing him here, his hard body covered in those elegant clothes, and the intense gaze promising a host of delicious indecent things.

What are you afraid of, Claudia?

Developing deeper feelings . . . becoming vulnerable . . . not measuring up to someone like him. Being used and discarded, like my mother. Losing the emotional independence I have worked long and hard to build. And being distracted from achieving the goals I've set for myself. I'm afraid of too many things.

I wish he was like other guys—just someone I could enjoy an uncomplicated and purely physical fling with. But there's too much history between us. We share too many memories. After taking a sip of water, I turn around and look him directly in the eyes. I need to dispel this tension between us. So I soften my tone.

"Rough day at work?"

He crosses his arms over his chest.

"Every day at my work is rough."

"It must be hard to manage a big company."

He lets out a deep breath. "I'm used to it."

I'm not sure why I want to keep having a conversation with him. I think it's the alcohol. I should be in bed already.

"Do you still sketch?"

His lips turn into a halfhearted smile. "Yes."

"Did you move past the stage of drawing Pokémons?" I tease, recalling the phase in his childhood when he was obsessed with sketching game characters.

He shoots me a forlorn glance. "That was a different time, so long ago."

I can't stop myself from giggling. I've annoyed him, and it's a refreshing change. "Sure, sure."

"I can show you my most recent drawings whenever you like. I've improved a lot." He sounds confident.

"I bet you have. You've always been clever, picking things up pretty quick."

He arches a brow. "Is that compliment?"

"Why are you shocked? I always loved your sketches. In fact, you—" I stop myself. I don't know if I should finish I was about to say.

"You, what?"

"I thought you could have become an artist."

The look of amusement on his face vanishes, replaced by deep sadness that I'm pained to see.

"We can't always become who we wish to be."

"Sorry, I—"

"You don't need to apologize." He smiles at me reassuringly

but the look of sadness stays. "I'm fine with who I am and what I do now."

Even though he sounds convinced, I know this is the opposite of the truth. As a kid, not once did he ever mention wanting to become head of Hidalgo Enterprises one day. This makes me see him in a different light. He appears so alone, so unhappy. It never crossed my mind that the power passed down to him was an unwanted burden placed on his shoulders. I remember his passion and excitement when he talked about his drawings. Fast-forward to now, when he looks so vulnerable and deprived of affection. Before I can rethink or regret what I am about to do, I place my glass on the table and walk over to him. He unfolds his arms and looks at me, astounded. I wrap my arms around him in a hug, and rest my face on his chest.

"You've done a great job." Although it takes him a few seconds to react, he reciprocates and encircles me in his arms. The sweet scent of his cologne is soothing. I can hear and feel the rapid beats of his heart against my ear. This feels right, even though it likely isn't. This hug feels wonderful, and I lose track of time. I am enjoying every second of it. When we come apart, my hands linger on his sides and we stay very close. Our eyes communicate the intense emotions surfacing and wrestling between us. Artemis leans forward, and his lips brush against mine. I pull my face back as quickly as I can. I take a step backward and attempt to leave. He reacts fast, grabbing hold of my wrist and pulling me toward him. Then, with his free hand, he grabs my face and plasters his mouth on mine.

A sudden burst of emotion rushes through me and clouds my reason. I kiss him back with an urgency that astounds me. It's not a gentle kiss. It's a fierce kiss loaded with years of longing. Our lips are in sync, moving furiously and passionately. My fingers are tangled in his hair, pulling him closer, while he grips me tightly by the waist. Our breathing becomes heavy and our movements are clumsy as we struggle to keep our passion under control. His scruff rubs against my face every so often, and it feels great. No one has ever kissed me like this. And I have never felt this way before.

Artemis presses his body closer, and my breasts rub against him. Though we are still fully clothed, I can feel the hardness of his body, and the intensity of the sensation is disorienting. His soft, wet lips are sealed to mine. He tastes like whisky. His tongue moves lightly over my lips, teasing, before he continues to kiss me with abandon.

I can't make myself stop.

He lowers his hands from my waist to my ass, and gives it a squeeze that elicits a moan from me. I feel him getting hard against my stomach. It frightens me how much I want him. Without breaking our kiss, he lifts and places me on the edge of the kitchen table, positioning himself between my legs. I am drunk with overwhelming desire. Every part of my body feels like a live wire. Artemis has put his hands inside my sweater and caresses my back and the sides of my waist. His fingers leave a delicious warm trail, marking everywhere they touch.

We pull apart by an inch and try to catch our breath. And then we resume our kiss with the same need and intensity. His hands move inside my sweater until they reach my breasts, and squeeze gently. His thumbs slide inside my bra and graze my nipples, triggering another moan. Instinctively, I've been rocking my body against his, rubbing myself against his hardness. I'm fully aware that I'm playing with fire, but how could I stop myself at this point?

Artemis unbuttons my pants and before I can react he slides one of his hands inside. I gasp in his mouth the very instant his fingers make intimate contact.

"Fuck, you're wet," he grunts against my lips. "Shit. You're so sexy!"

I am way too aroused and it won't take his fingers long to make me climax. His tongue is plundering my mouth while his finger is penetrating me. It's driving me crazy. I hold on to his shoulders. He halts our kiss and intensifies his skillful ministrations deep inside me.

"Open your eyes, Claudia."

I hadn't realized that they were closed, so I obey, and our gazes meet.

"I need your eyes on me when you come. I want you to moan against my lips, and tremble in my arms. I want all of you."

These words give me the final push and I reach my climax. I bite my lips in an effort to suppress my moans, but it's hard to contain them. Those intense brown eyes are staring at me with a passion that intensifies the incredible orgasm rippling through my body. I whisper a host of curse words while waves of pleasure wash over me—one after the other they batter my body, leaving me completely spent. Immediately after my orgasm, without hesitation, I quickly remove his tie and unbutton his shirt, revealing the bare chest that has been tormenting my thoughts since the morning when I saw him after his workout.

The sound of the main door opening and footsteps approaching brings us to a halt. I shove Artemis away from me. Still, there is not enough time for me to button my pants or for him to do up his shirt. Artemis places himself strategically with his back to the door so he can tuck his shirt in. My breathing is labored. Who could it be at this time? It's past midnight.

Ares enters the kitchen. He's running his hand through his hair, and wobbling. Is he drunk? When he sees us, he grimaces in confusion.

"Huh. What are you both doing awake?"

I'm having a hard time swallowing. My chest rises and falls at a fast pace.

"We were . . . talking."

Artemis faces us both. His shirt is buttoned up but his tie is a disaster.

"You've been drinking again." His voice has regained its familiar cool and composed tone.

Ares shoots us a silly grin. "Just a little." His gaze falls on me. "You're blushing. Are you hot?"

I exchange looks with Artemis, who conceals a smile.

"Yes. The heat is set too high."

Ares clumsily sits down at the table. "I must be plastered, because I don't feel hot or cold."

I get off the table and use the opportunity to button up my jeans. "I think it's time for bed," I state.

Ares covers his mouth as he lets out a long yawn.

I turn to look at Artemis, which is a big mistake. He sticks out his tongue and slowly licks his fingers before addressing me in a whisper. "I like the way you taste."

I look over at Ares in a panic. But he still has his hands covering his face.

"Ares, let's go. Let's get you to bed."

Ares uncovers his face to reveal a pout.

"I'm not a child."

I ignore his protest, and start to lead him out of the kitchen. Artemis waves at me with that one hand, looking cocky and pleased with himself.

"Good night, sexy."

I break into an impish smile as I walk out.

Eleven

And what if I am wrong?

CLAUDIA

Ares is boy of very few words when he's sober. When he drinks though, he turns into a chatterbox.

"Are you listening to me, Clauuuuuuu?" he howls while pointing at me.

"Yes, you've told me four times already."

He puffs like a deflating balloon.

"I don't know what's happening to me. Am I going crazy?"

"Ares, it's four in the morning. Can you go to sleep?"

He shakes his head. "I need to see her."

"Again, it's four o'clock in the morning. She must be in bed. Which is where you need to be right now."

I'm staying with him because he's set on going to Raquel's house. If he visits in this condition, god knows what kind of racket he'll make.

"I just want to see her for one second. Clau, please."

"Wait until sunrise. I'll even go along with you to see her. Right now, I need you to go to sleep, please."

Ares falls back on his bed and uses his forearm to cover his eyes.

"Clau, I don't know what to do with these feelings."

"You're in love, you fool," I mutter to myself.

After a few minutes spent in silence, Ares finally settles and falls asleep. I remove his shoes and unbutton his shirt so he can rest comfortably. I cover him with a blanket, and pause for a moment to watch him sleep.

He looks terribly vulnerable and innocent with his black hair all messy, framing his face. I'm happy that he's at last found someone who makes him feel something real, someone who's helped him break the pattern of shallow and meaningless one-night stands. I exit his room on tiptoes.

I try to keep my mind off what just happened between Artemis and me. My mind is still processing it. I go to bed with the memory of his lips on mine, his hands on my breasts and his finger inside me . . . argh. I bite my lip, thinking back to that exquisite orgasm.

I feel restless.

I don't want to face this feeling I've fought for too long, but I can't seem to shake it off. I'm apprehensive about seeing Artemis again. For some inexplicable reason, I don't regret doing more than kissing; letting him touch me and use his fingers to bring me to sweet ecstasy. I just don't know how to act around him now. I decide to go with the flow—I'll go along with whatever happens between us. I'm tired of constantly fighting these emotions, and trying so hard to prevent what's inevitable.

Perhaps he and I need to spend a night together to put this

attraction to rest; to close this chapter and move on.

But what if we spend this one night and I want more?

This is unknown and dangerous territory for me. I wouldn't dare try it with anyone else. But this is him. Artemis has always conveyed a sense of peace and security, and I want to believe that he won't hurt me.

But what if I'm wrong?

Well, I'll deal with it. I can't keep myself stuck in this safe space my whole life. Ugh, I don't even know what to think anymore; what happened is jumbling my thoughts.

The next morning, I'm gathering my hair into a messy bun as I make my entrance into the kitchen to prepare breakfast, and I almost die of a heart attack when I find Ares sitting at the table. He looks like he didn't get a wink of sleep. He's still wearing the same clothes from last night and has huge dark circles under his eyes.

"Good morning?" I address him inquisitively because he looks asleep even though his eyes are wide open.

He offers me a quick glance and goes back to staring off into space.

"I need to eat something so I can sleep," he says.

"Were you awake the whole time? I thought when I left you hours ago you were sleeping."

"I woke up at the crack of dawn." He fesses up. "As soon as the sun rose, I went to see her."

I can tell by his expression that the expedition didn't go well.

"Is everything okay?"

He lets out a deep sigh. "Clau, to be honest, I don't understand her. She . . . I just don't get her."

"Did you tell her how you feel?"

He nods.

"And?" I feel terrible for questioning him but I want to know what happened. The curiosity is killing me.

He grimaces. "She laughed."

Ouch.

I sense he doesn't want to talk about it. I know him well, and he'll share when he feels ready, so I busy myself preparing breakfast.

I serve him and watch him eat absentmindedly. His thoughts are elsewhere. Before he leaves, he hugs me and kisses the side of my head.

"Clau, thanks for looking after me."

"You're welcome." I smile as I watch him leave. "Ares, please get some rest."

After I take breakfast to my mother, I return to the rest of my duties in the kitchen. There isn't too much to do, except for preparing breakfast for Mr. or Mrs. Hidalgo, in case they choose to eat at home on a Sunday. Occasionally, my eyes dart to the door, expecting Artemis to show up, since he's usually one of the first to come down for breakfast on weekends. I want to see him so I can get over these nerves. I turn on the coffee machine and prepare an espresso. On cue, Artemis makes his entrance, just when I least expect it. He's shirtless again, slightly sweaty and wearing shorts. I gather he just finished his workout. I freeze right in front of the coffee machine, and look at him out of the corner of my eye.

Artemis sits across the table, and he has his eyes squarely on me. "Good morning, sexy."

I manage to contain a smile from spreading across my lips, and turn around. "Good morning, sir." I tease him.

Artemis shoots me a charming grin that makes my heart

race. His eyes have a mischievous twinkle that I've never seen before.

"What would you like to eat for breakfast?" I ask in a friendly tone.

He arches a brow. "Are you on the menu?"

I become short of breath. And the sexual tension is back on, as intense or more so than before.

"I don't believe so."

He sighs deeply. "That's a pity."

Artemis gets up and comes around the table. I'm rooted to the spot and watch him move, like prey watching a predator approach.

As he stands in front of me, I can see clearly every muscle and ripple defining his arms, chest, and abs.

"Last night you left me in a terrible state, Claudia."

"Oh, is that so?" I play dumb, pretending I don't understand.

He licks his lips.

"You were on my mind for the rest of the goddamn night."

He takes one step closer to me. Then he entraps me by bringing his arms forward on either side of my waist and placing his hands on the edge of the counter. Earlier, I had decided to let things between us flow. At this very moment, with him this close, I lose my courage and start to reconsider my decision. I'm fighting the urge to flee

"I'll forgive you under one condition," he suggests, while ever so slightly rubbing my bottom lip. "Kiss me."

I hesitate briefly, but his intense gaze makes all doubt on my part vanish. My hands encircle his neck and pull him into a kiss. Our lips meet. And just like last time, a delicious host of sensations erupts between us. The kiss starts slowly, our lips slightly grazing. It grows passionate when our mouths begin to press with force and move in sync. I could easily get lost in his kisses. He certainly knows what he is doing, and there's no doubt in my mind he has a lot of experience. No other guy I've been with has kissed me so well. Artemis knows how to move his lips and his tongue; he even knows when to bite my lips to get my pulse racing. I take my hands off his neck and use them to caress his chest and abdomen, tracing every line and muscle with my fingertips.

I need to pull away before this escalates. It's one thing to get carried away in the middle of the night, and another to let this continue in the light of day. We could get in big trouble if his parents or one of his brothers enters the kitchen and finds us this way. Our breathing is labored as I manage to free myself from his arms.

"I need air."

He gives me a cocky smile and grabs my wrist.

"Should we move this to my bedroom?"

I understand what he's implying, and I'm not offended one bit. We're both adults, and the attraction between us is undeniable.

I release myself from his grip. "Oh my, someone is impatient."

He laughs and raises both hands in the air. He looks like a spokesmodel.

"The offer stands till whenever you wish to accept it."

"Hmm, Artemis Hidalgo making things easier for a change. This will ruin the reputation of the unreachable iceberg."

He raises a brow. "Iceberg?"

"Yes. Cold as an iceberg."

"Last night you left me hard like an iceberg."

Heat rushes through me and turns my cheeks red. I give him my back, pretending I'm looking for something in the fridge.

"What would you like for breakfast?"

"Since you're not on the menu," he says, "the usual—fruit salad. Please."

I bring out the fruit and start preparing it. Artemis has positioned himself behind me, his breath caressing my neck. He brings his hands on either side of my waist and places them on top of my hands.

"How can you look so sexy while doing something so mundane?"

I can feel every part of his body plastered against my back. The flimsy shorts he's wearing are not much of a barrier, and I can feel all of him.

His lips make contact with my earlobe. "Come to my bedroom, sexy."

His hands leave mine and move up to slowly caress my breasts over the uniform I'm wearing. My chest is heaving. He definitely knows how to make a girl melt with the way he touches and licks.

"You know that you won't regret it. What happened last night was a preview of how I can make you feel."

I clear my throat. "Stop it, someone might come in." My voice sounds hoarser than usual.

His tongue makes its way down my neck. My legs are trembling.

Artemis comes back up to my ear and whispers, "I bet you're already wet."

This man is going to kill me with his touch, his tongue, and his words. I don't want to lose control but I'm one lick away from racing upstairs with him and letting him do with me as he pleases. I remove his hands from my chest and turn to face him, hoping to put some distance between us.

“That is enough,” I reply breathlessly.

Artemis looks at me with a wicked grin, and raises his hands as if to surrender.

“Fine,” he replies, before moving to sit on the other side of the table.

I finish cutting the fruit, and give my breathing time to settle back to normal. I present him with a plate. “You used to hate fruit.”

He grabs a slice of banana. “It’s healthy. In university I didn’t have much time to cook full meals.”

“I don’t believe you can cook, even if you had the time.”

He frowns. “And what do you mean by that?”

“That you cannot cook. Even if your life depended on it.”

He chuckles. “Is that what you believe?”

“I know so.” I fold my arms over my chest.

“For your information, I took a cooking class in university as one of my options and got the highest grade. There is nothing this brain of mine can’t assimilate.”

His arrogance doesn’t bother me. It’s one of the Hidalgo traits I’ve grown accustomed to.

“Oh really? You could never beat me playing video games.”

The arrogant smile vanishes from his face. “Video games are insignificant.”

“Sure, sure,” I concede, amused. “You could never beat me at board games either.”

Artemis shifts his gaze to me.

“Again, they are games, all trivial.”

“I had to help you with biology in school because you hated Mendel’s laws.” He opens his mouth and is about to say something. “Or are the laws of inheritance also insignificant and trivial?”

Artemis remains quiet and picks up another piece of fruit. I smile victoriously. Mrs. Hidalgo enters the kitchen, and my smile disappears in an instant.

"Good morning, son." She walks past Artemis while he continues to eat in silence.

I hurry to serve her breakfast the way she likes it, and give her the newspaper.

"Thank you," she responds before turning her gaze on Artemis. "I've told you that I don't like it when you walk around the house shirtless. It's in bad taste."

"I only do it on weekends right after my workout."

"I understand that you and your brothers think of Claudia as a sister, but she is still a woman. You can't go around looking like this in front of women. You'll make them feel uncomfortable."

I squeeze my lips to suppress a laugh.

Oh, lady, if you only knew.

"It's all right, Mother, I'll be more careful." Artemis finishes what's on his plate, then shoots me a playful smile before stepping out of the kitchen. "I need to go shower."

Twelve

Hello, iceberg.

CLAUDIA

Many days have passed since I last saw Artemis. This isn't out of the ordinary; when he works a lot he has a tendency to come home very late and leave early in the morning. I overheard his father explain that it's been a hectic week at the office. Even his mother is concerned with his eating habits, and Sofia comes into the kitchen Friday morning with a special request.

"I need you to prepare a well-balanced meal and deliver it to Artemis for lunch. Carl can take you." Artemis is so swamped that even his mother, someone who rarely worries about anyone but herself, has taken notice, and even offered her personal driver.

A part of me is excited to see Artemis. I miss him. I've grown used to his presence now that he lives in the house. It has also awakened in me a nostalgia that I wasn't aware I was harboring until now.

Artemis used to be my best friend; the one person I could

count on for everything. I've missed having someone in my life who's there for me unconditionally.

I prepare his lunch with care and make sure to include a fruit salad for dessert. I ride in silence with Carl to Hidalgo Enterprises headquarters. I'm glad that I changed my clothes—the last thing I want to do is step inside the building wearing a maid's uniform that looks more like a Halloween costume. I don't think I should wear it anymore. After all, the one who made me put it on was Artemis. I enter through the glass doors and am amazed by how shiny the floors are and how impeccable everyone looks. At reception an elegantly dressed brown-skinned woman greets me with a smile.

"How may I help you?"

"I've brought lunch to"—I almost blurt out his first name—"to Mr. Hidalgo."

She looks at me puzzled. "For our CEO?"

"Yes."

"And you are . . . ?"

"My name is Claudia. I'm the housekeeper for the Hidalgos."

She looks me over from head to toe. The jeans I bought at a garage sale last week are not fancy enough, even though when I first put them on I thought they were the cutest pair in the world. I suppose what's cute to me may be trashy to others.

"Is he aware you're coming, Claudia?" Her eyes land on my buttoned shirt, which I also thought looked pretty when I bought it on sale.

"I don't think so. His mother sent me."

She hesitates and scrutinizes me, making me uneasy.

I've been polite, and tried my best. "Listen"—I stare at the name tag she has pinned on her jacket—"Mandy, you can call whoever you want to confirm my identity. In the meantime, Mr. Hidalgo's lunch is getting cold while you judge my appearance instead of doing your job efficiently."

Her jaw drops and she looks stunned.

I continue. "Your job is to make a call, confirm who I am, and let me go up. Very easy. So stop wasting everyone's time and do what's necessary."

Mandy does as I say and calls Artemis's assistant. She issues me a visitor's pass, which I pin on my shirt, and lets me go upstairs. Artemis's office is located on the top floor, which doesn't surprise me—he's always loved heights. I bet his office has tall, wide windows so he can enjoy the view. When the elevator arrives, I'm greeted with a sweet smile from a tall, fuller-bodied male assistant, who is way friendlier than Mandy.

"Claudia?"

I nod. "Yes, hi."

"Go on in." He points me to the set of doors on the left.

I knock and hear Artemis say "Come in." My stomach flip-flops as I make my entrance. The sun streaming through the large windows in his office blinds me momentarily. Tall windows, just as I expected. I know him so well. Artemis is sitting behind his desk, buried in paperwork. He's taken off his tie, his shirt is wrinkled, and his hair is a disaster. I can see circles under his eyes. When our gazes meet, his face is overcome with relief.

"Hi, sexy."

"Hi, iceberg."

He smiles and gets up. "Just in time, I'm starving."

I empty the contents of the lunch bag, placing them on the table in front of the couch on one side of his office. Artemis sits and doesn't wait for me to finish plating before he starts eating.

Poor thing.

I missed you.

I can't bring myself to say it out loud.

"Having a difficult week?" I ask instead.

"You have no idea."

He reclines on the sofa when he's done eating and closes his eyes. He looks exhausted. When I place my hand over his, he opens his eyes and looks at me.

"I . . ." I stop myself. I can't tell him.

Artemis flashes me a sweet smile and intertwines his hand with mine.

"I missed you, too, sexy."

I quickly release his hand as I hear the sound of the door opening, and turn around to see who's there. It's the redhead he brought with him to the house the night of the surprise party. His girlfriend. Correction, his ex-girlfriend, according to what he said at his nightclub. She's wearing an elegant black skirt and a white blouse paired with red high heels that match her handbag. Her red hair is perfectly styled in a high ponytail and her makeup looks flawless. She carries a bag with food from a restaurant in one hand.

"Oh, hi. It seems I'm too late, and you ate already!"

My heart begins to pound erratically. I have a terrible queasy feeling in the pit of my stomach. The woman smiles as she walks in, stands in front of me, then leans across me and plants a kiss on Artemis's lips.

Oh no.

I can hear the sound of my heart shattering inside my chest. My stomach churns. Artemis avoids looking my way and keeps his eyes fixed on her. She turns her gaze on me.

"You must be Claudia. Pleasure to meet you. I'm Cristina, his fiancé."

Fiancé.

No. Girlfriend. Or is it ex-girlfriend?

So what in the hell was happening between us?

He told me he no longer had a girlfriend. So what am I, the other woman? I try to calm my breathing but I'm having a hard time inhaling.

"Are you not feeling well?" Cristina asks me politely.

I need to throw up. I feel like I'm about to burst into tears, so I stand up.

"I . . . need to go now."

For the last time, my eyes search for Artemis's, but he looks away.

"Have a good afternoon," I force myself to say.

I bolt out of his office. I feel stupid for believing that something great could happen to me, for letting him back into my life and into my heart when I damn well know we belong to very different worlds. Obviously, he only wanted to sleep with me. Love and devotion, on the other hand, are reserved for his fiancé. To someone like him, I'm just the other woman; I could never be anything more.

I've never felt a pain like this before. For the very first time I gave myself permission to be vulnerable. The bastard told me that he no longer had a girlfriend because he knew I wouldn't do anything if he was involved with someone else.

How could he lie to me like this?

How was he able to look cool and composed when his fiancé arrived?

Does he not give one damn about how I feel?

I keep my cool, and keep my tears from freely flowing until I get home. There, I run to the bathroom and stare at my eyes, which are turning red as big, fat tears roll down my cheeks.

Claudia, you are an idiot.

Did I really think he would leave someone like her for someone like me? What hurts the most is that she's engaged to him. Is he going to marry her? How could he kiss me and touch me the way he did when he's planning to marry someone else?

How could he be unfaithful and use lies to make me complicit in his deception?

The memory of his smile and his words that day in the kitchen are fresh in my mind. How could he do that when he was engaged to someone else?

I cover my face so I can cry with abandon. In this whole fucking mess I can't pinpoint what hurts most. I only know that the intensity of this pain points to deeper feelings I had started to develop for him beyond physical attraction.

It was much, much more than that.

Thirteen

Hello, sexy.

ARTEMIS

Five hours ago

Sitting around the U-shaped boardroom table alongside the heads of every department working for our company, I'm bombarded with numbers, figures, graphs, and a pile of proposals. I play with the pen in my hand while I listen. But my mind is occupied elsewhere.

Black eyes, red hair.

Claudia.

I still can't believe that after all these years, waiting and longing, I finally kissed her. The feelings she stirred in me with one single kiss frighten me. I can't shake the image of her flushed beautiful face, the desire in her eyes, her soft moans, how she desperately unbuttoned my shirt.

She is so precious to me.

I press my lips shut when I'm hit with the memory of how wet she was. The evidence that that she wanted me as much as I wanted her drove me crazy. I would have plunged myself inside her right there in the kitchen if it wasn't for Ares's unfortunate timing.

The last thing I need is an erection right in the middle of this meeting, so I push away the wayward thoughts.

"What do you think, sir?" Ryan, a project manager, asks me. I look up at him for the first time in the ten minutes of his presentation. Fortunately, my brain excels at retaining information after hearing it once, even when I'm not fully focused. Maybe that's the reason why university was a breeze for me.

"Brilliant. However, why the need to hire out-of-state contractors?"

Ryan proceeds to explain. "It will reduce the total cost, sir."

I turn to look at Alex, my best friend, who currently occupies the position of chief financial officer. "How much would we save if we worked with out-of-state contractors?"

Alex takes a quick glance at his meeting notes. He understands exactly what I'm asking without me having to go into details.

"Not much. We're talking about contractors bringing in out-of-town workers who will have to travel and will need room and board for the duration of the project. We also have to factor in the level of motivation of a crew of workers who won't be well-fed and may feel homesick."

"Exactly." I put down my pen. "We have an efficient local workforce. I believe we'll achieve optimal performance by creating work opportunities in our own community. Moreover, we'll be fostering a sense of ownership among the crew since they'll play an integral part in the further development of their hometown by putting up buildings and houses where they live."

Ryan lowers his head. "Understood. I was simply trying to save the company some money."

"I know. But as Alex pointed out, it's not much. And I believe we'll get better results if we generate new employment opportunities where we live."

Sasha, our chief of human resources, interjects. "I only want to add that we've worked with local contractors before, and they've been incredible."

"Well, then, it's settled," I conclude.

The door to the boardroom opens and everyone but me stands up when my father makes his entrance. Everybody here has great respect for Juan Hidalgo. He's a role model to many who choose to follow in his footsteps. He built this great corporation from the ground up and established an empire that comprises six branches nationwide, overseeing a multitude of projects in many states. I admire him too, although maybe not for the same reasons held by those present in this room. I know how much my father has sacrificed to accomplish all this. I know how hard it was at the beginning—all the sweat, tears, and what he had to endure to get here.

"Good morning. Please sit down," my father instructs everyone with a smile. "I've told you before this formality isn't necessary." He jokes with them while lightly slapping the shoulder of a department head. "Forgive me for interrupting."

Alex speaks to him in a friendly tone. "We were finishing up."

"Oh." His eyes finally land on me. "Then would you mind giving me and your CEO a few moments alone?"

The team promptly vacates the boardroom and my dad takes the seat at the other end of table, straight across from mine.

"I thought you were going to be away for a few weeks," I inquire, getting comfortable in my chair.

"I leave this afternoon," he answers, tapping his fingers impatiently on the table. I know why he's here, but I want to hear him say it. "Let me get to the point to save us both precious time." I gesture for him to go on. "I got a call from Jaysen this morning. He told me that he's reconsidering renewing their contract with us."

"Okay."

"Artemis, I don't like surprises. Particularly those with repercussions for our company. We had a deal. I let you choose which girl, and today I'm informed that you broke up with her."

I let out a deep sigh. "I don't think it's wise to mix business with my personal life."

"That's not what you told me a year ago when we spoke about this. You agreed, and have been involved with her ever since. And now you're changing your mind as if there are no consequences? In business, acting impulsively can be damaging."

The protruding vein on his forehead has become very visible. He's angry, so I choose my words carefully. "We can merge with another furnishing firm to fulfill the needs of our development projects. For instance—"

"Enough!" He raises his voice and cuts me off. "It is absurd to change suppliers in the middle of our projects. Do you have any idea how much that will cost us? We're not talking about hundreds. It will be millions. Jaysen & Associates is the best and most prestigious furnishing firm in the nation. The quality they offer is unmatchable in the industry. There is a long line of companies waiting and eager to partner with them. Hasn't it become crystal clear to you that we need them more than they need us?"

I run my hands over my face. "Father . . ."

"No. I'm not talking as your father now. I'm speaking to you as the president of Hidalgo Enterprises. You made a deal. You need to keep your word and avoid causing problems for this company. You are the CEO, and the well-being of the company needs to be your first priority."

My lips curve into a sarcastic smirk. "You haven't even asked why I did it."

My father scowls. "What are you talking about?"

"You haven't asked why I changed my mind. Is that not relevant?"

"It's completely irrelevant. The company always comes first." The coldness in his tone is unnerving.

Part of me wants to rebel against all this, challenge my father and do the opposite of what he expects from me. But he's right—I did give him my word.

I like Cristina a lot. Back then, I didn't think it was a terrible deal or that it would be difficult to follow through with an engagement that benefits both companies, not only from the publicity but by strengthening the relationship with Cristina's father. It seemed a natural part of doing our family's business.

My father gets up. "Cristina is coming by later. So fix it."

I simply nod as he makes his exit. After the door clicks closed, I punch the surface of the table with my closed fist in frustration.

Artemis, what are you doing?

I rub my face, thinking, unable to answer to this question. I keep thinking about Claudia. She finally allowed me to kiss her and touch her. And now I have to push her away again? Perhaps our destiny is to overcome many hurdles along the way. I like her a lot, but I committed to keeping the company afloat and successful at all costs. Nothing can derail me from my course, not even her.

Then why do I feel this way? Awful. I don't want her to think that I was playing with her feelings. But how am I going to explain this change of heart without sounding like a jerk?

Yes, I kissed you. Also, I'm getting back together with my ex.

I could ask her to wait for me. Or to be the other woman. She doesn't deserve either.

I'm not surprised to find Cristina waiting in my office when I return from the boardroom. She's wearing a fitted black skirt, a nicely tailored white shirt, and red high heels. She has her red hair pulled up in a high ponytail.

She greets me with a smile. "I'm sorry about what happened."

I believe her. She's trapped in this arrangement just like I am. "It's fine. This is how things work here."

"I want you to know that I made several attempts to reason with my father. I—"

I interrupt her with a smile. "You don't have to explain anything. I trust you tried your hardest. Our parents can't adjust to today's different standards."

She sighs. "Tell me about it. He's so old-school. Are we living in Victorian times, back when parents chose their children's spouses?"

"They don't treat us like their children." I can be totally honest with her since we share the same opinion. I lean over my desk with my arms crossed. "They think of us as assets they can make use of when convenient. Right now, we are simply an arrangement, an attractive publicity campaign that will benefit their respective companies."

She approaches me and places her hands around my neck. The scent of roses from her perfume fills my nose.

"I am glad that it's you," she states, as her eyes lock with mine. "I don't think I could bear it if it was someone else."

I caress her cheek. "Me either."

My eyes drop to her pink lips and I run my finger over them. "I missed you," I whisper as I put an arm around her waist.

She smiles broadly. "Wow. Artemis Hidalgo, being sweet. We should break up more often."

"From one to ten, how much did you miss me screwing you?"

She bites her lower lip. "Eleven."

I give in and kiss her. I've underestimated our attraction. We spent over a year together, and given the similarities in our upbringing we understand each other very well. I'd be lying if I said that my father is the only motivating factor that made me date her. I like her and feel at ease in her company. And the sex is incredible. She was a virgin when we met, and one of the advantages to being her mentor during her sexual awakening was teaching her what satisfies me in addition to helping her discover what pleases her.

When she pulls away, guilt washes over me when I think of Claudia. Then I immediately scold myself. This is my world, and this is how things work. There's no room for fleeting emotions. What I share with Cristina needs to be enough. It's an arrangement of convenience *and* I'm attracted to her. I can have total control over this situation. No surprises. No risks.

"Are you hungry?" she asks as she takes a step back. "Look at those dark circles. How long have you gone without sleep?"

"I'm fine," I reply as I round my desk.

"You don't have to do this all on your own," she tells me with reproach. "You know you can ask me for help, right?"

"You're already doing enough by reviewing the designs I send you every week. Thanks for your feedback—it's spot-on by the way." She's about to protest, but I keep talking. "You don't work for me, you're my fiancé."

I wake my computer and log in, navigating to the internal pages of the company server to check on a few things.

"I'd love to work for you already," she comments with a sigh as she sits on the edge of my desk next to me and crosses her legs.

I swivel my chair in her direction. "I find it difficult to wrap my head around making a job offer when you're already an executive director managing a company that's as big as mine."

She rolls her eyes.

"Precisely. You better than anyone understands the immense responsibility that comes with the title—dozens of employees, people with families and children to support, could lose their jobs if I were to make a simple mistake." She stares intently at one of the windows. "I would love to be just another employee and focus solely on doing my job right, putting food on my table and looking after myself instead of being in charge of hundreds of workers."

"I'm pretty sure that if one of your employees heard that, they'd think you're ungrateful."

"Fortunately, *you* are not one of my employees." She holds my hand. "And you understand what I mean."

I nod in agreement because she's right. Cristina and I understand each other very well.

"I'm going to get you something to eat."

"How do you manage to have all this free time?"

She winks at me, and leaves the office. My eyes feel heavy and I'm drowning in reports, but this project is very important, and I review every detail several times. If everything goes well, it will be a windfall in profits.

My assistant calls and I put him on speakerphone. "Sir, there's a woman at reception who would like to come up and see you. Her name is Claudia. She says your mother gave her orders to bring you lunch."

This takes me by surprise and makes my heart beat a little faster than usual. I haven't seen Claudia in days. "You can send her up."

I have a hard time focusing and my eyes keep darting to the door, anticipating her arrival. I play with the pen I'm holding, and keep twirling it, but stop when I hear a light knocking on the door.

"Come in."

Claudia enters. She's wearing a pair of hip-hugging jeans that are very flattering, and a blue buttoned-up blouse that accentuates her skin tone.

She looks good in everything she wears. Her black eyes meet mine and I can't help feeling a sense of relief sweeping over me.

"Hi, sexy."

"Hi, iceberg."

Claudia empties the contents of the lunch bag, placing each item on the table in front of the big couch in my office. I sit down next to her and start to devour the food laid out before she's even done unwrapping everything she brought.

She's looking intently at me. "Having a difficult week?"

"You have no idea."

I recline on the couch when I finish eating. It's a marvelous feeling when your stomach is full with homemade food, so I close my eyes and savor this special sensation, knowing it may well be the last time I spend with her like this. She places one hand over mine. The warmth of her skin makes me feel good, and I open my eyes and stare at her.

"I . . ." She stops herself, but I understand what she needs to say by her expression. For the very first time I'm able to read her face, and knowing how she's feeling takes my breath away. I turn my hand and intertwine it with hers.

"I missed you, too, sexy."

The moment we hear the door open, she immediately lets go of my hand as if it was on fire, and my heart hurts because I know the special magic moment we just shared is over. I turn around to see who is at the door, and Cristina struts elegantly in, carrying a bag of food.

I didn't, for an instant, fail to remember that Cristina would return shortly. I don't want to explain myself to Claudia; I'd rather she arrive at her own conclusions.

Claudia, please hate me.

Push me away.

Close yourself off again.

I'm a coward, I know. But I'm not good with words. Besides, I'm not confident I can look her in the eye and tell her that I'm back with Cristina, who is currently greeting Claudia with a friendly smile.

"Oh, hi. It seems I'm too late, and you ate already!"

I watch Claudia's expression change. Pain spreads over her beautiful face. And I can't bring myself to look directly at her. I don't want to see the hurt she's feeling written on her face. Cristina bends forward and gives me a quick peck. I fix my gaze on her when she straightens up. At this very moment, I'm having a hard time grappling with how deeply I've hurt the woman sitting next to me.

"You must be Claudia. Pleasure to meet you. I'm Cristina, his fiancé."

Cristina knows well who Claudia is. My mother has mentioned

her name many times when speaking about the house staff.

"Are you not feeling well?" Cristina asks her politely.

This makes me turn to check on Claudia, which I regret immediately. The pained look on her face makes my stomach churn. I can tell she's struggling to stay calm.

I'm a piece of shit.

Suddenly, I realize I've handled the situation in the worst possible way. Claudia leaps to her feet.

"I . . . need to go now."

I feel her gaze on me but I can't bring myself to look at her.

I can't stand seeing you like this, Claudia. It hurts.

"Have a good afternoon," she says as she leaves my office. And behind her, a deafening silence.

It's better this way, Artemis, I tell myself over and over again, trying to exorcise from my mind the pained look on Claudia's face. I need for her to hate me and to stay away from me because I believe I'm incapable of doing that on my own.

Cristina is watching me. "What was that?"

"Nothing." I get up and walk to my desk.

She folds her arms. "That did not look like 'nothing' to me." There's no reproach in her voice, just curiosity. "I was under the impression that we were going to be honest with each other if we became involved with someone else."

"There's nothing between us. Well, not anymore."

She understands what I mean.

"Was she why you broke up with me?"

Her question doesn't surprise me. I don't need to lie. Cristina is quite perceptive and good at reading people.

"Yes."

Cristina laughs a little.

"You have a thing for redheads, huh?"

I remain quiet. She lies down on the couch.

"She's very pretty."

Claudia is more than pretty.

"Are you jealous and making a scene?" I observe her inquisitively.

"Jealousy isn't something that factors into the type of relationship you and I have."

"Oh, I see. And what type of relationship do you and I have?"

Cristina gives me shrug. "A relationship of sex and convenience."

"And since when are you this cold and calculating?"

"Since the moment you acted in the same manner. It's the only way we can survive in our world, Artemis."

"And here I was thinking that you were madly in love with me."

She snorts. "You wish."

We stay silent for a few minutes, and I continue to fight the urge to go find Claudia and explain that I wasn't using her, that I was done with Cristina when I kissed her, and I'm not the kind of jerk who resorts to deception to get what I want. Unfortunately, I can't do that. I have a role to play in this company and for my family.

And there is no place for Claudia in this world.

Fourteen

They are older now, and are going to be fine.

CLAUDIA

My life is back to its old routine.

Yes, indeed. The monotonous day-to-day that I was more than accustomed to and did not mind at all until Artemis came back home and right into my life, turning it upside down only to make his way out again in the worst possible way. And now it seems this routine is not enough, and I feel unsatisfied.

At least I can blame him for ruining it all. I can't help but feel a painful squeeze in my heart when I think of him. He hurt me. I've come to terms with this truth. I let him in, made myself vulnerable, and he hurt me. Maybe in his twisted mind, this was getting back at me for rejecting him that Fourth of July, and now we're even. Still, this doesn't seem fair to me. I never played with his feelings: I was straightforward and let him down on his first attempt. I didn't lead him on or rub someone else in his face.

He now seems to be avoiding me, and I'm thankful even

though I know it will be nearly impossible to keep up, since we both live in the same house.

So it's only a bit of a surprise when I'm coming out of the laundry room just as Artemis enters the house through the main doors. His perfectly tailored suit molds against his nicely toned body well. The memory of my fingers tracing his chest and abdomen comes to mind, and I curse the vivid reminder. Our eyes meet, and I might have noticed a trace of sadness, but I'm too upset with him to care. Part of me wants to kick up a fuss but I'm not going to further degrade myself. I'm not giving him the opportunity to claim that he never said he was looking for something serious, or go about laying on the bullshit as I've witnessed Ares do on multiple occasions. I walk past him in silence, and go about picking up the plates and glasses Mrs. Hidalgo left in the living room after having friends over.

Artemis walks to the foot of the stairs and stops. He seems unsure whether to go up.

My hands are full and I take the first batch of items away. When I come back from the kitchen I want to slap myself for feeling disappointed when I notice he's gone.

Not even an apology, Artemis?

And what did you expect, Claudia?

Sunday is visitors' day with a very special someone in my life. I get off the bus in front of a large seniors' residence, and when I enter, the nurse on duty greets me with a smile and takes me to the garden. The facilities of this exclusive long-term care residence are impeccably clean, the staff is very well trained and friendly, the rooms are spacious, and the overall look is more luxury hotel than anything else. It is exactly what it ought to be: a nursing facility for seniors who have more money than they could hope to spend during the time they have left. In the garden that has become familiar to me over the past two years, I walk among the remaining beautiful flowers already at the end of their blooming cycle. Fall is on its way.

I can see him in the near distance, sitting on a bench next to a tall leafy tree facing the lake. Of their own accord, my lips curve into a smile as I near the spot where he's sitting.

Anthony Hidalgo is a sturdy and very tall man with brown eyes of a shade that's similar to that of his grandsons Ares and Artemis. The wrinkles on his face are a road map of the hard labor he invested earlier in life to get where he is now. Nevertheless, he is in great shape despite being almost eighty years old. He moved into this residence after his children came to an unanimous decision. Grandfather smiles back at me.

"I thought you weren't coming."

"And miss our wonderful Sunday date?" I snort. "Never."

Apolo was pretty much raised by his grandfather, and I'm happy Apolo has benefitted from this influence. Mr. Anthony takes a glass filled with lemonade from the table next to him and offers it to me.

"Very sweet, just how you like it."

My heart softens with affection. The way his face lights up when sees me every Sunday when I visit lets me know that he's lonely in this place, which, luxurious as it may be, is not home. Perhaps money isn't everything.

I take a sip of the lemonade and sit on the bench next to him. "Hmm, it's delicious."

"Do you want a snack? I can order your favorites."

I pat him on the shoulder. "I'm good. How are you?"

"I've got this headache that comes and goes, but it's nothing that I can't handle."

That worries me.

"Have you mentioned it to your doctor?"

He shakes his head. "It'll be fine. How are the boys? Apolo doesn't talk much about them."

Apolo visits him on Saturdays, and I visit him on Sundays. This way he has company two days in the week.

"They're fine," I respond, even though I'm sure this answer won't be enough.

"Apolo told me that Artemis has been bothering you since he came home."

Damn Apolo. He can't keep his mouth shut.

"It'll be fine." I regurgitate his previous answer. "I, more than anyone, am capable of handling the situation."

Grandfather lets out a sigh and looks at the beautiful lake in front of us, filled with dark-blue water shimmering with the sunlight.

"And what about Ares?"

Though most people will deny this, grandparents, or even parents, often have a favorite. And while Apolo was practically raised by his grandfather, Mr. Anthony has always had a soft spot for Ares. They both have strong characters, and are very similar. Of course, this has complicated their relationship, turning it into a game of emotional tug-of-war from time to time.

"He's fine. I think he's finally ready to settle down," I reply, thinking of Raquel.

Grandfather sighs again, and the sadness is evident in his voice. "Has he asked about me?"

I would love to lie and say yes. "You know what he's like."

Ares has only visited once the entire time his grandfather has been living at this nursing home. And when he left, he was on the verge of tears. He cannot stand seeing his grandfather here. The fact that he wasn't able to prevent his grandfather's admittance is something that eats away at him. Hence, he'd rather ignore the situation and act as if it's not happening so he won't have to deal with it. The boy with the bluest eyes is not capable of handling his emotions at all. On the outside he acts superior and seems imposing, yet inside he is uncertain and unsettled.

"I'd like to see him," his grandfather adds. "He must be taller. He hasn't stop growing since he was twelve."

I take out my cell phone, and click to open the photo gallery. "See for yourself."

I show him silly photos I've taken with Ares. There is Ares with his mouth stuffed with food flipping me off, his blue eyes catching the reflection of the flash. And Ares sleeping on the couch after watching a movie. There is one of him looking terrified as a bunch of Apolo's rescue pups encircle him. And another of Ares in his soccer jersey standing next to his teammate Daniel.

Agh, Daniel. That photo was taken the night I made the grave error of sleeping with him.

I put the phone away and clear my throat. Grandfather takes my hand.

"Ares and Artemis may appear cold, but it's a defensive mechanism, deep down they are kindhearted."

Not Artemis. I almost give way to my anger, but I know what he's telling me is true.

Artemis was good to me when we were growing up. I don't think I could ever forget how kind he was to me even though I'm deeply hurt by him now. I just have to keep away from him for the time being, and that's all.

Grandfather Hidalgo squeezes my hand.

"Please look after them. I feel at peace knowing that you're there for them. They never had a positive female role model, a woman who has stood by them throughout their lives."

It's clear he's talking about their mother, a woman who has been unfaithful to her husband many times, and hasn't been caring or nurturing toward her children.

"They're older now, and are going to be fine," I reply, staring at the shimmer of water gradually intensifying.

"They may be older but they have been deprived of love, Claudia. Their parents didn't show them affection when they were growing up, they gave them nothing. By the time I realized it was happening, it was too late. I was only able to give my love to Apolo."

I turn to face him. "And why are you telling me?"

His eyes meet mine and his gaze softens.

"Because I want you to keep this in mind if you ever reach the point when you feel like throwing in the towel and decide to shut them out. Apolo told me that Artemis has been pestering you. Please don't give up on them, and try to remember how much they care for you, all right?"

I give his cheeks a soft pinch and speak to him playfully. "Look at you, so adorable, worried about your ungrateful boys who never pay you a visit."

"They'll come one day." The certainty in his tone makes me roll my eyes in a dramatic way. He lightly taps my forehead. "Insolent girl making fun of an old man."

"An old man?" I get up, looking to both sides. "Where?"

He bursts out laughing, and I look at him affectionately. I am grateful for Grandfather's presence in my life; he is amazing. We spend the rest of the day talking. As always, he asks me about school, if I need anything. And as usual my answer is no—by paying my tuition and university expenses he has already done enough. I don't ever want him to think I'm taking advantage of his love by asking for more money.

With a smile on my face, I say my good-byes and head home.

It's four o'clock in the morning when I'm woken up by the ringing of the house's landline. I have a tendency to bring the cordless phone to my room so I don't have to walk to the kitchen and answer every time a call comes in. I stretch my hand from the bed to answer, hoping it's not a crank call.

"Hello?" My voice is hoarse and weak.

"Good evening." The formality in the tone of the woman on the other end puts me on alert. "I'm calling from the general hospital." I sit up immediately, imagining all sorts of scenarios. "We need to inform you that Mr. Anthony Hidalgo was admitted to emergency a little while ago." I stop breathing. "This is the number we have as his primary contact."

"What happened?" I'm unsure what to ask.

"He suffered a stroke. The doctors are currently working to stabilize him. I'll be able to provide you with more information when you get here."

"We're on our way."

She gives me a few more details before ending the call.

I dress in a hurry and don't even pay attention to the clothes I put on. My heart has formed a lump in my throat, and I can feel it beating hard.

"He's fine. He has to be fine."

I've got this headache that comes and goes, but it's not anything I can't handle.

Stubborn old man! If he wasn't feeling well why didn't he say something? A sense of dread courses though me and I dart out of my room.

My mother hasn't stirred one bit. She's a deep sleeper—not even a hurricane could interrupt her slumber. Meanwhile, I find Mr. Juan in his pajamas, with his cell phone to his ear when I reach the living room. It's clear that the nursing home reached out to him while the hospital was calling the landline. He can see the dread and desperation in my eyes.

"Should we go to hospital?" I ask.

My eyes move in the direction of the stairs and he reads my mind. "I don't want to wake them up right now," he says. "It's best to wait until morning, and then—"

But I'm already running past him and up the stairs.

"Claudia!" I hear him shout behind me. "Claudia!"

I knock on each of the boys' doors hard enough for them to hear, and come to a halt outside Apolo's room. Ares peeks out, his hair a spiky mess pointing in all directions. He has one eye closed and is struggling to keep the other open. "What's wrong?"

A shirtless Artemis also sticks his head into the hallway. "What the fuck is going on?"

I try to slow my breathing and make an attempt to sound calm, so I choose my words carefully. "Your grandfather . . ."

Apolo opens his door and stands in front of me. "What's happening, Claudia?"

"Your grandfather is in the hospital."

Understanding and fear is evident in the expressions worn by each of the Hidalgo boys when words fail to come out of my mouth.

They all scramble to put on the first scraps of clothing they can find while asking me a lot of questions. And then they follow me downstairs. Mr. Juan is waiting at the bottom of the stairs and gives me a disapproving look, but I don't care. Our ride to the hospital is quiet, yet the air is heavy with suffocating worry. Mr. Juan is driving and Artemis is in the passenger seat. I'm in the back, between the other two boys. Apolo cries silently, big tears rolling down his cheeks.

My heart is shrinking. I don't want to entertain the possibility of his grandfather not making it through. *He is strong and will be fine*, I repeat to myself over and over.

I take Apolo's hand and give it a squeeze. He rests his head on my shoulder and his tears dampen my shirt.

Ares is resting his elbow on the car window, his closed fist held against his mouth. His knuckles have turned white. The tension through his shoulders is obvious. He's mad. No, correction: furious. I assume he deeply regrets not visiting his grandfather. Perhaps we all thought Anthony was eternal because he always looked strong. I link Ares's other hand with my free hand and place them on my lap. When Ares turn his gaze to me, I see pain in his eyes.

"He's going to be okay." Ares goes back to staring out the window but doesn't let go of my hand, squeezing tightly.

Artemis turns around slightly and glances at me. He's trying to conceal his worry but his deep concern is written all over his face. I smile at him and whisper, "Your grandfather is going to be okay."

He nods and straightens in his seat.

They may be older but they have been deprived of love, Claudia. Their parents failed to show them affection when they were growing up; they gave them nothing. The words of their grandfather echo in my mind as I enter the hospital with the Hidalgos. One single thought takes up residence in my head: You've got to get well, you stubborn old man. Don't you dare die on us. If you do, I will make sure to bring you back and kill you myself.

My mind flashes to the way the wrinkles on his face appear more evident when he smiles.

He is the closest thing I have to a father figure, something I never had in my life.

I love you so much, you stubborn old man. Please get well.

Fifteen

My god, I am so sorry!

CLAUDIA

Anthony Hidalgo is stable.

The results from the MRI show that he sustained minimal damage, which is a relief. However, the doctor said something about having to keep him sedated and resting until the swelling in his brain comes down. After a couple of days of keeping vigil at the hospital, we were all sent home with the promise that they would contact us the moment he's conscious. I feel like I can finally breathe, though I won't be completely at ease until I'm able to speak with him. But at least now I know he'll be okay. Life at the house has almost returned to normal.

I bring my mother her supper after I'm done tending to Ares and his guests, which include Raquel, a boy with an infectious smile, and a girl who resembles Daniel. When I go back to the rec room with the refreshments Ares requested, I find it empty. Where did they go?

I go up to Ares's room and knock on his door.

"Come in."

Inside, I find that he's not alone—Apolo is with him, and I can tell something is going on by their expressions.

"I brought the drinks you asked for but your guests aren't there."

The disappointment on Ares's face is clear as the light of day.

"Have they all gone?" He knows I'm asking if Raquel has left.

"Yes. Everyone," he confirms, with a sigh. A flash of sadness appears in Ares's eyes, though he tries to hide it. Apolo smiles at him and leaves.

I gently rub my tense shoulders and make my way down the stairs. I have one last task to complete before turning in: I have to collect the dirty towels from the gym and put them in the washer. Now that Artemis is living in this house, I have to do it more often since he works out every day.

I slide open the door to the gymnasium and walk past the exercise machines, making my way to the entrance of the wash-room located at the end of the hallway. I yawn as I pick up the used towels from the basket placed right outside the shower stall, and check inside the stall to see if there are any towels in there. The stall is huge and long, and the shower is right at the end. I fantasize about Artemis having a shower, and suddenly I feel hot. I should not be thinking about that idiot.

In the laundry room, I place half the towels in the machine and start it up, putting the rest on the floor. I'm exhausted. I slide down until I come to rest on the pile of fluffy towels.

I must have fallen asleep, because the next thing I know, I wake from a scorching wet dream. I couldn't make out the face of the man in my dream, but he was giving me the best fuck I've had in my entire life. My frustration grows when I realize I'm drenched. Damn it.

Come to think of it, when was the last time I had sex? I can't even recall. No wonder my hormones are in overdrive. I can't even remember the last time I helped myself ease some of this tension. I open my legs and push up my skirt, and my eager hand slides inside my stockings. I shouldn't be doing this here, but I can't take care of it in the room I share with my mother.

I'm completely soaked and my fingers easily slide inside my most intimate place. A moan escapes my lips; I had forgotten how good this feels. I shift my stocking to one side so I can have better access. I know exactly what I like and my fingers move accordingly, deep inside. I close my eyes, drowning in a flurry of sensations.

I bite my lower lip and let out a few whimpers, which become louder as my fingers increase their tempo. I open my eyes and instead of finding the door closed, I see Apolo standing across from me.

I jump to my feet, roll my skirt back down into place, and try to stand, but my legs are shaky.

"Oh my god. I'm so sorry!"

I lower my gaze, mortified beyond belief. I wait for him to leave but he doesn't. Instead, I hear him close the door behind him and move farther into this small space. I look up to watch him but remain speechless. My breathing is in complete shambles. In all the years I've known him, I've never seen this expression on Apolo's face. It's neither innocent nor childish. It's pure lust. His eyes are shining bright, and show the determination of a man. He approaches slowly, as if he knows a sudden move could scare me. Once he's standing in front of me, he extends his hand to hold my chin and his thumb gently rubs my lips.

I'm trembling as I open my mouth. "What are you doing?" My voice is barely audible and the words come out in a whisper.

Apolo doesn't reply. Without taking his gaze off me, he leans in closer.

"Apolo . . ."

"Just feel," he answers hoarsely.

He is aroused and his breathing, like mine, is in shambles.

My mind is clouded by the sexual haze spreading between us.

He wets his mouth and leans in to kiss me. And I know I shouldn't, but when he moves his lips against mine at a slow, sensual pace, I lose all control.

He increases the pace of his kiss and presses me against the wall with his body. I release my mouth from his kiss to let out a groan.

I can't stop myself from gripping his shirt tightly, while my legs are a quivering mess. I close my eyes—he's a great kisser.

I need to stop this before it gets more out of hand, so I break the kiss, resting my forehead against his. The sound of our combined rapid breathing echoes in the small room. We're both panting. As the moments pass, I become more clearheaded and the realization of what I've done grows. I need to get out immediately.

I pull back from Apolo and step around him, exiting the laundry room, and when I walk into the living room, I run straight into Artemis.

He still has his suit on, and probably just came home from work. Artemis looks at me intently, without saying a word. I bet I look flustered, and my face is red.

"Pardon me." I turn around and walk away before he can work anything out.

I'd like to tell him that I feel guilty or something along those lines, but I don't. There is nothing between me and Artemis. I've lost all respect for him after he deceived me just to get a kiss. More so now that I know he has a fiancé. Not just a girlfriend, but someone he's engaged to.

Apolo, on the other hand, worries me. The last thing I want is to ruin our relationship or make things awkward between us. But we crossed the line the moment we jumped from platonic love to kissing, right? I'd always thought of him as a brother. Well, that changed today. I recall his grunts, and the desire burning in his gaze. I shake my head.

Claudia, you can't want him that way or you'll make life complicated. You have to switch back to thinking of him as the boy he is; the boy you have always regarded as a younger brother.

I realize I'm outside Ares's door when he opens it and finds me standing there.

"Claudia?"

I don't know what I'm doing here. I suppose I'm running away, though I'm not sure from whom exactly. Apolo is usually the one I seek when I need refuge, but I can't go to him now, not after what just happened. He must be feeling as confused as I am.

"May I come in?"

Ares steps to one side.

His bedroom is partially lit, the only light coming from the table lamps on either side of his bed. Lightning flashes through his window, and it's soon followed by thunder. Shortly after, rain begins to fall.

"Has something happened to my grandfather?" Ares doesn't try to hide the concern in his voice.

I shake my head. "No."

Ares is wearing a white T-shirt and jeans. It's getting late and I'm surprised he hasn't changed into pajamas. Maybe he's going out? He sits down on the reclining chair in one corner of his room.

"What's going on?"

I'm so embarrassed, and doubt I can tell him what just happened. How could I? *Well, Ares, two weeks ago I hooked up with Artemis, but it turned out he was a complete jerk because he was engaged to someone else. And today I hooked up with Apolo. So, what do you think?*

"I need to take my mind off things. Can I just stay here a little while?"

He nods, lets out a sigh, and rubs his face with his hand. He doesn't look well—something is up. Turning my attention to the problems of others always helps me forget about my own issues.

"Are you okay?"

"Yes." He grimaces.

"You don't look like you are."

I notice he still has his shoes on.

"Are you going somewhere?" He shakes his head, but the look on his face tells a different story. "Do you want to go somewhere?"

He doesn't answer. I think back to how Raquel and her friends left earlier this afternoon and how sad Ares looked when that happened. It's obvious that his grandfather's condition has been distressing to him. I sense he needs to unload how he feels, needs someone to lean on. I could be that support, but he already has someone who is better suited for the job.

"You should go see her."

Ares looks up. He knows I'm talking about Raquel.

"I can't."

"Why not?"

"She's angry with me."

I sigh. "Did you tell her what happened to your grandfather?" He shakes his head for a second time. "Why not?"

"I don't want her to see me like this."

"Like this, how? Like a human being with real feelings, who is sad about his grandfather?"

"I don't want to seem weak."

This bothers me. "For heaven's sake. Why do you think that loving someone and leaning on them is a sign of weakness?"

"Because it is."

"No, Ares, it is not," I respond, pressing my lips together. "You consider opening your heart to someone a weakness? It's the opposite—it's the most courageous thing a person can do."

"Ah, don't start with the lectures. You're as bad as Apolo."

"You idiot, I'm just trying to get you to see that being in love is not a weakness."

Ares raises his voice. "Yes, it is. You and I know that better than anyone."

He's referring to his mother.

"You can't use what happened as a shield and hide behind it all your life," I tell him.

"I don't want to be like him!"

"You're not like him!" I reply and get up. "You are not like your father. And I'm completely certain that Raquel is nothing like your mother."

He snorts angrily. "How can you be so sure?"

"Because I know you, and you would never get involved with a girl who is anything like your mother. Also, I've observed Raquel, and her openness and honesty impress me. And I bet those were the qualities that attracted you to her."

Ares looks mad, which is what often happens when he doesn't have a counterargument.

"You're encouraging this. You . . ." I can already see he's looking for a way to hurt me. It's his go-to defense mechanism when he feels cornered. "You, who's stuck taking care of her mother—someone who put you through hell when you were a kid. You're telling me that love isn't a weakness?"

"What my mother did, all the mistakes and bad decisions she made, all the terrible things she put me through—that is her burden, not mine." I pause. "If I were to let that define the person I am, then I make the choice to carry that myself, and that's my guilt to endure."

Ares is speechless.

"Go see her, Ares," I repeat. "Needing her doesn't make you weak. On the contrary, admitting that you need someone is the greatest proof of courage. So, go on—find her."

I watch him hesitate for a moment. Eventually he stands up and leaves his room.

He's a good guy.

Sixteen

To hell with the bro code?

ARTEMIS

I can't stop thinking about Claudia's face, and the way she looked. Her face was flushed and she was panting. It reminds me of the night when I kissed and touched her.

I watch her run up the stairs as if she's running away from someone other than me. I'm intrigued when I see a blushing Apolo appear from the same hallway she came from.

"What's going on?"

Apolo walks past me and avoids making eye contact. His shirt is wrinkled around the chest area, as if someone had a tight grip on it. I give him an eye roll.

What are those two up to?

And how is that any of your business, Artemis? You pushed her away.

Nevertheless, that doesn't mean that I'm okay with her being with someone else. Especially not one of my brothers. Even though I need to let her go, why am I still so possessive? Why do I think of her as mine?

Because you are a selfish idiot.

I had another tough day at work. After spending a few days at the hospital, I returned to the office to catch up on a pile of work. I barely made it home tonight to get some rest. I walk up to my bedroom and have a shower. The hot water falls on my skin and the steam fills up the stall. My wet hair covers my face and I press my fist against the wall. Every time I close my eyes, I'm tormented by the memory of that afternoon in my office and the wounded look on Claudia's face.

She didn't deserve that. She's been so good to Ares and Apolo. I recall the night we were on our way to the hospital and how supportive she was to both of them in the car. She's a kind woman, and I needlessly caused her pain by not explaining what she witnessed with Cristina. And what did I accomplish by that? By confusing her? I'm not even sure how to best explain my situation.

Regardless, the facts remain the same. We can't be together. Well, not for the time being. I rub my face and turn off the water. After I put on more comfortable clothes, I stare at the door.

Don't go looking for her, Artemis.

I clench my jaw and throw the towel to one side before I leave my room. I find her in the kitchen, wiping down the table, leaving it shiny and spotless. Her expression hardens the moment she looks up and sees me. She throws the rag into the sink and turns to leave.

"Claudia." She doesn't stop. When she tries to walk past me, I grab her by the arm and spin her to face me. "I'm speaking to you."

She shakes her arm free from my hold. "And I'm ignoring you."

Her anger bothers me.

"Is that what you plan to do? Ignore me from here on out?"

"Yes." She doesn't hesitate for a second.

"How mature." I see a spark in her eyes, and it's of pure anger. "I hoped at least we could be civil."

She takes a few steps back and crosses her arms. "And did you decide that before or after you lied to me to get closer?"

"I didn't lie to you."

She snorts. "You are shameless."

"Claudia . . ."

I'm unsure what compels me to raise my hand in an attempt to touch her face. She takes one more step back.

"Don't touch me."

I lower my hand. "Claudia, I—"

"Everything all right?" I'm startled by the sound of Apolo's voice right behind Claudia. I didn't see him come in.

Claudia turns around in an attempt to leave. "Yes. I was about to turn in."

However, when she tries to walk by him, Apolo shifts into her path. "Let's go to my room, we need to talk."

An electric current zaps through my veins and settles at the pit of my stomach. *Don't touch her*, I want to growl.

Claudia appears uncomfortable. "I don't think this is the right time," she says.

"I think it is. Let's go." Apolo starts to lead her by the arm.

"No, Apolo. Tomorrow."

I react before I think, and catch up to them. I pull her toward me by the arm that is free and release her from Apolo's grip.

"She said no."

Apolo turns to stare at me with a defiance I've never seen.

Apolo has always been intimidated by me, but apparently not this time. The tone of his voice is serious. "What I need to discuss with her is none of your business."

"I don't like the sound of this."

I feel anger in every fiber of my being—my jaw is clenched and my shoulders are tense. Claudia loosens her arm from my grip.

My full attention is on Apolo when I speak. "Anything that concerns her is my business."

Apolo doesn't hesitate. "And why is that?"

I feel the need to mark my territory. "Because she is involved with me."

Claudia looks at me, horrified.

Apolo's expression turns from defiant to confused. "What are you talking about?"

"Artemis, shut up. Don't say anything else," she says tersely.

"Apolo, she belongs to me."

Apolo's gaze turns to her. "Claudia?"

Claudia immediately shakes her head. "No. I'm not anything to him."

"That's not what you said when you were riding my fingers, Claudia."

Claudia throws me a murderous look. If she hated me before, I'm pretty sure she hates me even more now.

"You . . . with him?" Apolo is at a loss for words. Claudia moves toward him but I take her arm and bring her to a halt.

She shakes my hand off and screams, "Stop grabbing me and treating me as if I'm a fucking object! I don't belong to you!" She grabs Apolo by the hand. "Come with me, and let me explain."

And that's when everything turns red.

It feels like she's choosing him over me, so I walk to where they stand and I pull them apart.

"Why do you need to explain anything to him, huh?"

Apolo gets between us. "Enough."

I stare at her over Apolo's shoulder. "Claudia?" I say through clenched teeth.

She looks back at me and tells me without a hint of hesitation, "Apolo and I kissed today."

What?

My world comes to a stop. My anger boils. My chest rises and falls rapidly. I have never felt this furious. I grab Apolo by the collar of his shirt. "What did you do?" Apolo grabs my wrists and tries to free himself.

"She's made it very clear. She wants nothing to do with you."

"So, to hell with the bro code?" I remind him of the pact we made years ago when we each promised to stay away from girls any of the others were interested in.

For a brief moment Apolo seems genuinely guilty. "I didn't know that you and her . . . I didn't—"

"Fucking hell!" I tighten my grip on his shirt.

Claudia stands next to me.

"Artemis, let him go."

I look my brother straight in the eyes. "You and Ares have *always* known that I'm interested in her."

Claudia grabs my shoulder. "Let him go!"

I can't get a hold of myself. The thought of her kissing him makes my blood boil. Apolo speaks to me with an icy coldness that perturbs me. "She said she's not with you. It's not my fault you're stuck in a one-sided obsession."

His words burn, fanning the flames of my anger. I punch him

so hard that my knuckles make a cracking sound when they make contact with his chin. Apolo tumbles and falls backward.

"Enough!" Claudia slaps a hand on my chest. "Stop it! Leave!"

I grab her by the wrist. "Only if you come with me. I'm not leaving without you."

She hesitates. I can see she wants to protest, but she knows that would trigger Apolo. He'd jump to her defense and all hell would surely break loose between us. Apolo has crumpled to the floor, where he remains seated, holding his cheek and wincing in pain. This doesn't make me regret my reaction. He broke the bro code and knows he had that punch coming; it's likely the reason he didn't fight back.

I hold Claudia by the wrist and lead her upstairs.

"I'll be right back," I hear her whisper to Apolo.

The moment we enter my room, she folds her arms over her chest, furious.

"Have you lost your mind? Beating your own brother? What in the—"

"What happened between you two?" She's not expecting the question. "Tell me everything. I need to know every detail. How many times he kissed you. If he touched you. Everything."

She gives a snort and is visibly indignant. "You have no right to ask me that."

"Yes, I have every right to! I earned it weeks ago when you let me touch you. And now you're allowing my brother to do the same thing with you?"

"Are you listening to yourself?" She raises her voice. "Artemis, you lied to me. You have a fiancé—you let me in only to push me out. What gives you the right to make a scene? Have you lost your mind?"

I run my hand over my beard and my head. “Stay away from him.”

She lets out a sarcastic laugh. “You’re not even listening to me.”

“Claudia, you need to do as I say. You have no idea what I’m capable of.”

“I’m not afraid of you, Artemis.” She comes closer just so I can see the disdain in her eyes. “Listen to me, you idiot. You and I are nothing. I don’t belong to you, or to any other man. I am not an object, I am a human being. What I do with my life from this moment on is none of your fucking business. So please do me—and yourself—a favor and focus on your life and your fiancé, and let me live in peace.”

She turns and walks to the door.

“Not him, Claudia.” She stops but keeps her back to me. “Not with my brother,” I say through clenched teeth. “Not with my fucking brother.”

She glances at me over her shoulder. “I want you to know that it wasn’t my intention to hurt you.”

It never is. My shoulders slump in resignation.

“Don’t take this out on Apolo, he loves you and is your brother.” She pauses, choosing her next words carefully. “You and I were done before we even started. That’s how it is with us. Stop trying to make the impossible happen, Artemis.”

I walk up until I stand right behind her.

“How can I ever do that when it’s you?” She doesn’t say anything. I put my hands on her shoulders and rest my forehead against the back of her head. “I can’t do that, Claudia.”

I can feel her tremble a little at the sound of my words. She puts her hands on top of mine and tries to get them off her shoulders. I gasp in pain when her hand touches the knuckles of one of mine. I hadn't noticed they were bleeding. Claudia turns to face me and holds the hand that is injured.

"Oh, look what you've done." The coldness in her eyes vanishes and concern immediately takes its place. "Sit. I'll go get the first aid kit."

I do what she says and sit on my bed. She comes right back, leaving the door open, and sits down next to me. I quietly watch her disinfect my knuckles with utmost care. I frequently got into fights when I was a teenager and she was always there to scold me and tend to my wounds. She purses her lips as she treats my cuts with great care and attention.

It takes me back to a day . . .

"Artemis! Artemis!" The urgency in Ares's voice alarmed me. I paused my video game as he ran into my room. His eyes were red and tears streamed down his small cheeks.

"What's wrong?" I imagined a slew of devastating scenarios.

Ares was crying inconsolably and could hardly speak. I took his face in my hands.

"Ares, what happened? Tell me."

"I got . . . a good grade." He wiped his face with the back of his hand. "And I went to show Mom . . ." His face twisted in a grimace, looking anguished. "She . . . There's a man in there . . . She and that man . . . He's not our dad."

I was confused. "What do you mean?"

"Mom—she's doing things in her bed with that man who is not our dad."

A cold feeling settled in my gut. I knew damn well what was taking place.

Sadly, I wasn't proven wrong when our mother suddenly

appeared outside my bedroom door. She was naked under a white blanket wrapped around her body.

"Ares! Come here! Right this second!" Although her tone was commanding, I also detected fear. Her eyes searched my face, surely trying to assess if Ares had had a chance to tell me what he'd witnessed.

I catapulted to my feet, pushed Ares aside, and made my way in her direction. My sudden reaction took my mother by surprise. However, she wasn't my target, so I walked past her and made my way down the hallway.

"Where is he?"

My mother shook her head. "Artemis." She tried to grab one of my arms but I swiped her hand away.

I rushed to her room and kicked open the door. Inside, a strange man was just finishing buttoning his shirt.

I jumped on him in a flash and punched his face over and over, my muscles tight with anger. I was taller than him even though I was still a teenager, and my rage made me strong and unrestrained.

My mother shouted at me, demanding I leave him alone. I felt her hands on me as she tried to pull me away, but I couldn't stop

My mother's voice sounded like it was coming from far away, much like the memories of her standing next to my father when she was smiling and promising that our family would always be united and stay together.

Liar.

Hypocrite.

The only words that came to mind were insults that I would never dare call my mother; still, they roamed freely inside my head.

The grunts that came out of my mouth as I punched the man under me had an underlying tinge of powerlessness. My knuckles ached and burned, but I couldn't make myself stop.

I didn't want to stop.

A warm hand landed gently on my cheek, and I was about to flick it away when I heard her voice. "Artemis."

I stopped, holding my fist midair as I looked up. Claudia was kneeling in front of me, her unruly red hair framing her face. She took her hand off my cheek and used it to take my wrist. My breathing was fractured, making my shoulders rise and fall uncontrollably.

"That's enough."

I didn't think it was.

She entwined her fingers with mine.

"You're fine. This is enough. Let's go." I shook my head and she gave me a sad smile. "Please."

I released my wrist from her grip and reluctantly stood. I was about to resume my assault when my mother moved in to assist the man, kneeling beside him as he moaned in pain. I left the room to avoid turning into a murderer. Claudia walked behind me in silence. Out in the hallway, I turned my gaze to my room, where I'd left Ares. Claudia could read the concern in my expression.

"My mother is looking after him. She made some tea to soothe him, and she's trying to distract him. You should calm down before seeing him. And we need to tend to the cuts on your hand."

I was confused until I followed her gaze to my knuckles, which were bleeding profusely. They hadn't hurt until then, as I finally took notice.

Adrenaline? Or pure rage?

I walked away without saying a word about the state I was in, and went downstairs, with Claudia following closely behind. Although I never told her, I was grateful she followed me that day.

Fucking grateful.

When I finally snap back to reality, I'm welcomed by the sight of Claudia carefully bandaging my fist.

"Claudia, how can I stop wanting you? How can I stop myself when you've been by my side every time I've ever needed you? When we share too many memories?"

I sense movement, and when I glance over, Apolo is standing at the door. He's holding an ice pack to his cheek. I feel terrible for hitting him now that I've cooled off—I've never hit my younger brother. I'm about to say something when I realize he's not looking at me.

Apolo lowers his head and leaves. I turn back to Claudia, who is now gathering the contents of the kit she used to clean and bandage the wounds on my hand.

"Try not to move your hand too much, and make sure to change the bandage tomorrow morning," she orders as she gets up.

"Thank you."

She nods at me before turning to leave.

"Good night, Artemis."

"Good night, Claudia."

I watch her go. And although tonight I've let her out of my room, I know deep down I'll never be able to let her out of my life.

When it comes to her, how could I ever?

Seventeen

I was waiting for you, Claudia.

CLAUDIA

Grandfather has regained consciousness.

I was in school when I received the call, and the bus took a long time to get to the hospital, so I'm the last one to arrive. I was so relieved when I heard Mr. Anthony had woken up, but I need to see him with my own eyes to feel completely reassured. I'm a little surprised to find Raquel sitting outside the room. Ares must be getting serious with her if he brought her along.

While I'm happy for Ares, I can't hide the concern in my voice. "How's he doing?"

"Apparently, he's doing fine."

I let out a long sigh. "That's great. I came as soon as I heard."

She gives me a curious look. "Have you met their grandfather?"

"Yes. I've spent most of my life living in the Hidalgo house. My mother took care of him a bit before they put him in a nursing home. Anthony is very special to me."

"I would imagine. What's it been like to live with the Hidalgos most of your life?"

Her question makes me chuckle a little. *If you only knew, Raquel.* "It's been interesting."

"I can't begin to imagine. I bet one of them was your first crush."

I feel my cheeks getting warm so I lower my head.

"Come on, which one? It's okay . . . as long as it wasn't Ares."

I'm opening my mouth ready to answer when I hear the sound of heels heading in our direction. I turn around to find Mrs. Hidalgo.

She has deemed the occasion worthy of her presence.

Sophia makes her way toward us on red stilettos, wearing a white skirt that sits above the knee and a low-cut blouse. Her makeup is excessive, and her hair is up in a very tight, high ponytail. Her eyes land on Raquel.

"And who are you?" She does what she knows best, scrutinizing the poor girl with eyes filled with contempt. Raquel doesn't answer. "I asked you a question."

Raquel clears her throat.

"My name is Ra-Raquel." She politely extends her hand to greet Mrs. Hildalgo.

Sofia looks at her hand and then at her.

"All right, Ra-Raquel." She mocks Raquel's initial stutter. "What are you doing here?"

I step next to Raquel. "She came with Ares."

Sofia arches an eyebrow. "Are you joking? Why would Ares bring her along?"

I roll my eyes. "Why don't you ask him yourself?"

Sofia purses her lips. "Don't take that tone with me, Claudia.

The last thing you want is to provoke me. Where is my husband?"

I point to the room's door, hoping to get her away from us. Mrs. Hidalgo enters the room, taking her bad energy along with her, and leaving us on our own. Raquel looks pale.

"What a nasty lady."

I give her a smile. "You have no idea."

"You don't seem intimidated by her."

"I grew up in that house. I think I've mastered the ability to engage with difficult people."

"I can only imagine. I just thought that since she's your boss, you'd have to . . ."

"Let her treat me poorly?" I finish her sentence. "I'm not a kid who gets scared easily anymore." I sit and pat the chair next to me. "But enough about me, tell me about yourself instead."

"There's not a lot to say. Only that I've fallen under the spell of the Hidalgos."

"I can see that. I can also tell that you finally managed to get the idiot to confess his feelings for you."

"How do you know?"

"Because you're here," I tell her in all honesty. "Their grandfather is one of the most important people in their lives. The fact that Ares brought you along speaks volumes."

"I've heard a lot about this man, and would love to meet him."

"I hope you do very soon. He's a wonderful person."

We talk for a while, just enough for me to understand why Ares has fallen in love with this girl. She's charming, an open book. Her expressions give away how she feels and her gestures reveal what she thinks. We get along beautifully.

The younger Hidalgo men finally emerge from the room.

The mood turns awkward as soon as Artemis's eyes meet

mine. He presses his lips tightly together then makes a turn and heads down the hall. I look at Apolo, who greets Raquel with a smile but does his damnedest to avoid my gaze.

"We're going to get a coffee. Grandpa asked about you, Claudia. You should go in as soon as my parents come out." Apolo shares this update without looking at me. He follows Artemis down the hall.

The cold shoulder, again, eh? Well, Hidalgo boys, I can play the same game.

Ares doesn't look at me either; he's focused on Raquel and grabs her hand instead. "Come along, witch."

I'm not exactly sure why I feel the need to apologize. Though it wasn't my intention, I somehow feel responsible for causing an unpleasant scene and not handling it in the best possible way.

"I'm sorry."

Ares looks up.

"It wasn't your fault." Ares never lies and I know he's being sincere. "You should never blame yourself for his impulsiveness, Claudia."

It's obvious he's referring to Artemis, who's always been the most impulsive and volatile of the three brothers. I watch them leave, then Mr. and Mrs. Hidalgo come out of the room. Sofia's uptight expression lacks a hint of genuine emotion. I would say this lady's audacity still shocks me, but all these years have conditioned me to expect the unexpected when it comes to Sofia Hidalgo. Juan points me to the door.

"He's been asking about you since he woke up."

There's a trace of jealousy in his tone. I can't believe it. He doesn't get to be jealous of his father's affection. He lost that right the day he let Grandfather be committed to a nursing home. Juan gives me a friendly smile and leaves with his wife.

I find Grandfather lying on his bed. My heart squeezes tight in my chest. I run to his side and give him a hug.

"Stubborn old man!" Tears stream down my face, and he gently pats my back.

"I'm fine, I'm fine."

I pull back from him with lips trembling, trying to contain the urge to cry. He grabs my face with his hands and plants a kiss on my forehead.

"You stubborn old man. I love you very much."

He puts his hands on mine. I'm caught by surprise the moment I withdraw from our hug and we look into each other's eyes—he's not someone who cries easily, but his eyes are watery.

"And I too love you very much, daughter."

Daughter.

He takes note of the shock written all over my face.

"You are way more important to me than all these vultures, my so-called children. If it wasn't for you and Apolo, I couldn't have coped with the loneliness in that place." His hands caress my face. "Thank you, daughter."

"Old man . . ." My voice breaks.

"How about calling me grandpa? I think dad would be weird. Or is that too much? I understand if this makes you uncomfortable. I know you're grown woman now and . . ."

I place my hand over my heart. "It would be an immense honor to call you grandpa."

He smiles and all his wrinkles become noticeable. We talk until it's almost time for me to catch the last bus.

It was decided that Grandpa would finish his recuperation at the Hidalgo house, and I couldn't be happier. I can look after him and stop worrying about him being alone at the nursing home. I hug him tightly before I leave. Outside, Sofia Hidalgo is in the hall by herself. She looks at me from head to toe.

"You've grown, a lot, Claudia." I pick up the hint of malice in her tone. "You should use your attributes to accomplish your goals and get ahead. Or do you want to spend the rest of your life as a housekeeper?"

My mouth forms a fake smile. "I will never lower myself to your level. No, thank you."

She laughs. "Oh really? And here I was thinking you were already screwing the patriarch of the Hidalgos, sinking your hooks into the fattest fish in the pond."

I keep my fists clenched on my hips.

"Projecting your ways and methods on me? People aren't all like you."

"Like me? Or maybe, more like your mother?" She moves closer. "Or are you forgetting how she would trade her body for cheap drugs? I always wondered if she ever prostituted you, simply because, you know . . ."

The sound of the hard slap I give her echoes in the empty hallway.

I speak through clenched teeth. "You can say whatever you like about me but don't you ever mention my mother."

"Who do you think you are, laying your hands on me?" She snarls at me and raises her arm ready to strike, but I catch her wrist midair and push away her hand.

"I'm leaving now."

She gives me one last look with hate-filled eyes before I walk away. I barely make it to catch the last bus. Once on board, I stare out the window as I travel along the route taking me back to the house. I'm happy that my position in the family is secure enough I no longer feel intimidated by Mrs. Hidalgo. I'm not five years old anymore; I'm a grown woman.

Right after the supplementary reading class I'm taking at school, I went back to the Hidalgo house. I entered to find the fireplace lit, which was uncommon in the middle of summer. I was about to head to my room when I noticed Mrs. Hidalgo sitting across from the fireplace.

"Oh. Good evening. I hadn't seen you there, ma'am." I tried to limit my interactions with her.

"Claudia, I was waiting for you," she replied with a forced smile. "Have a seat." She offered me the chair that she was facing.

I obeyed and sat down across from her. I was about to ask her if she needed something from me when I noticed the small book on her lap. My diary.

"You know, I didn't expect to find this in your room. I walked in out of mere curiosity and lo and behold, this was in full view right on top of your nightstand." She shook her head. "You are quite stupid for a fifteen-year-old girl."

I struggled to swallow.

"You shouldn't take other people's private property," I squeaked out.

"This is my house and I can take whatever I damn please." I opened my mouth to reply but she carried on. "Which is something you seem to forget, Claudia. This is my house. And we took you and your mother in despite—" She scowled in disgust. "Despite everything your mother has done out there on the streets."

"And my mother and I are very grateful, ma'am."

"Oh really? How grateful are you, Claudia?"

Her question sent shivers down my spine.

"A lot."

"Very good. That means you'll do as I say without resistance or objection," she said as she opened my diary and began to read. "'Today, Artemis held my hand again. And my chest felt like it was going to explode. I felt nervous and my palms were sweaty, so I quickly let go, afraid that he would notice.' Aww, how sweet."

I put down my head, ashamed. She didn't stop there, but turned the page.

"'Artemis invited me to see the fireworks this weekend. He said he has something important to tell me. I hope he is going to ask me to be his girlfriend. Although he's older than me, and my mom will get mad, I don't care, my feelings for him make it all worth it. I know we are still too young but what we feel for each other is true love, like you see in the movies.'"

"Ma'am, please."

"Yes, I think that's enough. We welcomed you into this house, and you have the nerve to set your sights on our son?" The coldness in her voice frightened me. "Listen to me, Claudia. You're going to stay away from Artemis. He's leaving for university at the end of the summer. Then, he will be pursuing a future path that has been decided by his father and me. And you won't stand in the way. Agreed?"

"Ma'am, my feelings for him are genuine, I—"

"Silence." She put up her hand. "If what you feel for him is genuine, then you want what's best for him, right?" I nodded. "So, we agree. Because you, Claudia, are not what's best for him. You do know this, right? How could the daughter of a former drug addict and prostitute be worthy of a boy like Artemis?"

"I believe that's up to him to decide, not you."

Her expression hardened.

"Girl, you need to watch your tone. I'd hoped you would choose the easy way." She released a dramatic sigh. "Well, then it's the hard way. I've already discussed this with my husband, and unfortunately, if you decide not to go along with our decision, you and your mother will need to move out of this house—tonight."

The blood in my veins froze with fear. No. Not life on the streets again. And the countless men coming after my mother. She'd stayed clean for years. I couldn't let her go back to that life. And we had nothing to fall back on out there.

Mrs. Hidalgo crossed her legs. "Oh. Have I put you in a difficult position? You just have to make a choice between your mother and this childish crush."

Of course I would choose my mother, over and over again. And she knew this.

"All right, ma'am. I'll do as you say—I'll push him away." I got up when I felt tears welling up, clouding my vision. "I should go to bed now."

That night I wept in silence until I ran out of tears and my chest hurt from sobbing.

I spent the best night of my life with Artemis that Fourth of July, the night of the fireworks. He bought me cotton candy, ice cream, and even a stuffed pig, which he paid for when we both failed to win at one of those fairground games.

When it was time for the fireworks, we sat on the grass to watch the spectacle in silence. I snuck a quick glance at Artemis; his gorgeous face was illuminated by the colorful flashes, but that wasn't why I loved him so much. It was who he was deep down when we were together. He was so kind and understanding. He was with me for every one of my nightmares, and during my most vulnerable moments. He fought the bullies at school who picked on me for being poor, or because of my mother. He always stood by me, offering warmth with his gaze and calming peace with his beautiful smile. I wanted to stay like that with him for longer because after that night, all of that would be over. I was watching the show in the sky again, getting lost in the bright colors when I felt him place his hand on mine. My heart began to pound fast. But I didn't pull my hand away.

Don't say anything, Artemis. Please, let's stay like this a little longer.

I turned to look at him. Before I had time to process his intentions, he moved in swiftly, grabbing my face and giving me a kiss. His soft lips pressed against mine, and I melted on the spot.

My first kiss . . .

I was glad it was with him.

You need to make a choice: your mother or this childish crush.

I fought my aching heart, and I pushed him away.

Artemis pulled away from me. I tried to seem indifferent, but I was afraid that if I tried to speak, I'd cry instead. The wounded look on his face hurt me. I watched him get up and turn his back on me.

"Artemis . . ." I called, my voice breaking. But he was gone already.

I'm sorry, Artemis. I am so very sorry.

My mom is already in bed when I arrive home after visiting Grandfather. I sit next to her and watch her sleep. She's made many mistakes in her life, but she's my mother. I will always choose her over anyone. On the night table, there's the stuffed pig that Artemis bought me that Fourth of July. Of course I still have it. I pick it up and hug it tightly, feeling both nostalgic and anguished.

"I did want to be your girlfriend, Artemis," I tell the stuffed toy. "I wanted to be with you."

Eighteen

It's because of him, isn't it?

CLAUDIA

The days pass, and I can't wait for Grandpa to come home. I'm ecstatic he'll be staying at the house. I'll be able to look after him, and he'll get to spend time with his grandsons. Even though he doesn't say it, I know he misses them terribly.

The afternoon sun streams through the kitchen window, giving the table and utensils an orange hue. I take a peek outside to the patio where Apolo's dogs are playing.

I haven't seen Artemis. He must be leaving early in the morning and coming home late, doing a very good job avoiding me. After what happened with Apolo, I think we all need some distance.

I run my hand across the table. I can't deny that I sometimes replay what happened in this room that night with Artemis. I remember very clearly how his eyes were locked with mine, and the sensation of his breathing on my lips. How good I felt when

I kissed him, and the tingling feeling of his light scruff rubbing against my skin. And his deft hands running all over my body . . .

Why did you have to fuck it all up, Artemis?

What hurts me most is that he cheated on his girlfriend—which is so unlike him. Given what happened with his mother, I never thought he would be capable of being unfaithful. He disappointed me, profoundly.

Me having a girlfriend is what's keeping you from being mine?

I no longer have a girlfriend, Claudia.

Liar.

Someone clears their throat behind me, and Apolo appears in the doorway and leans his shoulder against the frame. He's wearing a pair of jeans and a red jacket that matches his sneakers. His chestnut-brown hair looks messy, like someone gave it a tousle on purpose.

"Hi," he whispers.

"Hi," I greet him, leaning my lower back against the edge of the table.

He peels himself away from the doorframe and stuffs his hands into the front pockets of his jeans.

"Sooner or later we have to talk about what happened, Claudia."

"Apolo . . ."

He takes one step into the kitchen. "Claudia, I—"

I raise my hand. "No, stop."

Apolo frowns. "You're not going to let me speak?"

"No." I shake my head. "I know what you're going to tell me, and I don't want you to say it. Because once you put it out there, there's no going back. And I'd rather not go through that."

His shoulders slump in defeat. "Then what do you want?"

"I want the old Apolo, the sweet boy who's like a brother to me." His face twists in confusion. "You're one of the most important people in my life. I don't want us to ruin that. Please."

"It's because of him, isn't it?"

I know he's talking about Artemis.

I wet my lips uneasily. "No."

"Don't lie to me." He takes a few long steps over to me, grabs me by the waist with one hand and holds my face with the other. "I'm not your brother, Claudia."

The proximity grants me a clearer view of his bright, brown eyes and his plump lips. As much as I wish it wasn't the case, he reminds me of Artemis when he was this age.

I clear my throat. "I know. But . . ."

He envelops me in a hug, and I'm wrapped in a familiar scent.

"But it's all good. I respect your decision." He kisses the side of my head. "I won't impose myself on you or pressure you. I'm not that type of guy."

I know. When he pulls away, he looks straight into my eyes. "I will always be here for you." He kisses my forehead and takes a step back.

I give him a genuine smile. "And I'm here for you."

He walks backward, never breaking eye contact until he finally turns around and leaves. And though he doesn't seem fine, I am sure he'll be all right. I know him too well, and have an idea what he believes he feels for me. I think he's confusing the affection he developed for me over the years with something deeper. His mother didn't spend time caring for him, and I'm the first positive female role model in his life. He's confusing romantic love with the sense of security and well-being he feels when he's with me. But they're not the same. I shouldn't have let the situation in the laundry room get out of hand. I got carried away by the attraction and comfort between us. But what's done is done. And the best I can do to remedy this situation is to let him find someone who can show him what true love is.

Good luck, Apolo.

Back in my room, my mother is sitting by the window, holding a cup of tea with both hands. Her hair is peppered with white strands, combining with the red. I've offered to dye it but she doesn't want to. She says she would like to show off her gray hairs with pride.

"You aren't going to the university today?" she asks as I lie down on my bed and cover my eyes with my forearm. She remains silent for a moment. "Are you tired, sweetie?"

I feign a smile and attempt to look energized, sitting back up.

"Of course not. I was just being dramatic, Mother."

She returns the smile. "How did it go with yesterday's presentation?"

I give her a thumbs-up.

"Wonderful. My daughter is very smart."

That seems to cheer her up. My heart fills with happiness when I see her smile. It's true that she's made a lot of mistakes, and my childhood was at times difficult, but I could never turn my back on her. It's too easy to get stuck on the faults of others. When I look at my mother, I don't think of her failings. Instead, I see a woman who chose the wrong man to have a child with. A man who beat her and abandoned her on the streets with a baby in her arms. A woman who starved on many occasions so that her child could eat and who sold her body for a roof over their heads. Someone who got hooked on drugs because she wanted to escape the reality of having to trade her body every night. I also see the woman who changed her ways when the opportunity of a stable job was presented to her. I see the woman who shook, cried, and endured the aftereffects of withdrawal when she got clean, and had the strength to never have a relapse. The moment she had the chance to fix her life, she gave it her all, and for that she will always have my respect.

Getting your life together when you've gotten off track requires way more strength and willpower than keeping it together when it's been that way from the start. For this reason, I don't mind being her support now. I lean over and kiss her on the forehead.

"I'm going to get ready for school."

"Take care of yourself, my daughter. God bless you."

"Amen, Mom."

"I hate my life." Gin has her head down on the table. I take a sip of water from my glass. She straightens in her chair and shoots me a sad face. "I am never falling in love again."

Things have not gone well for Gin with Victor. They spent a few nights together after our invitation to Artemis's nightclub, and now he's acting cold and distant with her. And when they talked a few days ago, he told her he's not looking for anything serious. My friend pouts.

"Be honest with me. Did I give it away too easy? Open my legs too soon?"

"Gin."

"I knew it. I should have played hard to get."

"Gin." I'm serious. "Why do you do this? Why do you always find a way to blame yourself? This guy's a fucking jerk. You're incredible and he's missing out. Period. End of story."

"It's just that I thought I had found a real one."

"That's exactly what you said about the last guy."

"I know, I know," she says. "But, Clau." She lowers her voice until it becomes a whisper. "He's a god in bed."

I roll my eyes.

"It's the best sex I've ever had in my miserable life." She groans.

"And that automatically turns him into the love of your life?"

"Of course!"

"Love is more than sex, you dummy."

"Oh sure, the love expert, Miss Claudia, has spoken. Meanwhile, you're the female version of him—screw them and dump them."

"I'm honest with them. Anyway, I've never received any complaints."

She quirks a brow. "And Daniel?"

"He's the exception." I can't believe Daniel keeps calling me.

"I want to be like you. But I can't have sex without becoming emotionally involved. I always fall in love, Clau."

I give her a shrug. "Nope. You don't fall in love, Gin. You don't spend enough time with those boys to figure out if it's love or just physical attraction."

"It could be love at first sight."

"In your case, it's more like screwed at first sight."

"Very funny." She sighs. "In any case, I may just agree to casual sex with him, on occasion."

"Are you kidding?"

"Clau, he's the best I've ever been with. Seriously. He makes this gyrating movement with his hips. . . Wow! Gets me right in my G-spot!"

"Too much information." I grimace.

Gin suddenly looks over my shoulder, surprised. "Speak of the devil."

I turn to see who she's referring to, and spot Daniel heading our way. "Oh no."

"I'm dying of curiosity, Clau. What in the world did you do to that boy to get him this hooked?"

Memories flood back of Daniel and me in a hotel room, our bodies in different positions, covered in sweat. *Maybe the better question is what didn't we do?*

"I have to go," I say.

"Clau, no."

I get up and run like my life depends on it, leaving Gin by herself in the university cafeteria. I hear Daniel call my name but I rush down the hallways I know like the back of my hand. What is he doing here? He isn't enrolled here. My god, this boy is way too intense.

I yawn and cover my mouth with one hand as I board the bus that will take me home. It was a long day. I look out the window and watch the stores and trees pass by. My restless mind wanders and recalls the jerk in the immaculate suit I haven't seen in days. I close my eyes and imagine Artemis's face close to mine. I need to stop thinking about him; it's not worth my time. As I doze against the window, his passionate kisses and sweet words invade my dreams. But that's all they are, dreams. Because whatever was between me and Artemis ended before it really began.

Nineteen

You're dumber than I am.

CLAUDIA

The bus driver wakes me up when we arrive at the garage where the buses park for the night. I clearly underestimated how tired I was. It's all Mrs. Hidalgo's fault. She's been working me extra hard, making me clean spots in the house that were already done. I suspect it's how she's retaliating for the way I treated her at the hospital.

I'm in trouble.

This was the last bus and the last stop. I'm a few miles from the house. The driver says good-bye and leaves me by myself. I hesitate about whether to tell him I have no way to get home. But he leaves on foot; I suspect he lives not far from here. I hang my backpack on one shoulder and reach inside for my wallet. The salary I earn working for the Hidalgos is spent mostly on medicine for my mother, books for school, and bus fare, so I don't have much on me. And though I'm very good at budgeting, having all those expenses makes it difficult to save.

I bite my lower lip and go back to counting the bills in my wallet. If I pay for a cab, I won't have enough money left to cover bus fare for the rest of the week. With this in mind, I put the wallet back inside my backpack next to my books. I guess I'll have to make my way through the streets. I have to admit it makes me nervous. But I have pepper spray on me. I also took a course on personal defense. I step out of the parking garage and look both ways. The street is completely deserted. I inhale deeply before starting to walk. The luminescent streetlights, the darkness at this time of the night, and the deserted street take me back to another night.

"Look at her hair! So disgusting!" A group of teenagers hanging out at a field in the park that served as a temporary home for me and my mom were making fun of me.

They had me cornered against the fence, and I squeezed my teddy bear.

"She does have a sweet face, though," one of them added. "I mean, after you scrub away all that dirt."

A boy crouched and placed his hands on his knees, leaning toward me.

"Where's your mommy, scum?"

Though I was still only seven years old, I'd grown up in difficult situations and had learned how to defend myself. "I'll scream if you don't leave me alone."

The boy laughed.

"Are you going to scream? Then go ahead, stinky brat." He stretched out both arms and pointed in either direction in the park, which was empty at night. "I'm pretty sure you won't have an audience."

My tiny fingers holding the bear trembled.

"Now, tell us. Where's your mommy? She owes us some merchandise, and if she can't pay for it we have other ways to get that money, and she knows it."

Even though I didn't fully understand what they intended to do with my mother, I knew it wasn't good because she always cried after they were done with her. When I didn't respond, another boy brusquely grabbed my face, digging his fingers into my skin with such force that it made me wince in pain. "I don't have all night."

I clenched my hand into a fist, and struck him between the legs with all the strength I could muster, just like my mother had taught me. Due to my small height and the fact that he wasn't expecting the blow, my hit landed hard. He grunted and fell to the ground, and I raced away, dodging between swings and slides until I made it to the small shrubs that encircled the park. Before I knew it, I'd reached the street. I looked over my shoulder to check that no one was following me. I slowed my pace but my chest kept rising and falling, recuperating from the run. The smell of freshly cooked food reached my nose and I closed my eyes to fully savor it.

Oh no. I was on the street with all the restaurants. My mom said I should never come this way because just watching the food is pure torture. I had, on occasion, made it this far, thinking that the smell would be more than enough. I stood outside restaurants with signs I couldn't read, and I could see everything through the clear windows. I fooled myself into believing I could taste what was being served just by inhaling the smells. There were soups, meats, bread, juices. I licked my lips, and my mouth watered. An elegant man sat at the head of one of the tables, smiling widely at the other people sitting with him. I realized he was with his family. There was a woman next to him and she had a baby on her lap, and a boy who appeared close to my age was seated beside her. Another boy who looked older sat right across from them.

A happy family. I wondered what it felt like to have a father.

Impulsively, I placed my hand on the glass. The boy who looked my age stood up, and then I could tell by his height he was younger than me. Without his family noticing, he made his way to the window and put his hand on the other side of the glass, exactly on the spot where I had mine. He had black hair and beautiful blue eyes.

I smiled at him and he smiled back.

I couldn't help the urge to ask him if he could share some of his food with me. Just a little. But I knew he wouldn't be able to hear me from this side of the glass, so I signed with one hand bringing food to my mouth while rubbing my belly with the other. He seemed to understand but before he could say anything, a hand jerked him away from the window: it was the woman. She shot me a cold and dismissive glance, then pulled him back to the table. My hopes for a warm meal were dashed when he left. I hung my head low, let out a sigh, and turned around to make my way back to the park to find my mother.

"Hey!" someone called to me. I looked around, fearful that it might be the guys who had been harassing me before.

It was the elegant man from inside the restaurant. His family stood behind him as a black car pulled up and parked in front of them. The lady helped the kids into the car; the boy with the blue eyes waved good-bye to me. And the older boy was standing, still staring at me, likely waiting for his father.

"Hey, there!" The gentleman greeted me amicably and gave

me a warm smile, then knelt down in front of me. "Are you hungry?"

I looked at him with trepidation. No one was ever nice without expecting something in return. That was what my mother told me all the time. But I was starving, and slowly nodded in response.

"Are you alone?" I shook my head. "Where's your mother?"

Unconscious. Right behind the swings, in a patch encircled by some bushes that had become our home.

"I'm not going to hurt you." He extended his hand. "My name is Juan. What's your name?"

I quickly glanced at his hand and decided not to take it.

"Claudia."

His smile widened.

"That's a pretty name. Great. Now, Claudia, I just want to help. Okay? Will you take me to your mother?"

My alarms bells went off. Was he one of the men who came looking for my mom only to make her cry? He didn't look like those men. My eyes landed on the older boy standing there, waiting for his father. They all seemed fine when they were having dinner together as a family. If this man had been bad, I didn't think the boy would be waiting for him like this. I grabbed the hand the gentleman offered me and guided him to where my mother was. When we walked by the older boy, the man spoke to him.

"Artemis, get in the car and tell your mom to head home. Albert will stay with me and I'll come home later by cab."

"Dad . . ."

The boy got in the car and we made a quick departure before they drove off. A tall man dressed in black had come out of the car and was closely following in our steps.

I tensed up, and the gentleman gave my hand a squeeze. "You can relax. He's here to protect us, okay?"

I nodded again. My mother was awake by the time we arrived at the clearing we called home. She looked worried. The man let go of my hand, and knelt to face me.

"I need a moment with your mom to talk. Could you go keep Albert company?"

I looked at my mother, and she nodded so I did as he asked. I didn't know what they discussed, or understand what was going on. I only knew that we left our spot in the park and got in a cab. The gentleman and Albert got in another.

"Mommy, where are we going?"

Her eyes were red and she hadn't stopped crying since she'd spoken with that gentleman.

"We're going to . . . My little girl, things are going to change." She grabbed my face with both hands. "I'm going to change, for you. That man has offered your mom a decent job."

"Are we going to have food?"

She nodded and smiled while tearing up. "Lots of food."

"And a bed?"

"Yes. And we're going to take a long shower."

I couldn't believe my eyes when we finally arrived at the house, and I stared at it with my mouth wide open. It was beautiful and reminded me of the houses I'd seen on the pages of the magazines my mother and I used as blankets. Mr. Juan introduced us to his family as soon as we came in. There was Sofia, Artemis, Ares, and baby Apolo. My mom bowed her head with gratitude. Right after he showed us to our room and took his leave, we ran to the bathroom to clean ourselves. This was the first bed we'd had in a long time, and we didn't want to get it soiled.

Mr. Juan left a few women's clothes from his wife for my mom. He also brought me clothes that belonged to the older boy, who was nine years old, and whose name was Artemis. The shorts and the T-shirt were way too big for me but I didn't mind because they smelled clean. My mom was exhausted and quickly fell asleep. I didn't blame her—the bed felt like a dream. However, I was very hungry. Mr. Juan said we could eat whatever we liked. In the kitchen, I opened the refrigerator and couldn't believe its contents. I let my impulses take over, and reached in to pick a little bit of everything I saw. Bread, jam, cheese, deli meats.

"You're going to get a tummy ache."

I froze when I heard a voice in the kitchen. With a hunk of bread in my hand, I turned to find Artemis.

"You need to eat slowly."

I chewed and swallowed the piece of bread I had in my mouth.

"I'm sorry," I whispered.

He gave me a friendly smile.

"I wasn't scolding you, dummy. You need to slow down when you eat or your tummy will hurt if you stuff yourself with too many things all at once."

"Don't call me dummy." He wasn't expecting my reaction, but I continued. "And you're dumber than I am." I regretted my words as soon as they were spoken. I'd have to behave better or they'd kick us out, like my mom had said. "I'm sorry."

"It's fine." He didn't look bothered. "Let me make something for you."

That night, Artemis made me the first proper meal I'd had in a very long time. Then right after, I went to sleep on a bed that wasn't made of grass or newspaper, with my belly full of real food instead of air. It was the best night of my childhood.

By the time I make the walk home from the bus depot, I'm exhausted. It was farther than I expected, and the nostalgia triggered by the memory from that night still lingers in my mind. I open the front door and rest my back against the wall. The room is dark except for the glow of the fireplace. The crackling noise of the fire echoes in the otherwise silent house.

I don't have to see him to know he's there.

His suit jacket is off and carefully laid over the arm rest of the couch. The top buttons of his white shirt are undone and so is his tie, revealing a patch of chest where his shirt parts. It's close to midnight. Did he just get home from work?

Artemis doesn't say anything and simply stares at me. When I see him, I never pick up on the coldness that Ares and Apolo often speak of.

Am I the only one who is capable of looking past it?

Am I the only one you allow to see through you, Artemis?

I'm struck by the sentiment that perhaps I'm the one person who knows him better than anyone else. I find it hard to believe he's the type who could be unfaithful—there must be more to him cheating on his girlfriend. Am I stupid for entertaining these thoughts? Am I refusing to face reality? Five years have passed; maybe he's completely changed and is no longer the sweet boy I fell in love with. So why can't I shake the feeling that whenever he's with me he's the exact same person he was before? He lowers his head, stands up, grabs his blazer, and turns to give me his back, heading toward the stairs.

"Artemis."

I surprise myself. What am I doing? He turns around but doesn't approach me. I peel myself off the wall and make my way to him cautiously, one step at a time. I come to a halt with a safe distance between us.

"Tell me the truth, Artemis."

He scowls.

"I'm giving you this one chance to be honest with me."

His voice is dead calm. "What are you talking about?"

"You know damn well." I'm exasperated and raise my hands when he refuses to give me an answer. "Forget it. I'm not sure what I was thinking."

I walk away, feeling like an idiot for seeing something that wasn't there. I'm about to step into the hallway that leads to my room when a pair of arms wrap around me from behind, stopping me in my tracks. Artemis pulls me tight against him. His chest is glued to my back.

He rests his forehead on my shoulder, and his voice is barely a whisper. "I didn't lie to you or toy with your emotions. I could never play games like that with you, Claudia."

I keep quiet and let him continue to explain, because I know he could not do it face-to-face. "I had broken up with her when I went looking for you that night at the club. You were never the other woman. I couldn't put you in that position."

"But you got back together with her."

He doesn't say anything.

"Why did you kiss me if you were going to get back with her?"

"Because I didn't want to get back with her, I wanted to . . ."

I turn in his arms so that I can see him, and grab his face with both hands. I force him to look straight at me, which is a terrible idea, since having him this close is too tempting.

"What did you want?"

The honesty in his eyes is explicit. "I wanted to be with you."

"I don't understand you, Artemis."

He presses his forehead against mine and his breathing grazes my lips.

"I want you to know that I wasn't playing games with you. That wasn't my intention."

I look him straight in the eye. "So what do you want now?"

He closes his eyes and bites his lips, unsure. I let go of his face and take a step back.

"You want to stay with her."

Artemis remains silent. I take that as his answer, and force a smile.

"It's fine, I understand. I appreciate that you've cleared things up about what happened. And now we can get back to keeping things civil between us without me wanting to murder you every time we run into each other." I wave. "Good night, Artemis."

I leave him in the living room. His shoulders are slumped and he looks like he lost a battle against a far superior adversary before it even started.

Twenty

This was a bad idea.

ARTEMIS

I can't stop looking at her.

I've tried to distract myself by discussing business with my father or talking about public relations with my mother. I even tried to start a conversation with Ares. Despite my best efforts, the moment Claudia walks into the room, I can't peel my eyes off her no matter how hard I try. And I don't like feeling this way. I can't stand not being in control of my emotions.

We're on our traditional family trip to Greece for the Christmas holiday. As customary, Claudia and her mother have come along. However, this time it's out of necessity, since Claudia is performing the role of caregiver to my grandfather. She seems quite at ease in his company, and they appear to have a close rapport. I've never been able to have that kind of relationship with him. I respect him greatly, and he's a role model I look up to, but we haven't deepened our bond.

On the hotel terrace, the late-afternoon sun paints the surroundings warm orange. Sitting at a long table, my mother is drinking her favorite wine, my father is occupied drawing graphs on his tablet, and Ares and Apolo are on their phones, chatting about a picture we took earlier that has apparently gone viral on social media.

Our grandfather has gone to take a nap, and Claudia is sitting across from me. She has on a blue bathing suit and a cover-up that doesn't really cover that much. In any case, I have a clear view of her cleavage. Her skin looks soft, and I can't help but imagine my tongue gliding along her neck and making its way down to her breasts. I shake my head.

Stop being a pervert, Artemis.

This woman is going to be the death of me. Ever since the night in the kitchen, my mind has become more depraved after having kissed her, tasted her, felt her . . . The sound of her moans has made me want more of her.

But you can't have her, so you need to stop fantasizing about her.

Claudia wraps her lips around a large piece of watermelon before taking a bite. Her soft lips become slightly redder while she eats the piece of fruit. I have the urge to get up, pull her closer by the neck, kiss her, and suck on lips covered in sweet watermelon juices. I can't concentrate when she's around.

Claudia notices the way I'm looking at her. She frowns and whispers, "What?"

I was just fantasizing about the many ways I want to fuck you.

"Nothing."

Her light tan brings out the freckles on her cheeks and nose. Claudia looks at me, puzzled, before continuing to eat. I need air, so I get up from my seat before my wild imagination turns into a hard-on right here in plain view of my family.

I take the elevator up to our suite, sticking my hands in the pockets of my shorts. A group of female resort staff get on at the same time. I hear them whispering and giggling after they check me out. I'm used to getting attention from women, but I know the fact that I'm attractive doesn't make me a better person. It makes it easier when it comes to the opposite sex, that's all. Still, it hasn't been much help in my efforts to win the girl who matters most to me.

In the suite, I find my grandfather sitting on the sofa. He's holding a bowl of popcorn and watching a movie. I greet him with a smile as I walk by, heading to my room. The hotel suite we occupy is immense.

"Artemis." My grandfather's voice brings me to a halt, and I turn around.

"Yes? Do you need something?"

He addresses me without making eye contact. "Cowardice is a flaw unbecoming to us Hidalgos."

"What are you talking about?"

Grandfather lets out a sigh. "I guess everything happens in due time. I just hope it's not too late by the time you decide to do something about it."

"About what?"

He looks at me and smiles. "Fighting for what you want." He pauses. "Or who you love." I'm about to say something when he raises his hand. "Shush, this is the best part of the movie. We'll talk later."

Puzzled, I head to my room, and fall back on the bed, closing my eyes. The images are vivid in my mind: Claudia in her cute swimsuit, her body, her curves, her smile in response to Ares's jokes, her pretend anger when our grandfather doesn't follow her orders. Or how she presses her lips together to keep from saying something she shouldn't, and her habit of wiping her mouth with her hand before she's about to tell a lie or when she's nervous.

Claudia, how can I push you out of my mind when you're everywhere I turn?

I truly would like to leave you in peace. I don't want to complicate your life or hurt you again. But how can I do that when I'm attracted to you with every fiber of my being and with an intensity I can't control?

In truth, it's a struggle to live up to my father. He wasn't always the calculating and cold man he is now. He was the best father in the world until my mother cheated on him. Though he was working hard building his empire during my childhood, he always found ways to spend time with us whenever he could. I can still recall vividly the night he found out what had happened with my mother, and the aftermath—the devastation evident in the redness of his eyes and the broken whisky glasses that littered the floor of his study.

"Dad?" I called to him as I carefully avoided the shards scattered on the floor.

My father was slumped behind his desk. "Get out of here, Artemis."

I was a teenager filled with anger and pain. In that moment, I needed my father.

"I'm not leaving you alone."

He stood and raised his hands. "Your father is a disaster and has failed as a husband."

"That's not true."

He burst out laughing. Probably to keep from crying, the only other way he knew to react.

"It's clear that even though I can build a million-dollar empire, I'm unable to keep my marriage together."

"It's not your fault, Dad. It's hers, she's a—"

"Watch it. She's still your mother, Artemis. Whatever happens between me and her doesn't change that."

"You don't have to stay with her, Dad. We'll understand if you don't want to be with her."

My father pursed his lips, and his eyes were wet.

"I love her, son." Tears rolled down and he wiped them away. "I don't want to be alone."

"You have us."

"You boys will grow up, build your lives, and leave me behind," he explained. "I'll end up alone in a nursing home."

"I won't do that." I took a step forward. "I will never abandon you, Dad. I promise."

"You're just a teenager. You don't know what you're saying."

"I do know what I'm saying. I'll always stay by your side and be there to support you any way I can, at the house or at the company. I promise. All right?"

He offered me a sad smile.

"All right."

I fall asleep with the fresh memory of the promise I'd made seared in my mind.

It's after ten at night when I wake up. I take a shower, then speak with Alex, who hasn't stopped calling me all afternoon.

He's talking nonstop about a personal issue on the other end of the line, and I give him monosyllabic answers. I can tell he needs to vent, so I let him take over the conversation. All the while, I head down to the first floor and make my way through the sliding doors that lead to the pool. The place looks empty at first glance. And then I notice someone sitting on the edge with their feet dangling in the water. It's Claudia. Alex keeps unloading on the phone. Meanwhile, I can't keep my eyes off the redhead who has occupied my thoughts ever since she was a smart-mouthed child.

Claudia is wearing a plain floral beach dress in a shade of red that matches her hair, which is gathered in a high bun. A few unruly strands that have come loose lightly touch her skin. The warm tone makes a nice contrast with the suntan from time spent at the beach these past days. She appears absentminded, and is moving her feet back and forth in the water.

What's going through your head, dummy?

Ever since she was a girl, she'd get so irked if I called her dummy.

I say good-bye to Alex and leave my cell phone on a lounge chair. I make my way in her direction, stopping by her side. She appears a little uneasy when she looks up at me, so I give her a friendly smile.

She turns her gaze back to the water. "Hello."

"Do you mind if I join you?"

"No."

I sit down next to her but make sure to leave some space. I'm fully aware there's still tension between us, maybe even more after my confession that I wasn't lying when I told her I didn't have a girlfriend. Unfortunately, what I feared most happened, and I ended up confusing her even more by failing to explain the true nature of the arrangement between me and Cristina.

The pool lighting illuminates the water, which in turn shines brightly in her eyes, giving them a lovely glow. This reminds me of the night that Fourth of July, of how the fireworks reflected in her eyes the same way. A part of me has always wanted to ask her why she rejected me. I'd been sure the attraction and feelings I felt went both ways—until that night. Obviously, I'd misread the signals when I made my move.

I don't ask her about it. I'd rather not know if she didn't reciprocate the feelings I had.

But I do need to break the silence lingering between us. "Are you still good at holding your breath underwater?"

She twists her mouth, making an expression that's hard to read. Annoyance, perhaps? "I'm still better than you."

I raise an eyebrow. "I've improved a lot."

"Your lungs are weak."

"Wow. No mercy."

"You don't deserve it."

I nod. "You're right. But I really have improved."

She lets out a chuckle, mocking me.

"What? You don't believe me?"

She folds her arms over her chest. "Prove it."

"How?"

She tilts her head, indicating the pool.

"Right now?"

"What's the matter? Afraid you're going to lose again?"

"Fine." I pull my shirt over my head, making Claudia blush and look away. My lips turn up in a cocky smirk. I can tell she's attracted to me, even though she won't admit it. I get into the water, which comes up to my waist since we're at the shallow end. There's a trace of mischief in her eyes as she watches.

"You have to swim from one end to the other and give me two laps, keeping underwater without coming up for air."

"What?"

"You can't? I've done it several times since the day we arrived."

It's not a small pool. But I think I can pull it off.

"And what's my prize if I succeed?"

"Maybe I'll change my perspective about you and go back to believing you're a human being."

"Yay."

She leans in, hands on the edge of the pool. "Good luck, iceberg."

"Thanks, dummy."

Claudia shoots me a murderous look. "You're dumber that I am."

I grin when I hear the familiar response. I head to the other side of the pool, accepting the challenge. I give her one last glance before I plunge in. I swim underwater as fast as I can, completing my first lap with success. In the middle of my second lap, my lungs start to burn, and I'm desperate for air. But I'm not ready to give up, especially when I have just one more turn left. I emerge from the water just as I reach my goal, taking in huge breaths. Claudia isn't on the edge of the pool anymore, and when I look around I see her walking to the doors.

"Hey, Claudia!"

She turns and gives me the finger. Oh no, this is not going to end like this. I leap out of the pool as quickly as I can and run after her. Claudia is through the sliding doors and into the hotel lobby, making her way to the elevator.

"Sir, you're wet and should . . ." a member of the hotel staff begins, but I ignore him. I keep moving until I reach Claudia and grab her by the arm.

She's surprised. I take advantage of the moment and bend

to lift her up, throwing her over my shoulder. Other guests are staring at us and whispering. I pay no attention as I carry her back to the pool area.

"Artemis Hidalgo! Put me down, now!"

I lower her to the ground near the edge of the pool.

"You throw a challenge at me then take off when you lose, and to top it off, you give me the finger?"

She crosses her arms. "I didn't think you could make it."

"But I did. And now you have to admit that my lungs are no longer weak."

"No."

God, she's too damn stubborn! She always brings out my playful side without much effort. I grab hold of her dress with one hand, twisting the top part. I spin her so she's barely standing on the edge of the pool, hanging over the water.

"Admit it."

"No."

I pretend I'm about to let go and she grabs my wrist, letting out a squeal.

"It's your last chance, Claudia."

She sticks her tongue out at me. "I'm not afraid of water. I'm not made of sugar."

At that very moment, I release my grip and let her fall backward into the pool. She emerges from the water, pushing hair that's come loose from her bun off her face.

"You're a jerk."

"And you are a sore loser."

She stares at me but shows no inclination to get out of the water, nor to admit defeat.

Don't jump in the pool, Artemis. You won't be able to resist the temptation if you get near her when she's wet and no one is around.

I switch off the rational part of my brain and dive in. The splash I make sprinkles her face, and moves her backward. Given our height difference, the water reaches just above my waist but comes to under her chest. My eyes move along the outlines of her exposed skin, traveling from her neck, now covered with tiny drops of water, and down to the rest of her body. Her dress floats and I watch her struggling to cover her legs. This was a bad idea.

"Don't look, pervert," she scolds me, holding on to her dress.

I keep my eyes on her face, displaying chivalry in response. She sucks in her lower lip, and my mind can't help but wander off to a very bad place. I need something to distract myself.

"Why are you so bad at losing?"

"Because I don't like to give you the satisfaction of winning."

"But I already won."

"Not until I admit you have."

I squint at her. "You're as stubborn as ever."

"And you're as needy to claim victory."

Realizing that we'll never get anywhere if we keep this going, I change the subject. "Despite all the renovation work, the swimming pool still looks like it did when I taught you to swim right here."

She quirks one eyebrow. "You taught me? Pretty sure I learned how to swim on my own."

"Do I have to remind you how you clung to me the first time we ventured to the deep end of the pool? Your nails left marks on my neck."

She shrugs. "I don't know what you're talking about."

I smile, victorious. "Yes, you do."

"The one thing I remember is you running and screaming

because a bee was chasing you all around the pool." She lets out a hearty laugh.

"I'm allergic! I had good reason to be afraid."

"Help me!" She imitates my cries of that day. "I'm going to die!" She keeps laughing. "The bee was long gone and you kept running."

I can't stop myself from chuckling. Looking back, my reaction was pretty funny. We both stop laughing and stare at each other. The tension that passes between us amplifies.

Do you feel what I feel, Claudia?

I take a step closer to her, and she moves back, clearing her throat. "I should go."

But I don't stop. I clench my hands at my sides, staving off the urge to touch her. I keep advancing, and she continues to retreat until her back hits the wall of the pool.

"Artemis." I don't listen and continue to corner her. She lets go of her dress and puts her hands on my chest to halt my advance. "Artemis."

I stare down at her body. Her dress floats, revealing her legs and part of her underwear. I bite my lower lip. Claudia's breathing is as fractured as mine. Her chest rises and falls unevenly. I raise my hand and gently rub her parted lips. I notice Claudia swallowing. She pushes my hand off her lips.

"I have to go." She is about to slip away when I grab her by the hand, forcing her to face me.

"I know you feel the same way I do."

She frees her hand from mine. "I never said I didn't." She gives me sad smile. "I'm not the one who needs to decide, Artemis. I know how I feel. I also know what I'm worth. And I won't belittle myself and play the role of the other woman while you figure out what it is that you want."

And with that out in the open, she takes her leave. I don't stop her. I know she's right. I'm the coward in this situation. I'm the one who won't fight for what I want. My grandfather's words replay in my head: *Cowardice is a flaw unbecoming to us Hidalgos.*

Grandfather, I guess I'm not much of a Hidalgo, after all.

Twenty-one

That girl has you whipped.

ARTEMIS

Three months later

Alex bursts in, looking smug as he dumps a small pile of folders on my desk. I wonder what he's up to, so I open the first folder and stare at the résumé of a girl still in university.

"What is this? Do you expect me to be part of the hiring process? Seriously?"

Alex points his index finger at me. "Oh, trust me, my friend. You're going to want in on this."

I scan the girl's résumé, and I learn that she's enrolled in her last year of school. I furrow my eyebrows.

"Are these the interns? You want me to help select the university interns?"

Alex plops himself on the chair across from my desk. "Yes."

I close the folder and push the pile toward him.

"Alex, I don't have time for this. Human resources can handle it."

Alex snorts. “You are not getting the hint.” He sounds frustrated. “Open the next folder.”

Begrudgingly, I do as he asks, hoping that eventually this little exercise will lead somewhere. My fingers freeze when they reach the folder I least expect to find in this pile. It’s Claudia’s. I gape like an idiot at the name at the top of her résumé. I stare at her qualifications and the rest of the information listed. She applied to do an internship with the company? I feel flattered, and extremely confused. Why didn’t she mention it?

“I’m waiting for a thank-you. If it wasn’t for me, you would have never known. It’s very likely she would have completed her internship here unbeknownst to you since you never venture down to that department.”

“Was her application accepted?”

Alex smiles. “But of course. Just take a look at her grades and the evaluation of her writing samples. She was the first to be accepted.”

And then it dawns on me. She never said a word because she wanted to get in based on her own merits. It’s also very likely she wanted to keep me from knowing that she was working here. Which is exactly what would have happened if Alex hadn’t told me.

“I am truly amazed at your ability to stick your nose into the affairs of every department in the company.”

He winks at me. “It’s a skill, I know.”

“Which department was she assigned to?”

“So you can spy on her like a fool?” Alex raises an eyebrow.

I give him a cold stare.

“First of all, I have yet to hear a ‘Thank you, Alex. You’re my best friend in the whole world. I don’t know what I’d do without you. Oh wait, I know. I’ll stay frozen like a damn ice cube, too hard to be melted by the summer sun.’”

Ice cube . . . iceberg . . .

A silly grin tugs at my lips, and Alex gasps in an overly dramatic way. "Oh, ladies and gentlemen, he smiles!"

"Alex."

"I'm not going to tell you where she'll be working."

"As if I couldn't figure it out on my own."

Alex smiles playfully. "That's where you're wrong. I know you. Why would the chief executive officer go out of his way to inquire about this year's interns when he's never shown an interest before? You know damn well staff will be suspicious if you snoop around, which will in turn put a target on the poor girl's back before she even starts."

"You're in the mood to play games today, aren't you?"

"Always. Also, I bet she didn't tell you because she doesn't want special treatment while working here."

"I don't—"

"Artemis, please, admit that you've been contemplating the many ways you could make her experience easy and pleasant from the very instant you found out she's going to work here."

He's right. I can't help myself. I want to set up her first office, get it organized and decorated to her liking. And outfit it with the best equipment and most sophisticated technology so she can do her work with every tool and resource at her disposal. I want to look at her smile and the excitement in her eyes when she finally sits in her chair behind her desk. But I know that interns aren't assigned offices, and they have to share desks with other interns. I rub my face with my hand.

"Alex, I'm not going to deny that the thought crossed my mind. But I respect her too much. And I understand she wants to start from scratch and earn her place with hard work. It would be disrespectful to her intelligence and abilities if I were to meddle in any way."

Alex's mouth drops in an exaggerated and dramatic way. "Shit. That girl has you whipped."

"And you have too much time on your hands."

"Ah, come on. It's Friday." He moves his eyebrows up and down. "How about a glass of whisky? How about we go to your bar? I've acquired an appreciation for its candlelight lounge."

"Listen, Alex, bringing up the fact that you almost kissed Claudia is not the best move on your part."

"Get over it. How was I supposed to know who she was? You should be thankful that I was able to put on the brakes before anything happened. Anyway, it was thanks to my call that you were able to come down to the club and seduce her. By the way, you never thanked me for that. I'm not feeling very appreciated as your friend."

"Oh, what should I say? Thank you, Alex, for holding yourself back and not sticking your tongue down my girl's throat?"

I purse my lips as soon as the words come out of my mouth, aware of the critical error I've made.

Alex smiles widely. "Your girl, huh?"

"You didn't hear a thing."

Of course, Alex won't let it go.

"Everybody is afraid of you in this company. You bring that cold and serious exterior wherever you go. If they only knew you were all soft inside, just like a—"

"Don't say it."

"Avocado."

"Get out of here, Alex. Go earn your salary."

"It's Friday and it's about"—he looks at his watch—"five

o'clock in the afternoon. Work finished at four, so please loosen your tie and come along with me to your club."

"This might come as a surprise to you, but drowning myself in whisky is not my priority at this moment." I hold the bridge of my nose between two fingers. "There's a new project I need to oversee, and lots of papers to sign and decisions to make."

Alex checks his cell.

"Wow. According to Instagram, your fiancé has been enjoying herself in . . . Barcelona? I thought she was in Rome."

"She's been traveling all over Europe this month."

"When was the last time you saw her?"

I shrug. "I don't know. Two months ago?"

"You don't sound like a very interested fiancé."

"I've been busy."

Alex brings his hand to his chin, pondering. "How do you survive this long without sex?"

"How do you survive asking questions like that?"

Alex winks at me again. "You can complain all you want, but deep down you know you can't live without me."

I feign a quick smile. "Oh, how I would like to put that to the test."

Alex gives me the finger.

His gesture makes me flash back to that night three months ago in December when Claudia gave me the finger following our challenge at the pool. Her words drew a line I haven't crossed. I've kept my distance, as it should be. She's absolutely right. I don't deserve to get close to her or seduce her—not until I figure out what will happen afterward.

Yes, it's true that Cristina and I are playing roles in a farce. Yet, to the world, we're still together. And I need to keep Claudia away from all of this. I'd never put her in an impossible and uncomfortable situation.

"Doesn't it seem to you that Cristina's taken a lot of photos with this man?"

Alex shows me a picture from Instagram in which Cristina is standing next to a tall man with a beard and sunglasses. She's in a lot of photos with him in different stops throughout Europe.

"I'm glad she's having fun. She needed a break from work."

Alex frowns. "Artemis."

"Yes?"

"Your fiancé is obviously having a fine time gallivanting around the best cities of Europe with another man, and you're not bothered one bit."

I let out a sigh. "I'm not a jealous guy, you know that."

"Sure." Alex nods. "You're not jealous. Except you punched your younger brother and you were on the verge of hitting me when you found out that I was this close to messing around with Claudia. My friend, this pattern begs to differ."

"Claudia . . . our situation . . . it's complicated."

"Okay, I'm going to straighten you out," Alex says tersely. "You don't seem to mind that your fiancé is very likely having an affair right as we speak. But you turn into a wild beast if anyone gets within an inch of Claudia. Ergo, you are in love with Claudia and feel absolutely nothing for your fiancé."

I snort. "In love?! For god's sake, Alex!

"What I don't quite understand is why you're with Cristina when it's obvious that you'd rather be with Claudia. Shit, this is some prime-time soap opera stuff."

"You need to find *yourself* a girlfriend so you can stop worrying this much about my life."

"Nah." His smile fades. "I'm not looking for anything serious for a while."

"Alex."

"Stop giving me that condescending look."

"It's been months. You need a fresh start."

"Not yet, she . . ." He licks his lower lip, and his voice is barely a whisper. "She destroyed something inside me that I'm not exactly sure I'll ever be able to get back."

"She was the one who cheated. She has no right to break you. Please don't give her that much power."

Alex stands up. "Well. If you wanted me to leave you alone, you've succeeded."

"Alex, wait, I didn't mean to . . ."

He gives me a half smile. "I'll be at your club enjoying myself by drinking and getting frisky in the candlelight lounge. Which, by the way, was a fantastic idea."

I roll my eyes. "It wasn't my idea."

"That's right, it was mine. Oops!" He turns around and heads for the door.

"Don't cause any trouble at my bar."

Alex waves. "I'll behave, old man."

Once he's gone, I read through Claudia's entire résumé. My chest swells with pride. Despite all the daily chores on her plate, she's managed to get high grades, and the quality of the work she put in her writing samples is impressive.

Hey, dummy? You can accomplish anything you set your mind to.

I admire her. She came from nothing, and her life hasn't been filled with rainbows and happiness. Yet she's never given up. She deserves more respect and recognition than someone like me, who never had to make an effort and had everything handed over on a silver platter. I didn't even have to study that hard in university and I finished my degree with honors. I had an easy time learning, and made it through effortlessly. Right after I graduated my father put me at the head of his company, and in charge of its large workforce. I never had to start at the bottom and work my way up. I simply came in, and the job was mine. It's possible that's why I feel stuck in my professional life. The CEO title is the highest on the ladder, and there are no more steps left to climb, no more goals to achieve here. Perhaps if I had started from scratch, every promotion would have felt like a victory and a step up leading to this title. Maybe I sound ungrateful. However, I often wonder what it would have been like to have the chance to make it on my own, and spend more time with each department; grow along with everyone else by building a rapport with the staff as I worked my way up to becoming their leader.

I run my finger over Claudia's résumé. "You have my respect, Claudia."

Though her passion for singing never ceased, at twelve years old she discovered she wanted to study advertising and marketing, although her aptitude and abilities were apparent much earlier. I recall one summer afternoon when we were kids. Our school had organized a lemonade sale to raise funds for a good cause and our booth wasn't selling very well.

"Let's see." Claudia grabbed our sign and crossed out the one dollar we were charging per glass and wrote "Now only 99¢ plus a complimentary sticker."

I looked at her incredulously. "What are you doing?"

She smiled at me. "I have a bunch of sheets of stickers that I won. Everyone loves stickers, so I just improved our pitch."

I rolled my eyes. “We aren’t going to sell anything.”

We sold out.

I suppose some people are born with inherent aptitudes that make them suited for specific careers. This memory makes me think of the night Ares begged our father to let him study medicine. I felt bad for my brother. To challenge and stand up to my father is completely out of the question. Sometimes I feel I can do it, but the urge dissipates when I come face-to-face with him. I don’t want to be a nuisance, disappoint him, or cause him any pain. It’s hard to pinpoint the cause of my unwavering loyalty. I’m not sure if it’s the promise I made to him or if maybe I don’t ever want to see him as broken as he was that night. The pain, the look of defeat, the tears rolling from his reddened eyes, they’re all seared into my mind. But I also want to support my brother.

It often feels like Fortune gets a kick out of placing me at a crossroads, forcing me to choose between who matters most to me.

Twenty-two

I am not talking to you.

ARTEMIS

I come out of the building, rubbing the back of my neck as I make my way to my car.

"Mr. Hidalgo!"

An older gentleman with gray hair wearing slightly wrinkled clothes approaches me.

"Yes?"

"I'm very sorry to bother you like this. I can see you're tired and are heading home."

"I'm sorry, but who are you?"

He clears his throat, "My name is Richard Perez, and I work in the cleaning department. Well, I used to work there."

"How can I help you, Mr. Perez?"

"I understand you're a busy man who doesn't concern himself with the trivial things, but today I was fired." And that's when I notice his eyes are swollen and red. "You see, I have four girls to feed. I've worked all my life with this company. Maybe I'm overstepping, but could you help me?"

"What was the reason given for your dismissal?"

He hangs his head. "I'm older now, and I guess it's affected my performance. But I always leave everything very clean, Mr. Hidalgo. I promise. Even if I take longer than someone who is younger."

I approach him. "How long have you been working with us?"

"Fifteen years, sir."

"May I call you Richard?" He nods. "What positions have you occupied over the years, Richard?

"I've only worked as a cleaner, sir. Simply because I never graduated from high school."

"Come with me, Richard." He follows me back inside the building and I take him up to my office.

Richard sits in front of my desk, wringing his hands in his lap. Sasha, the head of human resources, comes in a few minutes later. It was good fortune she happened to be working overtime. Her smile quickly fades when she notices Richard sitting with me.

"Good afternoon."

Richard gets up. "Good afternoon, ma'am."

"Sasha, Richard here has told me he was dismissed without just cause. Moreover, he wasn't given severance or any other compensation."

Sasha places her hands behind her back, looking nervous. "Mr. Perez has had difficulties performing his duties."

"Has he been able to complete his tasks?"

"Yes, but it takes him longer than the allotted time."

"I understand Mr. Perez has been working for this company for fifteen years and has four daughters to support. Were you aware of that?"

"Yes, sir, I was aware."

"Is this how we show gratitude for years of loyalty?"

"Sir, I think it's best we have this conversation in private." She shoots Richard a glance.

"No, Richard has a right to be here. He's been with this company longer than you. So do we treat him like he's disposable and let him go just because he's aging?"

"Sir, that wasn't at all my intention. I was just trying to improve the quality of the work performed by the cleaning crew."

Richard cuts in. "Sir, I don't want to cause any trouble."

"Richard, don't worry. It's me who should thank you for bringing this to my attention." I turn my gaze back to Sasha, who is visibly sweating.

"Sasha, who is the manager of the cleaning crew?"

"Mr. Andrade."

"And how long has Mr. Andrade been with the company?"

"One year."

"You're telling me that Richard, a man who's been with us for fifteen years, wasn't considered for a promotion to the position of manager? A position that's better suited for him since it requires less physical effort and is more age appropriate? In addition, he has more experience and knows the company better than Mr. Andrade, which in turn makes him the ideal candidate for a role he would excel at. Yet he was fired, just like that?"

"Sir, Mr. Perez didn't finish high school."

"And? He has fifteen years of experience under his belt and knows every member of the crew better than anyone."

"Sir, if I may, several important factors were considered before arriving at this decision."

"I'm having a hard time seeing these factors. What I see is a loyal worker who wasn't given a promotion he deserved. Instead, he was fired." I pick up from my desk the two files I requested. "Mr. Andrade's performance record is littered with complaints and mistakes throughout the one year he's been working here. Meanwhile, Richard's record is spotless, not one complaint in his fifteen years of employment. Sasha, please explain to me why you promoted someone who is undeserving?"

"Mr. Andrade is younger."

I smile sarcastically. "Be careful what you say. The point you are trying to make is dangerously close to discriminatory."

Sasha looks alarmed. "No, sir. I would never."

"Let me explain how we're going to handle this matter since it's Friday, and I'm sure we'd all like to go home." I walk around my desk and stand in front of Richard. "On behalf of my company, I apologize to you, Richard. I want you to know I value the years given to us, and your hard work."

Mr. Perez's eyes fill up with tears. "You really don't have to . . ."

I place my hands on his shoulders. "Your loyalty and dedication will not go unnoticed. I would like you accept the position of cleaning manager. Do you think you can take over the role?"

"Yes, sir." He quickly wipes away his tears.

"All right, Sasha." I turn to her, and I can tell she understands what I need.

She lowers her head. "My apologies, Mr. Perez. I did not mean to disrespect you in any way."

"Don't worry about it," Richard replies. "You were only trying to do your job."

I dismiss Richard and I'm left alone with Sasha. My voice turns cold. "Sasha, let this be the last time that you let the power you hold cloud your judgment and prevent you from appreciating the labor of those who work under you."

"Yes, sir."

This is a first time in a long time I've made it home while the sun is still up. So I'm not surprised to find the living room full of life rather than quiet and dark. Claudia and Apolo are on the sofa that's across from the television. I squeeze the door handle tighter than I should when I see Claudia laughing heartily at one of Apolo's jokes while playfully throwing popcorn in his direction. She looks relaxed in his company.

I would like to put up a wall between them.

I intentionally slam the door to get their attention.

The smile fades from Claudia's face; she clears her throat and turns her attention to the movie. Apolo does the same, and whispers something to her. The soft tone in his voice makes her face light up; she's clearly amused. Aw, they're whispering to each other now. How immature.

"Claudia, can you fix me something to eat, please?"

Apolo turns to me. "Don't be a party pooper, we're watching a movie."

Claudia looks at me, and her icy stare is crushing. "Your food is on the table, and you can heat it in the microwave. Or are you not familiar with how to use one, sir?"

Apolo keeps his lips pressed tight to prevent him from laughing. I move a little closer to the sofa.

"I want a fruit salad. I like it freshly cut and served."

Apolo snorts. "Don't be a pain, Artemis."

"I'm not talking to you."

Claudia stands up.

"It's fine, Apolo. Pause it, I'll be right back."

Apolo shoots me a hostile look but I ignore him and follow Claudia into the kitchen. I know I'm acting like a jerk. I just can't stomach watching them together. And I find it hard to control the urge to separate them. What if something else has happened between them in the past months? I imagine her in Apolo's arms, kissing him. Or even worse, making love to him. My chest tightens. *No, Artemis. Don't let your mind go there.*

Claudia efficiently chops each piece of fruit, and I can't stop myself from thinking back to the morning after the night when we kissed and she let me touch her. I recall how much fun I had teasing her.

She's wearing a comfy dress that looks more like a night shirt, reaching to just above the knee. Her red hair is loose and a little messy on the sides. It's grown a bit; it almost reaches her waist.

I miss you.

The words are stuck in my throat. Claudia finishes and presents me with a plate full of fruit. She then washes her hands and leaves the kitchen without giving me a second glance. I suppose we're back to the cold-shoulder treatment. I make my way back to the living room with my fruit plate, only to find that Apolo and Claudia are no longer alone. Ares and Raquel are seated across from them. Raquel smiles at me when she sees me enter.

"Oh, hi, Artemis." Raquel gets up. "I wanted to see you." She hands me an invitation. "It's for my birthday party. Maybe you're not interested, but it would be nice if you could come."

This girl's joy and positive energy are contagious.

"Ah. I'll try. Thank you for the invite."

"Great!" she replies, giving me a thumbs-up.

Ares eyes me with distrust. His expression immediately changes when she turns around and walks toward him. The doubt in his eyes is replaced by a look of pure adoration. Who could have imagined that this girl, who looks like a sprite, would bring my heartbreaker brother to his knees?

Ares gets up and takes Raquel by the hand. "We'll be in the rec room. A *Super Mario Kart* rematch awaits."

Claudia raises an eyebrow and shares a glance with Apolo. "Sure, a rematch . . ."

Raquel blushes. "Um, well. I hope to see you at my birthday." She follows Ares down the hallway that leads to the rec room.

Claudia and Apolo share an amused look, acting as if they know something no one else does. It bothers me that they can communicate just by looking at each other. I need to stop feeling this way; it's eating me up inside. I head to my room before I say or do something I'll regret, making matters worse, which tends to happen anytime I'm near Claudia.

After my shower, I go downstairs to get a glass of water. To be honest, I want to check if they're still sitting together on the couch, enjoying themselves. I've imagined the many possibilities and outcomes of what could happen between them. But when I enter the living room, I find it empty. I'm this close to cheering for the peace of mind this brings me when I notice them coming out of the kitchen. Both have wet hair, which I suspect is from having just showered, and they're dressed nicely. Are they going out? My stomach lurches. My god, this is a horrible feeling!

You're jealous. Alex's voice echoes in my head. It's beyond me how he can get a rise out of me without even being in my presence. Claudia is wearing a short skirt and a blouse with a plunging neckline. She carries her jacket folded on her arm. They greet me with smiles and walk past. I clench my fists and keep them glued to my sides. I want to keep my mouth shut, but I can't.

"Where are you going?"

They don't turn.

"Just out," Apolo replies.

Were they seeing each other all this time while I was drowning myself with work in order to avoid running into her?

"Out?" I let out a fake laugh. "Out is not a place."

Apolo turns to look at me. "It's none of your business, Artemis."

"Since when do you think you can talk to your older brother like that?"

"Since that brother stopped showing up for his brothers when they needed him most."

I know he means Ares and his desire to become a doctor. And me taking our father's side when he refused Ares's request for assistance.

I take a step closer to him, and Claudia moves to stand between us.

"You go ahead, Apolo. I'll catch up shortly. I need to clear something up with your brother."

Apolo is ready to protest but Claudia throws him a pleading look, and he makes his exit. My anger loses its steam with her in front of me. Her presence alone gives my emotions a boost.

"I want you to understand that the only reason I'm offering an explanation is that I don't want any problems between you and your brother," she says. "The only thing that's going on between Apolo and me is a lovely friendship. In fact, we're on our way to have dinner with the girl he's dating. So stop going around growling and making up excuses to come between us."

I'm not exactly sure why I'm smiling. Or why I like it when she clarifies what's going on. Maybe because I feel like there's hope for us if she believes that she owes me an explanation. Unfortunately, when it comes to Claudia, I couldn't be more wrong.

"Stop smiling." She shakes her head. "I'm not dating your brother. I'm not heartless, and would never do something like that." She moves closer. "But, Artemis, just because I'm not going out with Apolo doesn't mean I won't see other people. And when that happens, you better not get in the way since you have no right to."

"Are you seeing anyone?"

She shrugs. "Maybe. Anyway, that's none of your concern."

"Yes, it is."

"Oh yeah?" She crosses her arms. "How come? And maybe we should ask your fiancé how she feels about that?"

"It's complicated, Claudia."

"Artemis, to me it's quite straightforward. You're engaged. So stop meddling in my life and with my business. It's that simple."

I take a step forward and she takes a step back, keeping the same distance between us.

"See you later, Artemis."

I remain rooted to the spot while she walks away. That's what our life has become; I constantly watch her as she drifts further from me.

I'm certain the time will come when she'll no longer be on her own. Someone else will be by her side and I won't be able to take it. I know I have to make a decision soon or I risk losing her forever. Clearly, I can make decisions without difficulty when I'm dealing with company matters. However, when it comes to my personal life, I'm ashamed to admit I'm nothing but a coward.

Twenty-three

Playing hardball. Aren't you?

CLAUDIA

"Should I stay or go?"

I stand in front of the mirror. The purple dress I'm wearing is fitted and accentuates my shape. I'm not thin, but curvy. I love my shapely legs and hips. And I've never felt insecure about my figure. I have my red hair down, falling on each side to frame my face. My makeup looks natural and I'm wearing my favorite red lipstick. The only reason I hesitate to attend this birthday party is that Raquel invited Artemis, and we can't be in the same place together without having an uncomfortable moment. Though I'm hoping he won't show—social events aren't his thing. Perhaps he's afraid that if he socializes for too long with others his defenses might just melt. I smile to myself at the possibility. Damn iceberg.

I'm determined not to let him affect my social life, so I make my way over to Raquel's house. I will not let him take away my chance to share this very special day with her. I like her a lot and it was nice of her to invite me. I find a side door ajar when I arrive and make my way in. I run right into Raquel, who smiles at me, carrying a tray on her hand.

"Hey! You came."

Her smile is contagious.

"Indeed! Happy birthday." I offer my gift but her hands are full.

"You can put it on the table over there. The guys are in the back."

I can't stop myself from asking. "All three?"

"Yeah. Go ahead. I'll join you after I pass this food around. Okay?"

I place Raquel's gift on the table next to the others and make my way to the garden. As soon as I arrive I spot Raquel with Daniela, Apolo's girlfriend. They stand next to each other, staring at something. I join them, and notice they're watching Artemis and Apolo, who are surrounded by a group of girls.

"Who are they?"

Raquel jumps, clearly startled by my sudden appearance.

"Those are my cousins," she explains, letting out a deep breath.

I purse my lips. "I need a drink."

Daniela feels the same way. "Come with me. I know where the vodka is."

"Hey, go ahead and enjoy yourselves." Raquel gives us a thumbs-up. Daniela and I exchange a look in agreement, and we each grab one of Raquel's arms and drag her along with us.

Vodka shots come and go, and I'm enjoying myself. I feel quite at ease with Raquel and Daniela. The only friend I have is Gin, so any opportunity I get to hang out with other girls makes me happy. I'm not saying that Gin's company isn't enough; it's just nice to talk with different people.

We sit in a corner of the courtyard. Raquel leaves our side every so often to spend time with other guests, which doesn't bother us in the least. After all, this is her party and we don't want to keep the birthday girl all to ourselves. In the end, she always makes her way back to us after she's done playing hostess.

"Cheers!" Dani raises her glass. "To the stupid brothers Hidalgo!"

I join their cheer. I truly enjoy the great vibe I get from these two girls.

"Cheers!"

Dani grumbles after finishing her drink. "Look at her. She's making eyes at him, putting on an innocent act to snare him."

I follow her gaze to Apolo. He and one of the girls are alone together, talking. I examine the girl from afar—she has a baby face and appears younger than him.

"Nah. I don't think he's into her. She looks about his age, and Apolo tends to like girls who are a little older than him."

I'm not saying this because he was confused and tried something with me; I just know him. Even though Apolo is young, he's very mature for his age, so he's always been attracted to girls who measure up to or exceed his level of maturity.

Dani looks hopeful. "Really?"

"Without a doubt. Apolo, unlike his siblings, has always been easy to read."

Raquel shoots me a curious look.

"You mean Artemis, right?"

I smile in response to her question. Her inquiry doesn't end there.

"Do you get along with him?"

I glance at the iceberg and watch him as I speak.

"He is . . . someone who can be difficult."

"Oh shit," Dani mumbles, getting my attention. "Is there something going on between you and Artemis?"

I burst out laughing when I notice Raquel biting her nails. Her curiosity is adorable. My eyes move from her to Dani, aware they're waiting for me to answer.

"It's complicated."

"It's complicated," Dani repeats, shaking her head. "Don't give me a relationship status line from Facebook."

"Let her be, Dani." Raquel saves me from the interrogation.

I stop talking when I see Ares, Apolo, and Artemis casually walking in our direction. Ares says something to Apolo, which makes him laugh and shake his head. Artemis shoots them a tired look. I give myself permission to give Artemis a lingering look. He has a black suit on, no tie, and the top buttons of his shit are undone. His hair is combed back, and his light scruff accents his strong jaw.

"Do you mind if we sit with you?" Ares asks when they reach us.

Ares sits down with Raquel, and Apolo sits next to me, which prompts Artemis to take the spot on the other side. *Very mature, iceberg.* Ares takes Raquel's hand and gives it a quick kiss.

"What are you all drinking?" he asks.

"Just a little vodka," Dani responds.

Apolo extends his hand to Dani. "May I have some?"

Artemis raises an eyebrow and Apolo pulls his hand away. I roll my eyes and give my glass to Apolo. "Take it."

Artemis twists his lips. "Claudia."

I smile at him. "Loosen up a little, iceberg."

"Iceberg?" Raquel asks.

"Yeah. That's what she calls him." Ares laughs.

I gesture at Artemis with my hands. "Can't you see how tall and cold he is?"

Artemis purses his lips. "I'm right here."

Raquel laughs heartily.

"That's a superoriginal nickname," she adds, giving a thumbs-up.

I take a bow in an exaggerated and mocking way.

"Thank you, thank you."

"We should play Never Have I Ever," Raquel suggests.

I don't think that's a good idea. But how can I say no to the birthday girl? We all share a look and she raises her glass. "I'll go first."

It's a long wait until Raquel starts the game. She's deep in thought, and I suspect she's thinking of something that involves Ares, because she can't stop staring at him. She's crazy about him, isn't she?

It truly makes me happy that Ares's first love is so real and pure—he deserves it. It's about time he met someone who showed him there are good women left in the world. Women who can be trusted blindly and who are worth a chance.

"Raquel?" Ares's voice seems to bring her back. "We're all waiting."

Raquel begins. "Okay, for those who have never played, it's like this: if I were to say 'Never have I ever eaten pizza,' and you have, then you drink. You don't need to explain anything, just have a drink if you've done the thing mentioned. Or not drink, if you haven't. Everyone gets a turn. Is that clear?"

Okay, that can't be that bad.

"Never have I ever watched porn," Raquel declares.

Uh-oh. This game is not as innocent as I thought it was going to be.

We all share a look, feeling slightly awkward, and we each take one drink. Ares has a wide smile plastered on his face. He drinks and raises an eyebrow, waiting for Raquel to have a drink. She blushes the moment she takes a sip. This makes me laugh.

And now it's Dani's turn. She looks slightly unsure, then her eyes fix on me. I'm not getting a good feeling here.

"Never have I ever kissed someone standing in this circle."

Dani takes a drink. So do Ares, Apolo, and Raquel. I hesitate and play with my glass. I look over at Artemis but he avoids my gaze and takes a drink, so I do the same. It's sheer torture thinking of his kisses. For the first time in my life, it felt so good and so right—our lips fit perfectly, as if they were made for each other. I need to stop my mind from wandering back to that night. It was a fleeting moment. He had some fun before getting back with the girl he wants to be with.

And now it's Apolo's turn.

"Never have I ever lied by claiming I'm not interested in someone, when truth be told, I'm dying to be with that person."

Ares smiles and shakes his head. "That's deep, bro."

Apolo, Artemis, and Raquel don't drink but Dani does. Shortly after, everyone is staring at me while I play with my glass, again.

"Claudia?"

I can feel Artemis's stare on me. I give him a tortured smile and proceed to take a drink.

It's my turn, at last. I shoot Ares a playful look, and he seems worried. "What?"

I clear my throat. "Never have I ever stalked the person I know is stalking me, and smile like a fool every time I see them."

Everyone turns their heads to look at Ares, who grins.

"Showing no mercy, huh?" He drinks. I'm amused by the look of surprise on everyone's face.

It's Artemis's turn, and I stop breathing for a second. I know him. He was drinking before he came here. His eyes are bloodshot and have a slight twitch. This means trouble. That volatile, unfiltered part of Artemis only comes out to play when he's had too much to drink.

His tone is cold. "Never have I ever kissed two guys presently sitting in this circle, and caused a fight between brothers."

Silence.

I knew it. My chest tightens in reaction to his words, aware of how deliberately he's trying to make me uncomfortable. Everyone looks around, wondering who will take a drink.

Artemis raises his glass at me. "Aren't you going to drink?"

Every cell in my body vibrates with rage. I grip my glass and throw its contents in Artemis's face.

"You're a goddamn jerk."

I get up and make my way through the middle of the circle. I don't want to create a scene at Raquel's birthday party. It would be too mortifying.

"Claudia, wait." I hear Apolo's voice behind me, but I keep walking.

The night breeze brushes my skin, and the wind blows my hair back. My eyes are burning. I don't want to give Artemis the pleasure of seeing me hurt like this, shedding tears because of his stupidity. He's not worth it. To be frank, what bothers me most is that I was just starting to form a friendship with Raquel and

Daniela, and given the fact that it's hard for me to make friends, he just ruined my chances. It's likely that Daniela might hate me. As for Raquel, I'll become the girl who fools around with two brothers. I want to hit him so badly, and hurt him emotionally in so many ways. But I know that won't solve anything. Although it would be extremely gratifying to kick him in the balls—maybe he would learn not to be such a jerk.

I lock myself in my room. My mom watches me from her bed.

"You're home early."

I make an effort to smile.

"Yes. I had a lot of fun." I answer while removing my earrings and necklace.

I change into my shorts and T-shirt pajama set, then lie down next to my mother.

I can't sleep.

For what feels like hours I stare at the ceiling in the dark. Pent-up rage courses through my veins, making my heart beat fast and clouding my mind. I need to shake him out of my system so I can get some sleep, but my brain refuses to cooperate.

How could he embarrass me like that in front of everyone?

Does he not feel an ounce of consideration? Or respect?

A faint sound of shattering glass jolts me from my bed. I look over to my mom and she's still sound asleep.

I run out of the room, and just as I'm about to enter the living room, I hear Ares speak in a worried tone, so I stop and remain hidden in the hallway.

"Apolo, you need to calm down."

Apolo sounds furious. "I'm telling the truth. Just look at Claudia."

I grab hold of my chest and back against the wall, listening carefully.

"It's no secret that I've always liked her but although she won't admit it, she only has eyes for that idiot I call brother who treats her like shit." He laughs sarcastically. "And after all I've done to win Daniela's heart, what happens? She rejects me. I should be like you two, admit it. I have no fucking idea why I thought acting and being the total opposite would turn out better."

"Shut up. Don't ever say shit like that again." Ares sounds determined. "You have no idea how lucky you are that you didn't turn out like us. How I wish I could be more like you and get the girl I love without putting her through so much along the way, without having to face so many fears, without having to fight my inner self every time I want to show her a small sliver of how I truly feel."

"But I always get hurt."

"That's a risk we all take in love."

"Let me go. I don't want to cry in front of you. I know what you think of anyone who cries over girls."

"I'm a different person now, Apolo. If you need to cry because your heart is broken, go ahead. Men cry too."

"I opened my heart to her. I know I'm not experienced, but I gave her all of me. And it still wasn't enough." Apolo's voice sounds so broken.

I listen to Apolo openly sobbing, and my heart breaks into a thousand pieces. I can't believe Daniela turned him down; she seemed crazy about him. I don't get it. I hear footsteps, and I suspect Ares is taking Apolo upstairs to put him to bed.

I go back to my room but it's obvious I won't be able to sleep unless I do something to find a release.

When was the last time I had sex?

Come to think of it, it's been months. I haven't had a sex life since Artemis came back to this house. And why is that? It's not like he deserves any kind of loyalty. What Apolo and I shared were kisses and touching. It wasn't full-on consuming and draining sex, the kind that leaves you worn out and elated after an incredible orgasm.

Feeling restless, I pick up my phone and scan through the countless texts from Daniel. Maybe it's a mistake to reach out to him, but I have to admit he's the best I've had so far. The fact that he's a soccer player helps—his endurance is impressive.

I text him a simple hello, and he immediately responds.

Daniel: Hello.

Me: What are you up to?

Daniel: I just dropped off my drunk sister at home, and I'm heading to meet some friends at a bar. Why?

Me: I want to see you.

Daniel: Really? I admit, this is a surprise.

Me: I enjoy surprising you.

Daniel: Oh yeah? Do you want me to pick you up?

Me: If you want.

Daniel: Want? With you? Always.

Me: Great. It's a plan.

Daniel: I'll pick you up in 20 minutes, babe.

Me: Perfect.

I take a quick shower then put my purple dress back on but make sure to wear sexy lingerie underneath. Every time Artemis pops into my head, I push him out. Instead, I picture him fucking his fiancé, so that he won't spoil my one night of great sex. I head out of my room dressed and made up, looking for a drink of water before I leave. I nearly have a heart attack when I'm startled by Artemis sitting in the dark, like a ghost, at the kitchen table.

"Shit!" I blurt, putting a hand to my chest.

I don't want to deal with him, so I turn around and go to the living room. I hear his footsteps right behind me.

"Claudia, wait." He grabs me by the arm but I slap his hand off me.

"I don't want to talk to you."

"I'm really sorry, I'm a jerk. I don't know what came over me. I—"

"Stop." I raise my hand. "Save your apologies. I don't want to talk to you, Artemis."

"Please forgive me. I lost control. I don't know what's wrong with me."

"What do I have to do to get you to leave me alone?" I ask, not hiding the anger in my voice. "Let me be in peace."

"I'm sorry," he mutters, hanging his head.

If it wasn't for my raging anger, I would accept his apology. "Whatever. Just go to sleep."

"Where are you going at this hour?"

I ignore him and walk to the main door. He moves to stand in my way, forcing me to take a step back.

"Let me through, Artemis."

"Where are you going?"

My phone rings in my hand, and he watches me intently when I answer.

"I'm outside," Daniel says.

"I'll be right out, just give me a minute."

I hang up and Artemis cocks his head.

"Who was that?"

I don't know how to make him understand that this is none of his business. That I want him to leave me alone. And that his indecisiveness only complicates my life. So I reply, holding my head up.

"My boyfriend."

I wasn't expecting the look of hurt I see overtake his face. "You're lying."

I shrug. "I really don't care if you believe me or not."

He holds me by the arms.

"Look me in the eyes, Claudia. You've never lied to me. Please don't start now."

"I'm not lying," I respond coldly. How dare he ask for honesty after everything that he's put me through?

He releases me, looking defeated.

"You had your chance and you wasted it, Artemis." I make this very clear. "I'm not waiting my whole life for you when you can't even bring yourself to acknowledge the feelings you claim to have for me right now. Good night."

I bid him farewell, leave the house, and get into Daniel's car. My heart aches but I need to turn the page. I can't put my life on hold for someone who won't fight to make me a part of his. It's not worth it.

Twenty-four

It's never too late to change your life.

ARTEMIS

"Grandfather is waiting for you in the study."

My father and I exchange a glance in response to Claudia's words, delivered right as we arrive home from work. She gives me a cold stare before leaving.

"Do you know what this is about?" I ask.

"No," he replies, loosening his tie.

We enter the study, and I begin to understand what this may be about when we find Ares already on the couch sitting across from our grandfather. Ares asked our father for his support to study medicine and was turned down. And when he asked our grandfather for his help, he also said no. I suspect this may be the reason behind this meeting.

"Father, what's the matter? We're both busy, and have a video-conference scheduled in ten minutes," my father explains.

"Cancel it." Our grandfather smiles as he gives the order.

My father protests. "Dad, it's important."

"Cancel it!" Grandfather raises his voice, surprising us.

My father and I share a look. He nods, so I call to cancel the meeting, and we take a seat. My father lets out a sigh. "What's going on?"

My grandfather regains his composure. "Do any of you know why Ares is here?"

My father gives Ares a cold-eyed stare. "I assume to ask for your help again."

"That's correct." Our grandfather nods.

I try to guess what's really happening, and speak up. "Given that you previously said no to him, I can imagine his insistence has bothered you."

Ares stands up. "There's no need for this, Grandfather. I understand."

"Sit down."

Ares obeys, and Grandfather turns slightly to face me and my father.

"This conversation is much more important than any goddamn deal you're trying to close. Our family is more important than any business, which is something that you both have clearly forgotten."

No one says anything, and Grandfather continues. "But don't worry, I'm here to remind you all. Ares has always had everything handed to him. He has never had to fight for anything, or had to work in his life. He came to me asking for help and I turned him down because I wanted to see if he would give up on the first try. On the contrary, he surpassed my expectations. For months this boy has been busy around the clock applying for scholarships and grants, fighting for what he wants.

I never anticipated this would happen. Ares working? Not giving up?"

Grandfather looks at Ares with pride.

"Ares has not only won my support, he has also earned my respect. I'm proud of you, Ares. I'm proud you have my last name and that my blood runs in your veins."

Our grandfather has never looked at me like that. Or expressed those words to me. His smile fades as his gaze falls on my father.

"I'm extremely disappointed in you, Juan. Our family legacy? I'd gladly let death claim me if I ever thought our family legacy was determined by material possessions. A family's legacy is made of loyalty, mutual support, and affection. And it entails passing all those positive qualities and attributes down to future generations. The family legacy is not a goddamn corporation."

The silence when he's done his rant is unnerving.

Our grandfather, however, has no problem filling it. "Just because you've turned yourself into a workaholic as a means to avoid dealing with your wife's infidelities it doesn't give you to permission to make your children as miserable as you are."

My father clenches his fists. "Dad."

Our grandfather shakes his head. "Juan, it's shameful that you turned your back on your own son when he begged for your support. I never thought you would disappoint me this much." Grandfather's eyes fall on me. "You made this one pursue a career he hated, and have done everything in your power to turn him into you. And now look at him. Do you think he's happy?" I open my mouth to protest but my grandfather raises his hand to silence me. "Be quiet, son. Though I understand you're the product of your father's poor parenting, it bothers me that you turned your back on your brother, chose not to stand up for him, and failed to give him your support. I pity both of you. At this very moment, it would not bother me if you two were not tied to our last name."

Shame drags my head down.

"I hope you learn something from this, and can improve as human beings. I have faith in both of you." Our grandfather turns back to Ares. "I've begun your enrollment process in the faculty of medicine at the university you mentioned to Apolo." Grandfather presents him with an envelope. "This is a bank account I opened in your name with enough funds to cover your full tuition and all related expenses. Inside, there's also a key to an apartment I bought for you, located near the campus. You have my full support, and I'm sorry you had to witness your own father turn his back on you. On a positive and constructive note, you were able to experience what it feels like to work for what you want. I believe you will become a great doctor, Ares." Grandfather shakes his hands and slowly gets up. "Well, that's all. I must go and have a rest."

My father follows him, keeping his head down. Ares and I are left alone. I can read from his expression that he's still processing what just happened.

The words from our grandfather were painful to hear, though they were honest. The fact that I didn't support Ares will always weigh heavily on my conscience.

I can't pinpoint the exact reason why I refused to support him. Perhaps I didn't want to contradict our father. Or maybe I was jealous that Ares would be able to choose what he wanted to study. No matter the reason, what I did was indefensible. I acted like a terrible person and a bad brother.

I get up from my seat. "I'm truly sorry. And I'm glad that you'll be able to pursue your dreams." I try to smile. "Ares, you deserve it. You, unlike me, had the strength to veer off the path that was laid down for you. Our grandfather has good reason to be proud of you."

I expected Ares would derive some gratification from the reprimand that my father and I received, but there's no trace of joy in his expression. He appears receptive of my apologies, and understanding of my actions. He's definitely a better person than I am.

"It's never too late to change your life, Artemis."

"It's too late for me. Good luck, brother."

I find Claudia in the hallway outside the study. We pass each other, keeping our eyes down. I go up the stairs and head to the terrace. From up here, I can see the main entrance, the garden, the fountain, and the parked cars. I sit down on one of the metal chairs and lean back, closing my eyes. I massage my forehead with my fingers. My grandfather's words keep repeating inside my head. When I open my eyes, I find my father standing with his back to me. His hands are on the balcony railing and his eyes are fixed on the sky. He looks over his shoulder and back at me. And for the first time in a long while, his expression is not blank. He looks very sad.

"Why?"

I frown. "Why what?"

"Why did you break your engagement with Cristina months ago?"

I recall the conversation we had when he found out I had broken things off with Cristina, when he said my reasons were irrelevant and that the company should always come first.

Dad, is this you trying to change?

"Because I was interested in someone else," I tell him.

He remains silent for quite a while. Then he lets out a long sigh. "You no longer have to worry about marrying Cristina."

I immediately stop breathing. I'm speechless. My father tightens his grip on the railing, his shoulders visibly tense. Even though he's facing away from me, I suspect his expression is full of emotion.

"I don't believe in apologies, Artemis. I think actions are best when making amends for mistakes we make."

"Dad . . ."

"I'm not quite sure when I became a terrible father. I guess my heart has been hardened by the pain I've endured. I can't promise I'll change overnight, but I can start to do things differently. So, please, be patient with me."

My chest tightens. This man standing in front of me is the father I loved so much as a child, before he was changed by what happened with my mother. We would have water gun fights and bicycle races. He would also take me to the movies. He bought me my first soccer ball even though I sucked at playing. This man would display my Pokémon drawings in his office, not worried if clients or partners would see them. My father. He starts to leave but stops next to me and puts his hand on my shoulder.

"After all I've put you through, you never left my side, and you kept your promise, carrying a burden all these years that wasn't yours to carry. But it stops now, my son. You've done an amazing job."

He goes back inside the house, and his words remain suspended in midair. It's like a great weight has been lifted off my shoulders, and I can finally breathe. I feel free. I become aware of how trapped I've felt all these years. And the first thing that comes to my mind is Claudia.

I reach for my cell phone and call Cristina, who is finally back from her trip. She sounds sleepy when she answers.

"Artemis? If this is a last-minute booty call, I can't . . ."

"It's over."

"Wait, what?"

Is that a hint of excitement I pick up in her voice? I believe I wasn't the only who was miserable in this arrangement.

"Cristina, we're free."

She lets out a long sigh of relief. "Really? Thank goodness. No offense intended, but you can't begin to imagine how happy I am to hear this."

"Don't worry about it."

"We can still be friends, right?"

"Of course. Good luck, Cristina."

"Good luck, Artemis."

I go inside and hurry downstairs, looking for Claudia. But I can't find her in the living room or the kitchen. She must be in her bedroom. I knock on her door, feeling impatient. I've turned back into a fucking teenager. Martha opens the door with a smile on her face.

"Artemis."

"Hello. I'm sorry to bother you but I need to talk to Claudia."

I look around the room but it's empty. My eyes zero in on the nightstand next to the bed where I notice the stuffed pig I gave Claudia that Fourth of July. She still has it? While my heart fills with hope, my brain fogs with confusion. She rejected me that night. Why did she keep a memento?

"Claudia went out. She said she'd be back in a few hours."

"Do you know where he went?"

She shakes her head.

"All right. Good night, Martha."

I take a seat in the living room and wait. I take off my jacket. I scroll through emails on my phone. When the clock strikes midnight, I go outside and sit on the front steps, hoping this change in location will speed up her return.

Eventually, a car pulls up and parks in front of the house. I can spot Claudia inside. She's saying good-bye to someone. Is that Daniel? Is she dating Ares's teammate? I restrain myself before jealousy spoils my chance to tell her what needs to be said. Claudia gets out of the car and waves. She's wearing a casual minidress with a floral pattern that's flattering, and she stops in her tracks when she sees me waiting. As usual, my thoughts get all mixed up when I'm in her presence, and my head fills with doubt. Her gaze is on me, and I can read in her expression the questions running through her mind. *What are you doing here? What do you want now?*

"Did you have a good time?" I don't bother adjusting my tone.

"That's none of your business."

"I was waiting for you."

She walks over, and folds her arms over her chest. "Why?"

I rub the back of my neck with my hand and begin my explanation, choosing my words carefully. "Cristina and I are finished."

She doesn't seem affected by the news; it could be that she she's good at hiding her emotions.

"What does that have to do with me?

"It has a lot to do with you." I take a step closer to her. "I want . . . I want to be with you, Claudia."

But the cold-eyed stare remains in place. Why?

"Tonight," she begins. "So you want to spend the night with

me, then tomorrow you can get back together with your girlfriend like nothing ever happened? I'm tired of your games, Artemis."

"I'm not playing a game," I assure her. "The engagement is over."

"And why should I believe you?"

I inch closer until she's forced to look up and meet my eyes.

"Because it's you. Because you're the only person who can see through me."

She slowly parts her lips and I conjure all my inner strength to keep myself from kissing her. I don't want to scare her. Besides, she says she has a boyfriend. Even though I don't want to believe it, I wouldn't want to put her in a difficult situation. I've already caused enough problems. It's obvious she's not sure what to say, so I speak instead.

"I'm not asking you to be with me right this moment. First, I want to win your trust." I cup her face with both hands, feeling the softness of her skin under my touch. "I don't want to act like a coward anymore, Claudia. There are no more obstacles impeding me from being with you."

She licks her lips. "I told you, I'm seeing someone."

"We both know that no one makes you feel the way I do."

A smile plays on her lips. "You're conceited."

"And you're a dummy for dating someone else."

Shè puts her hands over mine on her face. "You're way dumber I am."

The silence settles between us. And I lose myself in that beautiful pair of jet-black eyes. How can they be this intense and mesmerizing? I run my thumb along her lips, imagining how they would feel pressed against mine. She takes a step back, breaking the connection between us.

“Fine. If you want to fight for me, go ahead. But I make no promises.” She walks past me, heading for the door. She turns around just as she’s about to go inside. “By the way, I don’t have a boyfriend. I wasn’t telling the truth. I just said it to annoy you.”

I open my mouth to protest, but she’s already gone. I’ll fight for her, and I will not rest until I have her in my arms. I contemplate the many ways I can seduce her and make her fall in love with me.

This is going to be fun.

Twenty-five

Artemis, I don't like the dark.

CLAUDIA

I'm not good with good-byes.

I suppose this is normal, considering I've had very few in my life. The day Artemis left for university, we didn't even say good-bye. I couldn't look him in the face after I pushed him away. In a nutshell, situations like these are rare and far apart in my life. My lack of experience makes it hard to prepare for the moment, so it's difficult to predict how I'll behave when it happens. Ares is going away to study at a university in another state. Raquel let me know that his flight leaves in a few hours. I just left her in the kitchen, eating with the rest of the family.

I notice that his door is ajar and peek inside. His room looks organized and clean, but it also appears empty in a way that's hard to describe. Ares is wearing jeans but is shirtless. His hair is wet, and he's having a hard time trying to fit something inside one of his suitcases.

Though I knew this day would come, I'm shocked by how much it pains me now that it's finally here. As I watch him pack his bags, I realize I'll no longer run into him in the hallway, or catch him making faces at me, or find him in the rec room playing video games, or spend time chatting about silly things wherever we happen to be hanging out in the house. I underestimated how used to his presence I am, and how much I'll miss him. He smiles at me with sadness when he sees me, and there's a glimmer in his blue eyes.

"All set?"

He nods, and sighs. "I guess so."

I'm not sure what to say or how to say it. I've always put up a strong front around him, and I'm not sure how he might react if he sees me crying. A memory of Ares as a little boy comes to mind. He's inside the restaurant and his hand is pressed on the glass where I have mine. His smile is warm and innocent. He's always been kindhearted. These boys have truly been family to me.

"What are you thinking about?" he asks.

"Nothing. Just reminiscing, that's all." I have a lump in my throat. "I'm not going to the airport."

He doesn't ask why, or look disappointed. He simply nods, understanding that farewells at airports are not for everyone.

"I guess you're here to say good-bye, then." The closer he gets to me, the more I struggle to contain the tears that are welling up in my eyes.

"Umm, I . . ." My voice breaks, so I clear my throat. "I wish you the best in the world and I know that you'll do great. You are incredibly smart." I stop talking for a moment; my vision is getting foggy. "You're going to be an amazing doctor. I'm really proud of you, Ares."

His expression saddens, and his eyes turn red. Before I can continue, he pulls me into a tight hug.

"Thank you, Claudia," he whispers against my shoulder. "Thank you for everything. For being a good woman, and teaching me everything that my mother couldn't." He places a kiss on my hair. "I love you so much."

I let the tears flow down my cheeks at the sound of those words. "You dumbass, I love you too."

Ares wipes away my tears with his thumbs when we pull apart.

"Dumbass?"

We both laugh.

"Don't worry. I'll be here every other weekend. And Thanksgiving and Christmas. You're not going to get rid of me that easily."

"You better do that. All right, I'll let you finish packing," I tell him as I sniff through my stuffed-up nose.

"Okay." Ares kisses me on the forehead. "And remember, no matter what happens with iceberg—"

"You'll always be my favorite."

He winks at me.

"Good girl."

I leave him to finish packing and make my way downstairs. Everyone is waiting for him in the living room. Artemis and I exchange a quick glance before I head to my room. I don't even want to be present when Ares leaves with his suitcases in hand. Farewells are a newly discovered personal weakness. I run into my mother in the hallway.

"Is he leaving already?" my mother asks with a sad smile.

"Yes, he's about to come downstairs."

"I'll go say good-bye." I nod and step aside to let her pass.

My mom loves the three Hidalgo boys very much. She's spent more time with them than their own mother. I let out a sigh when I enter my room. Ares's flight departs early, but it's not yet dawn, which means I have a few hours left to sleep. Sunrise is in three hours and I'll need all the energy I can get. I crawl into bed.

I want . . . I want to be with you, Claudia.

I roll to my side and rest my cheek on my hands. Artemis's words keep circling inside my head. Several days have gone by and I haven't seen him other than just this morning, but I can't stop thinking about him.

Because it's you. Because you're the only person who can see through me.

How can he say those things and disappear, just like that?

I roll over again, and this time I'm lying on my back with hands outstretched on either side.

"Stupid iceberg."

I close my eyes, and take a deep breath. I really need these three hours of rest or I'll perform poorly during the day. Moonlight sneaks through my window, invading the darkness of my bedroom, and the trees outside make shadows on the roof.

A wistful smile forms on my lips.

"What are you doing?" I asked with trepidation when I was eight years old, watching Artemis place some sheets on the floor of his room before turning the lights off. My fear of the dark from spending so many years living on the streets still tormented me. So I closed my eyes, feeling afraid.

Artemis took me by the hand and led me over to where he'd put down the sheets, and we both lay down on our backs. I kept my eyes closed because I didn't want to see the monsters around me.

"Artemis, I don't like the dark."

"I know," he whispered. "Open your eyes and look at the ceiling."

I slowly opened my eyes and discovered that the ceiling was covered with glow-in-the-dark stickers. There were stars, planets, and constellations, all in different colors. It was a beautiful sight.

"Wow."

"You don't have to be afraid, Claudia. You can also find beauty in the dark."

After that night, we shared other moments together in the dark and he showed me so many beautiful things. Eventually, I came to associate positive experiences with the dark and overcame my fear. I doubt anyone else knows how kindhearted Artemis really is. I wonder if he's shown that side of himself to anyone else.

At last, exhaustion wins and I fall asleep with that question lingering in my mind.

"This is the list of your daily tasks," Mrs. Marks concludes, giving me a sheet of paper. "And Claudia, I want to reiterate that we're very happy you accepted this internship. Your résumé and writing samples are impressive."

"Thank you very much. It's a great compliment coming from you, Mrs. Marks."

"Oh, please, call me Paula. 'Mrs. Marks' makes me feel old."

"All right, Paula."

Paula is the manager of the marketing department at Hidalgo Enterprises. She introduces me to the rest of the staff and to Kelly, the other intern. I take a seat on one side of the large desk Kelly and I share.

I still can't believe it's the first day of my internship. The very first time I have the opportunity to put into practice what I've been learning in school all these years; a chance to do what I like. It goes without saying that I'm grateful to Mr. Juan for letting me take over the housekeeper position when my mother fell ill, but I don't plan to work for the Hidalgos forever. I have many goals and aspirations, and this is one of them. My connection to the Hidalgo family didn't influence my desire to work for this company; I was objective in my selection process and made my decision based on the fact that this is one of the most successful companies in the state. Their marketing department has a strong reputation and it's highly respected, having launched some of the most creative and innovative marketing campaigns I've ever seen. I knew this was the place I needed to be whenever I came across one of their projects or read about its team.

I'm pretty sure Artemis won't find out I'm here. This building is immense, and I'm just one intern of many working three days a week during the afternoon shift. I can't completely abandon my position at the Hidalgo house, so I'm glad the internships aren't full-time.

"Are you excited?" Kelly asks me.

"Yes. And you?"

"Extremely. I've heard that they received over a hundred applications. One hundred! And here we are, you and me. We're so lucky."

I smile at her. "Yes. Indeed we are."

I spend the first hours of the afternoon setting up my half of the desk and organizing the desktop computer assigned to me so I can perform well and do my work the way I like. During the afternoon break, Paula gives us the company credit card for the coffee run. Kelly and I go to the cafe across the street and pick up drinks for the whole team. This is one of the tasks on our list of duties, so I'm not bothered in the least. Caffeine is often considered the fuel of the workplace, and we are the newest members of the team. When we make our way back to the building and walk through the revolving doors, I come to an abrupt stop and nearly drop the tray of coffees I'm carrying.

Artemis is coming out of the elevators, dressed in an impeccable dark-blue suit paired with a light-blue tie. His handsome face wears the cold expression he shows to the world. His cell phone is plastered to one ear while he's riffling through some papers with his hands. Two men in dark suits follow closely behind him. I move before he can see me, trotting to one side, where I hide behind a potted plant that's slightly above my height. I'm amazed I manage to avoid spilling one drop of coffee—I should add that skill to my résumé. I sneak a peek, sticking my head out from behind the potted plant and notice that Kelly is frozen in place. She gives me a "what the fuck" kind of look. Her gaze turns to Artemis, who walks right by without noticing her and exits through the revolving doors.

I let out a deep and long breath. That was close. Kelly comes near, waiting for an explanation. "Claudia? What's going on?"

"It's . . . complicated."

"Why are you hiding from the CEO?"

"How do you know he's the CEO?"

"Because he's the face of the company. He appears in tons of the promotional materials and ads. And how could he not be—he's gorgeous."

And he's also a great kisser.

"It's just that, you know, I felt intimidated. He's the big boss. Maybe it's first-day jitters."

"I completely understand. To be honest, I felt shivers when he passed by. He looks terrifyingly intense and intimidating."

"Exactly."

We go back to our desks after we deliver the coffees to the team, for which they're all very appreciative. I still can't believe Artemis almost saw me; that was a close call. I can't say exactly why, but I'd rather he didn't know I work here. I guess I don't want to be treated differently, and want to avoid any discomfort resulting from the team finding out he and I are acquainted. I want them to value my work based on my own merits, and not the people I'm connected to. Even if they were to deny it, I'm certain the dynamics would change if the staff here found out I have a close relationship with the CEO.

By the time I get home, I'm exhausted. After I was done at work, I had classes at the university. I may have underestimated the demands of this internship—it's amazing how even a few hours can wear you out. I'm not surprised by how still and quiet the house is when I make my way inside. I head to the kitchen because I'm starving. I let out a yawn, covering my mouth with my palm. I nearly choke on my own saliva when I find Artemis inside.

This is the first time we've been in a room alone together since the night he said the words that keep tossing and turning inside my head. It's not so much his presence that catches me by surprise, but his attire. He has on an apron over a white dress shirt and he's cooking something that smells delicious. His back is turned to me, so he hasn't seen me yet. I lean against the doorframe, watching him. It's a very nice view.

"How long are you going to stand there staring?"

His voice catches me off guard. How did he . . . ? He answers by pointing his wooden spoon at my shadow on the wall next to him, anticipating the question I was about to ask. Shit.

"It's an unexpected sight, that's all."

He turns to face me, and my heart warms. That face, with the light scruff—every detail of his appearance is so masculine and sexy. Even when he's wearing an apron he manages to look so damn handsome. But it's his expression that stirs so many emotions in me. His warm gaze is the opposite of the look I saw on his face this afternoon. He's a completely different person when he's with me.

"I'm almost done. Have a seat." He points to the kitchen table.

I arch an eyebrow. "Are you cooking for me?"

"Why do you look surprised? Who prepared the first sandwiches you had when you first came to live with us? Who taught you how to make pancakes? Huh?"

"Okay. Yes, I get it."

He smiles. And I feel the urge to grab his face with my hands and kiss his lips.

Calm down, Claudia.

I take a seat and watch him cook then plate the food he's prepared.

"You look exhausted," he comments.

"I am. It's been a long day." I would love to chat with him about my internship. With the exception of what his horrible mother did to me, I'm not used to hiding things from him. He puts the plates down on the table, and everything looks delicious.

"Wow." The presentation looks incredible, just like it was done by a professional chef.

"Wait until you have a taste."

He takes the seat next to me and grabs my hand, placing a kiss on my knuckles, which sends shivers all over my body. He looks me straight in the eyes, his hand still holding mine.

"I'm sorry I've been absent for the past few days. A new company project has taken up all my time. I even slept in the office a few nights."

"Don't worry. You don't owe me an explanation."

"Yes, I do. I can't make a declaration swearing that I'm going to win you over then disappear only to come out of the woodwork as if nothing happened. You deserve better than that."

His proximity is making it very hard to resist the urge to kiss him. This need for him has intensified over the months spent fantasizing about him. I clear my throat and pull my hand from his grasp.

"Time to taste your famous food. Let's have a try."

Artemis watches me expectantly as I take my first bite. My face contorts with disgust, just to bug him.

"What's wrong?" he asks, alarmed.

I chew and smile, then speak after I'm done swallowing.

"It's delicious, I was just teasing you."

He rolls his eyes, and without much warning, sneaks in a quick peck on my cheek.

"Hey!"

The jerk grins at me. "I was just teasing you."

I look away when I feel the heat rise and warm my cheeks, and get back to eating the food on my plate. I wash the dishes when we're done with our meal, which was simply divine: fried shrimp, rice, and salad. Artemis is on the other side of the table, right across from me. We're chatting about work. I leave out any mention of my first day interning at his company.

"It must be difficult to manage such a large company," I tell him, while washing a glass.

"You're one of the very few people who think that," he replies, rubbing his face with his hand. "Most people think it's easy being the CEO, that I spend my time sitting in a big office, enjoying the view from my window."

"I bet you look sexy in your office."

He bites his lower lip. "Are you flirting with me, Claudia?"

I shrug. "Maybe."

"You know what they say about those who play with fire, don't you?"

I finish with the dishes and dry my hands with a towel.

"And why should I be afraid when I *am* fire?" I point to my hair.

Artemis laughs. He keeps his eyes locked with mine as he stands and walks around the table, slowly dragging his fingers along the edge.

"You are fire . . ." he whispers, and I have a hard time swallowing.

I have to lift my face to look at him when he comes to stand in front of me. My heart is racing, and I try to control my breathing. My god. What is this tension I sense in the air? I've never felt anything like it before. Artemis licks his lips, observing me attentively. He extends one hand to me and uses it to cradle my cheek.

"I missed you."

I want to tell him that I missed him, too, but the words are stuck in my throat. So instead I lift my hand and touch his cheek, feeling his light scruff under my palm. I reply with a smile. The dim lighting in the kitchen makes his brown eyes appear black. I'm in awe at how much his features have aged and the maturity of his appearance. Part of me is on guard and doesn't want to be vulnerable again—the hurt from a few months ago is still fresh—but this time I know he's being honest. Artemis lowers his gaze, staring at my lips. I can see desire in his eyes. It's evident he wants to kiss me, but he's not sure if it's something I want, given everything that's happened between us.

"You are so beautiful," he whispers as he strokes my cheek with his thumb.

"I know."

He raises an eyebrow. "Very well, then."

He lowers his hand and steps back, breaking all physical contact between us.

"Tomorrow after class I'll pick you up at campus and take you out to dinner."

"Hmm, let me think about it."

"You'll think about it?"

"Fine, I accept. But it's just because the food tonight was delicious."

"Good. Also, I'm not sure if clarification is needed, but just in case: we're going on a date. Okay?"

"Okay."

He waves. "Good night, Claudia."

"Good night, Artemis."

He gives me a smile, then turns his back on me and walks away. I move fast and catch up to him. I grab his arm to turn him around and grab him by the collar of his shirt to kiss him. He immediately reciprocates with kisses as hungry as mine. Our lips brush and I become wet as our passion ignites. My entire body is burning up from one kiss. The moans coming from his lips indicate that he feels the same. I move my head slightly to one side and deepen the kiss, enjoying every second.

That's enough, Claudia. Or you'll end up screwing him right here on the table.

I pull away from him but he grabs me by the waist. He presses me against his body and tries to kiss me again. I put my thumb on his lips to block his attempt and he shakes his head.

"You're not the one in charge," I tell him, freeing myself from his arms. "It's me who's in control."

And I walk away, leaving Artemis alone in the kitchen, breathing heavily and wanting me.

After all he's done to me, from this moment on I will be the one who decides if something happens between us.

I am fire after all.

Twenty-six

You make my heart ache for you.

CLAUDIA

I play with my hands while I wait for Artemis in front of the university building. This is the first time I've felt nervous before going out on a date with a man. But he's not any man—I honestly don't know why I'm surprised by my current state. He was my first love—my only love. And this is our first official date. I'm restless so I keep adjusting the neckline and the hem of my knee-length floral dress. My hair is down and parted in the middle. I'm glad that it's warming up so I can wear nice clothes without carrying a coat, hat, and other accessories to cover myself up.

I lick my lips, thinking of my kiss with Artemis from last night; of his heavy breathing and the pent-up tension in his body. To be honest, I don't think we're capable of being alone and keeping our hands off each other. If this date wasn't in a public place, I'm pretty sure it would lead quickly to sex.

Given the long history we share, and all the years of

accumulated desire, it's incredibly difficult to keep our hands to ourselves. Add to that the fact that Artemis is superattractive, and I get all hot and bothered just thinking of him. I take a deep breath and try to steer my mind in the direction of more innocent thoughts.

Who am I kidding, as if I could ever do that. My heart starts beating fast as soon as I notice him parking his elegant black car in front of me. I'm about to take a step toward the passenger door when he gets out. He's wearing a black suit with a shirt and tie of the same color. It looks like the driver matches the car; both elegant and dressed in black.

His eyes fall on me and I try my best to appear calm, pretending that I'm not affected by how drop-dead gorgeous he looks.

Artemis smiles at me as he opens the door. "Hello."

"Hello," I reply with a smile, and get into the car.

The interior is also black with dark-blue accents. The contrast makes for a sophisticated look. The AC blows refreshing cool air in my face. The car smells like his cologne and him. I put my seat belt on while Artemis gets back into the car.

"Nice car," I say, watching him put on his seat belt.

"And now you tell me? This isn't the first time you've been inside." He pulls the car onto the road.

He's talking about the night at his bar when he drove me home. The same night we nearly defiled the kitchen table but didn't because Ares interrupted us, god only knows why. Oh well, I guess I was saved from greater humiliation since not too long after Artemis got back with his girlfriend.

Don't think about that, Claudia. Don't ruin the night before it's even started. Live in the moment.

Maybe I need to change the subject.

"How was work today?" I remember there's a new project that's taking up most of his time and focus. The marketing team kept talking about it yesterday; they said it was crucial to close the deal, and that it was a multimillion-dollar venture. If it moves forward, our department will have to dedicate a substantial amount of work formulating project-specific public relations and marketing strategies.

Artemis rubs the back of his neck with his hand. "It's been . . . intense, but it's nothing I can't handle."

"I never imagined you would be interested in business management. You never mentioned it when we were growing up."

"Because I wasn't interested."

This revelation saddens me, though I had my suspicions he chose to pursue studies in business administration out of obligation and not by choice. I thought that with time, he might have grown to like it. I watch him for a moment. He has one hand on the steering wheel and the other is rubbing his neck. His eyes look tired and so does his posture. Artemis is still young but he carries a heavy burden on his shoulders; he's responsible for something he never wanted in the first place.

How could you stand doing something you didn't like for this long, Artemis? How much have you endured? Are you frustrated?

If he's miserable, he's done a good job of covering it up. He's never complained or cursed his father; hell, not even his mother after what happened with that man. I have great admiration for his capacity to put up with so much, as well as his ability not to lash out.

He quickly glances back at me, feeling my gaze on him.

"What is it?"

"Nothing." We'll talk about it one day, but not now. I don't want to discuss sad things and spoil this night. "Where are we going?"

"First is dinner. And after, wherever your heart desires."

Your bed, maybe? Claudia, for god's sake.

"Where are we going for dinner?" I ask out of curiosity. I look at the streets, at the houses and the trees passing. We are far from the university campus, heading in the opposite direction of the downtown core.

"You'll see."

And then I notice a familiar street. My chest tightens when I recognize every house and restaurant on this strip. The place looks like it's been frozen in time. Artemis parks the car, and I don't wait for him to open my door. I get out quickly and go to stand in front of the Greek restaurant where I saw the Hidalgos for the first time.

A wave of emotions washes over me. Nostalgia is the first one I recognize. It's incredible how vividly I remember the hunger I felt that day and the smell of the food, as well as my fear of the men who were after my mother. The image of the Hidalgo family that night is imprinted in my mind. They were seated at that table, and looked like one of those idyllic portraits of happy families. Artemis comes to stand next to me. We stay silent for a few minutes, absorbed in watching our surroundings and reliving the memory.

He breaks the silence. "I thought it would be nice to come back to the place where it all began."

I turn to look at him, and he's watching me attentively. I suppose my reaction to this moment matters to him. He begins to speak when I can't find words.

"If you're not okay with this place, we can go somewhere else.

I just thought that no other restaurant, no matter how high-end and exclusive, would have as much significance as the one where I first saw you. Maybe those times don't bring back the best memories for you, but that was the day your life changed for the better. Also, it was the day you came into mine."

I don't know exactly what to say so I lick my lips instead. He's right, this place holds a special place in my story, and I don't see it in a negative light. Instead, it's the place where my life had a new start.

"I love it," I reply and take his hand, a move that seems to surprise him.

He clears his throat. And is that a blush I see? Artemis Hidalgo is blushing?

"Fine. Let's go in."

The restaurant is well preserved, and has kept its very distinctive classy appearance. The clientele is made up of predominantly well-attired men and elegant women. Although it's not in one of the best districts in town, the place has managed to maintain an ambiance suitable for its distinguished patrons.

We follow the waitress, who takes us to the table in front of the window—the same table where the Hidalgos sat many years ago. Out the window, I can almost see the child version of myself standing outside staring at the food inside.

"What are you thinking about?" Artemis asks. The dim lights of the restaurant make his face glow across the table.

"Nothing. I was just remembering." I try to smile happily, but it feels bittersweet. "Your father did a very generous deed that day. He saved my mom's life and mine."

"That's the version of my father I always carry with me."

"You know, it's not a version of him. It's who he really is.

I believe that deep down, that it's his true self. You need to be patient. Your grandfather still has a lot of faith in him."

"You're very close to my grandfather." He points this out without a hint of annoyance in his voice, just curiosity.

"How can I not be? He's so loving."

"Is he your favorite Hidalgo, by any chance?"

"To be honest, yes, he is. But don't tell Ares. I promised him he'll always be my favorite. Though in reality, he's a close second to his grandfather."

Artemis smiles at me. "I don't think I can settle for third place in the list of your favorite Hidalgos."

"Who said you were third? After Ares, there's Apolo."

His smile has disappeared, and he clenches his fists on the table. Apolo. Still a sensitive subject between us, huh? He needs to get over it. There's a glimmer in his eyes, and I'm having a hard time figuring out what that's about. I raise my glass of water to take a sip.

"We'll see who your favorite Hidalgo is after I screw you senseless and give you the best orgasm you've had in your life."

I cough, nearly choking on my water. I put my hand on my heaving chest and try to clear my throat. How can he say that while sitting so calmly and with such a straight face? Artemis gives me a sly grin with a hint of mischief. And I shoot him a contemptuous smile.

"You're feeling very confident about your abilities."

"I'm just a man who knows what he's doing." He raises a glass half-filled with wine. He swirls it first, then sniffs it. "I can get you wet without touching you. Mmm, I made you feel hot just now."

"Oh yeah?"

I slip my foot out of my sandal and stretch it out under the table, just enough to place it on his thigh, not too far from his crotch. Artemis becomes visibly tense. He wasn't expecting that. I give him an innocent smile.

"And I could give you an embarrassing erection. Don't you ever forget that."

"You really don't like to give up control, huh?"

"That's something you'll have to earn."

"Is that a challenge?"

Our gazes meet, and the intensity electrifies the air around us. The waitress shows up at our table with a friendly smile and asks if we're ready to order, breaking the moment. I put my foot down and go back to behaving myself.

It's going to be a long night.

Twenty-seven

My silence is your answer.

CLAUDIA

This is a whole new level of sexual tension.

The car ride home is quiet, and the magnetism between us is palpable. In all honesty, I've always prided myself on being able to rein in my impulses. But this is different; I've never wanted someone as much as Artemis. Maybe it's built up over so many years, and the fact that there's nothing standing in our way anymore makes it hard to resist the urge to rip his clothes off and . . .

I need to keep my imagination under control.

Artemis puts his hand on my bare thigh, and I jump when his warm palm makes contact with my skin. I watch him, but he keeps driving like nothing is happening. I can feel my heart hammering with every heavy breath I take. It's as if all my senses are on high alert.

"How come you're so quiet?" His voice sounds deeper in the car's interior.

"Just thinking about how much you've grown."

"And you haven't seen it all."

"Artemis!"

He laughs a little, giving him the appearance of a charming and naughty boy with a soft, scruffy beard that makes him look even sexier. The selfish person in me is glad he never shows this smile to the rest of the world. Artemis parks the car and we walk to the front door.

When we step into the house, we share an uncomfortable moment. There's no awkwardness between us; it's just that since we live in the same place, we don't know what to do at this point. How do we end the date and say good night? Or do we even have to? We come to a stop at the bottom of the stairs.

"I really had a great time with you tonight," he says, making me smile.

"I had an okay time." He raises an eyebrow. "I'm kidding. It was an amazing date, thank you."

A heavy silence lingers and we look into each other's eyes. I lick my lips and he looks away.

"Good night," I finally blurt.

"Good night."

I turn and start to walk away. I grimace, frustrated now that I'm out of his sight. Suddenly, I feel his hand on mine, turning me and pulling me toward him. Before I can blink, he lifts me up in his arms and walks us to the stairs. My heart is in my mouth, and I look at him. His neck is tense, his veins are popping out, and his breathing is a disaster.

"You want this as much as I do, don't you?" His voice is thick with desire. He carries me up the stairs. I find it sexy, the way he holds me with ease. The answer to his question is my silence as

I nod. When we reach his bedroom, he closes the door and puts me down. My feet have barely touched the floor when he pushes me against the door and kisses me with urgency. I don't hesitate and return his kisses with the same urgent need, because . . . my god! I want him as much, perhaps even more. Our mouths move in sync, wetting our lips. I hold on to his tie and tilt my head slightly to the side to deepen the kiss. Artemis has his hands on either side of my face, holding me firm against the door, visibly trying to keep himself under control.

To hell with self-control.

His kiss intensifies and becomes more passionate, more demanding and intent on driving me wild. Our breathing and the sound of our kisses echo throughout the room. My body burns from his touch. When I feel him press his fists against the door, I lightly push myself away from him.

"Stop holding back," I whisper, nibbling on his lips.

His voice is husky and sensual. "I'm trying to be gentle."

"Fuck gentleness." I suck on his lips harder. "Lose control and screw me like you've always wanted to screw me."

And I watch as his restrain crumbles. His hands find my breasts and squeeze them gently, provoking a soft moan from my lips.

"I'll screw you the way I want," he growls against my mouth.

He crushes my lips beneath his and deftly massages my breasts before reaching for the straps of my dress. He pulls them off my shoulders and jerks the top of my dress down, exposing my bra. My skin is burning hot, dying for his touch. He leaves my lips and kisses my neck while his hands unhook the clasp of my bra, freeing my breasts.

A moan escapes my lips when I feel his mouth on the skin

of my naked breasts, sucking on them. I throw my head back, enjoying the sensation. He deftly sucks and licks, switching from hard to soft. The perfect combination, making my legs go weak. Good god, I might have an orgasm just from this alone.

Impatiently, I grab his face and make him look at me so that I can kiss him. I remove his tie and throw it to the side. Without breaking the kiss, I unbutton his shirt and push it off his shoulders while simultaneously removing his jacket. I run my hands over his chest, feeling every contour and ripple of his muscles. I trail down until I reach his toned abdomen. He momentarily breaks the kiss to watch me, and takes a hold of my wandering hand, guiding it a few inches lower.

"Touch it."

I obey, and cup him through the fabric of his pants.

"I want you to feel how hard you make me."

And he's really hard. I massage him through his pants as he slips a hand up my dress and rids me of my panties in one swift yank.

I gasp.

"The way I want," he reminds me, as his fingers find their way to my most intimate place, making me forget about my torn underwear. I'm so wet, making his fingers slide, which seems to excite him even more. His breathing becomes more erratic, and his shoulders rise and fall. I can't wait any longer.

I unbutton his pants and take them off along with his boxers. My mouth waters when I see the man standing before me. He's so fucking gorgeous. Every line on the muscles of his arms, chest, and abs is well defined.

My dress falls to my feet and I am completely naked. I pull him closer, pressing my body against his. I groan when I feel the skin-to-skin contact between his aroused member and my sensitive core. I can't wait anymore. I turn around in his arms, giving my back to him. I rest my palms on the door and expose myself to him.

But Artemis has other plans and grabs my arm, flipping me around and throwing me on the bed. I land on my back then push myself up to rest on my elbows so I can watch him. He pulls me by my ankles, dragging me closer to the edge of the bed.

"I want you to look me in the eyes while I fuck you."

"Fine. I'll let you be in control. But just this once, iceberg."

Artemis maneuvers himself between my legs, and swoops down for a kiss. The friction created by our naked bodies grinding against each other makes me moan with anticipation. He halts the kiss briefly to look deep into my eyes. His hard member brushes against my center. I'm about to beg him to take me, when in a one fluid movement he thrusts inside hard, making me arch my back.

We both groan at the sensation, but he doesn't give me time to recuperate and begins to hammer into me with growing urgency, burying himself deep over and over again. His eyes are fixed on mine, and there's a look of intense passion on his face. His grunts and moans amplify the intensity of the moment. I wrap my legs around his sides in an attempt to feel his thrusts deeper.

"Aah, yes," I moan, wrapping my arms around his back.

He is fucking me hard, like a wild beast, exactly how I wanted him to take me. The sound of our bodies slapping hard against each other blends with our moans of pleasure. I never thought I would feel this good. It's not the first time I've had sex without a condom, but the sensation of my heated skin pressed against his is too much to bear.

I get lost in Artemis's brown eyes, feeling him so deep inside me. Each thrust brings me close to orgasm. He knows exactly what to do, and his mouth breaks from mine to whisper in my ear.

"You're so hot and wet inside." The sound of his moans intensifies my arousal. "You're driving me crazy."

He leans back and carefully lifts me up, bringing our hips to the same level and deepening his thrusts. My breasts tremble with each thrust. I bite my lower lip, struck by how sexy he looks when the muscles in his abdomen and arms contract with each movement he makes.

"Artemis!" I groan on the verge of orgasm.

"Yes. That's right. Moan my name." His whispers are laced with pure desire. He rubs my most sensitive spot with his thumb while he keeps thrusting inside me. My eyes roll and I'm overcome with the urge to explode. "Like that, sexy. Moan your pleasure, let go while I'm inside you."

"Ah, god."

I grip the sheets at my sides. My orgasm sends shocks all over my body, rushing through my nerves and overpowering my limbs. I moan loudly. His name and a host of profanities escape my lips. Artemis doesn't stop; instead, he accelerates his movements, making my legs tremble while he speaks between grunts.

"Can I come inside you?"

The thought of letting him finish his release inside me sounds sexy as hell, and I'm on the pill so I nod my response.

His punishing pace picks up speed. His eyes never leave mine. Arousal makes his face contort as he comes to his release. I can feel him inside me, still hard and throbbing. He falls on top of me, his heart thumping madly against mine. Our breathing is in shambles, and I'm unable to stop the silly postorgasmic grin plastered on my face.

Artemis rolls over, and lies on his back next to me.

"Wow," he exclaims, turning his face toward me.

"Not bad, iceberg."

He gives me a roguish smile.

"Likewise, fire."

"Fire?"

He reaches out to me with his hand. His finger caresses my neck, then moves down to my cleavage.

"You once told me you were like fire, and I now have confirmation." He pauses. "Getting burned by you is totally worth it."

His feathered touch trails down to my tummy, and I hold my breath, enjoying the contact. He lets his fingers skim along my sides, drawing small lines on my skin that point to the places it has stretched whenever I've gained and lost weight. He does it with such tenderness and adoration, making me smile. I've never felt ashamed of my body. And why should I? All these marks are part of my history and what I've been through. I'm a healthy person and that's what matters. Everything else is trivial. His hand moves lower until it reaches the outer part of my thigh. He brushes against the old scar there, and whispers.

"Fourth grade, you fell from a bicycle. God, there was a lot of blood and you didn't even cry."

I laugh at the accuracy of his recollection. "You were pale. I honestly thought you were going to faint."

"I almost did. But if you ever tell on me, I'll deny it."

He sits and puts his finger over another scar on my knee. "First year of high school while roller-skating. I told you not to go down that street because it was so steep."

"As if I ever do anything you tell me to do."

He lies back on his side and cradles his head with one hand so he can stare at me. His hand travels to my waist, where there's a nearly unnoticeable scar.

"Appendicitis," he continues. "It was the first time I saw you cry, and it broke me."

I reach out to cup his face, and feel his light scruff against my palm.

"You are a very sweet man, Artemis. You have always been."

"Sweet?" He arches an eyebrow. "No. How about sexy? Devilishly handsome?"

"Yes. Physically speaking, you are very attractive. But that's not what made me"—*fall in love with you.* He waits for me to finish my sentence, so I do—"notice you."

"So you're telling me that it was my sweet disposition?"

"Yes."

"You are aware that everyone else in the world says I'm a bastard, that I'm detached, that my aura is icy and cold."

"I am not everyone else in the world."

He uses the palm of my hand to lightly rub his face. "Would you like to be a part of my world?"

"I think you're still high on postorgasmic endorphins."

He rolls and lies on his back, gesturing for me to lie on his chest. And I do, hugging him and placing my arm on his abdomen. He drops a kiss on my forehead. "What are the chances that . . . ?"

"We are not going to do that again."

"It can't hurt to try."

After we spend a moment in silence, I get up and climb on top of him. I kiss him passionately, and when I pull away I notice he's watching me with an amused look on his face.

"I thought you said we weren't—"

"I lied."

And I kiss him again, letting all the emotions stirred up by our first encounter flow freely. I'm terrified by everything I'm feeling. Sex has never meant that much to me, and now I know why. In spite of the fact that so much time has passed, I have confirmation that subconsciously I've been saving my heart for him and only him. Sex didn't mean much to me until it happened with him. Artemis Hidalgo, my beloved iceberg.

Twenty-eight

I thought you had already melted me.

ARTEMIS

I didn't want to wake you up. You were sleeping so soundly. Sorry I had to leave like this, but I have to go help my mother get her day started. I'll see you later, iceberg.

—Clau.

I smile at the note left on the nightstand and stretch as I get up, still fully naked. My gaze falls back on the bed and its disarray. The memory of Claudia gripping the sheets while I was fucking her raises the temperature of my body. How I love that woman! She drives me crazy. Sleeping with her has far exceeded my expectations.

I've never experienced such intense feelings while having sex. The emotions, the looks, the warmth in my heart when I kissed her . . . everything made it the best sex I've had in my life. I shower, then get ready for work. I put on a suit and notice a red mark on the lower side of my neck when I fix my tie. I get closer to the mirror and tug the collar of my shirt open to inspect the spot. It hurts a little when I touch it. I try to recall the moment when this could have happened. Claudia on top of me. She's moaning, moving up and down. She leans forward to kiss me on the mouth first, then moves to my neck where she sucks hard while she amps the speed of her movements. I let out a groan in pain because she was sucking too hard, then she pulled away to look at me.

"Sorry, I got carried away."

"Never apologize for moving like that, ever."

It was worth it. I head downstairs, ready to leave for work. I'm in a good mood and have a big smile plastered on my face simply because. When was the last time I woke up feeling this great? I can't recall. I enter the kitchen, and try to hide my smile when I spot Claudia preparing my morning coffee. I move closer and hug her from behind, which makes her jump as I catch her by surprise.

"Hey," she complains, turning in my arms.

"Hi, fire," I say before giving her a quick kiss. Her soft lips greet mine momentarily. Now that I'm finally able to kiss her and hold her in my arms, it's all I want to do.

"Good morning, iceberg."

"I thought you'd already melted me."

Her lips curve up, forming a smile. "I was under the impression it was the opposite: I made you hard."

Her reply causes me to arch an eyebrow. "I think we need to confirm that."

She feigns innocence. "I have no idea what you're talking about."

"By the way"—I caress her face gently—"do you think you could wear your uniform when we're alone?"

"I'll think about it."

"You have no idea how many times I've fantasized about screwing you in that uniform."

"Oh, I might."

I rub my nose against hers. "Was I that obvious?"

She nods and I pull her in closer for a kiss packed with emotions, feeling every inch of her lips against mine. The kiss picks up tempo and she brings her hands around my neck while our lips deepen their contact. The beating of my heart increases. She was the first girl I liked, the first girl who made me feel nervous and awkward, the first one I declared my feelings to, the one I showed my vulnerable side, and the one I cared for on so many occasions. So I'm not shocked by the intensity of my feelings when I hold her in my arms. For me, it has always been her.

Claudia ends the kiss. She reaches past me, searching for cups to serve the coffee. "Your parents or Apolo could come down at any time," she reminds me. "And your grandfather and his nurse are living here now, so we have to be careful."

I let out a sigh and step aside, watching her pour coffee into two cups. She hands me one.

"Don't you have to go to work today?" I ask her, and when Claudia frowns, I almost slap myself. She still doesn't know that I'm aware she works at my company. Shit! "I mean, do you have plans today?" I hide my face behind the coffee cup as I take a sip.

"Not until much later."

I glance at the clock on the wall. I need to go now; I have a meeting in half an hour, and I slept longer than usual.

"I have to go." I give her another quick kiss and put the cup down on the table.

She hands me a container. "Fruit salad. It's important to have breakfast."

That makes me smile like an idiot.

"Are you worried about me?"

"Why are you so surprised?"

"I'm not surprised."

"Then?"

I look her straight in the eyes. "I like it."

She blushes and looks away. I'm trying hard to resist the urge to kiss her again, and so I ask her another question instead. "Should we do something tonight?"

"I have plans. I'll see you later when you come home."

"What kind of plans?" I ask, and she raises an eyebrow. "I'm just curious."

"Relax. They're not plans to meet a man."

"I'm relaxed." I give her a wide smile. "Can't you tell?"

"All right, Mr. Relaxed. Get out of here or you're going to be late." She pushes me in the direction of the door.

"Is it a girls' night out? To a club? You could go to my club. I promise I won't bother you if—"

"Good-bye, Artemis."

I reluctantly make my exit.

After a rather long two-hour meeting, I'm dying to eat and grateful to Claudia for the fruit salad waiting for me in my office. To my great misfortune, when I walk into my office I find it occupied by Alex, who is lying on my couch, holding two ice packs to his head. His eyes are closed, and he grimaces in pain.

"Don't you have your own office?" I ask.

"Can you please have mercy, I'm on my deathbed," he replies in a low whisper. Perhaps if I ignore him, he'll go away of his own accord. At my desk, I uncover the fruit cup and begin to eat. The sight of Alex stretched out on my couch looking like a rag doll is not the best view, but maybe he won't be his usual chatty self since he's not feeling well.

Alex turns his head in my direction and opens his eyes. He watches me for a few seconds. "I'm not seeing the moody aura that's often around you."

"Alex."

He squints while studying me from afar. "Where has the tension in your posture gone? Or on your face? I'm not getting the icy chills when I'm near you." He sits up and puts the ice packs down. "So what happened? How did you manage to turn back into a human?"

"Very funny, Alex."

He smiles at me, but winces in pain. "Ow, this headache is going to kill me."

"Should I be concerned about your alcohol intake?"

"Nah. I only drink once a week, so I'm fine. But thanks for worrying about me." He makes eyes at me.

I give him a tired look.

"Alex, don't you have an office of your own? Where you have a couch that's identical to mine simply because you've always been a jealous guy?"

"But I'm alone in my office and don't have you by my side."

I'm not even going to acknowledge his comment with one of my own, so I keep eating. Alex stands up and tilts his head to one side, looking at me as if I have three heads.

"What?" I say.

"I made a joke and you didn't growl once. What—" He comes to a full stop when his eyes land on my neck, and I quickly pull my shirt up to cover it. "Artemis! Is that a hickey?"

I clear my throat. "No, it's a mosquito bite."

"Sure, a very sensual mosquito." He stands in front of me. "What are you not telling me? If you broke up with Cristina . . ." He walks to one side, holding his chin and looking deep in thought. "Was it Claudia?"

I look away, pretending I'm not interested.

"Bingo!" he exclaims. "Wow, if I had known that Claudia would change your eternal bad mood, I would've played Cupid a long time ago."

"Didn't you have a headache?"

"Yes, but it's not every day that your best friend finally gets together with the girl he loves. You were never able to get over your first love, huh? It's because you're a hopeless romantic."

"Alex, I'm going to punch you."

He pats me on the shoulder. His voice loses its playful tone, and he gives me a genuine smile. "I'm happy for you, Artemis."

"Thank you," I reply. "Now get back to work."

"Your wish is my command, Mr. Chief Executive Officer. By the way, try to stay inside your office as much as possible. The mosquito bite will attract too much attention."

He winks at me, picks up his ice packs, and leaves.

At this moment, I wish my face didn't appear in so many of the company's ads. It's nearly impossible for me to go unnoticed among my employees—everyone knows that I'm the CEO. They either scurry away in fear or they try hard to impress me with the most perfect version of themselves by giving one hundred percent to their jobs. I even suspect they hold their breath the moment they spot me. I had the intention of paying a visit this afternoon to the marketing department, where Claudia's doing her internship, hoping to watch her from a distance for a little while. And now I know it won't be possible—I have yet to reach the floor where her department is located, and I've already passed several members of staff who fell silent or looked petrified.

I don't look that terrifying, do I? I'm younger than most of the staff. Why would they be afraid of me? I understand that I hold the highest position of authority in the company, but I've decreased the rate of layoffs since my father appointed me to the role. Job security is the most stable it's ever been. So what is it, then? Do they see me as an iceberg?

I think back to that word Claudia uses, which doesn't make much sense since she's one of the very few people who knows I can be warm and kind. I give up. Since I'm near the finance department, I decide to pay Alex a visit. Maybe he can come up with an answer.

However, I stop when I spot his secretary, a young woman with a cherubic face, wavy hair, and a voluptuous figure. She's applying lipstick and adjusting her hair before going into Alex's office. I think that my best friend's secretary has a crush on him. Alex, you're such a cliché. I go back to my office in defeat.

The sound of my cell phone ringing wakes me up. I squeeze and rub my eyes with my thumb and forefinger before opening them. My office is cloaked in darkness. How long was I asleep? I stretch out my hand and reach for my phone, which keeps ringing insistently. I become fully awake when I notice Claudia's name lighting up the screen. This is the first time she's called me on this line.

"Hello?"

"Iceberrrrrrrg!" she shouts in my ear, forcing me to peel my head off the receiver, ever so slightly.

"Claudia?"

I hear female laughter, chatter, and music playing in the background.

"Iceberg, I think . . ." she whispers, as if divulging a state secret. "I'm drunk." She giggles.

"Claudia, where are you?"

"Relax a little. Loosen up, Artemis. Aren't you exhausted being tense aaaallll the time?"

"Claudia." I say her name in a harsh tone. "Where are you?"

"At . . ." She is slow to complete the sentence. "The street."

"Which street?"

"The street where all the bars and clubs are." A girl makes a comment about the lights in the background, and Claudia laughs. "I tried to get into your club but I was told only VIPs are allowed. I hate you. Why do you have a club if you don't let people inside? Bad Artemis."

I stand up and collect my suit jacket from the side of my desk.

"I'm on my way. Don't leave."

She gives me an exaggerated snort. "Even when I stand still, everything keeps moving."

I've never heard or seen her that drunk. She's always in control.

"Stay there. Claudia. I'll—" She hangs up on me. I have never in my life left the building in such a hurry.

I immediately call my club's head of security. "Put tonight's doorman on the phone."

"Peter speaking, sir," the doorman answers a few seconds later.

"Peter, a red-haired girl tried to get in the bar with her friends a few minutes ago. Did you see her?"

I get into the car.

"Yes, sir. But they didn't have a pass; that's why I—"

"I know. Do you see her right now? She's still out there somewhere on the strip. Could you go look for her and bring her to the club, please? I'm on my way."

"I'll try, sir. There are a lot of people on the street now."

"All right, thank you."

I drive as fast as I can within the speed limit. The club district is not far, but there's a lot of traffic at this hour. I know I may be overreacting, and that Claudia is a woman capable of looking after herself, but I can't help it. How can I not worry when she means so much to me? I park in front of the bar and immediately spot Peter, who anticipates the question I'm about to ask.

"They're inside, sir. In the VIP section."

I let out a sigh of relief and enter the club, which is packed as usual. I climb the stairs and head to the VIP section. My shoulders relax, and I'm overcome by an immense sense of relief when I see her. Claudia is sitting between two guys who look familiar, and there's a girl next to them. Where have I seen them before?

"Iceberg!" Claudia shouts when she sees me. I move closer to them. They attempt to appear serious. "You came."

"Always, dummy."

There's a glimmer in Claudia's eyes, and she gives me the most adorable smile, making me want to kidnap her and take her away from everyone. The girl sitting with them stands up and wobbles over to me.

"I think Claudia has had a little too much to drink."

"Is that what you think?"

The guys also stand up.

"Well, well, here's the ice-cold prince you've been talking about the entire night. Time for us to leave." They grab the girl by the hand. "Let's go, Gin. Claudia will be fine."

"Will you take care of her?" Gin asks me, and I nod. She pats me on the back. "Good boy."

They leave, and I turn my attention to the drunken redhead seated a few steps away from me. Claudia is covering her mouth and giggling. "Am I in trouble?"

I sit next to her. "You have no idea."

"Do I deserve a spanking?" she asks, blushing.

"Do you want a spanking?"

"From you, I want it all."

Heat spreads over my neck and travels down my chest and abdomen. I shake my head. She's drunk.

"Let's go home."

She cups my face with her hands. "You're so handsome."

I'm unable to hold back a smile.

She pulls her hands away and runs her index finger along the contour of my face, my lips, and nose. "You being here, close to me, is enough to turn me on." She leans in to kiss me and I stand up, pulling her up with me.

"Let's go," I tell her, needing to get out before she gives me an erection right here in the middle of the lounge.

I grab her by the waist and walk her down the stairs. She stumbles several times, but I have a tight grip on her and keep her steady.

As soon as we're in the car, I put on her seat belt and drive away. She lets out a sigh. "I'm happy."

I shoot her a quick glance. Hearing her say that fills me with joy.

She gestures broadly in the air as she speaks. "I always keep everything organized, and in control. I don't drink that often. But today . . . I said . . . fuck everything. Today I woke up next to the man I have loved my entire life, and I had a good day at work. My boss even congratulated me in front of everyone. So why not get a little drunk? I'm entitled to lose control."

"I suppose you are," I tell her.

"It's exhausting," she admits, whispering. "Keeping everything under control, it's so . . . exhausting. I'm twenty years old, not forty. I've always lived my life with caution, but I'm"—her voice breaks—"so tired." She lets out a sad laugh. "So today I got drunk and didn't care if I acted like a fool. I've never acted foolishly, so what's one time in my life. Right?"

"It's nothing," I say and reach out to hold her hand. "You can do whatever you want, and I'll take care of you. You're no longer alone, Claudia. I'm here. You can lean on me and let me carry some of the burden for you."

"You're so adorable." She grabs my cheeks, giving them a squeeze before she straightens in her seat.

Upon our arrival, I realize she won't be able to walk in without making a racket. She could wake up everyone, including my mother. And that's a terrible idea. So I carry her in my arms while she keeps laughing quietly.

"What a true gentleman." She buries her face in my chest. "You smell so good."

I make it across the living room and head down the hallway leading to the guest room, because I don't think she'd like to go to bed next to her mother in this condition.

"No." She grabs my shirt. "I want to sleep with you, please. I want to wake up next to you."

Shit. This woman is going to melt my heart.

"I won't seduce you, I promise," she murmurs, and I can't help but smile.

I take her up to my room and lay her down on my bed, covering her with the sheets. She sits up, fidgeting. I can see it won't be easy to get her to settle down and fall asleep. I take off my jacket, shirt, and pants, but leave my boxers on. I walk around the bed and sit next to her. Claudia stares at my abs shamelessly.

"Claudia, my eyes are up here."

She bites her lower lip. "Can I tell you a secret?"

"Of course."

"I love your penis."

I choke and beat my chest. I'm at a loss for words, and Claudia covers her face with the pillow. I take the pillow off her face.

"Tell me more."

She shakes her head. This is more fun than I thought it would be. It appears the alcohol has removed all her filters and the self-restraint she exercises diligently. She moves closer to me, and gives me a side-hug, resting her face on my neck.

"It's always been you, Artemis. Always," she whispers. Her voice tickles against my skin. "If it wasn't for her, we would have been together a long time ago."

I furrow my eyebrows in confusion. Who is 'her'? Cristina?

"I was so happy that Fourth of July by your side. I wanted it to be the first of many Fourth of July celebrations that we would spend together."

She's bringing up something that has always puzzled me.

"You still have the small stuffed pig we won at the fair that day," I tell her, recalling what I discovered on her bedside table. "Why?"

"Because I wanted to be with you, idiot. I've always wanted to be with you."

"But you rejected me that day." It still pains me to say it.

She yawns as I wait for an explanation.

"Claudia?"

"I didn't turn you down because I wanted to. I had to."

I lean forward, and sit up straight. I cup her face with both hands and force her to look at me. "What are you talking about?"

Her eyes are half-closed. "Your mother . . ." she begins in a whisper, "she threatened me. She told me that if I didn't reject you and push you away she would kick me and my mom out of the house."

The blood boils in my veins, and I clench my jaw.

"I couldn't let that happen, Artemis. My mom and I couldn't land on the street again. You understand, don't you?"

I pull her close. Of course I understand. Her mother means everything to her, and I would never be angry that she chose her over me. I'm furious, but not with Claudia. I'm mad that she was forced to choose. The fact that my mother put her in that position turns my stomach. And now everything makes sense. I always felt that Claudia reciprocated my feelings. It was why her rejection rattled me. I didn't understand how I could be so wrong when it was blatantly obvious that she liked me. But my mother's intrusion ruined everything.

How much more are you going to destroy for us, Mother? Do you even care in the slightest about us? Tomorrow, I will make you listen to me.

Claudia sighs as she falls asleep in my arms, and I kiss the side of her head. I guess we're destined to be together, because in spite of all these obstacles, she's here in my arms, just as it was meant to be.

Twenty-nine

Act natural, Claudia. Pretend you forgot it.

CLAUDIA

A light knocking on the wood panel wakes me up. I open my eyes, expecting to find the ceiling of my room. I furrow my eyebrows when I realize it's not above me. My head is. I immediately sit up, and take stock of my surroundings.

Artemis's room? Wait. . . How did I . . . ?

"Artemis, are you in there? I'm coming in."

The sound of Apolo's voice makes me curse under my breath. I barely have time to jump out and hide behind the bed. From under the bed I watch Apolo's feet parked by the open door.

"That's strange. I thought he was here."

Apolo leaves and closes the door. I let out a long breath and stand up. However, the youngest of the Hidalgos seems to have remembered something and he finds me frozen in place when he opens the door a second time. Apolo's small brown eyes open wide, and his mouth forms the shape of a wide *O*. I clear my throat. I'm pretty sure my hair is a mess and that I look like I recently woke up.

It's obvious that I slept here—my smudged makeup and messy outfit from last night are very telling.

"Good morning." I wave to him, feeling awkward.

Apolo snaps out of his shock and runs his hand through his wet hair. He just showered, and is wearing a white shirt with a pair of jeans. He has his towel hanging around his neck.

"Good morning . . . I—" He coughs a little. "I needed to ask Artemis something."

"Aah. He must be downstairs, or maybe he already left for work."

I have no idea what the time is, but if Apolo is still here and not at school, it means that it's still early.

"Then . . . I'll go . . . downstairs."

"Okay."

"Okay."

We remain silent for a moment, and then Apolo smiles at me before he turns to leave. I pull at my hair in a dramatic gesture and fall backward on the bed. How did I end up here?

Think, Claudia. Think.

I went out with Gin, Jon, and Miguel to celebrate the great day I was having. Soon after, I had too many shots of vodka followed by a few more of tequila. And that's when my memory starts to go foggy. I make an effort to remember every detail, but anytime I recall something, the flashback is more embarrassing than the previous one. There's Artemis picking me up at his bar, then bringing me home. God, the things I said to him.

Do I deserve a spanking?

Do you want a spanking?

From you, I want it all.

Blood rushes to my cheeks. I cover my face and growl in frustration. Have I gone mad?

Can I tell you a secret? I love your penis.

How am I going to face Artemis after saying all those things to him? Even if I was being honest, those were my innermost thoughts, which I usually keep buried.

Well, it appears that it only takes a few shots of vodka and tequila to dig out those deepest thoughts. I walk out of Artemis's room, combing my hair with my fingers in an attempt to look presentable. I come face-to-face with the nurse caring for Grandpa. She's carrying a tray with breakfast for him. She raises an eyebrow, and tries to disguise a smile.

"Good morning."

"Good morning." I return the smile, and keep my head down.

Am I going to run into everyone in this house?

I hurry downstairs, praying that I won't meet anyone else. I let out a sigh of relief when I reach my bedroom. However, as soon as I open the door, I freeze. Artemis is sitting in front of my mother's bed, and he's laughing at something she's said. He's wearing one of his suits, and his hair is combed back, showcasing his finely chiseled face. My mother has a tray of food in front of her.

Did he bring her breakfast?

My heart is touched by the gesture. Maybe he planned to wake me up later but wanted to make sure that my mother had something to eat before he left for work. If that was indeed the case, how can I not love this man?

"Clau!" My mother looks at me confused. "You look like . . ."

Artemis turns his head around and glances at me over his shoulder. A slight smile forms on his lips.

"Good morning," he whispers.

"Artemis told me that you drank too much last night and that you slept in the guest room. Are you okay?"

Artemis tries to hide a smirk. God, I can't look him in the face. So I stare at my mother.

"Yes. I'm going to shower," I inform them, and close the door.

Once I'm showered and wearing fresh clothes, I head to the kitchen, where I find Artemis cleaning up the breakfast tray he brought to my mother.

Act natural, Claudia. Pretend you forgot everything.

I walk past him and pour myself a glass of ice-cold water, hoping it will help my upset stomach feel better. Why did I drink like that? Why?

"You're very quiet." The hint of amusement in Artemis's voice is hard to ignore.

I drink my water and set the glass aside. I look everywhere except at him.

"Well," he says as he approaches. I smell the scent of his cologne. "I have to go to work. Are you not going to say good-bye?"

I smile nervously at him, and he raises an eyebrow.

"Are you feeling awkward and nervous around me?" He leans over and I take a few steps back. "That's not like you, unless . . . you remember everything you said to me last night and you're embarrassed."

"I don't know what you're talking about."

Artemis purses his lips but the corners of his mouth curl upward and give him away. He's trying hard not to laugh.

"Ah, so it's a no?" He comes even closer and I take another step back until my lower back hits the table that's behind me. I'm trapped and have nowhere to run. "Shall I refresh your memory?"

"No, thank you."

He chuckles, and gently grabs my chin. The morning sunlight that streams through the window is reflected in his eyes, making his brown eyes appear a lighter shade.

"I have to go." He tilts his head to one side and closes the space between us. I melt the second his lips graze mine. Artemis kisses me softly. His lips press against mine, making my heart and breathing speed up.

I grab the jacket of his suit and kiss him back.

Artemis wraps his hands around me and pulls me closer. The kiss becomes passionate. The memory of how heavenly it feels when he's inside me makes my body temperature shoot up. I want to feel that again, all of him. We kiss as if there's no tomorrow, and the sound of our fast breathing can be heard all around the small kitchen. Artemis holds me even tighter, and I sense the evidence of his growing hardness against my waist.

"What the hell is this?" I've never moved away from someone that fast. I react by pushing Artemis hard, making him move two steps back.

Sofia Hidalgo is standing in the kitchen door, wearing one of her fitted black dresses. Her face is red, and her clenched fists are jammed on her hips. Her eyes are on me, sparking with fury. I must admit that I'm scared.

"What in the hell does this mean, Artemis?" Her question lingers in the air as she moves in my direction, looking furious. "You freeloading bitch!"

Everything is happening so fast that I barely have time to react. Suddenly, my face is forced to one side by a hard slap delivered by her hand. My cheek burns. Sofia pulls my hair and tries to drag me away, but Artemis steps between us and pulls her wrist away before she has the chance.

"No! Don't you ever lay your hands on her!" I haven't heard that cold tone in Artemis's voice in a long time.

Sofia snorts and looks indignant. "Of course you defend her. She probably has you under the spell of her young pussy, just like the conniving bitch she is."

It's my turn to push Artemis aside, and I slap Sophia across the face with all my might.

"How dare you!" She cradles her cheek with one hand. "You and your mother better pack your things and get the hell out of my house!"

"Stop it." Artemis speaks in a whisper, and I sense his rage. Artemis is one of those people who appears cool and collected before he blows up.

Sofia ignores him. "What are you waiting for? Get out! We put a roof over your head, and you had the audacity to screw around with my son. I guess when you're from the streets, it's hard to shake off the filth."

"Stop."

"Not surprisingly, with a mother like . . ."

"Damn it, shut up!" Artemis's shout is deafening. "Neither she nor her mother are going anywhere. Have you lost your mind? On what moral ground do you stand to justify this behavior?"

"What's happening here?" Mr. Juan arrives, looking alarmed. He probably heard Artemis shouting. Apolo follows closely behind, looking worried.

"Juan, she hit me!" Sofia points at me. "She's shown her true colors. She's after our son, so both she and her mother need to leave this house."

Juan remains silent, assessing the situation.

"*They* have to go?" Artemis says between clenched teeth. "Just like five years ago, Mother? When you threatened Claudia, forcing her to reject me?"

I hold my breath. Did I tell him that story when I was drunk?

"What are you talking about?" Sofia looks cornered.

"Did you know about that?" Artemis asks his father, and Juan shakes his head. Artemis goes back to staring at his mother.

"Artemis, I don't know what lies this woman has told you, but I—"

"Shut up!" His shoulders rise and fall with every breath he takes.

"I won't let you speak to me like that! I'm your mother! You have to respect me!"

"Fuck respect! You've never respected this family, my father, or my brothers. The only thing you've accomplished is fucking up this family, why?!" Artemis strides angrily toward his mother. "Why?!"

Juan steps forward. "Artemis, we need to calm down."

"No," Artemis growls; his eyes have turned red. "I can't keep quiet any longer. I can't let this go on anymore. You . . ." His voice breaks. "You've taken so much from me. It's your fault I had to take on a role I never wanted because I couldn't abandon my father, not after all he suffered because of you. And now I find out that you took away the girl I adored. What did we ever do for you to want us be so miserable?"

Sofia tightens her lips, and tears roll down her cheeks.

"I'm just saying out loud what no one in this house has dared to speak until now." He breathes heavily. "I'm simply telling the truth. Why have we never been enough for you? Why?! Why do you look to other men to fulfill you? If that's what you needed, why didn't you leave my father so that he could rebuild his life? Why did you sentence us to years of watching him consumed by pain to the point that he turned into someone so cold we don't even recognize him?"

Apolo's eyes fill with tears and he looks away. My chest grows tight. The pain and frustration is palpable in Artemis's voice. "Why, Mom?"

And right there, in front of almost all his family, two big fat tears roll down Artemis's cheeks. I've never seen him look so vulnerable. It's as if he's revealing this sadness and how difficult this experience has been for him for the first time. Juan's eyes have also reddened. He's just become aware of how much his children have suffered in silence.

"Artemis," Juan begins, but Artemis raises his hand to stop him while keeping his eyes fixed on his mother.

"Answer me!" he exclaims, wiping away his tears. "Have we ever mattered to you?"

Sofia bows her head and cries.

"Answer me!"

I move closer to him and take his arm. "Artemis."

He looks at me over his shoulder, and I can see the anger in his eyes begin to subside. It reminds me of the time when he found his mother with another man and almost beat him to death.

I grab his wrist. "Enough." I entwine my fingers with his. "It's all right. That's enough. Let's go." He shakes his head and gives me a sad smile. "Please."

I remember it clearly, as if it was yesterday. The anger radiating off him is very similar. So I bring my other hand down and interlock it with his, and return his sad smile.

"It's enough."

I take him away from there, holding hands. The silence is deafening. Not even Mrs. Hidalgo dares to protest or throw an insult at me as I walk away holding her son's hand. This morning's discussion has been a wake-up call for this family. Artemis never imagined how his words would change the course of our lives. Sometimes it takes one person to speak the truth out loud to bring about change. I stare at Artemis over my shoulder. He follows me with a sad look on his face, and squeezes my hand, looking like he's afraid of getting lost if I let go.

Thirty

Me, in love? With that iceberg?

CLAUDIA

"I want to be alone."

His request doesn't surprise me in the least. This is Artemis's reaction whenever he's going through something that's emotionally heavy.

He reacted in a similar way the day he found his mother with another man, making the exact same request after I tended to his injuries.

Leave me alone.

I guess some things don't change. Part of me wants to stay with him, hug him and whisper positive words of encouragement in his ear. But I know him better than that. He needs time alone to process everything that just happened, including what he divulged to his mother and the rest of his family.

I'm confident he'll come to me once he processes everything, just like he did a long time ago. This time won't be different. Still,

I owe him the chance to reconsider in case he's changed over the years that have passed.

We're in his father's study, so I sit next to him on the couch. "Artemis."

"No." He shakes his head and avoids looking at me.

And that's my answer. He needs to spend this time by himself, which doesn't bother me. I, too, have had moments in my life when I needed to be left alone in silence to assess things.

"Okay," I reply, standing up. "I'll be in my room." He knows he can come to me when he's ready to talk.

"I'm leaving for work in a few minutes," he informs me. "I'll see you later this evening."

The coldness in his tone doesn't surprise me, but it also doesn't please me. His cold-as-stone defensive walls tend to go up when he feels vulnerable. I don't believe he's aware he does this; it just comes naturally to him. I refrain from saying another word and walk over to the door, taking a quick glance over my shoulder. He remains seated, in his impeccable suit, with his elbows resting on his knees and his hands massaging his face. The expression he wears is a mixture of pain and rigidness. I briefly reconsider whether I should turn back and hug him, but decide to respect his wishes. After I leave the study, I run into Apolo in the living room. He's sitting on a sofa, in the same posture as his brother. He's even rubbing his face with his hands. I guess they're related after all. It breaks my heart to see his eyes red and the sadness on his face. He looks at me but doesn't say anything. I let out a sigh and sit next to him. He immediately reacts by turning to hug me.

"I had no idea," he whispers against my neck. "I didn't know the truth, I . . ."

We pull apart, and I notice the color of his eyes has been intensified by recently shed tears.

"What are you talking about?"

He twists his lips before licking them in attempt to suppress the urge to cry. "I didn't know he had suffered so much."

I understand he's speaking about Artemis.

"Apolo."

"No. I always thought he was a coldhearted idiot because he wanted complete control over my father's company. I just assumed—" He looks away. "I didn't know about the pain my own brother suffered, Claudia."

I open my mouth to say something, but he continues.

"What kind of brother am I? He's lived with this bottled-up frustration, backed my father one hundred percent, and helped him get back on his feet. And what do I do? I judge him."

"Apolo." I take his face in my hands. "You haven't done anything wrong. Please don't blame yourself for anything that's happened. This entire situation is extremely messed up and yes, it has hurt your brother in so many ways. But it's not your fault. The blame lies with other people and their terrible decisions," I say, thinking about his mother. "And you are not responsible, now or ever, for the outcomes."

"Do you think he holds a grudge against me?"

"On the contrary, I think he loves you guys so much, and you've been his greatest motivation to carry the weight of the promise he made to your father. He didn't want you or Ares to be burdened with the responsibility."

"Who told that idiot he had to sacrifice himself for us?" he asks, and I let go of his face. Apolo wipes away his tears.

"I don't know," I joke, trying to lighten the somber mood.

"He really fooled us all with his iceberg act when in reality he's too kind, almost bordering on foolish."

This makes Apolo smile. His cute little face, reddened from crying, lights up.

"He hasn't fooled us all." Apolo keeps smiling. "He hasn't fooled you. Is that why you fell in love with him?"

"Me, in love? With that iceberg?"

"I guess I understand now." He runs his hands through his hair. "I used to think you were crazy because you liked him, when all along, you were the only person who could see through him."

I stay quiet. His words register in my head because I know that what he's saying is the truth. As children, I noticed how differently Artemis would act around me from how he was with everyone else. Even before what happened with his mother, he was always reserved and unsociable. So I was always surprised by how differently he would behave in my company. Maybe his gentle and protective side switched on when I, a street child, came to live at his house. I still remember the day he found out about my nightmares and sleepwalking.

It was my second week living at the Hidalgo house when I experienced my first nightmare and walked in my sleep. I was trembling and barefoot, standing in the middle of the kitchen with tears rolling nonstop down my cheeks.

I was trying to leave the house but was stopped and woken up by Artemis, who had come down to the kitchen for a glass of milk.

He was standing in front of me, the strands of his hair pointing in all directions—messy evidence he'd just woken up. His puffy eyes gave him away. He was wearing blue onesie pajamas with a zipper down the middle. Artemis stared at me, looking as confused as I was about what had just happened. We were small, naive children who didn't know a thing about sleepwalking or night terrors. Yet, for whatever reason, he knew I needed him, and flashed me a huge smile.

"Don't cry." He took a step closer. "You're safe now."

He didn't know how much those words meant to me. As a child, it was difficult to feel safe and secure from the bad men who were after my mom, the ones who would threaten or beat me up when they couldn't find her. I wiped my tears quickly. Artemis grabbed the hood of his onesie and tugged it down until it fit snug around his head, showing two tiny cat ears on top.

"I'll protect you," he promised. "I'm Supercat."

That made me smile because it was something I didn't expect from him. During those days at the house, I had noticed he was often alone and would seldom interact with the people around him. This smiley and cheerful version of him was new to me. Maybe he instinctively knew that it was exactly what I needed.

"Supercat?" I sniffed.

He nodded.

"Yes. And I'll protect you, so don't cry anymore. Okay?"

"I don't want to close my eyes again. I'm scared."

"Do you want me to read you a story?"

I nodded, feeling shy. Anything was better than going back to sleep and having awful dreams. We went to the living room and sat on the couch. Artemis turned on a lamp and brought down blankets and pillows from a hallway closet. Once we had wrapped ourselves in the blankets, Artemis sat next to me and proceeded to read. He sounded lively and completely involved with the story. He even made up different voices for every character. I couldn't help but forget about the nightmares.

And I fell asleep right there, with my head on his shoulder. He was always there to help me deal with my nightmares. My very own superhero, my Supercat.

I'm overcome with nostalgia and a sense of gratitude that takes my breath away. I firmly believe the support Artemis showed me back when we were just a couple of kids has played a crucial part in my life. And I feel a great need to give some of it back to him. I give Apolo another hug and a kiss on the cheek.

"You're an amazing guy, okay?"

He nods. I get up and go back to the study. Artemis doesn't look up when I come in and close the door behind me. I take one of the chairs from against the wall and place it in front of him. I sit facing him, then place my hands over his and pull them down from his face. His expression still looks wounded, and I can't help but notice how handsome he looks despite his current state.

"Claudia, I told you that—"

"Hush," I interrupt him.

"What are you doing?"

My mind goes back to all those moments when he did the very same thing for me.

"Creating a space."

His eyes open slightly.

"This is your space, Artemis."

He doesn't say anything, so I carry on.

"If you want me to keep quiet and just hold your hand, I'll do that. If you want to tell me everything and talk about it, you can do that too. But I'm here for you, just like you've been here for me so many times before. You need to stop thinking that you have to deal with problems on your own. And that you and only you can carry the burden." I give his hand a squeeze. "I'm here for you."

He lets out a long breath, as if he was weighed down by something really heavy.

"I . . . never felt I had any permission to—" He stares at our intertwined hands. "To feel awful, and express my emotions. Don't ask me why. I don't really know. Maybe silence is the easier way out when you'd rather not hurt the people you love."

"It's not the best approach when some of those people are the ones hurting you."

"Yeah, but she's my mother, Claudia," he tells me with a sad smile. "I would like to say that I hate her because, as we both know, she's not a good person. But I can't. Even now, after saying all those things to her in the kitchen, all of which I know are true, I feel terrible for hurting her because I still love her very much."

"And that's okay, Artemis. You have a noble soul, and there's nothing wrong with that. But you can't keep everything to yourself forever. It's not healthy for you. Remember that this is your space—you share anything you want and I'll never bring it up ever again. We'll just pretend that it never happened. What are you feeling now, Artemis?"

And this question is the one that finally knocks down the walls guarding that place inside him where he keeps his emotions locked up. His eyes get wet, and he breathes deeply.

"I'm so tired, Claudia." His lips tremble. "I spent five years studying something that didn't interest me. I got up, went to class, and got good grades so I could assume the huge responsibility of running the company." He pauses, and his hands squeeze mine tightly. "You can't begin to imagine how incredibly difficult it is to wake up every day so I can work at a job I never wanted. I'm frustrated! And then I immediately feel terrible for thinking this way because my father needs me, and I don't want to regret the decisions I've made because he's my father and I love him."

"I get that you love him, but what about you? Your love for him shouldn't cancel out your feelings."

"I do it subconsciously. I always prioritize the people I love."

"If you can't prioritize yourself, then I will make you a priority of mine. Your well-being is the most important thing to me. It's enough, Artemis. Your father has already released you from many company obligations and responsibilities. You only have to train the person who'll replace you so you can finally be free," I tell him with a smile. "You can do whatever the hell you want, and I'll be there to make sure it happens. Okay?"

Artemis lets go of my hands and caresses my cheek. His eyes meet mine. He slowly moves in and kisses me tenderly.

It's a slow, gentle kiss loaded with emotion. I feel like my heart is stuck in my throat. I squeeze his hands, resting on my lap. His soft scruff brushes against my skin while his lips softly graze mine. He rests his forehead against mine when we break away. I slowly open my eyes and get lost in the intensity of his gaze. His voice is barely a whisper.

"For me, it's always been you." His words warm my heart. "Claudia, I love you."

And there, in his space, Artemis Hidalgo takes my breath away.

Thirty-one

Are you flirting with me, Artemis?

ARTEMIS

Claudia didn't say it back. She didn't tell me that she loved me too when I made my declaration. I didn't realize how much it meant to me for her say it back, and how badly I hoped she would.

I remember in great detail her expression, and how her small face twisted, looking surprised. And how her lips slowly parted yet not a single word came out. At that precise moment, Apolo knocked on the door to inform her that mother was asking for her. And she left, disappearing from my sight right after I had confessed that I loved her. I twirl the pen I hold in my hand. It's later in the day and I'm in my office, but I keep replaying that scene over and over in my head. A part of me is glad that my mind is preoccupied with that moment and not the argument I had with my mother.

I run my hand over my face, stroking my beard, and sigh. I glance at the paperwork in front of me. I have to take care of so many things before I leave my job. I wish it could be as easy as stop coming in one day and that's it, it's over. But since I'm CEO, I need to proceed at a slow and thoughtful pace in order for this transition to have as little impact as possible on the company's daily operations.

Though it wasn't a personal choice to work for the company, I want to make sure my decision doesn't affect my father or the rest of my family in any way. I've also developed a sense of belonging and a great respect for this company during my time here. This is my family's business, which my father built from the ground up with a lot of effort, sacrifice, and dedication. It's thanks to this place that my brothers and I have enjoyed a comfortable life and have never wanted for anything. So I have great respect for my father now and always. I pick up my phone and press a button to connect with my secretary. David promptly responds.

"Please call the chief of finance to my office."

"Yes, sir. Right away."

I can't believe I'm calling Alex. As annoying as he can be, and as hard as it is to get rid of him, we need to talk. I need to bring him up to speed with all aspects concerning the transition. Ten minutes later, I'm turning a page from a document, one of the many piled on my desk, when Alex arrives, adjusting his red tie as if the fit is too tight.

"Mr. Hidalgo," he calls in a mocking tone.

"Don't call me that."

"Why? Because it makes it sound like you're an old man?" Alex sits on the other side of my desk. He's finally loosened his tie. "Why'd you ask me to come?"

"How are preparations going?"

Alex sighs. I put down the papers, rest my elbows on the desk, and look straight at him. "What's wrong?"

"Look." Alex purses his lips. "I appreciate that you recommended me to your father for the promotion to CEO. But to be quite honest, I don't think I can do it."

"Why? Does the position not interest you?"

"It's not that. You know better than anyone that it's the last step in the corporate ladder. So it's an honor, but I don't know if I meet all the requirements for the job."

I pick up on the hesitation in his words, as well as his insecurity. Alex comes from a family of very modest means. He got a scholarship to attend university, and had to maintain high grades to stay enrolled. After he graduated, he went through a few internships in which he did a phenomenal job. The letters of recommendation were endless. He was an intern here first, then he was offered full-time employment, and quickly moved up to occupy the position of chief financial officer. Now he's financially secure and can help support his family. I still remember how he cried from happiness when he was finally able to buy a car for his mother, who'd worked hard throughout her life but couldn't afford one. I've always admired him, but I've never told him that. I don't think anyone has ever told him how inspiring he is. Hence, the self-doubt and hesitation he's showing at this crucial moment.

"Alex," I say in a serious tone, "do you think I made the recommendation to my father because you're my friend? You don't think I'm capable of keeping my friendships separate from my work relationships? Or that I would put the future of my father's company at risk just because you're my friend?"

Alex says nothing.

"I recommended you because you exceed the expectations.

Because I've never met anyone as hardworking and dedicated as you. Because you've fought your way to the top. You've also amassed a stellar employment record throughout your time here. You deserve it, Alex. This is not a promotion out of friendship. It's a promotion based on merit."

He looks uncertain, but as usual, he smiles and makes jokes to conceal his emotions.

"Are you flirting with me, Artemis?"

I smile back at him.

"No more self-doubt, okay? You're going to be the fucking CEO of this company. So start celebrating."

"Yes, sir."

"Now, let's get to work."

We begin to go over the documents on my desk. There are acquisitions, potential projects, contracts, subcontracts with other companies, partnerships, etc. The day flies while we try to cover everything; we move to the couch. There are papers everywhere—on my desk, on the small table across the couch. Our ties and suit jackets have come off.

We're interrupted by a knock on the door, and I let whoever is on the other side know it's okay to come in. It's Alex's secretary. Now that I see her up close, I notice she looks very young. She has a pink twinset on and a skirt that hits at her knees. Her hair is wavy, and loose curls fall on each side of her face. She's holding a bag in her hand.

She clears her throat. "Pardon me." She sounds nervous. "Sir." She addresses me with respect, and I smile in an attempt to calm her down. I forget how much I intimidate everyone who works here.

Alex keeps flipping through papers and doesn't look at her. "What's wrong?"

Her delicate hands have a tight grip on a bag she holds out.

"I went out on my lunch break, and I thought, well . . . I brought you lunch," she says, licking her lips. "When I called Mr. Hidalgo's secretary, he told me you hadn't eaten, so I thought . . . I hope I'm not bothering you."

I sit up straight. "What's your name?"

"Chimmy. I mean, Chantal. It's just that my friends call me . . . It's Chantal, sir."

She's adorable, and reminds me of Ares's girlfriend.

"Nice to meet you, Chantal."

Alex gives her an answer but continues to avoid her gaze.

"You can leave the lunch on the table, Chantal."

I can see the disappointment on the girl's face. "Yes, sir."

I give my best friend a cold stare, and smile at Chantal when she places the bag on the table.

"Thank you very much, Chantal. Thanks for thinking of us. It's very kind of you," I tell her genuinely.

The disappointment that marred her expression earlier fades away, and her small face lights up. "You're welcome, sir. I hope you enjoy it."

As soon as she leaves, I punch Alex on the shoulder.

"Ow!" he complains. "What was that for?"

"I thought the cold one in this duo was me."

"What did I do now?"

"Why do you treat her like that?"

Oh, the irony. I'm interrogating Alex and asking why he's cold with a girl. It's likely I see myself in him, the version that had just come back home who treated Claudia so poorly. I still regret my behavior.

"How so?" Alex seems to be unaware.

"She brought us lunch when she didn't have to. And you didn't even look at her or thank her."

"She's seeing someone."

"Huh?"

Alex sighs and slams the papers down on the table.

"Chimmy is seeing someone."

"Chimmy? I thought only her friends called her that."

"We were friends."

"You were? Alex, I don't understand."

"Or we are friends. I don't even know anymore. It's just that, I can't explain, since she started seeing that idiot, I get angry every time I see her."

Oh.

"You like her."

"No."

"Oh, you're crazy about her."

"No, Artemis. It's just—" He opens the bag and takes out his lunch. "She's always been in love with me, ever since she started working as my secretary. By pure fluke I overheard her a few times chatting with other female staff about her crush. She's always been resigned to leave it at that, and I never encouraged or misled her in any way. You know I'm not that kind of guy."

I nod and motion for him to go on talking.

"She's always been there for me, including the time when . . ." He doesn't need to mention his fiancé's infidelity. "I suppose I got used to being her everything."

"So what happened?"

"She confessed her feelings to me, and I turned her down. We remained friends, and everything was fine until . . ."

"Until she started dating someone else and you stopped being her everything."

"Exactly. It's not that I like her. Maybe I'm just being selfish."

"Alex."

"What?"

"I think, for the first time, it's my turn to give you some love advice," I tell him in disbelief. "Who would have thought! You can deny it all you want, but I think you like Chimmy. In fact, I believe it goes beyond that. It's just that you're afraid that she'll make you fall in love with her and make you vulnerable again."

"You're crazy."

"Either way, it's not right that you treat her like that just because you lack self-control. Don't be like me—you'll regret it later when you think back to the times you mistreated her. You can apologize all you want but that won't turn back time."

Alex looks at me with a concerned expression. "It sounds like this happened to you."

I let out a sigh, pull the other lunch container out of the bag, and remove the lid.

"Is everything okay?"

I'm not sure if it's because we just discussed the topic of declarations, but I go ahead and share what happened with Claudia.

"That must hurt," Alex replies, before taking a mouthful from his meal. "But look on the bright side, Artemis. At least she was honest. It's very easy to lie and say I love you without reciprocating those feelings simply because you don't want to embarrass someone. And she didn't do that."

"I thought she and I felt the same way."

"Oh, come on. After all you two have been through, don't

doubt her feelings just because she didn't say she loved you back. We're all different. And our feelings develop at our own unique paces. The time will come when she'll say it back."

"I hope so."

I'm greeted by silence and emptiness when I enter the house, and I'm glad that's the case. I don't want to have another confrontation with my parents or Apolo. In all honesty, I don't even think it's a good idea I see Claudia after my unreciprocated love declaration. Nevertheless, it's strange that the lights in the kitchen and the hallway that leads to her room are turned off. Maybe she's still at school?

I loosen my tie and climb the stairs to my room. Instead of finding it cloaked in darkness when I open the door, I notice dim candlelight. I frown as I enter and my heart tightens when I spot Claudia sitting on my bed.

At the sight of her, my body immediately feels as if it's been lit on fire. She's wearing her uniform. Her hair is styled in two braids falling on either side of her beautiful face. The top of her uniform is slightly open, and I can see the swell of her gorgeous breasts. She's hiked up her skirt, exposing her creamy thighs. The same thighs that were wrapped around me the other night. The memory alone makes my body heat rise, moving from my abdomen down to my already hardened member. I haven't even touched her, and I already feel like I'm about to come in my pants, like a novice teenage boy. I swallow with difficulty and lock the door behind me. And she shoots me a naughty smile when I turn around.

"Welcome home, sir."

Thirty-two

You're very sexy, Artemis Hidalgo.

ARTEMIS

Get a grip, Artemis.

I need to scold myself when I see her on my bed wearing the uniform I've fantasized about on more occasions than I care to admit.

She stands up and gives me a naughty smile. She's so fucking sexy. I hold my fists clenched to my sides to prevent myself from jumping her like a brute. Claudia moves closer and stops right in front of me. She reaches out to grab my tie, and bites her lip before she speaks.

"Are you tired, sir?" I'm only able to nod, and her smile widens. "What can I do to help you relax?"

She pulls me by my tie and guides me to the bed, then pushes me down gently until I land sitting on the mattress. She stands in front of me. My eyes travel to her legs and move up to the tops of her stockings. I reach out to touch them but she slaps my hands off.

"No. I'm the one in control now, sir."

"Okay," I breathe.

She first removes my tie, then my suit jacket. She bends down to unbutton my shirt, granting me a perfect view of the valley between her breasts, and I lick my lips. I don't know what I've done to deserve this woman standing before me, but I'm not complaining. I'm already hard and she's only removed a few pieces of clothing. Her slow movements and the sensual way she's doing everything are driving me crazy. I pay attention to every detail about her uniform, her skin, and every curve and swell of her body.

I'm left in my boxers after she takes off my shoes and pants. She picks up my clothes and places them on the chair next to my bed. She bends on purpose, allowing me to see the skimpy black underwear she's wearing under her short skirt. I feel like I'm going to burst.

"Claudia . . ." I'm not sure if she can hear the desperation in my voice, but I try nevertheless. She straightens and is once again standing in front of me.

"What would you like, sir?"

"You."

"Oh, would sir like to touch me?" She takes my hand and guides it to her breasts, letting me brush against them for a brief moment, which feels heavenly until she removes it. I protest with a grunt. She brings my hand down between her legs, and I can feel through her stockings that she's wet. A sigh escapes my lips. "Would sir like to fuck me?"

Before I can say anything, she moves my hand away and pushes on my chest, forcing me to lie back. She brings her legs on either side of my hips and straddles me. I'm dying to touch her, to ravage her from head to toe. But this time she's in control, and I restrain myself. However, I don't know much longer I can hold back. She leans forward and fixes her eyes on mine. Then she tilts her head, gets closer to my mouth, and moves in for a kiss. I groan when I kiss her back desperately and urgently. I'm starving for her and brimming with desire. Our breathing becomes faster. We kiss with passion and urgency. It's the kind of kiss that can only happen in the privacy of my room, and not in public. She starts to gyrate on me, and I stifle a groan in response to the sensation of her inner thigh and crotch rubbing on me. I raise my hands in an attempt to touch her but she grabs them and brings them down, taking her mouth off mine.

"No, sir."

"I'm on the verge."

She sits up straight on top of me, then runs her hands over my chest and down to my abdomen.

"You are very sexy, Artemis Hidalgo."

"Thank you. You're beyond sexy, and I'm two seconds away from losing my self-restraint and fucking you senseless."

"It's too bad I'm in charge. Right, sir?" She begins to undo the top buttons of her uniform and I stop breathing. It feels hot in here.

With each button she releases, she reveals more of her breasts.

She stops at her waist and opens the shirt of her uniform, presenting beautiful breasts contained in a black bra that brings out the color of her skin.

She is beautiful, and she knows it. The confidence she exudes as she puts her body on display is thrilling. There is no hesitation, no shame, just power and self-confidence in her gestures and expressions. She takes my hands and puts them on her breasts, allowing me to give them a light squeeze that fuels my desire even more. Though I'm having a hard time tolerating this slow torture, I trust our coupling will be even more explosive once it finally happens. She keeps moving on top of me while I caress her breasts. She bites her lower lip and moans softly. I can feel the heat from her crotch. I can only imagine how wet she must be and how good it will feel when I finally penetrate her.

"You are so hard, sir." Her voice is fueled by desire, and lights my whole body on fire.

My member becomes harder when she pulls down the straps of her bra and bares her breasts to me. My hands make direct contact, and I groan in response to the sensation. My thumbs start working on her pert nipples, making her throw her head back and eliciting a much louder moan. Her swiveling movements on my lap are becoming more rapid and unruly.

"Claudia, I don't think I can take it anymore, I—"

She puts her finger to my lips. "Silence."

She removes my hands from her breasts and stands up. She pulls her undergarments down and steps out of them. She keeps her skirt on and grabs the elastic band of my boxers. She takes them off and exposes me to her.

She straddles me one more time. And the skin-to-warm-skin contact prompts me to grab hold of her hips to anchor me, praying I can control myself.

"Ah, Claudia."

She uses her wetness to lubricate her grinding movements, forward and backward. My grip on her hips tightens. I need to be inside her now. Not having control is driving me crazy.

"I want you inside me, sir," she whispers and slides slightly off me. I hold my breath as I watch her guide my member toward her entrance. "Ah." She moans, and I close my eyes as she completely encases me. She feels warm, soft, and wet inside; the sensation leaves me speechless.

This feels like fucking paradise.

Claudia slowly gyrates, tantalizing me and intensifying the sensation and my arousal. Her moans match the rhythm of her movements. The torture she's put me through is close to taking its toll and I may just come from all of this. But I fight hard to suppress the urge to lose myself.

"God, this is unbelievable," I murmur. She leans forward, and her breasts are dangerously close to my face. I don't hesitate and proceed to ravage them. I lick them, kiss them, and suck on them. The way she's shuddering is a clear sign that she's enjoying it.

"Yes. Artemis. God." She's lost control and her movements have picked up the pace. The sound created by the friction of our intimate parts echoes throughout the room, and it intermingles with loud moans of pleasure. "I'm going . . . to . . . Oh, god."

I can tell she's close to reaching orgasm and I kiss her. I move my hands down to her ass and squeeze it. I jerk my hips upward, burying myself deeper inside her. Claudia gasps into my mouth. She shudders and trembles. She's lost in the throes of her impending orgasm and I feel her pulsations on my member. She's getting wetter, and I know I won't be able to hold back much longer.

Her pace becomes fierce, and the sound of our bodies coming together gets even louder and more primal.

"Ohh, Claudia. I'm going to come if you keep moving like that," I admit, doubting my ability to resist the urge.

"Do it. I want to feel it." The warmth coming from her rapid breaths is driving me crazy. "Artemis, I want to feel you come inside me."

And that's all I need to hear to reach my climax. I tighten my grip on her ass, moan, and let myself go. Claudia drops on top of me and our breathing is ragged. I can feel her heart erratically beating, much like mine. She peels herself off me, and falls to my side. We lie on our backs, stare at the ceiling, and try to recover the ability to speak following the most incredible sexual encounter. My hand finds hers and gives it a light squeeze. I try to find a compliment that will do justice to how amazing this was, but my mind fails me.

"I may just take control more often." She breaks the silence, and I turn to look at her.

"As many times as you want."

She smiles at me. The dim yellow light coming from the candles illuminates her bare skin, and I'm moved by the need to repeat the words again.

I love you.

But I hold back. I don't want to put her on the spot. The last thing I want is to make her feel uncomfortable. Seeing her lying here naked next to me, with a bright smile that lights up her face, makes me realize how much I love everything about her. What began as affection between children who protected and looked after each other has evolved into a growing attraction that has culminated in the feelings I have for her today. Feelings so overwhelming they terrify me.

"What are you thinking about?" she asks, as her hand cups my cheek.

How much you mean to me. That I love you, and I'd like to shout it from the mountaintops. And that the intensity of what I'm feeling frightens me.

"What do you think?" I conceal my thoughts with a provocative smile.

She laughs, and I stare at her like a fool in love.

"I guess sir enjoyed his surprise." She winks at me.

"Call me sir again, and I'll screw you again."

"Oh, I'm scared!" she teases me, and I climb on top of her.

Our warm, naked bodies fit each other to perfection.

"You should be afraid of me," I tell her before kissing her softly, enjoying the taste of her lips and slowly savoring the way they feel. Claudia takes my lower lip between her teeth and smiles.

"I'm terrified."

I keep kissing her. The rubbing of our wet lips intensifies little by little. Her breathing accelerates. I rest one hand on the mattress while I caress her breasts with the other.

"Artemis." She moans against my lips, and I know I've got her where I want her.

"Spread your legs for sir," I order, teasing her.

She obeys, and gives herself to me all over again with unbridled passion. And though she still hasn't said she loves me, I feel love in every kiss, in each caress, in every glance—and that's more than enough.

Thirty-three

I did something stupid.

CLAUDIA

I've never been a sound sleeper.

I blame it on all those restless nights from my childhood, back when I was always on alert in case something might happen. And now the smallest sound wakes me up, like the beep from a notification on my phone.

I ignore the first message because I'm wrapped in Artemis's arms, who sleeps soundly behind me. I don't want to move. But I open my eyes to look at my phone on the nightstand when it beeps for a second time, then a third, and a fourth. The alarm clock next to it indicates it's 3:45 a.m.

Who is texting me at this hour?

I carefully extend my hand and grab my phone. I look at the screen, which is lit up with notifications. It's Daniel. I scowl as I read his messages.

3:40

Daniel: Claudia, I miss you.

3:41

Daniel: I'm drunk and I can't stop thinking about you.

Daniel: I did something stupid.

3:42

Daniel: I need to see you, please.

Daniel: Just once.

And it's the last message that brings my breathing to a complete stop.

3:44

Daniel: I'm in front of your house.

Daniel: I'm not leaving until I see you.

Shit!

Artemis squirms behind me. I lower my phone and bury it under a pillow so that the light coming from the screen doesn't wake him up.

Okay, Claudia. You need to think of the best way to handle this situation. Or it's going to spiral out of control in too many directions.

I doubt there's a right way. I entertain the option of not going out to meet him and shutting off my phone, hoping he'll get tired of waiting. But I know Daniel, and when he's drunk he tends to fall asleep wherever he happens to be. Besides, I'm not so heartless as to abandon him to Fortune's mercy when I don't even know how he got here. What if he drove? There's no way I can let him leave on his own. Argh! I had a feeling that sleeping with him one last time was a terrible idea. I knew he had feelings for me, and I shouldn't have taken advantage of him.

I carefully untangle Artemis's arms from my waist and get out of bed. I steal a brief glance at him lying naked. The moonlight streaming through the window illuminates the muscles of his back. His hand is outstretched, reaching to my side as if he's searching for me in his sleep.

Artemis Hidalgo.

My iceberg.

I don't want anything to ruin this, especially not a misunderstanding. I know that if I wake him up to help me with Daniel, he won't understand and will become jealous, and god knows what he'll do. Artemis can be very impulsive. He punched his own brother when he found out what happened between us. I can't begin to imagine what he would to Daniel, even though what we had is in the past. I whisper a curse when I realize that the maid's uniform is the only thing I have to wear. I quickly tie my hair up in a ponytail, put on my uniform, and quietly exit the room.

I carefully walk down the stairs and hurry to the front door under the cover of darkness. I deactivate the alarm next to the door before I open it and step outside. The night breeze makes me shiver but I don't let it bother me. And sure enough, Daniel is sitting on the steps of the small staircase at the entrance. He rests his head against a post, and his car is badly parked out front. The door is open. Dear god. How did he manage to get here in one piece?

"Daniel," I say firmly.

He lifts his head and turns to look at me. I can tell his eyes are red; so are his nose and cheeks. He's very drunk and has been crying, which makes me feel terrible. It was never my intention to hurt someone like this.

"Hi, baby," he says with a sad smile.

"What are you doing here? It's almost four in the morning, Daniel." I walk down the stairs to face him. He remains seated; I doubt he's able to stand.

"I needed to see you," he says softly. "I miss you. Why can't I get you out of my head?"

"Daniel . . ."

"I've never felt this way about anyone before, Claudia. No one. Please give me a chance."

"Daniel, I was very clear with you right from the start. I—"

"Yes, yes, yes. It was just fucking—no strings attached. I know. But other girls who've said the same thing to me before, they've always wanted more. I thought that you wanted more too."

I shake my head. "It was just sex, Daniel. To me, it was always just that."

His eyes are watery, and he licks his lips.

"Fuck me, it's just my luck that I would fall in love with the one girl who actually honors her end of the no strings attached bargain." He lets out a sarcastic chuckle.

"You can't do this. You can't show up at my house like this. It's not okay. You need to go."

He stands up and staggers toward me. "I love you, Claudia," he says with tears in his eyes.

There's something about that phrase, and those three words that doesn't sit well with me.

"No. You're just obsessed with me because you can't have me, because I haven't fallen in love with you like all the other girls you've been with. You still don't know what true love is."

"And you do?"

I remain silent.

"Are you with someone? Who is it? Is he better than me?"

"Daniel . . ."

"Answer me!" he shouts in my face, and I take a step back.

"Daniel, lower your voice."

"No, tell me who it is."

"That's none of your business."

"So there is someone."

I don't want to tell him anything that may hurt him even more, but my patience is wearing thin. He stretches his hand toward my face, and I take one more step back.

"You're so beautiful."

"Daniel, I'll call you a cab. You can't drive in this state."

"Are you worried about me?"

I comb through the pockets of my maid's outfit, searching for my cell phone. And when I can't find it, alarm bells go off in my head. I've left it in the room.

"Daniel, please tell me you didn't send any more texts after that last one telling me you were in front of my house."

He scrunches his eyebrows, as if he's thinking.

"I sent you one more, and called you after, but you didn't answer."

Oh god. I hope it didn't wake Artemis up.

"Daniel, you have to get out of here. Give me your phone, I'll call you a cab." He reluctantly gives me his cell and I call a cab that will be here in ten minutes.

I give Daniel his phone back, and quickly look back at the main door of the house, which remains closed. Good. He hasn't woken up. If he had, he would have been out that door in a hell of a hurry, exploding with rage after seeing those texts. Daniel takes advantage of my distraction to move closer and grab both of my arms. He's quite strong for someone who's this drunk. He leans his face forward in an attempt to kiss me, but I turn my head and push him away.

"You haven't listened to me at all!" I tell him, boiling with anger. "I don't want anything to do with you. Nothing. Daniel, please go on with your life and leave me alone."

"Just one kiss good-bye," he begs me.

I laugh. "No way. You've lost your mind."

The cab arrives and I help him get in.

"I'll keep the keys to your car. Tomorrow you can come by and get them. This has to be the last time you do something like this, Daniel. Next time, I'll call the police."

He nods before closing the door, and I watch the cab pull away and disappear down the road. I make my way back inside the silence and darkness of the house and head upstairs, relieved that that didn't end up being as bad as I expected.

I open the door to Artemis's bedroom and the first thing I pick up is the dim light coming from one corner in the room. My heart accelerates when I notice that his bed is empty.

I rest my back against the closed door behind me, and my eyes find Artemis's eyes. And that's when I stop breathing. He's shirtless, has a pair of pajama pants on, and is sitting on a chair next to the window. His hair is messy and the expression on his face is so blank it gives me the chills. I notice he's holding a tablet in his hands. He turns it around to show me.

There are black-and-white screenshots from the security camera at the front of the house. He's watched everything. To make things worse, these cameras record without sound. Which means he was only able to watch me talking with Daniel at four o'clock in the morning right after he sent those revealing texts. *It's just a misunderstanding. Just choose your words wisely.* My throat tightens when I look into his eyes, while he waits for an explanation. His shoulders and arms are tense, making the outlines of his muscles more pronounced.

"Are you going to tell me what's going on?" he asks, tossing the tablet on the bed.

"It's not what it seems." I hate this clichéd response overused by liars and honest people alike. "He was drunk and I didn't want him to drive home in that state."

"Did you fuck him?"

"What does that have to do with—"

"Did you fuck him?" He stands up. "Oh wait, let me read you his last message: 'I can still remember what it feels like to be inside you.'" The rage that his body language is giving off intensifies.

"My past sex life has nothing to do with you."

"Yes, it does, when my girlfriend slips out in the middle of the night to meet up with a guy she's fucked. Have you continued to see him?"

"No, of course not. This happened before you and I started seeing each other."

"I don't want you to see him again. And I want you to block him on your phone."

That makes me raise an eyebrow. "Who are you to tell me what to do?"

"Do you want to keep on seeing him?"

"No. Absolutely not. But I'm the one who decides what to do with the people in my life."

That makes him angrier. He knows he has no power over me. I have been and always will be independent.

"Listen to me. I'm sorry. Tonight, I didn't handle the situation in the best way. But I knew you would be angry, and I wanted to save you the aggravation. I just wanted to send him home in one piece."

Artemis turns his back to me and runs his hand over his head. And I honestly don't know what the hell is wrong with me, but seeing him angry and jealous is turning me on. The way his muscles are flexing, the displeasure in his eyes, the tension in his jaw and neck. I want him to use that rage to fuck me with everything he's got. I shake my head, reacting to my fantasies. Sex with him has clearly done a number on me. He still has his back turned, so I make the first move. I wrap my arms around his waist and rest my cheek on his back. I can hear the beats of his heart and the loud breath he lets out in frustration.

"Do you know how close I was to coming out and beating him to a pulp?" he confesses, confirming what I already knew. "But I held back. I know how much you hate violence. I thought of you, even after seeing you talking to another man in front of the house. And that's because I'm madly in love with you."

I plant a kiss on his back. My hands travel down his firm abdomen and slide inside his pajama pants. Artemis is caught by surprise and tenses.

"I've been a bad girl," I whisper against his back. "Why don't you fuck me to get rid of your anger?" I move my hand up and down, and he lets out a sigh.

"If you think sex is going to solve this . . ." He turns to face me, and pulls my hands out of his pants. The desire in his eyes gives him away. "You are absolutely right."

And he kisses me desperately, pressing my body against his with passion. He pushes me backward until my lower back comes in contact with the desk. He picks me up by my thighs and places me on its surface.

He positions himself between my legs, one hand holding me by the waist while the other rips my underwear off. His lips move aggressively, almost with rage, against mine. And I'm enjoying it. I enjoy everything about this man. We kiss each other madly. I slide my fingers to the waistband of his pajama pants and drag them down in one swift pull. I let out a moan when I feel his erection graze my inner thigh, and he's barely started. He stops kissing me and his eyes search mine.

"I love you," he tells me, and kisses me. And before I have the chance to say a word, he enters me in one single thrust.

And right here, against this desk, we make up over a round of angry sex that brings out our wildest and most wicked urges. And though I have not given him my answer with words, I finally have one. Yes, I do know what love is. And it has been by my side, all my life.

Thirty-four

We've met before. Haven't we, Claudia?

CLAUDIA

I love you.

Three simple words. Why can't I say them? Why do they get stuck in my throat every time I try? What's stopping me? I explore deep inside my head and in my heart, looking for a reason and a logical explanation. Am I not in love with him? No, it's not that. Artemis has always been the love of my life, and occupies a place in my heart. Even when I refused to admit it all those years ago. So then, what is it?

I love you. Please forgive me, Martha. I was drunk, I won't do it again. I swear on the love we have. I love you.

As a child, those were my father's words after he would hit my mother. The constant use of I-love-yous between other proclamations. At my tender age, as time went on and the beatings persisted, I learned that those I-love-yous were lies and meant nothing. We never hurt the ones we love.

After we ran away from my father and ended up on the street, my mother met other men while we squatted in abandoned caravans and condemned buildings. These men promised her a better life and many other things if she worked for them, trading sex for money while giving them a cut of what she earned. That was when I heard those words again. *I love you, Martha*. And again, they were just lies.

It seemed, to me, that those words were often used as tools by people who wished to manipulate and justify keeping someone tied to one place until they delivered their next blow.

Perhaps in my subconscious those words still have a bitter taste. Even if they're just words, they trigger an unpleasant sensation in me when I'm about to say them. Which is the opposite reaction I have when Artemis says them. All I feel is a reassuring warmth in my heart when I hear him say those words while looking at me with his chocolate-brown eyes filled with emotion.

Am I totally screwed up because I'm incapable of saying a sincere and honest I-love-you the way he does? An I-love-you that's not tied to negative memories from my past? Just a genuine and pure I-love-you? I don't want to say the words just for the sake of saying them. I guess I need time.

"Claudia?" Kelly, the other intern at the company, calls my name. "Are you listening to me?"

"Sure, sure." She frowns a little but lets it go.

"I was just telling you that Carl loved your marketing proposal for the next project."

"Really?" I say, holding a hand to my chest. Carl is the right-hand man for my boss, Mrs. Marks. I spent several nights doing market research and devising the perfect strategy to promote the company's new condo development, which will kick off construction in the coming months.

"I have to admit, I'm envious. I'm pretty sure it'll be chosen during this afternoon's meeting. They're going to let us sit in so we can watch and listen."

"I have to get ready," I tell her, and get up to go to the bathroom to fix my makeup. If they choose my proposal, I'm sure they'll have questions to ask, so I should make myself presentable. I need to hide these huge circles under my eyes, which will be worth the trouble if my idea is chosen. I hope it will be my first project.

I look in the mirror and give myself words of encouragement.

"You can do this. Hard work does pay off."

I walk out of the washroom and stop dead in my tracks when I see him. You have to be fucking kidding me. It's Alex. The man I almost kissed the night I went to Artemis's club. At least he disappeared before anything could happen.

He's wearing a light-blue suit and no company identification, unlike the majority of the staff, which means he's likely the head of a department. This is too much of a coincidence. I turn around and I'm about to go back into the washroom when Carl calls to me and ruins everything.

"Claudia!"

I press my lips together and begrudgingly turn around to face Alex, who greets me with a handshake and doesn't appear at all surprised to see me here. Carl introduces us. "The chief financial officer is paying us a visit today. Sir, this is—"

"We've already met. Haven't we, Claudia?" The playful tone in his voice does not go unnoticed. Carl gives us a puzzled look.

"How do you know each other?" Carl can't help but ask and I sigh, feeling uncomfortable.

Well, you see, Carl, we almost kissed but he disappeared before things went any further.

“From hanging around,” Alex replies.

“Carl!” Mrs. Marks calls him to her office. Carl excuses himself and rushes off, leaving us alone. Before this gets more awkward, I decide to clear things up. But he beats me to the punch.

“There’s no need to worry. Artemis is my best friend.”

“What?” I didn’t expect that.

He smiles at me. “That night at the club, I left as soon as I realized you were the girl my best friend has been pining for his entire life. I was also the one who called him to come get you.”

I take it all in. That’s why Artemis arrived out of the blue. Now everything makes sense.

“I have to say, I’m glad your friend interrupted us and told me your name. I don’t think Artemis would have ever forgiven me if I’d made out with you.”

Well. It’s a small world, and it certainly loves to put me in strange situations. Although there’s nothing strange about Artemis’s friend hanging out at his club.

“Let’s start over again,” he says. “Nice to meet you, Claudia. I’m Alex.”

“Nice to meet you.” I smile at him, but the smile fades when I immediately realize this could have other implications.

If Alex knows I work here, and he’s Artemis’s best friend . . . could it be possible that Artemis knows? I sincerely hope not.

“What’s wrong? You look pale.”

“Does Artemis know I work here?”

Alex is momentarily taken aback by the question, yet the guilt I spot in his eyes is a dead giveaway.

"He won't meddle in any way, shape, or form," he reassures me with an easy smile. "He promised."

That little liar. He's known all along and has been playing dumb. Oh, Artemis Hidalgo.

"Well, I'll let you get back to work. It was nice meeting you, Claudia." He waves good-bye, and I let out a long breath.

"Excellent proposal, Carl!" exclaims Mrs. Marks after Carl is done presenting my idea. I lick my lips and feel nervous because I know he'll soon call my name. Everyone is clapping and I stare at him with anticipation. But Carl says, "Thank you. Thank you. It was an idea that came to me out of the blue."

My mouth opens, and my heart drops. He's talking about the idea as if it was his, and getting all the credit, when I was the one who stayed up nights working on it.

"Wow. You've really impressed me this time, Carl," adds Mrs. Marks. I forget how to breathe. It's unbelievable. Next to me, Kelly looks tense. The meeting comes to an end and people start to make their way out.

I wasn't expecting this at all. I'm paralyzed with disbelief for a few seconds. And then I snap out of it just before everyone heads for the door, and I stand up.

"Excuse me, I have something to say." Everyone stops and looks surprised that the new intern is speaking up when we're only there to watch and listen. "This idea—"

"Claudia." Carl cuts me off. "You are only here to watch. Please abstain from sharing your opinions."

"It's not an opinion, I—"

Kelly takes my hand and gives it a tight squeeze and then whispers to me.

"Don't do it. If you confront him in front of everyone he could fire you."

I bite my tongue because I know she's right.

Everyone else leaves when I remain quiet. Carl gives me a smile as he walks by on his way out.

"Goddamn bloodsucking thief!" I bang my forehead against the desk. "How could he do that? How could he shamelessly take my idea? He didn't even hesitate for a second."

"I know," Kelly agrees. "I guess that's the way things work here. The higher-ups take advantage of the newbies to further their careers and make an impression."

"It shouldn't be that way."

"Tell me about it. Carl stole my campaign idea for a commercial mall the company is building next year. He presented it as his own last week." Kelly takes a sip of coffee. "I didn't find out until I was given copies of the proposal and noticed that it included my idea. It was a punch in the gut, so I know exactly how you feel."

"Is there anything we can do?"

"Complain? To our boss? Carl's her favorite."

"She has to have a boss, doesn't she?"

"She's the department head. Her boss is the CEO." She snorts. "As if we could talk to the head of the company."

Artemis. I bite my lower lip, thinking. And then I shake my head. I'll find a solution on my own first. I get up and make my way to Carl's office. He looks annoyed when he sees me.

"Yes?"

"Why didn't you give me credit for my idea? It's not fair, and—"

"Claudia, you're an intern. Your duties don't include developing entire campaigns for the company. I made the decision to use your idea and develop it. You should be flattered."

"It's my idea."

"No one is saying anything to the contrary."

"Then why did you tell everyone it was your idea at the meeting?"

He sighs, stands up, and slips his hands into the pockets of his pants.

"What were you looking for? An ego boost? If I had presented the idea as yours it would have sat on your desk collecting dust. As I said, introducing new projects is not part of your job description. No one would have paid any attention to your proposal."

Anger speeds through my veins. No matter how elaborate his explanation or excuse is, it doesn't change the fact that what he did was wrong.

"I want you to tell Mrs. Marks the truth, and I would like a chance to take the lead on the development of my proposal."

He snorts and laughs. "And what if I don't?"

"I'll tell her myself."

"Okay, go ahead." He shrugs. "It's the word of a new intern against mine. Go on, run along and let her know. But one thing is certain, I'll make sure you're not hired once you complete your internship."

"You're an idiot," I tell him before I leave his office and head to see Mrs. Marks. She's on a call when I arrive, and I have to wait for a few minutes before she can see me.

After I finish telling her everything, she says, "Oh, Claudia. I had no idea. Unfortunately, even if it was your idea, Carl is right. As an intern, I can't assign you the responsibility to lead a project of this magnitude. He has more expertise to flesh out a concept like yours. But I'll make sure that you get some credit at the next meeting for the idea, okay?"

"I—" I actually don't know what to say.

"I'm a little busy. So could you please go back to your desk?"

That didn't end as I had hoped it would, but at least I didn't stay quiet.

Kelly takes out her lunch bag and opens it when it's time for our break. The smell of bacon hits my nose, and while I've never been overly sensitive to smells, I can't help but grimace with disgust when she's not looking at me. I discreetly cover my mouth and get up from my chair. I come around my desk and head to the washroom. I have the urge to vomit.

"Clau?" I hear her voice, calling me from behind.

"Washroom," I murmur before I disappear down the hallway. I hurry into one of the stalls and lean over a toilet to empty the light breakfast I ate this morning. How disgusting is this?

I turn around and rest my back against the stall. What's wrong with me? This is the second or third time I've thrown up this week, and I'm getting scared.

My stomach gets upset when I'm about to get my period. But I've never vomited.

And I can't be pregnant. I started taking the pill six months ago to help regulate my hormones. I would have never allowed Artemis to finish inside me if I wasn't taking a contraceptive. I'm not an idiot.

So then what's happening to me?

Could it be the stress of the new job? Maybe all the years of working full-time while studying part-time are finally taking a toll on my body.

I come out of the bathroom feeling a little dizzy. Unfortunately, I find myself face-to-face with Carl. He's the last person I want to see at this moment.

"Oh my, Claudia. You look pale. Are you all right?"

"Don't worry about me." I walk past him, heading back to the desk I share with Kelly. But the nausea returns the moment I spot her still eating, so I walk by.

"I'm going out for some air," I inform a disconcerted Kelly.

I instantly feel better when the fresh air hits my face. Perhaps it was the tension of the work environment in the office. I find a bench and sit down. I stretch out my arms and lean back. I try to see all the way up to the top of the Hidalgo Enterprises building.

Artemis, you're probably up there busy working, wearing your fine suit, giving off that icy detached vibe that fools the rest of the world into believing you're not warm and don't possess a gigantic heart.

I'm still looking up when a shadow moves in, blocking my view. I lower my gaze to the person standing right in front of me.

It's Artemis. Mr. CEO of this giant company. My heart starts to beat faster and my lips slowly curve up to form a smile. He has the gift of making me feel safe when I'm not feeling well. Yet he's not smiling; his expression looks serious, and I can read worry in his brown eyes.

"Are you okay?" His voice calms me.

"Yes, I just needed some air."

"You look very pale." He extends his hand to gently caress my cheek, and the gesture makes me briefly forget where we are.

"You're freezing, do you want me to take you home?"

I take his hand in mine, and take it off my face.

"I'll be fine."

"Claudia."

"Artemis," I reply playfully. But he's not playing along, and looks worried. "I'm fine, besides, I only have a few hours left before I finish for the day."

"Don't worry about it. You don't have to work like that, I'll—"

"Artemis, I'm okay."

He twists his lips and sits down next to me. Our hands are intertwined. I remember that we're sitting right outside the company building, and I move my hands away. He arches an eyebrow. "Does it bother you if someone sees you with me?"

"No." I shake my head. "But this is my place of work and I think if people see us together it'll create complications. Haven't you heard about sexual harassment in the workplace?"

He points to himself. "Are you accusing me of something?"

"I'm just kidding. Still, it's not good for us to be seen together," I tell him in all honesty. "When we're not at work, it's a different story."

"Stop trying to seduce me, Claudia. I innocently approached you to make sure you were okay, and you come up with this."

"You? Innocent?"

He rolls his eyes.

"I am." He leans back next to me. "I was a lonely iceberg until a fire girl came along and melted me, robbing me of my innocence."

I laugh and lightly punch him on his shoulder. "I really missed your overly dramatic takes."

I'm hit by a wave of nostalgia, and think back to all those times Artemis would come up with creative and overly dramatic lines to justify himself as the victim. I stare at him like a fool. There, in the light of day, I examine every detail of his face—his light beard and the tiny wrinkle that forms between his eyebrows—when he catches me staring.

"What?"

"Nothing."

I arrive at the realization that when the moment is right, I'll tell him exactly how I feel about him. And that it doesn't matter that he's already made his declaration while I haven't. What binds us together is stronger and more resilient, beyond what anyone could ever imagine.

In spite of what happened this morning with Carl, Mrs. Marks, and the discomfort I feel, I'm very happy right now here in the company of the man I used to call Supercat when I was a little girl because he was going to protect me against all evil. I want to stay like this for the rest of the day. However, life has a way of complicating things when we least expect it, which in this case, is the moment right after I stand up, when I become dizzy, faint, and end up in the hospital.

Thirty-five

You had me worried!

CLAUDIA

A very bright white light is the very first thing I see when I wake up. I blink in discomfort, trying to adjust to the intensity. The blurriness in my vision starts to wear off, and a white ceiling lamp I don't recognize comes into focus. What happened? Where am I? I'm assailed by a sudden wave of dizziness as I try to organize my thoughts. I remember I was at the company, there was a meeting, and Carl stole my idea, there was Alex, I threw up, I went outside to get some fresh air, and ran into Artemis. Then I stood up and . . . and? It all went dark. Did I faint? I cough a little, and look over to my side. I'm lying in a hospital bed and my left arm is hooked up to an IV.

"Claudia?" I hear Gin's voice coming from the other side of the room. I turn my head in the direction of her voice. "Oh, thank god. You're awake. I came as soon as I heard."

She gets up from a couch with an expression of deep concern.

"You had me worried!" She comes to my side and takes my hand. "How do you feel?"

I wet my parched lips before I speak. "I'm fine."

"Come on, please don't give me this bullshit about being fine, that nothing's wrong. That's what landed you in the hospital and looking like this!"

"Gin . . ."

"No, Gin nothing. I have to go and tell the doctor that you're awake. And you better follow his orders so you can get better."

Gin can tell by the look in my eyes the question I want to ask. "Artemis has gone to get some food," she says. "The doctor suggested you should have something healthy to eat when you wake up."

"Is he all right?" I ask, because I know him. Artemis has never done well at hospitals, and had difficulty handling situations in the past when I was sick.

"Are you seriously worrying about him now?" Gin raises an eyebrow. "I'm sorry, but who's the one lying in a hospital bed?"

"I just know that he worries too much."

"And no wonder. Girl, what did you expect? You fainted in his arms."

I grimace as I move my left arm. There's a burning sensation where the IV is inserted.

"Please tell me you haven't called my mother. I don't want her to be worried."

Gin snorts. "Look at you worried about everyone else." She sighs. "Calm down. We didn't tell your mother."

"What happened to me? What did the doctor say?"

"Well, not much. They're doing several blood tests, though he suspects it could be anemia, perhaps a nutritional deficiency or something along those lines. That's all he's said. Have you been skipping meals and not eating?"

"Of course I'm eating. I've had a couple of stressful weeks, that's all."

"Claudia, you can lie to me all you want but you have to be honest with the doctor. If you're not having your meals on time or are skipping them altogether, or if you're not eating enough to save time during the day, you have to let him know."

I don't respond, and she goes to find the doctor. Dr. Brooks is a significantly older man, with white hair and thick eyebrows of the same color. He gives me a reassuring smile, typical of doctors in these situations.

"Hello, Claudia, I'm Dr. Brooks. How are you feeling?"

"A little weak and confused," I confess.

"I have your test results." He reviews the papers on the clipboard he holds in his hands. "I'm sorry, but in keeping with patient confidentiality, I must ask first if you agree to have your friend present while I share your diagnosis and the results from the tests?"

"Yes."

Gin stands next to me and takes my hand. Fear spreads through me, and I'm grateful she's here. What if this is something serious? What if I'm really sick?

"All right, then." The doctor looks at the results. "Okay, Claudia, it appears I was right. Your iron is very low. Anemia is not a big deal since we can treat it once we zero in on the cause, which we have."

A sigh of relief escapes my lips. "What was the cause?" I go over in my head the instances when I've eaten in a hurry or skipped a meal. It doesn't happen often, but I should really pay more attention to my health and listen to my body.

The doctor smiles at me. "You're pregnant."

And right at that moment, my world comes to a complete stop. I stare at the doctor, unable to form words to respond.

"Congratulations." The doctor speaks again in an attempt to snap me out of the state of shock I find myself in.

"I don't . . . That . . ." I mumble incoherently. "That's impossible, I'm on the pill."

Next to me, Gin looks petrified.

The doctor sighs. "I would love to say that the pill is one hundred percent effective. However, there is a small chance you could still get pregnant if you're not consistent and happen to skip a day or two."

I try to recall if I've skipped a day recently. These last few weeks have been a disaster.

"I—"

At that moment, Artemis opens the door, and I find myself unable to breathe. Artemis just stands there. He has one hand on the door handle, and a bag of food in the other. He's removed his tie and suit jacket, and is only wearing a white dress shirt and pants. His brown eyes search for mine, and he frowns when he notices the look on my face, which to be honest, I'm sure isn't a good one.

"Everything okay?" Artemis comes in and puts the bag down on the small table next to the couch. The doctor smiles at him then looks back at me; his eyes appear to be asking if he should keep talking and I shake my head.

"Well, I'll leave you to get some rest." The doctor adds, "I suggest you spend the night here so we can get some nutrients into your system via IV and monitor your progress. If you feel better tomorrow, you can go home."

"Thank you very much, Doctor."

Artemis comes closer and leans over me, kissing my forehead.

"You can't imagine how scared I was," he whispers before he pulls away. And I'm still speechless.

I can't be pregnant. I've been careful, and I've always been very responsible. I've always had in my head a clear list of items I want to achieve in life, and when I want them to happen. An unplanned pregnancy is something I never envisioned. I'm not exactly sure how I feel, what I think, or what I should do. I'm stupefied.

I don't know why, but I feel the urge to cry. My emotions are a complete mess.

"Claudia?" The sound of Artemis's worried voice next to me makes me look up. I look at him standing there, so handsome with his light beard marking the outline of his chiseled jaw, and those beautiful eyes that give off so much warmth anytime he looks at me.

Gin comes to my rescue. "She's been a little groggy since she woke up." She lies because she can tell I'm still processing.

"Oh." Artemis walks back to the table. He empties the contents from the bag and arranges the food containers.

Gin and I exchange looks, and she mouths something to me without making a sound.

What happened?

I've been careful, I reply.

Artemis puts a container of white rice and chicken in front of me. Everything's going well until I see a few pieces of bacon on the side. Oh no, no, no. Bacon. I press my lips together as I cover my mouth with one hand, shaking my head. Gin seems to understand and removes the container from my sight as fast as she can. Artemis looks at me, confused.

"I'm very sensitive to smells," I explain as soon as the nausea wears off. "It's because of the—"

"Anemia," Gin finishes for me. "The doctor told us that Claudia is anemic."

Gin explains what the doctor said without telling him about the pregnancy. Of course I know that I have to tell him, but first I need time to think, and figure out how to best share the news. I still can't believe it. As soon as night falls, Gin says her good-byes and leaves after giving me a tight hug, assuring me everything will be fine. I'm lying on the bed and resting on my side, and Artemis is sitting on the couch that's just a few steps away from the bed.

"Rest." His soft voice invades the silence of the room. "I'll be here all night."

"I'm okay."

"Sure," he murmurs. "So okay that you ended up in the hospital."

I don't reply and keep watching him. He sits resting his elbows on his knees, clasped hands in front of him. Always looking so handsome.

And then it happens—I imagine him with a baby, holding a boy or a girl, and I feel my heart tightening because, in my head, it's a beautiful sight.

You're going to be a father, Artemis.

How can I tell him when I don't know how he'll react? It's not something that we planned. We're in the early stages of our relationship. It's true we're not teenagers, but we're still young. He has responsibilities, as do I. What if his reaction isn't the one I expect? I'm terrified that he might take it badly or somehow blame me. We were equal participants in the sex but I did let him finish inside me. I thought we were safe and protected. One way or another, he trusted me.

"What are you thinking about?" The curiosity in his eyes is obvious.

"Lots of stuff." I sigh. "Thanks for being here."

"You don't have to thank me for anything. Supercat will always be your personal hero." He winks at me, and that makes me smile.

"You've been acting really cheesy lately," I tease him. "There's no trace left of the iceberg."

"I guess that's what happens when you get too close to fire," he replies playfully.

"Artemis."

"Yes?"

I close my lips tightly then relax them, and think carefully about what I'm about to say. I'm unsure if this is the right time. But I don't think there's ever going to be an ideal moment, so I should just go ahead and tell him now.

"There's something I need to tell you." He sits up and unclasps his hands, reacting to the serious tone in my voice.

"What's wrong?"

"I—I . . . umm." I blurt, "I'm pregnant."

Thirty-six

Don't joke around about that stuff, Claudia.

ARTEMIS

What?

That single word keeps spinning nonstop in my head. But I keep smiling because Claudia must be joking.

"Very funny. But I'm not falling for it," I reply, shaking my head. "You probably thought you could trick me like the time you had your appendix removed and you told me the doctor ordered you to eat obscene quantities of ice cream. You got ice cream every day for an entire week until I realized you'd been lying to me."

She half smiles when I bring up that story, but there's no joy in her expression. She licks her lips and puts a lock of hair behind her ear. Then she stares down into her lap, where her clasped hands are resting.

"Come on. Don't give me that," I say, laughing a little. "Superb acting performance."

"Artemis . . ." Her voice is barely a whisper.

"Don't joke around about that stuff, Claudia."

She looks up at me—straight in the eyes. And I understand she's serious. My smile slowly fades and my chest feels tight.

"I'm not joking." Her tone is flat and defensive.

I open my mouth to say something but immediately close it because I really don't know what to say.

My mind goes back to that one word, still spinning in a hamster wheel of disbelief because I didn't see this coming at all. I want to say something and soothe the fear and hesitancy evident in her expression. I just don't know what to say.

She's pregnant.

I suppose that's possible since we had unprotected sex—I'm not stupid. Although, I thought she was on the pill. Claudia has always been meticulous and careful in everything she does, so an unplanned pregnancy seems out of character for her, and has completely caught me off guard.

Say something.

Claudia bites her upper lip then slowly releases it. The tension is obvious in her shoulders and her body language.

"I'm sorry," she says with a sad smile. "I must have missed a day of the pill or something. I still can't figure out what happened, but this is my fault. You trusted me. You don't have—"

"Stop."

She stares at me with a puzzled look.

"Please stop talking, because I know I'm not going to like what you're going to say. I know you, and I can tell what you're thinking."

She is silent, and eyes me warily. I get up, and the back of my neck is so tight that I try to massage out some of the tension.

"We're both adults who knew what we were doing. Even though you're on the pill, we knew there was a risk of getting pregnant if we had unprotected sex. No one is to blame here."

She looks away. This is the first time I've seen her look so vulnerable.

She's afraid. This situation is probably as much of a surprise to her as it is to me. I glance at her stomach and suddenly heat spreads inside my chest. And the shock is replaced with a feeling of warmth.

Claudia is pregnant. My child is growing inside her. I'm going be a father.

Me? Someone's father? How can that be possible when I'm a disaster? After many years, I've just barely started to mend the relationship I have with my own father. My immediate plans didn't include a baby. But if it's with her, the woman I've always loved, it must be a good thing. After all, it's always been her for me.

"Claudia."

She looks at me, and I give her a genuine smile.

"Everything is going to be okay," I promise her as I move closer. The warmth I feel in my chest spreads all over. And I'm assailed by a volley of unruly emotions now that I've fully processed the news. "I know this is something we didn't plan, but I'd be lying if I didn't say that knowing I'm going to be a father makes me very happy." I cradle her face with my hands. "For me, it has and will always be you, Claudia."

Her eyes fill with tears, and I can tell she's struggling to keep them from falling. I know she doesn't like to cry, always fighting to maintain the remarkable fortitude that's part of her character. So I have to help her see that it's okay to be vulnerable and scared.

"I—" Her voice breaks. "I had so many plans, I had things I wanted to accomplish, wanted to improve about myself before I had a baby," she confesses. "Because I never want a child to go through what I experienced."

This breaks my heart.

"And that won't happen, Claudia. You are not alone." She closes her eyes, and two fat tears roll down her cheeks. "Hey. Look at me." She opens her bloodshot eyes. "You are not alone. I am here by your side, just like always."

"I'm so afraid, Artemis." Her lips tremble as she cries. "I didn't expect something like this—a baby, a life, someone I could mess up if I don't get it right . . . and I've always been terrified of giving birth. And . . ."

"Hey, hey." I try to calm her down. "Let's take one step at a time, okay? Put one foot in front of the other," I tell her, wiping away her tears with my thumbs. "I'm here, and everything is going to be fine. I'll take care of you and our baby, Claudia. Do you trust me?"

She nods.

"So trust me when I say that everything is going to be fine. And I'm going to be here every step of the way. Because I love you like I never imagined I could ever love someone. And I'm certain that I'll love this baby even more."

"What if we mess it up? What if we're not good parents?" She shares all her fears, and I'm glad she's able to share these emotions with me. "And what if something goes wrong? I've got so many fears and traumas. How can I be responsible for another human being? Me, who can't even say I love you without having my stomach churn, thinking back to all the men who said it to my mother."

It brings some peace to know the reason she hasn't said it back. She needs time, and I'll give it to her. I lean in and kiss her softly, tasting the salty tears on her lips. I smile at her when I pull away.

"Let me say it for both of us. I love you, Claudia." I look at her. "And I know you love me, too, dummy."

She gives me a half smile through her tears. "And you're dumber than I am."

I return her smile and kiss her forehead before wrapping her in my arms. She buries her face in my chest.

"Everything is going to be fine, Claudia," I promise once again, and I don't mind repeating it because I know how much she needs to hear it.

"I still can't believe it," she whispers against my chest.

"Neither can I," I admit.

"Promise me we won't screw this up. That regardless of what may happen between us, this baby will always be our first priority. Promise me that we will put their well-being above all else."

I understand her concern. We've both had bad experiences with our respective parents. I rest my chin on the top of her head.

"Claudia, you are you. And I am me. We are not our parents."

She sighs and I continue to speak.

"Let's use our parents' mistakes as examples of what not to do. I'm not saying we'll always get it right, but we'll be the best version of ourselves for this baby."

"I guess I melted you enough to accidentally create a mini-iceberg."

At least she's making jokes again.

"Or a mini-fire."

We pull away, and she wipes away her tears, letting out a long sigh.

"I hate you."

I arch an eyebrow. "Why?"

She taps my arm lightly. "Of course you had to get me pregnant."

"Excuse me? I don't remember you protesting while it was happening. I mean, not in a negative way."

She falls back on the bed, stares at the ceiling, and I sit next to her.

"You need to rest. Tomorrow is another day."

"I'll still be pregnant tomorrow."

"I know."

She reaches for my hand. "I'm not alone."

"You are not alone," I repeat back to her, and lift her hand to give it a kiss. "Now rest."

She closes her eyes. I watch over her until I notice her chest rising and falling in an even rhythm, confirming that she's finally asleep.

Down the hall outside the room, to my surprise I find Apolo checking room numbers, probably looking for Claudia's. How did he find out?

He rushes in my direction when he spots me, visibly concerned. My brain is still feeling a little disoriented.

"Artemis!" he calls to me. "How are you? What happened?"

"You're going to be an uncle."

The words spill out of my mouth freely and unfiltered. What has happened to me? What the fuck has happened to me? Claudia is going to kill me. Apolo freezes in his tracks and his jaw drops in shock.

"What?"

I clear my throat. I can't say any more. Apolo's face lights up.

"I'm going to be an uncle?" A smile spreads across his lips. "You're not screwing with me, right? I guess not, you wouldn't joke about that." He holds his face tightly, looking surprised. "Really?"

"Oh shit." I run my fingers through my hair. "If Claudia asks, I didn't tell you anything."

"I can't believe it. Congratulations, Artemis." He wraps me in a hug. His excitement is contagious. When we come apart, I notice his smile is wider. "I honestly thought Ares would be the first to make me an uncle."

I scowl.

"Oh, come on. We both know how much sex that savage has had," he adds before glancing at the door of the room. "How's she doing?"

"Surprised and a little scared. And I don't blame her—it wasn't something we planned."

"The best things are never planned."

"In this case, I fully agree. However, you're just finishing high school, so no unplanned pregnancies for you."

"As if I have sex," he mutters, but I don't believe him at all. "Anyway, can I see her?"

"She's resting. It's been a complicated day."

"I can imagine." Apolo grabs his head. "I just can't believe it. I'm going to be an uncle. I bet I'll be the favorite uncle."

"I've missed a few calls from the house. Was that you?"

"No, it was Grandfather. He's really worried. I'll call back and let him know she's fine."

"Apolo, you can't tell anyone that Claudia is pregnant. I need to talk to her first about how she wants to share the news. I told you by accident."

"Lots of accidents lately, huh?" he jokes, and I give him a murderous look. "Okay. Too soon?"

I don't say anything and head back inside to look after Claudia while she sleeps. I've never felt a fear as pure and as deep as when she fainted in my arms. So I'm staying put for a little longer. And now that I know she's pregnant, I feel even more protective than I did before.

"Artemis, you're exaggerating."

Claudia crosses her arms over her chest and refuses my assistance when we get back from the hospital. I want her to lean on me and let me help her walk to the house the moment we get out of the car. The early morning sun shines on her messy red hair and brings out the small freckles on her cheeks.

"I can walk just fine," she informs me as she goes by. I let out a sigh while closing the door of the car, and follow her.

When she enters the house, her mother and my grandfather are there to greet her with a hug. She reassures them that she's fine. However, I notice my father standing in the hallway that leads to the study. Apolo is next to him. They both look serious and worried.

What's happening?

"Claudia." My father greets her. "I'm so glad you're here. You gave us a good scare."

She smiles at him. "I'm stronger than I look."

All of a sudden, the person I least expected to see is coming down the stairs. His black hair is longer than the last time I saw him. I'm happy to see him, but what is he doing here? And then I remember the coming Fourth of July holiday weekend, and I realize that it's been a year since I came home, since I came back to her. Ares rushes over to give Claudia a hug.

"I know you were excited I was coming home but passing out is a little too much, don't you think?" says Ares playfully.

"Idiot." Claudia hits his shoulder before hugging him again. "It hasn't been that long, still, I've missed you a lot."

Ares moves toward me when they pull away, and I raise an eyebrow. "I'm not going to hug you."

He puts his hand on his chest. "Always so cold."

"No, it just hasn't been that long, Ares."

He hugs me anyway, and I grimace.

"Stop it with the uptight act," he says quietly into my ear. "You and Claudia, huh? Finally. It took you long enough."

Apolo can't keep anything to himself. He already told Ares about me being with Claudia. I just hope he didn't spill about the baby because I will definitely kill him—right before Claudia kills me.

"Ares and Artemis, we need you both to come to the study for a moment." My father's voice reminds me of the worried expression I noticed when I first walked into the house. Ares seems as confused as I am.

My dad turns around and walks down the hallway. Apolo smiles at me before he turns and follows him. Claudia knits her eyebrows, looking at me. And I shrug, because I have no idea what's going on, and make my way down the hall.

I close the study door behind us. My confusion grows when I see our mother sitting on the couch. Her eyes are puffy and red, but there's no trace of tears, as if she hadn't shed them at all. Apolo and my dad sit next to her. Ares and I share a glance before we take a seat on the couch that's across from theirs.

"What's wrong?" I ask, looking at the faces of my family and searching for an answer.

"We're taking advantage of Ares's visit and decided to gather you all here to hear what we have to share," our father begins. "We were thinking of doing this last night when he arrived, but Artemis spent the night in the hospital, so . . . well, your mother and I have decided to separate."

What?

"We've already started divorce proceedings." My mother speaks up. "I'm moving out of the house after the Fourth of July and into the vacation home I bought some time ago, the one next to Apolo's favorite river." She smiles at him, and Apolo looks devastated. Ares has his hands in his lap, and they're clenched into fists so tight his knuckles have turned white.

A painful ache catches me by surprise. I thought I would feel relief. This is what we always wanted—for them to separate because they had hurt each other so much. But now that it's actually happening, I feel my chest burn, and I can see the pain in my brothers' expressions. Regardless of all the mistakes they've made, they're still our parents, always together. I suppose we, their children, secretly hoped they'd work their problems out and find a way to keep our family together. Our parents are waiting for one of us to say something. When we don't, our mother tightly purses her lips, and manages to recover her strength.

"I know I've made too many mistakes and caused you all a lot of harm by being selfish. I have no excuse and don't expect you to understand. I just want you to know that I have loved you and will always love you. And that the doors of my house will always be open to you. That"—her voice breaks—"you will always will be my children, and I will always be your mother."

Ares snorts, though he seems to be on the verge of tears. "Now she wants to be our mother?"

Apolo lowers his gaze, tears running down his cheeks and falling from his chin.

"Ares . . ." I try to soothe him.

"No." He shakes his head. "After all the shit you've put us through over the years, now you've finally come to this realization." I sense the pain in his tone. He's doing what he always does, hiding behind coarse, cruel words. Our mother's eyes fill with more tears.

"Don't cry," Ares orders her. "You have no right to cry, you don't—" His voice chokes with the emotions he's trying hard to suppress. "What the fuck took you so long? If you had figured this out before, if . . ."

"We can't live in the *ifs*, Ares," I say, making him turn his attention to me. "Mistakes were made and people were hurt—all that already happened. We can't change the past."

My voice sounds colder than I expected. I suppose this is what I do. I hide behind cold composure. A sad smile forms on my lips as I realize Ares and I are more alike than I thought.

"It's okay, Artemis," Mom says as she wipes away her tears. "He has every right to vent to his feelings. Ares, son, you may insult me, say whatever you want to me—I deserve it."

Ares says nothing and covers his face with both hands.

My father speaks again. "You can visit her whenever you want, and she can come over to see you whenever she likes. Even though we're parting ways, your mother and I hope to remain amicable."

"We understand," I respond on behalf of my brothers. "I'm glad you're handling this situation in a levelheaded and nonantagonistic manner."

My mom stands up. "I need to start packing my things." My chest tightens but I try my best to give her a smile. "I am truly sorry, my children. I hope one day you'll find it in your hearts to forgive me."

She walks out of the study, leaving us still and silent.

Ares massages his face, looking frustrated. Apolo tries to hold back his tears. And our father simply gives us a sad smile.

"I, too, owe you an apology. Your mother is not the only person at fault. I chose to stay with her in spite of everything that happened. I chose not to get a separation when I should have, so I am partly to blame."

"It's okay, Dad," I reassure him.

Ares rises and exits the study without saying a word. Father sits next to Apolo and comforts him. And I need to get out of there.

I climb the stairs, heading to my room. I feel the eyes of everyone waiting in the living room directly on me. But I don't look back at them. I sit on my bed and run my hand over my face and hair. The image of my mother's flushed face haunts me. Someone opens the door, and Claudia enters. She closes the door behind her and studies me with worried eyes. I release the tension from my shoulders and let my guard down. I don't need to hide how I feel when I'm with her.

She slowly makes her way over. "Are you okay?"

I grab her by the hips and hug her. I rest my face on her stomach; the smell of her relaxes me. "I'm going to be a good father." I make a promise I know I will keep. "I'll try my very best, Claudia. I promise you."

Claudia strokes my head gently. "Of course you will, Artemis."

My goals in life, now and forever, are to love this woman and give my all to raising my baby. I can't change the past or erase the wounds it has inflicted. But I can forge a different future for us.

Thirty-seven

I'm already a mess.

CLAUDIA

I have successfully avoided hospitals my entire life with the exception of the time I had my appendix removed, and for my mother's appointments. Unfortunately, those days have come to an end. Now that I'm pregnant, checkups and ultrasounds will be frequent events in my life. Surprisingly, I feel more ready and calm than I thought I would be. Who is not feeling quite the same is Artemis, currently pacing back and forth in the gynecologist's waiting room. He runs his hand through his hair and keeps loosening his tie while I let out a sigh.

"Artemis, can you sit down?"

He comes to a halt in front of me, his chest puffing. He takes a deep breath and exhales. His beautiful brown eyes watch me. They appear to be searching for the serenity he needs to calm his nerves.

I don't get why he's so nervous. Perhaps one of the reasons

I'm calm is because he's so wound up. It wouldn't work out if we were both panicking. Come to think of it, I've always been better at handling my emotions. Artemis, on the other hand, only knows how to conceal them in order to avoid dealing with them. Or unravel, like he's doing at this moment.

"Please," I tell him, and he sits down next to me.

"I don't know how you can be so calm."

"It's only our first appointment." I take his hand and turn to him. "Everything is going to be fine."

"I should be telling you that. But no, look at me, I'm already a mess."

"No, you're not."

I caress his cheek, and feel his light beard against my fingers. I can't resist his lips when I move in closer, so I kiss him. I enjoy being able to kiss him whenever I want to. I no longer have to hold back or hide the attraction and affection I've always felt for him. I'm free to pull Artemis Hidalgo by his tie and kiss him with all my heart. He slowly opens his eyes when we come apart.

"You should have calmed me down like this from the beginning."

"Don't get used to it."

"Claudia Martinez," a nurse calls from the door.

The nurse leads the way to Dr. Diaz's consultation room. Dr. Diaz is a woman in her forties, with black hair and eyes. She smiles when she sees us. Her eyes linger a little longer on the man next to me, and I don't blame her. Artemis is far too attractive for his own good.

"A pleasure to meet you." She shakes our hands. "My name is Katherine Diaz and I'm very happy you chose me to be part of an important phase in your lives. It's Claudia, right?"

I nod, and she looks over at Artemis.

"Artemis Hidalgo," he replies cordially.

"Hidalgo?" Dr. Diaz raises her eyebrows in surprise. "From Hidalgo Enterprises?

"Very well," she says from the opposite side of the desk, while she looks over the forms I filled out a few days ago. "First of all: congratulations on your pregnancy, Claudia. According to the information you've provided, you are eight weeks along. Today, we're going to do some blood tests to check that your levels are normal in light of the medical scare you went through recently due to a mild case of anemia."

"Yes, she fainted," Artemis adds.

"How do you feel now, Claudia?"

"Good." I tell her the truth. "I get nauseated from time to time. And my breasts hurt, but I assumed that was normal."

"Right. We're going to check your progress and conduct an ultrasound to confirm that everything is all right."

She leads us to an adjacent examination room, where I lie on the table next to an ultrasound machine with a fairly large screen. Artemis sits next to me and takes my hand. Dr. Diaz puts on her gloves and spreads a gel on my lower abdomen while I take a deep breath. My eyes remain fixed on the screen, hoping I'll be able to see everything.

"There it is," she murmurs. Artemis and I exchange looks because I can't see anything on the screen except for gray-and-black images. Dr. Diaz smiles and points to the smallest circle I have ever seen.

I squint and try to get a better look until she enlarges the image.

"It's still too early to get a good look in a sonogram but I wanted to make sure everything was fine because you had anemia," she comments while she carries on with her assessment.

Artemis is spellbound. His eyes are fixed on the screen. I smile at his reaction and turn back to look at the monitor.

"And here's the gestational sac, and inside we can see the small embryo growing."

An unfamiliar sensation seizes my heart, and for the first time since I received the news, I feel absolute happiness. I never thought it was possible to love something this quickly, but perhaps seeing it has changed everything.

You're a tiny circle, baby.

"Very good, everything looks normal," she says as she completes the exam. "I'll set up an appointment for tomorrow so we can get your blood work done. For now, continue to take the vitamins prescribed by the emergency doctor, and keep a healthy diet," she explains with a smile. "I'll see you in two weeks to check that everything is coming along. Once again, congratulations, Mrs. Hidalgo."

My mouth freezes as it's about turn into a smile. Mrs. Hidalgo? Artemis and I respond at the same time.

"No . . ."

"No . . ."

We both stop and exchange glances, and I can feel the heat on my cheeks.

"We're not married," I clarify with a forced smile.

"Oh." Dr. Diaz blushes. "I apologize, I didn't mean to assume."

An awkward silence settles around us. I stand up and say good-bye, and we rush out of her office as soon as she gives me the slip with the information for the next appointment.

On the way home, I start to grow nervous. I'm impressed

with how calm I was during the doctor's appointment, which is a big contrast to how I'm feeling as we make our way to face what I think is the most difficult and uncomfortable challenge in our current predicament.

Our families.

Artemis and I agreed to break the news to them right after we confirmed everything was okay with the baby. Also, we wanted to take advantage of Ares visiting and the fact that Mrs. Hidalgo hasn't moved out yet. Today is the last day all the members of the Hidalgo family will be together at the house. Still, I can't help but be nervous about how they'll all react to the news.

As we get out of Artemis's car in front of the house, the sky is covered with clouds, and thunder rolls in the distance, signaling the coming rain. I lean back against the car, cross my arms, and stare at the Hidalgo house. I've spent a large part of my life in this place. I can almost see all of us as children, running out the front door and playing with water guns, fighting each other.

"Claudia." Artemis's voice brings me out of my thoughts. "Are you okay?"

He stands in front of me, and there's concern in his coffee-colored eyes.

"I'm fine."

"It's normal for you to be nervous, but you're not alone. We're doing this together, okay?" He offers me his hand, and I take it.

It doesn't take us long to gather the whole family in the study.

"Artemis?" His father arches a brow expectantly.

Their gazes are fixed on us. Sofia gives me a quick head-to-toe glance, disapproval evident in her expression. Going by what Artemis shared with me, I suspect she's playing the role of repentant mother. She may fool her sons and husband, but she doesn't fool me. I know exactly the kind of person she is. Sure, we all deserve second chances, but I don't think that's exactly what she wants. Her promises to change her ways are not and will never be sincere. This is an act so that just in case Mr. Juan one day decides to cut her off financially she can fall back on her children to provide her with the kind of support she's accustomed to. I don't fault her boys for wanting to believe in her; she's their mother and they love her. Who knows, maybe she truly feels regret.

"Claudia and I have something important to tell you." Artemis takes my hand and Sofia grimaces while my mom smiles. Artemis looks at me and I nod so that he may continue, because there is no way I'll be able to finish what we need to say.

"Claudia and I have been dating for a couple of months," Artemis explains.

"With all due respect, Artemis," Grandpa says, "we already knew that. You both may think you're very good at keeping your relationship under wraps, but you're not."

"This is true, my daughter," my mom agrees.

"There's more." Artemis clears his throat. Ares looks confused while Apolo bites his lips and tries hard to hold back a smile. Does he already know? I'm going to kill Artemis.

Everyone waits, and Artemis squeezes my hand. I turn to look at him. He's turned pale and is having a hard time swallowing. Drops of sweat trickle down his forehead, even with the air-conditioning on full blast. If he stays like this, I'm afraid Artemis will have an attack of some sort before he has a chance to share our news. As before, his nervousness gives me the strength to pull through and remain calm under pressure.

"I'm pregnant."

Simple. Clear. Straightforward.

There's complete silence. No one speaks; no one moves. There are a few looks of surprise. My bravery appears to give Artemis a push.

"Even though it's not something we planned, we are very happy." He smiles as he waits for their response, watching everyone. Sofia excuses herself and leaves the room.

Grandpa claps and breaks the silence.

"Congratulations!" he tells us with a smile. "I'm going to be a great-grandfather!" He puts his fists up in the air. "I never thought I would be around to meet a great-grandson or great-granddaughter."

"Congratulations, son." Mr. Hidalgo's expression is a mix of amazement and pride. "And I never expected I would be a young grandfather."

I notice a movement out of the corner of my eye but I barely have time to turn around when suddenly I'm enveloped in Ares's arms. He hugs and lifts me off the ground.

"I'm going to be an uncle!" he says over and over in my ear, and his joy makes me giggle. As soon as he lowers me, he cradles my face with both hands and plants a kiss on my forehead. "Congratulations, lovely."

"Thank you, you idiot."

Ares keeps teasing and congratulating Artemis. Apolo also gives me a hug.

"It's always been him, huh?" Apolo jokes as he pulls away.

My mother opens her arms to me. "My baby," she whispers. "I know it's unexpected. But it's a great relief to know that I'll be around to meet my grandson or granddaughter, and that you are no longer alone."

Tears spring to my eyes because I understand the true meaning of those words. Her doctors are not optimistic about the progression of my mother's illness. I can still remember my heart breaking the moment we were told that she had one year left, maybe two at best. Her relief pierces my soul, yet I'm glad that this, although unexpected, brings her some peace. I suppose sometimes there are positive outcomes to what's unexpected.

That thought takes up residence in my head as I watch them smiling, looking overjoyed and showering us with congratulations. This was not the reaction I expected. The excitement in their expressions makes me feel like I'm a part of something; it makes me feel like I belong to a family. The tears that my mother's words brought to my eyes are swelling in size because I never thought I could have this. I never imagined I would have the support of people who care about me; people who are this happy for my son or daughter. I blame the pregnancy hormones for the tears that I shed, and quickly wipe them away.

"Do you know if it's a boy or a girl?" Apolo asks me, and they wait for my response with bated breath.

"Not yet, it's too early."

"I bet he's a boy," Grandpa adds. "No Hidalgo has had a girl for many generations." It almost sounds as if he would prefer one instead.

"Maybe Clau will break that tradition," Ares says encouragingly.

"A Hidalgo girl," Mr. Juan mumbles. "That'll be interesting."

"Have you thought about names?" Apolo asks.

Ares grabs him by the shoulder. "Don't be so intense."

"Well, forgive me if I want to learn more about my future niece or nephew."

"Doesn't matter. I'll still be their favorite uncle," Ares replies arrogantly.

Apolo snorts, then turns to me. "Who do you think will be the favorite uncle, Claudia?"

I play dumb and simply shrug.

I find myself surrounded by Ares and Apolo's childish quarrel, my mother's words of encouragement, Grandfather's joy, Mr. Juan's acceptance, and Artemis's look of pure love. And I smile like I have never smiled in my life because I realize that I'm not on my own, and I won't ever be alone.

The small girl in me, the one who grew up on the streets, is smiling back at me because now she has the one thing she longed for with all her heart: a family.

The Final Chapter

CLAUDIA

Artemis and I had our first fight as a couple in the third month of my pregnancy.

"Claudia."

"No."

"You haven't paid attention to what I'm trying to say," he remarks in agitation while waving his hands in the air. The morning sun is streaming through the blinds in his bedroom. I'm almost finished getting ready to go to work.

"I have heard you and the answer is still no."

Artemis wants me to leave the internship with the company and stay at home all day. The fact that I'm pregnant doesn't make me less capable at my job. Also, my contract is for six months, and I only have two months left. I'm pretty sure I can handle two more months. I'm not even showing yet. The Hidalgos have already hired a girl to do the housekeeping. Artemis would not consider letting me continue to look after the housework, for obvious reasons.

"I don't know what you're trying to prove," he says.

"I'm not trying to prove anything. I'm being responsible. I signed a six-month contract and there are two more months left in it."

"A contract with my company that you don't need to finish. I can render it fulfilled."

"I'm going to work."

"Agh!" He turns around and brings his hands to his head. I fold my arms over my chest when he looks at me. "Do you have any idea how many people would kill to not work and stay at home?"

"Well, I regret I'm not one of them."

"Claudia." He purses his lips. "You're so stubborn. I should have known better and had you fired."

Ha!

"Go fuck yourself." I turn to leave but am hit by a wave of morning sickness, and rush to the en suite bathroom, where I lean over the toilet, ready to hurl. Artemis leans against the doorframe with arms crossed. I get up to wash my mouth and send a death glare to his reflection in the mirror above the sink.

"Claudia . . ." he starts again, trying to sound as though he's being logical.

"No." I face him. "Listen, Artemis, I get that you're worried. And I'm not unappreciative of the offer to stay home. But this is my life. And I choose to complete the internship. I need to show that I'm reliable and have an immaculate work ethic. I want to continue working, period."

"Do you want to open up your own publicity agency? I can . . ."

"Oh my god!" I cover my face with my hands. "It's like I'm talking to the wall."

He blocks the door on my way out. "Wait, wait. Don't leave like this."

I take a deep breath. "Do you realize you're acting like a complete idiot this morning? Considering giving orders to have me fired? Are you serious?"

He rubs his stubble. "I'm sorry, very sorry. I don't know what my problem is. I would like to . . . it's just—" He takes a step in my direction. "I just want to make sure that you're safe. If anything were to happen to you . . ."

"Artemis, I'm fine," I assure him. "Do you think I would do something that could put the baby in danger?"

"It's not that." He sighs and cradles my face with his hands. "I'm an idiot. I'm sorry."

I give him a fake smile. "I appreciate the apology. However, I'm depriving you of my company at night for a week. Enjoy sleeping alone, idiot."

I make an exit. I hear him call my name but I keep walking.

By the time my belly is showing in the fifth month, I've completed my internship and Artemis has left his job as CEO and appointed his best friend Alex to the position. He's done with his commitments to the family company and is free to do what he wants. Now he only oversees business projects of his own. I even convinced him to enroll in an illustration course to rekindle his passion.

Returning home from the checkup when we finally get to find out the sex of our baby, we find everyone waiting for us in the living room. Grandpa, my mom, Apolo, and Mr. Hidalgo are here. Ares joins us via video on a tablet placed in the middle of a table.

"Well?" my mother asks.

"It's a girl!" I inform them, elated. Though they've never said as much, I'm sure they were all crossing fingers, hoping for a girl.

"I knew it!" Grandpa smiles and gives Apolo a high five. "A Hidalgo girl!"

"Yeaaaaah!" I hear Ares shout excitedly from the tablet. "Apolo, you owe me twenty dollars."

"Did you make a bet? Seriously?" I scold Apolo, who shrugs.

"It was Ares's idea."

I bend and get closer to the screen to say something to him. "Idiot."

Ares smiles at me. "You love me and you know it." He winks. I give him an eye roll and straighten up.

My mom gives me a hug, and Mr. Juan comes up. "You're making Hidalgo family history," he comments. "She'll be the first girl in our family branch. My brothers and I have only had boys."

"My first granddaughter," Grandpa interrupts him. "Have you started getting her room ready?"

"Are you using one of the rooms upstairs?" Mr. Hidalgo asks. "Ah, but the stairs might be a problem. What are you planning?"

"Uh . . . we haven't . . ." Artemis and I glance at each other.

"You'll live here, right?" Grandpa asks, worry clearly etched on his face. "This house is enormous. I also think that the grandparents"—he points to my mom and Mr. Juan—"would love to have their granddaughter close to them."

"We haven't discussed that, Grandfather," Artemis replies, and I shift my weight from foot to foot, feeling a tad uncomfortable. How have we not thought about this already?

We talk with everyone a little longer before heading upstairs to Artemis's bedroom. I yawn and stretch my arms in the air before I sit down on the bed. Lately, I feel very tired even when I hardly do anything. I completed the internship and the new girl who looks after the housework is doing a thorough job. I no longer complain about Artemis being overbearing. I can't imagine what it would be like if I was still in charge of running the household.

Artemis unbuttons his shirt and takes it off while I gawk. My hormones have made me insatiable lately. He leans over and gives me a soft peck while gently caressing my face. I grab him by the neck and pull him forward until we land on the bed with him on top.

"Again?" he whispers against my lips.

"Are you complaining?"

"Absolutely not."

When I reach the ninth month, it's hard to walk very far without having my ankles swell up, and I become short of breath doing the simplest of tasks, never mind the stress on my back or trying to find a comfortable sleeping position. Artemis and I have decided to spend the first year of our daughter's life in this house. We would love for Grandpa, my mom, and Mr. Juan to enjoy her company for as long as they can. We'll decide later whether we'll live somewhere else long term.

We haven't heard from Mrs. Hidalgo, which doesn't surprise me. She probably doesn't want anything to do with me and my baby. And I'm perfectly fine with that. I'd rather not have someone with such terrible energy anywhere near my daughter. Artemis is way more relaxed now that he's no longer working for Hidalgo Enterprises and has only his own business ventures to oversee from time to time. He's truly having a great time getting back to drawing since he began his illustration course months ago. Although it hasn't been long since he started, his artistic sensibility and aesthetic have improved a great deal. I guess time is inconsequential when you have innate talent.

We're almost finished setting up our daughter's room and have paid attention to every detail with tender loving care. It's Valentine's Day weekend, which means everyone is home since we decided to have a party together. Gin and Alex have dropped by to help with the final touches. Apolo and Ares are in the living room assembling a piece of furniture that came with complicated instructions. I can hear them arguing over it from here. Alex is helping Gin put up a sign with my daughter's name on it up on the wall next to her crib.

"More to the right! It's crooked!" Alex complains.

"That's just what you said to me last night," Gin replies.

"Gin!" I shoot a reproachful look in her direction.

"I'm joking. Anyway, Alex is no saint," she proclaims in her defense.

Alex and Gin love bantering with each other. Thanks to Artemis and me they've become close friends. I suppose they're our best friends, so they have no other choice.

"Alex," I call to him. "What happened with Chimmy?"

"Chimmy?" Gin asks. "Oh yeah, the secretary. Right?"

"Nothing. Why? Is there something that should happen?" Alex does his best to sound puzzled.

Artemis coughs into his hand and mumbles, "Coward."

"I heard you. You're not my boss and I can kick your ass."

"My apologies, Mr. CEO of Hidalgo Enterprises," I joke.

"Don't encourage him, Claudia. I need someone in my corner."

I push against the arms of my chair to lift myself back up to my feet.

But when I straighten, I feel a warm liquid roll down my inner thigh and drip on the floor. Everyone looks at me in shock.

"Oh." It's all I can say. "I think my water broke."

Then everything turns into chaos. Artemis keeps asking if I'm doing okay every other second. Gin and Alex are pacing from one side of the room to the other. I hold my belly with one hand and reach for Artemis with the other for support as we make our way out of the room and down the stairs. Ares and Apolo look up.

Gin is hot on our heels, and she screams at them. "The baby! She's coming!"

The chaos intensifies. My mom, Grandpa, and Mr. Juan come out of the kitchen where they were preparing the meat for the barbecue.

Everyone is trying to talk to me and calm me down at the same time. Meanwhile, they're the ones who have lost their minds.

"I'm fine," I keep repeating.

The ride to the hospital is much quicker than I expected. Upon our arrival, we check in and fill out the paperwork. Although I can walk, they put me in a wheelchair.

I wish I could say that the entire birthing experience is wonderful. At first I thought being exposed to a team of doctors would be uncomfortable. Modesty, however, is far from my mind at this moment. Everything becomes irrelevant when all you want is to bring your daughter into this world, and for the pain of labor to end.

Artemis holds my hand the entire time. He looks so pale anyone would think he was the one giving birth.

"Come on, Claudia. One more push." Dr. Diaz encourages me. I make an effort to push while holding my breath. "Hold it. Hold it. Just like that. Good, nice."

I put all my remaining strength into my last push to get this baby out. I'm out of breath, light-headed, with nothing left. But none of that matters when I hear my daughter's cries. Dr. Diaz cleans her before placing her in my arms, and I can't keep back my tears. I've never felt love for someone this way, so deep and fast. Artemis leans over, and his eyes are wet. He strokes the tiny head of our baby with such gentleness, as if she's a delicate treasure so fragile she could break from his touch.

"Hello. Hi, my love," I whisper between sobs. "Welcome to the world, Hera Hidalgo."

Artemis kisses her forehead before giving me a quick peck. When he pulls away, he gazes at me with eyes that gleam with affection, and for the first time I'm ready to fully reciprocate what I see in them.

"I love you, Artemis."

I'm no longer afraid. These are the words I've heard from his lips every day these past months. The ones I've heard him whisper to my belly. Now, when I hear these words in his voice, I think only of the kind boy I grew up with and this beautiful baby in my arms. Artemis smiles at me.

"I know, my precious." He says this without a hint of arrogance, sounding more like the words are confirmation of a truth he's known all along. A truth I don't need to explain because he's aware of how hard it is for me to put into words what this all means to me. "I love you, too, Claudia."

I'm discharged on the third day. And Hera becomes the center of attention at the Hidalgo house. Everyone fights over who gets to hold her, who gets to change her diaper, and who gets to put her to sleep. It's quite clear that her being the first Hidalgo girl is a monumental occasion. On the upside, their generous assistance affords Artemis and me the chance to rest on occasion.

Hera is a beautiful baby. The color of the sparse hair on her tiny head is brown. Her facial features are adorable, and her eyes are blue, though the eye color of babies tends to change with time. I didn't expect her eyes would turn out to be this shade. Maybe it's a trait that skipped a few generations. My mom says that my father had blue eyes, very much like Ares and Artemis's mother.

Regardless, Ares makes use of this opportunity to tease Artemis. "I'm sorry, brother," Ares says in an overly dramatic way. "I tried to resist, but Claudia can be very persistent. She—"

Artemis slaps the back of his head.

"Show some respect, Ares."

Ares gives us a wide smile.

"Always so serious." Ares shakes his head, leaning over the crib and reaching for. "Hello again, my precious. Who is going to be a heartbreaker just like her uncle, huh? Who?"

Apolo rolls his eyes. "A heartbreaker? Are you serious? You couldn't think of something else—like intelligent, or something along those lines?"

Artemis sighs and sits next to me on the bed. I'm still feeling a little sore.

"Do you need anything?"

I shake my head. We sit together and watch everyone fight over who gets to hold Hera.

Fourth of July

Artemis and I are alone for the first time in months. Hera is at home with her grandparents, who were more than happy to look after her. I believe this is the first Fourth of July that we're spending alone together. Just like the night when we were teenagers and I rejected him because of his mother's threats.

We've come to a beautiful and secluded beach a few hours away from the house. A gorgeous moon adorns the dark sky, and its reflection shines brightly on the water. We sit on the sand. Off to the side, where the beach turns inward, there's a boardwalk where a small crowd lingers. The wind blows back my hair, and I look over at the man sitting next to me.

"This is beautiful," I attest. As I rest my head on his shoulder, I notice that he's shaking. I straighten. "Are you cold?"

Artemis shakes his head. "No."

"But you're trembling."

He doesn't look at me and points in the direction of the boardwalk, above which fireworks suddenly shoot over the ocean and explode in a multitude of different colors. I open my mouth, surprised and genuinely impressed by the magnificent display. I stand up and move closer to the shore to get to a better view of the light spectacle. I should have guessed Artemis would have prepared for this moment.

"It's wonderful," I tell him when he comes to join me. "I love it, it's—" I stop midsentence when he bends in front of me, going down on one knee in the sand. I cover my mouth in shock.

"Claudia," he begins. "I'm not good with words, but here under these fireworks, I'll try my best. We grew up together. You were my friend, the one who stood by me, and my first love."

The memory of him sticking out his tongue when we would fight as kids comes to mind.

"Together, we have overcome so much," he adds.

I think back to all the times he was there for me when I would sleepwalk, or when I was terrified of the dark. And the times he would get into fistfights and I tended to his cuts. And how he would come to my defense when the other kids would pick on me at school. And the way his brown eyes would calm me as he created a safe space for me.

"Our journey hasn't been easy and had many obstacles. But we've been together for over a year and we've welcomed our precious Hera," he continues, overcome with emotion. "And I know, without a doubt, that you are the one I want to spend the rest of my life with, the woman I want to build a home with. For me, it has always been you."

Big fat tears roll down my cheeks.

"And so this iceberg, Supercat, and a man who is crazy in love has a question to ask on this Fourth of July: Will you marry me?"

He brings up one hand holding a box with a ring inside. I put down the hand that was covering my mouth and smile through my tears.

"Yes. Of course. It's a yes!"

I lean forward and hug him. Fireworks explode and illuminate the night sky. When I pull away, he places the ring on my finger and gives me a kiss. It's a kiss packed with emotion, love, and promises. He stops and places his forehead against mine.

"You're not rejecting me this time, huh?" he jokes.

I caress his face, brush his soft scruff, and answer his question with a soul-destroying kiss.

Epilogue

Ten years later

My dark shades protect me from the unrelenting sun hitting the South Carolina beach. I enjoy the warmth on my skin and the soothing sound of the waves.

I needed this vacation. I've been worn out, with very little free time since I started running my own advertising company and looking after several foundations I've established with the help of Artemis. With that being said, I always make sure to spend enough quality time with my family. Most importantly, with my children and my husband. Our summer vacation is sacred quality time.

"Mom!" Hades, my youngest, runs toward me holding seashells in his sand-covered hands, his wet red hair sticking to his face and framing its small features. The sunlight makes his honey-brown eyes look lighter in color, and brings out the freckles on his cheeks. "I found so many this time."

His older sister follows closely behind. She has her arms

folded across her chest and looks frustrated. Sometimes I think she acts like a miniature version of an adult. I prop myself up on my elbows and smile at them.

"Wow. That's a lot," I tell him. He likes to collect tokens from the places we visit. His room is full of all kinds of souvenirs from countries around the world. "You have to choose the ones that you like best for your collection."

"As if he doesn't have enough in his room already," his sister replies.

"Hera."

"It's true, Mom. You can't fully open the door to his room anymore."

"You're exaggerating."

"I asked for her opinion, Mom. And as always, she's bitter." Hades rebukes her.

I wonder who she takes after.

"Who are you calling bitter?"

And this is the beginning of an argument. I calm them down, and we have the same old discussion about the need for respect and tolerance between siblings.

Hera lets out a sigh. "I'm sorry, volcano." Her nickname for Hades comes from the color of his hair.

"It's okay," he replies. His adorable pout could convince anyone, even his ill-tempered sister. Hera leans closer to him and playfully messes up his hair.

"Good. I'll help you choose the best ones," she tells him.

"The very best?" His pout vanishes and joy spreads across his face. Hades is cute. Both children are. My babies, my children.

I watch them walk back to the shore, joining their father along the way.

My husband has just emerged from the water. These past years have been good to him. How is it possible that the older he gets, the better he looks? It's not normal.

He continues to exercise on a daily basis and the water trickling down his muscles contour his well-toned chest, abs, and arms. The light, scruffy beard I adore so much still adorns his chiseled jaw. He shakes his head in an attempt to dry his wet hair before running his fingers through it. I bite my lower lip. I believe I'll be licking those abs later today when the kids go to bed.

Artemis comes over to give me a kiss and sits by my side.

"Claudia, the expression on your face gives you away every time you look at me while entertaining dirty thoughts."

I smile.

"Is that a complaint?"

"Not at all." He brings his mouth close to my ear. "In fact, I was thinking that perhaps today when the kids go to bed . . ."

As usual, our minds are set on the same goal. The same goes for all our responsibilities: his company and mine, the children, the foundations. We've had a few stretches when we've lacked the time for intimacy. The urgency and intensity of our couplings are dead giveaways of how long it's been. I guess this is what it's like to be an adult.

"It's late. We have to go back to the hotel and book our reservations for the fireworks show," Artemis tells me while caressing my exposed back.

I'm wearing a two-piece bathing suit. I'm confident in my skin and don't mind showing the scar from my C-section and the one from my appendectomy, or the stretch marks from my pregnancies. I owe this attitude to my mother, who taught me to love myself the way I am.

My beautiful mother, may she rest in peace. She passed away at few years ago. She managed to live longer than the doctor's prognosis. I firmly believe the birth of Hera and Hades were her motivation to hang on—her grandchildren were a source of strength and motivation to live. I find comfort in knowing that she treasured the time she had left because it was spent in the company of her grandchildren, and that that made her very happy.

I aspire to be as good a mother as you were, Mom. Even though you made mistakes you always showed me love, and fostered in me self-love and self-worth. I hope I don't let you down.

"What are you thinking about?" Artemis brings his arm around my shoulder and pulls me into a side-hug.

"My mom."

He plants a kiss on my head, and I shake off the sadness. After all, that's why we've come on the Hidalgo family vacation. It was five years ago when we started the tradition of celebrating the Fourth of July at the beach. Members of the Hidalgo clan from all over the country gather here for a yearly family reunion. And it's worked.

We call the kids and head back to the hotel to shower and change. We struggle to keep Hades from falling asleep on the sofa after his shower. It's a family tradition that we all watch the spectacle together. We walk down to the beach where the show takes place and sit on folding chairs. Hades is on my lap and Hera stands behind her dad and hugs him from behind, leaning on him for support.

The fireworks show starts right before our eyes.

"Wow!" Hades exclaims and looks at me to confirm I'm not missing anything.

"Impressive, right?"

He nods repeatedly.

I turn to stare at the man of my life and his gorgeous face illuminated by the colorful fireworks. He turns to look at me, feeling my gaze on him. Suddenly, we transform into the awkward teenagers from that Fourth of July many years ago. Artemis takes my hand and brings it to his lips for a kiss.

"Happy Fourth of July, fire," he whispers.

"Happy Fourth of July, iceberg," I reply.

I never thought it was possible to be this happy. Or that he and I would find our way back to each other and rekindle old feelings as well as commit to each other for the rest of our lives. I give his hand a loving squeeze. This time I'm not letting go.

Notwithstanding wounds and time, we all have the capacity to be loved and love truly and madly with all our hearts. In spite of life's fickleness, with its many ups and downs, sooner or later you find that someone who will hold your hand in the good times and the bad. That one person who can see through you.

About the Author

Ariana Godoy is the author of the bestselling novel *A Través De Mi Ventana*, which was adapted into a film by Netflix Spain. A Wattpad star, Ariana has over two million followers on the platform and her stories have accumulated over eight hundred million reads. She is also very active on social media and is a successful YouTuber. Ariana enjoys K-dramas, coffee, writing and spending time with her dogs in her house in North Carolina.

Ariana Godoy's globally loved, steamy romance series comes to an end with

Through the Rain

Coming Fall 2023

Turn the page for a sneak peek!

One

APOLO

I've missed jogging.

It took me two weeks to fully recover and get the go-ahead from the doctor to start exercising again. Physically speaking, I've healed. Mentally, well, that's a different story. I still have nightmares of the guys who brutally assaulted me. What's more, every time it rains, it puts me in a shitty mood.

It's half past six in the morning when I enter the apartment. I shut the door and make my way down the hall that stretches before me partially cloaked in the predawn darkness. I switch the light on when I reach the spacious kitchen. A disheveled Gregory pokes his head out from the hallway that leads to our bedrooms.

"Why are you up at this hour?"

"I went jogging."

"At . . ." He squints to read the time on the microwave. "At six o'clock in the morning?"

"Six-thirty."

"Not even my grandfather would get up at this hour to go for a run."

"Your grandfather didn't run," I remind him, placing the keys on the counter of the kitchen island.

"Exactly."

"What are you doing up?" I ask as I open the fridge to grab a bottle of water.

"Uh . . ."

"Good morning!" someone squeals from down the hall. I turn to see a perky brown-skinned girl with a familiar face make her way past Gregory to the kitchen.

What's her name again? Kelly, Gregory's I've-no-fucking-clue-what-I-should-call-her who frequently spends the night at our apartment. Sometimes they act like a normal couple. Other times, they don't even acknowledge each other when they cross paths. To be completely honest, I don't understand what their deal is, but I'm not going to be a busybody and ask.

My goal is to get along with Gregory. Though I met him through my brother Ares, he's become a good friend, and now a roommate. Living together has been a great comfort during these first weeks at college. I haven't felt as lonely as I might have. Gregory's always coming up with things to do, which doesn't leave me with too much time on my own to feel depressed or homesick. I still miss my grandpa, my oldest brother, Artemis, his wife, Claudia, and my dogs. But most of all, to my surprise, I miss Hera. I never thought I would miss my niece this much.

"Apolo?" Kelly stands next to me and waves her hand in front of my face. "Are you still asleep?"

"Good morning," I reply with a sheepish smile.

Gregory yawns and joins us in the kitchen.

"Well, since we're all awake, should we have breakfast?" he asks.

I raise my fist to bump his. Gregory is a great cook, an underrated skill that's only truly appreciated when the time comes to live away from home. I'm not good at cooking at all. The only thing I can manage are desserts, and I'm afraid we can't live on buns and cupcakes alone.

"What do you fancy today? A continental breakfast? A full American?" Gregory suggests, bending down to get the pans out of the drawer.

Kelly seizes the opportunity and moves behind him. She grabs him by the hips and begins to gyrate against his backside.

"Stop!" Gregory whispers as he turns around to kiss her passionately, holding her against the island's counter.

I grimace and shift from side to side while staring at a rather interesting painting of a pear that hangs on the kitchen wall. I should be used to this by now.

After breakfast, I take a shower and spend more time than necessary under the spraying water with my eyes closed. I lower my head, stretch my arms forward, and rest my hands against the wall. The water washes over me, but I feel as if I'm not exactly present. My body may be standing here, but my mind is disconnected. I feel numb, as if I'm falling deep inside a void. Such is the irony of my life, I came here to study Psychology and during my first week I had a traumatic experience in the form of a violent beating. I smile sadly and turn off the faucet. I stand still for a brief moment, shake my head in an effort to get rid of the excess water, and snap back to reality.

Each bedroom in the apartment comes with its own private bathroom. And my bedroom is quite spacious. I quickly dry off but soon realize that all my underwear is in the dryer, so I go to retrieve it wearing a towel wrapped around my waist and another placed on my neck. Kelly is lying on the couch in the living room, fiddling with her cell phone.

She notices me walking by and puts down her phone, arching an eyebrow.

"So you've been hiding *all that* behind your nice boy exterior?"

I frown when I hear the word *boy.*

"And what makes you think that I'm a nice boy?"

"Oh, please. You give yourself away too easily." She props herself up on her elbows. "I bet you're also a virgin."

Her remark makes me laugh. I turn and continue toward the laundry room, putting an end to our exchange. It could be my imagination, but it sounds like she's flirting with me. Maybe it's the way she was looking intently at my abs and arm muscles. The last thing I need right now is to create problems between me and Gregory.

When I pass by on the way back to my room, I find her sitting on the armrest of the couch, staring at me with amusement.

"Did I scare you?" she asks.

I recall listening to Ares explain the various flirting techniques used by different people. *I call this particular approach the Challenger; the questions are meant to pose a challenge with the sole purpose of proving an assumption is wrong. The overall goal is to get you to confirm something that's already established.* It's hard to believe how often that idiot's sweeping generalizations happen to be spot-on. I suspect his former life as a confirmed heartbreaker has granted him considerable experience in that department. And one thing is certain, I've yet to meet someone who's broken as many hearts as my idiot brother. However, I'm not the type of person who makes assumptions about others, so I smile at Kelly and decide to give her the benefit of the doubt.

"Not at all," I answer with a shrug.

She smiles back at me. Then she moves to stand right in front of me. She presses a fist against my naked abdomen and cocks her head to one side.

"Nice boy, you have a lot to learn."

There's that word again. I clench my jaw and wrap my hand around her wrist in an attempt to remove it from my stomach.

"I'm not a boy," I reply, keeping my cool. "But you're entitled to your opinion about me. I have no intention to prove you wrong."

I let go of her wrist and walk back to my room.

The first few minutes of my morning class is spent finishing up orientation, so it's easy. It mostly consists of tips and advice to help guide us through our first year in college. The classroom is packed with students, and the professor is going over some information about the cafeteria and the breaks between classes. My notebook lies open before me, and my restless hand begins to scribble something in pencil on a blank page. When I'm done, I read what I've written down: *Rain.*

That's her name.

Rain Adams came to my rescue that night. She's registered as a student here. And that's all I know about her. That's all the information the doctors who cared for me were able to provide when I woke up the morning after my assault. From what I understand, she cooperated with the police and gave a statement in my case, which is still open. The investigation is ongoing because the attack didn't fit the profile of a typical mugging. The police said it was too violent considering that I willingly gave them everything I had on me.

Nevertheless, I haven't seen Rain again. All I have is a faint memory of her from that icy-cold night: her voice, her silhouette, the scent of citrus perfume, and nothing else. I would like to find her and thank her. I have to admit that I want to see what she looks like and get to know her. I've tried searching for her on social media. But when I type *Rain Adams*, all the results I get are about weather. Maybe I'm thinking too much about her; meanwhile, she's probably already forgotten about me.

I break into a smile.

C'mon, Apolo. You just started college and here you are, obsessing over a girl.

"Do you like the rain?" A feminine voice pulls me out of my reverie. I look up, searching for its source. An attractive girl with glasses and wavy hair is standing beside me, looking over my shoulder.

It takes me a few seconds to answer, simply because I'm taken aback. This is the first time someone has talked to me in class.

"Actually, I no longer enjoy the rain."

She nods and sits down. "And here I was expecting a speech detailing how much you love the sound of the rain, how it relaxes you, and makes you feel nostalgic."

Her coffee-colored eyes sparkle slightly when she talks. I'm speechless. She smiles and offers me her hand.

"I'm Erica, and I'm retaking this course." I shake her hand, and I'm about to introduce myself when she cuts in. "It's nice to meet you, Apolo."

"How do you know my name?"

She arches an eyebrow. "Apolo Hidalgo, everyone knows your name on campus."

"What are you talking about?"

"Your name has been mentioned in the campus bulletin for a couple of weeks," she informs me. "I'm sorry about what happened to you. Are you all right?"

I detect pity in her look, and it bothers me.

"I'm fine," I tell her and get up, pretending to go to the washroom.

Instead, I head straight to the faculty bulletin board. A handful of articles about me have been posted with my full name and photo. I realize that my story is being extensively covered in the college news.

Surely, Rain must have heard or read about me somewhere. She knows my name, my major, and where to find me. I reluctantly consider the possibility that Rain has no intention of looking for me. And why would she? She saved me, and she doesn't owe me anything. I rub my face with one hand and turn away.

I feel my cell phone vibrating inside my pocket. I pull it out and read a text from Gregory.

> **La Cucaracha:** Housewarming party at our place! See you tonight, Looooooser. And save my contact under a different name, or I'll kick your ass.

I snort and text back a reply.

> **Me:** Dream on, Cockroach. Who did you invite?

La Cucaracha: A few friends from campus. I'm throwing you a 'debutante' bash so wear your best suit.

Gregory has been enrolled in this college for a year, so he has a wide social circle. Meanwhile, I'm new here, and he's my one and only friend. I missed the first two weeks of classes due to my recovery. In other words, I skipped the crucial phase in college life when most students had the chance to socialize and meet people.

I feel left out yet again. I've never been good at getting to know people on my own. In high school, I met people through my brothers. I ended up being friends with their friends simply because I happened to be around. I'm not complaining. This is how I've met some of my very best friends. Still, I've never managed to hit it off with new people without help.

Me: How many people did you invite?

La Cucaracha: Numbers are abstract concepts entrapped in space.

Sometimes I wonder if everything is all right inside Gregory's head. I've yet to figure out exactly how his brain works.

I let out a sigh and give him a call. He answers, and I hear a racket in the background. I wonder if he made it to class or skipped it to hang out with his friends.

"How many people?" I ask wryly.

"Twelve and a half." He laughs, which makes me squint.

"And a half?"

"One of the girls is bringing along her dog."

I love dogs, so this news makes the whole situation more tolerable.

"What's her dog's name?"

"Cookie."

"Okay. Fine."

He mumbles something else and hangs up. And then I realize that he may have exploited my weakness for dogs in an effort to distract me. I have a feeling he's going to squeeze a crowd in our apartment. I guess this is my chance to make new friends.

The hallway leading back to class is packed with people. Some look at me with curiosity, others with pity. Even though the bruises are gone, I still have stitches on the left side of my jaw and above my right eye. I look down and pretend to check my phone.

Citrus.

I look up when I catch the scent of a citrus perfume. It immediately takes me back to that night, the cold, the pain, and the words softly whispered in the midst of it all.

You'll be okay.

When I turn around, I focus in on a group of boys and girls walking away, leaving me behind. They're about to blend in with the rest of the crowd. I stand still in the middle of the moving mass and stare. I barely manage a glimpse as they keep moving further down the hall.

Stop it, Apolo.

I start walking back to class, but my mind is stuck thinking about her again.

Will I ever find you, Rain?